The

Overwhelmed

Prophet

By

Susan Davis Sandberg

SusanDavisSandberg@gmail.com

ISBN-13: 978-0-9849923-9-3
ISBN-10: 0984992391

Cover Design by John Sandberg
Cover Photograph © chloe7992, shutterstock.com

To
My daughter Dana

For a glimpse
into the mind-set
of a red-head

Chapter 1

It was still dark outside, but Aleta could tell it was snowing. The falling flakes crossed the light beams streaming from the lights in the bedroom. Stanley saw no reason to dress in the dark when Aleta would wake up if he lit a candle.

She watched him selecting his clothes with the same care he did everything else. He laid out her clothes on the bed for Bertha to dress her when she came. The dreaded wheelchair sat waiting near the doorway that led from the bedroom straight into the living room.

It was an unusual arrangement, but when she'd met Stanley less than six months ago, he was building a bachelor pad as he was over thirty and unmarried, not that he ever entertained women. He'd been as celibate as she and their honeymoon had been a wild exploration into the joys of sex resulting in a pregnancy earlier than Stanley had planned, but welcomed nonetheless.

"It'll be over two hours before Bertha gets here," Aleta complained. "Why do I have to have the slings on so early?"

"Because you'll be alone for two hours," Stanley said. "And knowing you, something will come up and you'll get up and wreck the progress you've made."

"Other people's bones heal in six weeks," she grumbled. "I think you and Dr. Cook conspired to keep me immobile."

"The fact is that a broken clavicle takes up to twelve weeks to heal, and you have broken ribs besides, to say nothing of the torn muscles and tendons in your other arm which take longer to heal. And you have a head wound on top of that."

"The head's fine," Aleta said annoyed. "The list's long enough without that. Why do you keep bringing it up?"

"Because your hair is so short," Stanley shot back.

"Don't measure it again," Aleta quipped. "It grows seven inches a year, not a month."

"My beard grows faster than your hair."

"Your scar still shows too."

Stanley stopped dressing and walked over and kissed her lightly on the forehead.

"Stop fretting, Aleta. Just think about how blessed you are to have survived and still have me. You know being married to you would have chased away a lesser man."

"A lesser man would let me have the remote," Aleta said.

"So that's what this pouting is all about?"

"I'm only going to watch the news."

"That's what I'm afraid of."

"Stanley, look at me! For heaven's sake! I'm minus the use of both arms so even if I wanted to do anything, I couldn't. I have to wait for Bertha to arrive to even brush my teeth."

"Dr. Cook and I still don't trust you. He wants all your war wounds to heal before you rush into battle again."

"I want one arm for Christmas!" Aleta declared.

"Ask Dr. Cook today," Stanley suggested.

"Bertha will be there," Aleta protested.

"Of course, she will," Stanley answered, stating the obvious. "You expect to push the wheelchair while you're sitting in it?"

"When she's there, he talks to her and not me," Aleta complained.

"That's because she listens to him and makes sure you follow his instructions," Stanley said. "She was a great hire."

"Being engaged to my Dad has made her even more protective," Aleta pouted. "She'll defy me now."

"That's because she knows we will all support her," Stanley said. "Listen, Aleta, I know it's been hard for you to be so helpless and maybe after Christmas that'll change a little."

"Is Dr. Cook going to let me use my arm after Christmas?"

"Not a chance."

"You spoke with him?"

"Yes," Stanley said, tying his tie and then turning as usual and asking, "How do I look?"

"I wouldn't change a thing. You look great."

Stanley smiled. "I keep remembering that you think bulldogs are gorgeous."

"Is Scooby alright?"

Stanley looked over at the chocolate Lab pup in the pen.

"Still sleeping. I didn't know pups slept so much."

"We've got him on a schedule. Waking at five isn't in his schedule."

"Bertha did a good job housebreaking him."

"I wish I could hold him and pet him," Aleta said wistfully.

"He loves you," Stanley assured her. "You take him for long walks."

"But Dad's always there holding on to me so I won't fall. How do I know...?"

"For heaven's sake, Aleta, in a month or two you'll be out throwing sticks for him and he'll be yours for life. And you're doing it again."

"Doing what?"

"You know what," Stanley said looking at his watch. "I'm late. I have to go. Love you."

Aleta saw the remote on top of the television set.

I could go get it, she thought.

"Stay in bed!" Stanley called from the front door.

Aleta had to smile. The man read her mind.

She watched the snowflakes fall and envisioned the expanse of land beyond, a bare flat area used for years as a path for tractors and other farm equipment between the sheds and the barn.

This was going to be her first real winter. Born and raised in Northern California, winter meant rain and the greening of the hills, dried to a golden brown from the summer sun. In Illinois winter meant the covering of dead grass with snow, ice on the roads and bitterly cold winds. The winds had already arrived and she'd found her fleece-lined boots essential. Her cape was heavy enough to keep the wind from piercing its double lining to her barely covered back and arms, but it couldn't keep the cold from inching up around her torso. She couldn't walk fast enough to work up the body heat she needed to stay warm, but she said nothing.

She looked forward to getting out of the house for a walk past the apple orchard toward the fields beyond the barn. She loved stopping off at the barn to see Jocelyn's horse Yudi, and Sterling, the 20-year-old Morgan with the fractured foot that had been designated Stanley's horse because Stanley didn't ride. Her sister Jocelyn had been given the task of finding a rescue horse to keep her jumper company. Yudi had been moved from California to Stanley's newly restored barn, but the trip had unsettled him. It had been decided that he needed the company of another horse. Jocelyn and her dad had found Sterling and liked his gentle nature. Jocelyn took care of both horses in exchange for barn privileges.

There were riding trails nearby and Jocelyn had made friends of other teenagers who rode competitively. Her uncle Paul who administered her trust fund made sure she knew there was money for training for both her and her horse, but Jocelyn had been afraid to touch it.

Aleta discovered that Sterling liked being talked to and would answer back. He was a sweet horse, definitely worth saving. And he had a purpose. With him there, Jocelyn's jumper was easier to handle. A high-strung horse, Yudi didn't do well alone and the trip from California had left him slightly skittish. Sterling's calm presence proved to be the key to settling him.

As she lay in bed, Aleta realized she'd been unreasonable earlier. Stanley was following Dr. Cook's orders, and Dr. Cook's sole purpose was to see that she was restored to her former healthy state.

And while Stanley complained about her short hair and insisted on measuring it, she knew he was searching for new growth along the line of her old scar that had been hairless since the bullet had skimmed the surface of her head. During the operation to repair a subdural bleed, Dr. Cook and Dr. Taekman had supposedly repaired the scar. Stanley knew it was important to her to have her hair as full as it had been.

Suddenly, the television clicked on.

Aleta looked around apprehensively. Scooby didn't waken. She wasn't certain whether he was old enough to sense that someone else had entered or if he was still sleeping because no one had entered.

The remote still lay on the stop of the set.

Aleta decided to stay where she was. She couldn't do anything in her present condition even if there were an intruder.

She lay still and waited, listening intently for any movement. The television appeared to be on mute as no sound came from the set.

After a few minutes she began paying attention to the scroll across the bottom of the set.

Who had set it for the hearing impaired, she wondered.

She began reading the news as if rolled past, glancing at the pictures above. The headline event was the third murder of a wealthy executive at a North Shore Christmas Eve Open House. While the bullets recovered tied all three together, there was no other connection.

What did Stanley think I was going to do about this, she wondered. I'm not a detective, after all. I'm a lawyer. A corporate lawyer.

The former intrusions into the world of criminal activity had been completely accidental. It had just happened. She couldn't help it. Still she absorbed every bit of what was being presented and her mind began to ponder possible connections between the victims.

She woke from her mental meanderings when the newscaster announced, "A series of killings among the homeless has also plagued the police in the northern Tri City area of Willow Glen, Arborville and Oakwood."

Aleta almost sat up, but the straps holding each shoulder in place kept her flat on her back. They stopped her long enough for her to remember not to rise unaided.

Her towns were involved. That meant that somehow she'd be involved.

She thought about that for a moment.

I can't be, she told herself. I'm not even allowed to leave the grounds. I'm seeing no one new. If I were at the office, maybe I could do something.

Her mind focused on the reasons she couldn't be expected to respond.

If I could use a telephone, maybe then I could act, but someone has to hold the phone when I make a call. Bertha fields the calls coming in and she has a private list buried somewhere in her head and no one that's not on her list gets through, so no one can even contact me.

Finally, she reached what she considered the only reasonable solution.

I'm just fantasizing. This isn't any kind of message. It absolutely couldn't be. Absolutely.

The next thought piled on top of her conclusion.

I can't tell Stanley. He's worried enough now. He's just beginning to relax. And he's right about my needing to heal.

While her mind was busy protesting against becoming involved, it was at the same time processing the information flashing across the television screen.

Then, abruptly the television screen went dark. Bewildered, Aleta lay staring out the window as the black night turned into the gray dawn of a snowy day.

As she lay there she realized this was the day before Christmas Eve. She was seeing a Christmas Day broadcast which was forty-eight hours from this moment.

"You know God, you could let me predict a Christmas tree fire. Stanley wouldn't hate that. Everyone would be grateful. Lives would be saved. There wouldn't be any aftermath to worry about. Murders mean murderers are involved. Murderers don't like people who stop them. They'll come after me again. Stanley likes life in the slow lane. He doesn't want… No, I take that back… I don't want the 'til death do us part' to happen just yet… I know we talked about this and I know I said I'd obey, but I have no idea what I'm supposed to do."

She lay still for a long time mentally drawing her cloak of extreme disability around her as a shield against the winds of change that involvement would bring

In the end, she sighed her compliance, "Tell me what to do and I'll do it."

After that she lay still for a long time.

Why would she get the vision when both Martha Cook and her own grandmother were both well-respected prophets?

Neither of them was so helpless as she. True, Martha was ninety and Grams was seventy and she was still in her twenties, but she couldn't believe age had anything to do with it. There had to be a reason though. And, as usual, Aleta tried to figure out what it could be. And, as usual, she couldn't.

At a quarter to eight, after Aleta had been watching the snow slowly cover the tree limbs and the barn roof for an hour, the side door to the laundry room opened. Bertha stomped her boots on the rug. The puppy woke up and began yipping. Bertha walked through the family room, kitchen and living room and entered the bedroom.

"Take care of Scooby first," Aleta said. "I can wait. He can't."

"Be back soon," Bertha said as she picked up the pup and headed straight for the front door which was closer. Aleta knew she'd walk him around the house to the back and that would be enough for him to take care of his business and be ready to eat.

After Bertha bathed and dressed her and she was wheeled to the breakfast table, Aleta said, "I need to talk to Lyle West this morning--personally."

"You have your doctor's appointment at nine and we are short on time," Bertha responded politely.

"This can't wait," Aleta said. Her tone was firm.

"Yes, Ma'am," Bertha said.

She dialed West's private number and held the phone to Aleta's ear.

"Lyle, it's imperative I talk with you as soon as possible," Aleta said. "I have an appointment at the clinic that I'm not going to cancel."

"You think Wayne's going to take one of those arms out of a sling, don't you?" Lyle West surmised.

"I'm hoping."

"Not a chance."

"That's what Stanley said this morning. How come you know?"

"Stanley told me."

"Well, I'm giving it my best shot."

"When are you leaving?"

"As soon as Bertha stuffs some breakfast down me. Toast and eggs this morning, so we'll be out of here pretty soon."

"Should I bring Tom or Alan?" he asked, naming the other Tri City police chiefs.

"How'd you know what I was going to say would affect them too?"

"I didn't," West replied. "But it always seems to affect the whole area whatever it is. You know, Martha Cook's predictions are much more localized."

"Gram's aren't," Aleta shot back.

"Hers are localized to the Tontine members," West said. "Yours are all over the map."

"I'm not even sure what I saw."

"We'll meet you at the hospital. I understand Wayne is going to do an MRI."

"Why not the clinic?"

"Too busy," Lyle replied. "Don't worry. We'll find you."

At the clinic, Aleta sat in the waiting room with a number of people. Most were poorly dressed.

"Nice cloak," the woman next to her said. "It works like a blanket at night, don't it?"

Aleta looked at the older woman with a well-worn face and smiled. "My mother-in-law had it made for me. The wind blows up it, but you're right it would be a great blanket."

The woman eyed her again and then realized it wasn't just the cloak that was nice.

"Whatcha doing here?" the woman probed, annoyed. "This is a free clinic, you know."

"I pay," Aleta replied.

"So this doc's cheaper than any other docs, huh?" she asked.

"He's the most expensive doctor in town. And he won't take insurance, so I have to pay his whole bill."

"So why do you come here?"

"He's the best."

"Really? I got the best doc in town," she said then grinned. Two front teeth were missing.

"Yep," Aleta replied.

The woman in the chair on the opposite side of the crowded room said, "See, I told you."

"Yeah, but you gotta come here same as me. She's got a choice."

The nurse came out and told Aleta that the doctor wanted the MRI done before he talked with her. Bertha wheeled her out the door, down the sidewalk, past the unfinished physical therapy wing and into the hospital.

When Aleta reached the hospital floor where the MRI was located, three police chiefs in full uniform were waiting for her. Lyle West wore his uniform because Martha Cook, Arborville's most powerful citizen, insisted upon it. Tom Milani, Willow Glen's chief, was bound to follow suit because his town considered itself higher on the social ladder then either of its neighbors. Alan Peets, Oakwood's new police chief and the first black chief in the area, wore his so there'd be no mistake as to his authority. It was an impressive group and even Aleta who'd had all three as guests at her dinner parties was slightly overwhelmed by the sight. She heard Bertha draw in a breath of air when she saw them.

"We're first," Lyle said. "Then the MRI. I okayed it with Wayne. He said you weren't to go anywhere but here or home, so we found us an empty room down the hall. Bertha, you need to go get a cup of coffee. Take at least half an hour."

"Yes Sir," Bertha said and left.

Once inside the room, the three chiefs settled in chairs and Lyle said, "Start from the beginning and tell us everything."

"I saw a news broadcast on television after Stanley left," Aleta began. "He left the remote on top of the set. It turned itself on."

"Some sort of electrical surge," Peets guessed.

The other two said nothing.

"It was a Christmas morning newscast," Aleta went on. "Three CEO's were killed at various holiday parties in Chicago's North Shore homes."

This time Peets stayed silent and waited with the other two.

"But that wasn't all," Aleta continued, "The newscaster said that the Tri City police were baffled by a series of deaths of homeless people in their cities. There were seven deaths altogether."

"Seven?" the three chorused. "Who?"

"No names. Just autopsy photos to try to get them identified. But I remember every one of those I saw."

"What about the CEO's?" Peets asked.

"I remember their names and the companies they work for," Aleta said. "Only I can't call them."

"Why not?" Tom Milani asked, "Aside from the arm thing."

"First they wouldn't believe me."

"How about the police in those towns?" Milani asked.

Peets jumped in. "They won't believe her either. In the Hoskinson case, I went on your word that it was no hoax, Tom, but I wouldn't have if I hadn't worked for you so many years and knew you personally. On top of that it wasn't risky.

Hoskinson was an old man in a nursing home who was sick. We're talking CEO's here. Who kills CEO's?"

"Give us the names," Tom said. "We'll take it from there."

When he had the names, Peets asked Aleta if she could describe the homeless people that were killed.

"Have you got another police artist or is Lyle the sole artist for all three towns?" Aleta asked.

"Seven people," Lyle said. "That would take all day. We need to do this at Aleta's house. She can't sit in this room for six or seven hours."

"I think others were shot," Aleta said. "But only seven died.

"A regular blood bath," Peets moaned. "On a night we have fewer patrols out. Wouldn't you know!"

"Why our towns?" Milani said. "We aren't ignoring the problem. We even have housing going up outside Arborville that'll serve all three towns."

"One thing we know for sure," Peets put in, "the CEO's don't live in our towns. So we've only got to deal with the deaths of the homeless."

"That's something," Tom agreed, "It's not much, but it's something."

"I have to get busy with the sketches," Lyle said. "Can you two take care of the CEO thing?"

"We need more," Peets said. "A motive or some connection that makes these three targets."

"Can we afford to call in Ed?" Lyle asked. "He might be able to find a connection. Then our warning would have teeth."

"I hate to be provincial," Peets put in. "But with a massive crime wave about to hit us we need to focus on our own catastrophe."

Tom Milani, Willow Glen's chief, weighed in.

"The CEO's all were killed at holiday parties," he said. "We can give the local police the time and location as well as who. That's a lot. I say we don't call in Ed. I'm over my budget as it is."

"Before you go," Aleta said, "please don't tell anyone I'm your source. If you do, you'll be back to guarding me full time again."

"As I said, I'm over budget now," Tom responded.

"I don't even have a budget," Peets said. "Everything I spend is over what Ramage spent which was nothing since all the men did was hand out traffic tickets. The police department was a source of revenue. Oakwood's not used to paying for police services. My lips are sealed."

"You have my word too," Lyle promised. "Now let's get you that MRI."

In the next room, Justin Conway, Tri City Register's young black reporter, using a borrowed stethoscope plastered against the wall of the adjoining room, heard every word.

He spent several hours at each police station waiting for some report of a crime other than a stolen car or minor vandalism to come in. The police had confiscated his radio twice when he beat the forensic team to the scene, so he was dependent on watching the three chiefs all of whom rolled if anything important came up.

This time he'd been in Oakwood chatting with Alan Peets when the chief got a call on his private line. Peets left immediately afterward, leaving word at dispatch that he'd be at the hospital.

Using back roads and breaking the speed limit still didn't get Justin there first. He had to scout the hospital before he saw all three chiefs waiting outside the MRI lab. He ducked into the utility closet and waited with the door cracked just enough to see what was happening.

When he saw Aleta Praetzel being wheeled down the hall, he knew something big was going down. When the four entered a room, he dashed down the hall and entered the room next to it.

The patient in the bed was too startled to protest. Justin held up his hand and hissed, "Don't touch the call button."

The old hand trembled as it dropped the call device as if it were a snake. The woman shrank away from the intruder, her eyes wide with fear.

Justin took pity on her. "I'm not going to hurt you. Just lay still and I'll be gone in five minutes."

The woman fixed her eyes on the clock and watched the second hand move around its defined circle. Five minutes later she cleared her throat. The chiefs had all just pledged their silence.

Justin took a step away from the wall and, looking at the old woman, said politely, "Thank you."

And then to her relief he left. He was in the elevator when Peets and Milani emerged from the room.

"What's Justin doing here?" Peets asked.

"I'll check out the next room," Milani said.

After he talked with the old lady, he radioed Peets. "Catch him. Bring him back."

"What charge?"

"No charge, yet," Milani said. "He listened from the next room. Scared the patient nearly to death."

"But be nice," Milani told his former lieutenant, "we may need his cooperation,"

"Tom, when am I not nice?" Peets asked.

"Be nicer than that," Torn said.

Peets laughed.

Lyle chatted with Aleta as she was wheeled into the room where the MRI would be taken. She would lie motionless in the tunnel of the machine designed to take radiographic images of any section of her body. It was a slow process which would take upwards of forty minutes to scan Aleta's brain and upper body.

It was a painless, albeit dull procedure, but Aleta was hoping it would show that she had healed enough to be able to use at least one arm normally.

"Justin Conway heard our discussion," Tom Milani told Lyle West when he left Aleta's side. "What can we offer? We can't let him write what we heard."

"We let him file the story," Lyle decided, "minus Aleta's name."

"Don't we want to stop him?" Milani asked leading West to the room where Peets was holding the young reporter.

"It could work to our advantage," Lyle said. "It'll let the homeless community know what we're doing. We might get more cooperation."

"And the CEO's?"

"They aren't really our problem, and it just might scare off the killer who's targeted them."

"And if nothing happens, we look like fools." Tom worried.

"If nothing happens," Lyle responded, "we'll have a quiet Christmas. All we need to do it say we're investigating and are taking steps to protect our homeless population. That's what we're supposed to do."

"So we are following up on a tip," Milani accepted.

"Will Peets let me speak for all of us?" West asked as he put his hand on the door handle.

"He's no fool. He'll let you stick your neck out."

After the MRI was finished, Lyle took Aleta back to the room where they'd met with the chiefs. He didn't mention the long discussion he'd had with Justin Conway. He just had her describe the first victim and began sketching. Bertha fetched coffee and doughnuts.

Dr. Cook arrived on the floor an hour later and studied the MRI's before sending Lyle and Bertha outside while he talked with Aleta.

"I'm not talking about our sex life," Aleta declared before the door was closed.

"So you two are being sexually active after I told you your body couldn't take that kind of activity," Cook pressed.

"Sort of" Aleta hedged. "But we're not violating any of the perimeters you set up."

"What perimeters?" Cook asked then added, "You mean the ones you created on the basis of Stanley's grilling?"

"Yeah, those," Aleta smiled.

"Well, whatever you're doing is okay. Just don't do more. Everything is healing nicely."

"Stanley's not going to be happy with that."

"I can guess why," Dr. Cook said knowingly.

Aleta changed the subject quickly. "So can I take off the sling on my left arm?"

"No way!" he proclaimed. His tone was adamant.

"But no bones were broken," she protested.

"Bones heal in six to twelve weeks. In the case of tendons, that translates into months. They have almost no blood supply. And when you reinjured the tendons you set yourself way back. The sling is because this time they need a great deal of time to heal."

"What about therapy? Will that speed up the process?"

"Maybe after Christmas," Dr. Cook said. "By then your ribs will be healed. By the way, your head looks fine. No hidden surprises there, so I can have a relaxed Christmas, right?"

"You're coming to our Christmas Eve blessing of the animals, aren't you?"

"The twins can hardly wait," Dr. Cook said. "I think they're hoping for a dog and cat fight."

"We're doing it in the barn. Dad and Jocelyn set up a manger scene. They were both delighted to be starting a new tradition. Jocelyn handled Thanksgiving just fine, but the first Christmas after a divorce is harder.

"Dad'll walk me out," Aleta said. "It will be so nice to do something on my feet."

"Aleta, you will stay in your wheelchair. The walks with your father are only to happen when you're alone. Got it?"

"Is that an order?"

"Has Stanley rescinded his order that you're to obey me yet?"

"I'm not sure he ever will," Aleta replied. "I don't think I realized how extensively he was going to use my wedding vow."

"Your problem is you made only one. You left yourself no loophole. That wasn't a smart move for a lawyer."

"He hasn't really misused it," Aleta said defensively.

"Just remember I'm not either. Yes, I'm ordering you," Dr. Cook said. "But I'm going to give you one exception as a Christmas gift."

"Really? What?"

"You want to open your present two days before Christmas? "

"I want to know so I can look forward to it."

"You're just like the twins."

As Dr. Cook turned to go, he saw Lyle's first sketch lying on the table. He picked it up and looked at it. "Who's this?

"A homeless man in my vision," Aleta responded.

"Oh, Aleta, you aren't going to make me work on Christmas, are you?"

"Afraid so," Aleta said.

"He sure looks like the homeless man that was brought in. Different chin and nose, but they could be brothers. Is Lyle looking for him?"

"Yes."

"When he finds him, maybe he will be able to tell us who our homeless man is."

"Can't the homeless man speak?"

"He's had a stroke. No one understands him."

"Do you want me to see if I can understand him?"

"I want you to go home," Dr. Cook said. "Haven't you noticed that I haven't called on you lately?"

"I thought you didn't have a need."

"You're my patient too. I need to protect you from further injury."

"Well, I'm already here," Aleta said. "So why not let me stop in and find out who he is. Then you can call his family."

"Just his name," Dr. Cook said.

Aleta smiled. It was good to be useful again.

Lyle was upset with the doctor. "You'll get involved and I need you. We've only just begun."

"Ten minutes," Aleta said. "You can time me."

"Ten minutes," Lyle grumbled.

He showed her the sketch he'd been working on while waiting.

"Much more hair. Longer and very stringy. Lips are much fuller. More like Peets."

Lyle rapidly made the adjustments telling her he'd catch up in a few minutes. Bertha took charge of the wheelchair and followed Dr. Cook down to emergency.

"What happened to all your patients?" Aleta asked thinking of the room full of patients in the clinic.

"My interns took over. You know I'm on call for emergencies during the day."

"What's the quid pro quo?"

"Free prescriptions at the hospital pharmacy for my clinic patients."

"You work a lot of hours," Aleta commented.

"I write a lot of prescriptions," Dr. Cook said evenly.

Bertha wheeled Aleta into the room and they were greeted by a jumble of sounds from the man in the bed.

"Don't swear at me," Aleta responded. "I'm here to help.

More sounds poured out, none of them intelligible to either of the nurses, Bertha or Dr. Cook. Aleta didn't even look around. She already knew she was the only one who could understand him. It had happen several times before.

"No, I'm not going to give you a shot or empty your bedpan. I'm also not going to clean your room and if you don't stop yelling at me I'm not going to translate what you're saying either."

The man spit out what sounded like a bunch of angry syllables. His eyes searched the faces for some sort of understanding of what he'd just said. He saw puzzled frowns, but that was all.

"Satisfied?" Aleta asked without rancor.

His next outpouring was brief but harsh.

"I am not going to tell anyone to leave," Aleta said, "until you ask me nicely and even then some get to stay. And I get to choose."

The next mumblings were calmer.

"Yes, I'm a lawyer. My name's Aleta Praetzel. I am not, however, licensed to practice in Illinois. I can't give you any legal advice."

His mumblings were fraught with vexation.

"Why do I call myself a lawyer, then?" Aleta asked for the benefit of those listening. "Because I'm the House Attorney for the Tontine Trust and am able to represent that group in this state, but no one else until I pass the bar in February."

A new mumbling surprised her.

"Really? Why doesn't Dr. Cook know you? "

The mumbling was brief.

"Because he's her grandson," Aleta responded.

"What is he saying about Grams?" Dr. Cook asked.

"That your grandmother knows him. He says he's rich enough to have the best care."

"Aleta, that tears it. You're done. I was happier not knowing what he was saying," Dr. Cook announced.

The sick man shouted at her as Bertha took hold of the wheelchair.

"Money is not what motivates me," Aleta said icily as Bertha turned the chair. "Besides my husband would give me ten times that amount to leave now."

Bertha began to push the chair when another shout of jumbled syllables emerged.

"Wait," Aleta cried. "I want to reply to this one."

She was turned back.

"Sir, I have the best doctor in town and he's standing beside me. And if you truly aren't homeless, then you'll be paying double the usual rate for his services. He hates rich people."

A low mumble emerged.

Aleta laughed. "No, he doesn't hate me. He still charges me though. But I think you've just lost him as your doctor. You say you can spot a lawyer a mile away. Too bad you can't spot a good doctor."

The old man mumbled a string of syllables.

"I understand," Aleta said.

She turned to Dr. Cook. "He says he has a DNR order on file at most Chicago hospitals and he wants to rescind that order. He's afraid that, if he tells you who he is, his relatives will execute that order and he'll die before he has time to make changes to his will."

"Stanley's not going to like this," Lyle moaned from the doorway.

The murmur from the bed stopped Aleta from telling Bertha she was finished.

"Yes, Stanley Praetzel is my husband."

Another murmur followed.

"Yes, he's a child advocate. But I can tell you right now he won't take you on. You aren't a child."

An answering murmur caused her to stare at the man in the bed. She hadn't really looked at him before.

"Lyle, clear the room," she said. "Except for Dr. Cook."

The nurses reluctantly filed out. Bertha went as well.

The door was closed. Aleta's face was drawn. Dr. Cook reached under her sling and took her pulse.

"Her heart's racing," he told Lyle.

"What did he say?" Lyle asked.

"He's one of them," Aleta responded.

"One of whom?" Dr. Cook asked.

She looked at Lyle.

"One of the targets."

"Keep her here," Lyle ordered. "I need to get men on her and him. And I'll call Stanley."

He'd been through this before. Once she was personally involved, she always wound up in danger.

"What is it?" Dr. Cook asked.

"Calm her!" Lyle ordered. "Stanley is not going to be angry."

"Oh, yes, he is," Aleta choked out as Lyle dashed away.

Her words were squeezed through a constricted throat.

Dr. Cook pulled over a chair and sat down and took her hands in his. "Stanley doesn't get angry with you. He gets worried about you."

"It comes out the same," she squeaked.

"You stepped into another mud puddle of trouble didn't you?" Dr. Cook asked already knowing the answer. "Stanley is not going to be angry. He told me you answer to a Higher Power now. That's why you called Lyle, isn't it?"

Aleta nodded.

Tears began to flow. Still she spoke.

"He told you that?"

"He wanted me to understand that if you disobeyed me, it was because you'd been given a directive from God. Fortunately for you I'm my grandmother's grandson

"The baby...," Aleta sobbed.

"Is also in God's hands," Dr. Cook said. "God has a purpose in all of this. But you still can't get out of that wheelchair until I tell you that you can."

Aleta smiled through her tears. "Men do nothing but give orders, don't they?"

"And we take them too," Dr. Cook said. "You'll notice I was ordered to stay in here, didn't you?"

Aleta's smile broadened.

"Lyle does like that part of his job."

"So it wasn't anything our mystery patient said that upset you?"

Aleta shook her head.

"Can you ask him a question for me?" Dr. Cook asked.

"You can ask your own question. I can tell you what he says."

"Sir," Wayne Cook asked, "how do you know my grandmother?"

Aleta translated his answer. "Her lawyers are working on my new will and the setting up a guardian for my youngest son."

"And my grandmother suggested Stanley Praetzel?" Dr. Cook pressed.

The old man nodded.

Dr. Cook smiled, satisfied. "Ah, Aleta. My patient has taken you off the hook. This time you didn't embroil Stanley in a touchy situation. My grandmother did."

Lyle pushed through the door. "We need to move this man up to the fourth floor where my men know the nursing staff. Can that be done?"

"Yes," Cook replied. "My grandmother?"

"Two men in uniform are at her door explaining their presence as we speak. They've been told that if she says no they are to stand outside."

"She won't make them do that," Dr. Cook said.

"I know," Lyle said smiling.

"And Stanley?" Aleta asked.

"He's on his way. He told you to stop worrying. He's learning to accept the fact that God is not going to ask his permission before He acts."

"But is he angry?" Aleta asked.
"Doc, let's get this man moved," Lyle insisted.
His avoidance told them both Stanley was livid.

Chapter 2

Twenty minutes later Stanley walked into a room on the fourth floor where Aleta was busy describing another victim. Aleta started when he entered. An apology sprang to her lips, but when she looked up at him, he took her head in his hands, leaned over and kissed her fully on the mouth. He waited until he felt her relax before he stopped.

"Does that answer your questions?" he asked straightening up.

"I was so pouty this morning," she said sadly.

"Pregnant women do that."

"Not me!" she declared, suddenly annoyed. "I'm in charge of my emotions."

He smiled at her. "I'd take advantage of the excuse Dr. Cook gave you--hormones."

"I don't need an excuse," she announced firmly. "I was pouty. It was me. Not hormones. And I apologize."

"I accept," Stanley said evenly, and then switched topics. "I spoke with Martha Cook on my way over. She told me what was going on with Wayne's mystery patient. Foster Mize told her all about his investigative journey."

"Investigative journey?" Aleta queried.

"He wants to leave a substantial bequest to the Homeless Shelter Julia is building and he wanted to find out what the homeless wanted in such a place, so he became one. Evidently, he does that sort of thing frequently."

"Lyle thought you were angry."

"I was."

"What calmed you down?"

"I guess realizing you couldn't help being yourself and I married you because I like the person you are."

"I interrupted your day."

"My secretary rearranged my schedule, but I promised I'd be available between one and three."

He turned to Bertha, "You can drive my car home. I believe Mr. Locke and Jocelyn are coming over to put the finishing touches on the manger scene and they'll need lunch."

"Yes, Sir," Bertha said. "Will you be home for lunch as well?"

"Not today," Stanley replied smiling. "Today I'm going to treat Aleta to lunch at one of our favorite restaurants."

Aleta's protest was immediate.

"I have to help Lyle."

"Lauren will be waiting for the three of us at noon."

Lyle added his protest.

"I can't finish by noon. I only have two sketches done as it is."

"You can sketch while we wait for our lunch. Aleta needs a little outing after finding out she's not going to have even one arm for Christmas."

"I thought you told her."

"Why aren't you sketching now?" Stanley asked. "I've seen you sketch and talk. And I did tell her. She didn't believe me."

Lyle went back to sketching, muttering, "Lawyers don't boss police chiefs."

"At one, you're going down for a nap," Stanley told Aleta, "You aren't used to this much activity."

"What activity?"

"You've been up since five," Stanley explained. "You're short of sleep."

"You aren't going to give me a choice, are you?"

"Nope."

Because Aleta had to translate for Foster Mize, Lyle accompanied them into the hospital room and continued sketching, checking with Aleta on a continual basis while Stanley talked with his client about his mentally handicapped son.

Stanley glanced over as Lyle showed Aleta his nearly completed sketch.

"Looks like Mr. Mize here," Stanley remarked.

"That's what Dr. Cook said about the first one," Aleta said.

"So, you believe the real target is Mr. Mize?" Stanley asked his wife.

Lyle looked up surprised. That idea hadn't occurred to him.

"Could be," Aleta said. "That would explain why I'm so sure he's a target."

"Have you shown Mr. Mize your sketches?" Stanley asked.

Lyle stood up and flipped over the pages of his sketchpad.

Mr. Mize mumbled a short couple of syllables.

"That's Butcher," Aleta repeated.

Another page was flipped.

"Slick."

Finally, the most recent one was shown to him.

"Gomer."

"Street names?" Lyle asked.

Mize nodded.

"What's your street name?"

"Cheesy," Aleta responded, translating his short utterance.

"How'd you get that moniker?" Lyle asked.

Aleta laughed as she translated, "He said he was so pompous when he first entered the community, they dubbed him the Big Cheese. Now he's just Cheesy."

"Who else looks like you?" Lyle asked.

"They don't look like me," Mize protested through Aleta.

Lyle tried again.

"Who could be taken as a brother or cousin?"

Mize calmed down.

"Kingpin, Preacher, Sarge and maybe Doc," Aleta repeated.

He uttered a string of syllables and Aleta replied to his comment without translating it.

"Chief West was going to find out anyway. He's a good friend of Martha Cook's. I mean, a really good friend. And Stanley and Chief West are better friends. Neither of them is going to tell the news media. Neither wants anyone to know that you're here."

Mize uttered another string of syllables.

"Lyle, he wants to know what you plan on doing with these men."

"Put them up in a motel for the next few days."

"They've got friends," Aleta responded for Mize, "and plans. Christmas dinner is always special at the food kitchens. They won't want to miss that."

"We only want them off the streets Christmas Eve."

Mize mumbled again and Aleta translated, "Give them each two pairs of warm fur-lined leather gloves, one for them and one to give to a friend. And maybe new socks and galoshes."

"We can do that," Lyle said.

Aleta was delighted to be in a restaurant for lunch. Lauren was waiting at the table near the tree.

The conversation was lively as the two were both delighted to be sharing a noon meal with their husbands. Lyle continued sketching, but as he could sketch and talk, no one minded.

A couple of men entered the restaurant. Glancing at them made Lyle quickly flip over the page to hide the sketch he'd been working on.

"You didn't show that one to me," Aleta commented.

"It wasn't coming out right," Lyle said sharply. "I'd rather start over.

"Shall we order?" Stanley asked evenly, noticing the entrance of the same two men. He recognized one as the editor of the Tri City Register. The other one was a reporter of long standing.

After the food was ordered, Lyle busied himself with his sketching not pausing until the soup was served. He handed the sketch to Stanley. As he expected, the reporter left his table and came over and took a peek.

"It's a good likeness," the newsman said.

Lyle greeted him warmly. "Just fooling around. You know she'd never voluntarily sit for this."

The newsman laughed. "You're right there!"

Shortly after that the two newsmen left. Stanley handed the sketch to Lauren.

"It is good," she said.

"I gather you sketched me," Aleta said. "But why?"

"I'm guessing Justin filed his story minus your name. They're guessing it might be you because I'm here," Lyle said.

Aleta nodded. "So if you were sketching a man they'd know I was your source. And you picked me to sketch because I wouldn't want a reminder of being practically bald."

"You're going to destroy it, aren't you?" Lauren asked her husband.

"No, he's not!" Stanley said. "He's going to give it to me. I like it."

"Are you going to let me see it?" Aleta asked.

"After dessert," Stanley said.

Lyle went back to sketching the fourth portrait. He finished by the end of the meal.

"I have enough to get the men started," he said. "Having names helps."

"Aleta will be available after three," Stanley said as they parted.

Stanley got Aleta into the house at ten to one. He escorted her straight to their bedroom and after helping her use the toilet, he undressed her halfway.

He drew the drapes before helping her to the bed.

"We never draw the drapes," Aleta protested. "What's going on?"

"You're sleeping in the nude."

"I am not."

"Well, half-nude. I haven't time to fuss with the slings," Stanley said positioning his hands behind her back as he lifted her legs into bed. "You like sleeping this way, so stop fussing."

"Not in the middle of the day!" Aleta cried softly.

Lying in bed half-dressed with people coming and going made her nervous.

"Relax," Stanley said.

He drew the covers over her legs.

"I want you to rest. Please indulge me. Think of it as your Christmas gift to me."

Aleta relaxed as her head sank into her pillow.

"A kiss would help."

"Always," he said as he leaned over, both hands cupping her head gently between them. "I love you, Aleta.

You are always delightful company. And with or without hair you are the most beautiful woman in the world."

After having said that, he left. The room was dark and quiet and sleep came quickly.

Bertha turned off the phone as soon as Stanley left the house. The Tri City Register hit the newsstands while Aleta was sleeping.

The answering machine was turned off as well. Stanley had explained to Bertha that everyone who knew him had his cell phone number. His secretary would handle the other callers. Her job was to make sure no one bothered Aleta.

His Christmas surprise for Aleta was being delivered and hidden in the barn. The hiding part was the hard part as the blessing of the animals was taking place in the barn the next evening.

Stanley wanted to surprise Aleta on Christmas morning.

The story in the Tri City Register carried Justin Conway's byline. On the basis of that, he received numerous calls asking him who the mysterious psychic was.

Justin turned most of these calls around to find out the reason for the query. He had three lists. One was for crackpots, which included everyone who believed in psychics; a second was for suspicious people. Cops from Chicago and surrounding towns went on the third list. He tried for quotes from them. If the predictions panned out, the quotes would be gold. He actually garnered quite a few.

Not a single police department involved took the predictions seriously and most asked if he had a snitch and was just dressing up his story by claiming a psychic was his source.

Justin didn't like the innuendos. He looked forward to them all eating crow when the next day's paper came out. He had saved the homeless group for that edition. He wasn't allowed to interview them so he had to let the sketches tell the story. These men were targeted for death. It was a good banner.

As for the CEO's, they had all been non-communicative, but Justin didn't let that stop him. Using the news files from the Chicago Tribune he tracked each man's history as a CEO and found all three targets had something in common.

He got photos from the archives when they were first hired, every one approximately five years ago. He proposed the headline: Snake Oil Specialists? His editor was taken aback by it, but after he read the accompanying sketch of each man's actions once taking over, he went with it.

Each man came in at the top, immediately laid off several key people and moved his own people into their spots. Within months the pension plan was changed and the new CEO was immediately vested. It was a matching plan with the CEO able to sock into it a sizeable percentage of his salary before taxes were taken out. Profits were cleverly recalculated showing a rise under the new management. These were inflated by the repeated culling of the work force. Employees earning the highest salaries were downsized or let go.

In each case in five years or less after starting, the CEO either retired or moved on to another company to again bring the profits up to a fast rise by his hatchet method of streamlining.

Justin had followed the fates of the companies these particular CEO's had left before taking their present job and found that they each had left a financially unstable company minus its most experienced people. Interestingly the blame was not laid on the men who left, but on the ineptness of those left behind. One company filed a Chapter 11 within six months; the other two were struggling to recover but financial analysts predicted they would not recover.

Justin saw a series in the making and his editor agreed. Who targets men with such a track record? And why?

The Tri City Register wasn't read by many outside the area, but certain media men were alerted by its brazen headline. Psychic Predicts Ten Deaths on Christmas Eve.

It was a bold headline. The seven homeless in the Tri City area were hardly worth notice; but the three CEO's who lived in Chicago's North Shore were another matter. Curiosity aroused speculation. Theories were quickly formed and touted. Odds were set. Bets were placed.

Television news services contacted Justin with offers of various types. He turned them all down, not out of any loyalty to the paper, but because he was sitting on a gold mine and he wasn't giving up his claim. He had the inside track. The offers would get better.

When the predictions hit the airways, all three CEO's were upset. Simon Jackman immediately cancelled his Christmas Eve plans. Charles Ludwig told two of his company's security guards they were his personal bodyguards and would accompany him everywhere the next several days. Joel Cockerton dismissed the whole thing as ludicrous.

"Psychics are con artists," Cockerton announced. "I don't take them seriously nor should you. By Christmas Day, you will agree with me."

"So you're making no plans to protect yourself?" the TV newsman asked.

"Absolutely none!" he declared.

Chapter 3

Aleta was awakened by a kiss. The drapes were open. Dusk was settling down over the farm.

"You were tired," Stanley said. "I came back at three but you slept through my kiss."

"What time is it?"

"Four thirty," Stanley said. "The police have twelve men in protective custody. They gathered up any who looked like the men in the sketches. Lyle needs to do the other sketches."

"Is Lyle here?"

"I told him I'd wake you at four-thirty. He's here."

"Did we make the paper?" Aleta queried.

"Yes

"Any calls?"

"I turned off our phone. My office handled the calls," Stanley said. "The television media has picked it up. They're concentrating on the CEO's."

"My name come up?"

"Not yet. Justin kept his word."

"So once I help Lyle finish the last sketch, we'll be done," Aleta broached hopefully.

"When they picked up three of the men you described, everyone marveled at how accurate Lyle's sketches were."

Aleta felt a shiver course down her spine. The result was she felt cold. Even seeing the tree was lit and sensing the warmth of the fire in the fireplace didn't help. She noticed more gifts had been added to those already under the tree and smiled. Stanley needed time to wrap presents.

That thought only warmed her a little. She desperately wanted the whole affair to disappear.

If only I could stop now, she thought. Oh, God, please give me a way out."

"How's your memory of this morning's vision?" Lyle asked. "Still there I hope?"

Aleta saw the door open in that query. God had provided an escape. She could walk away. They had three sketches. They had twelve already in protective custody. Everyone would understand if her memory became vague or even failed altogether. Everyone. Even God would understand and forgive.

Then Stanley spoke, "We'll have to go back to the hospital so Mize can tell you the names, won't we? Actually, that is okay by me. I want to show Aleta some of the more fantastic displays around town."

"Aleta, you ready to go to work?" Lyle asked.

"My memory…," she began, then hesitated.

Stanley would know she was lying. He knows the visions last a long time. He knows I'll see the vision of those faces in my dreams. She shook off her desire to escape. Men's lives were at stake.

"My memory is still strong," Aleta said. "Let's do it."

Several sketches later, Lyle paused with a query.

"Aleta, earlier you said Mr. Mize was one of the victims, I haven't drawn him yet. Why?"

"There's one more face to go," Aleta said. "But it's not him."

"I wonder why not," Lyle mused, picking up his sketchpad.

As soon as Lyle finished, Aleta was put in the van and Lyle suggested they not bother with the wheelchair.

"We'll borrow one at the hospital. It's getting late."

At the hospital Foster Mize identified Sarge, Smitty, Boston and Frog.

"We've already picked up Sarge," Lyle said. "I'll check our look-alikes against these latest sketches. That I can still do tonight."

Foster Mize mumbled and Aleta nodded. She turned to Lyle.

"Do you want more names?" she asked. "Mr. Mize said there are three more possibles. Scratch, Meddler, and Crow."

Lyle nodded as he wrote the names down.

"Mr. Mize, there'll be a man on you day and night until this is over," Chief West promised.

Chapter 4

Boston, Frog and Meddler had been picked up as look-alikes, Lyle discovered. The search was now narrowed to four: Butcher, Smitty, Scratch and Crow.

Christmas Eve morning the Tri City Register was given the sketches. Justin asked Lyle West if a photographer could photograph the men in custody. West gave his permission. The paper ran the photos alongside the sketches.

All three chiefs hoped that the publicity might deter the attacks.

Justin was ecstatic. His profile of the three CEO's would dominate the front page. The homeless men and that story would take up the whole third page and both would carry his byline.

The photos gave veracity to the predictions.

The homeless were faceless dirty people, featureless, characterless, just bodies cluttering up the spaces beneath the bridges, the benches in the bus and railway stations, the dark corners in the alleys behind the stores and the deep shadows in old buildings. These men had been gathered from all of these places in all three cities. Justin noted that fact also in his story. He ended with the question, "How did she describe six homeless men with such unerring accuracy?"

His editor had upped the number of papers that rolled off the presses with Justin's first story. They sold out. He increased the number on the Christmas Eve edition even more in anticipation of a rise in interest. That the wire services were picking up this story had boosted the paper's reputation.

He pressed Justin for the name of the psychic but the young man firmly refused to reveal it.

"I promised," he said. "And that's why I have an in on all new developments in this case."

The editor had to admit his new reporter was writing great copy. That Justin not only was given copies of the sketches, but also was allowed to photograph the men in protective custody indicted that he'd struck a bargain with the local police. That in itself surprised the editor because none of the three chiefs were usually amenable to the intrusion of the press into their investigations.

At nine o'clock Christmas Eve morning, Aleta's grandmother, father and sister arrived at the Praetzel house to help Stanley string lights down both sides of the long drive. Bertha had breakfast waiting and Stanley joined them.

"Is she still sleeping?" Harriet asked.

"We stayed up late last night," Stanley said. "We had the tree lit and a fire in the fireplace and we spent the time with my quizzing her in preparation for the bar exam. She's going to be the most prepared person ever to walk into the exam room."

"I thought that maybe the excitement of Christmas would take over," Harriet said.

"I want her to be totally surprised. I had to keep her going so she wouldn't pry the surprise out of me."

"And you want me to distract her this morning?" Harriet surmised. "Suppose I take her for a ride. I thought we might go see Martha."

"That'd be perfect!" Stanley exclaimed. "I'll get her up now. Give me half an hour."

"I need to help Jocelyn," Robert Locke said. "Is Huck Dirkson coming over?"

"I was going to have him come this afternoon, but, Harriet, if you can take Aleta away for a couple of hours, I'll change that."

"I've got my dogs with me," Harriet said. "I'm going to give them a good run before we go to Martha's. Then I can drop them off at my house on our way."

Stanley finished his coffee and entered the bedroom. He ran Aleta's bath.

Aleta stirred but didn't waken until he kissed her. He didn't stop with one kiss and Aleta noticed the drapes were closed.

"What's happening?" she asked.

"Jocelyn is here to take care of the horses, Robert's here to help me with the lights and your grandmother is running her dogs out in the back field."

"Why didn't you wake me earlier?"

Stanley kissed her again as he slowly removed the covers his eyes feasting on her loveliness.

"Did I ever tell you I love a woman who sleeps naked?"

Aleta smiled. "My bath water will get cold."

"That's not your bath water," Stanley said, kneeling beside the bed and kissing her again. "That's so Bertha won't come in."

"Dr. Cook didn't tell you he was going to let me forego the tape on that keeps my hands locked together, did he?"

"He doesn't even know about the slings being off at night," Stanley murmured, kissing her behind the ear. "And that's not his surprise."

"What is?"

"No more twenty questions. I'm busy."

"Stanley we can't have sex. And we can't fool around. This place is swarming with people."

"I sent them all away," Stanley said. "Now be quiet and enjoy this."

And Aleta did as she was told.

Forty minutes later, Harriet walked in the front door. "Bertha, I need a cup of coffee. It's cold out there. Aleta, you're up. You look refreshed."

Aleta nodded and swallowed a smirk.

"Nothing like a warm bath in the morning, is there?" Harriet said.

She turned and addressed Bertha. "Mrs. Praetzel and I won't be here for lunch."

"Where are we going?" Aleta asked.

"To Martha's."

"For lunch?"

"I go there frequently. This time you're invited."

"I don't think I'm dressed properly," Aleta worried.

"It's just lunch. With Martha it's always simple," her grandmother assured her. "Stanley, put her in her good slacks. The blouse is fine."

"What about my wheelchair? Doesn't she have stairs?"

"Lyle has a police officer stationed there. Let him help you up the stairs," Stanley said. "Harriet can clue him in."

As Stanley wheeled Aleta toward the bedroom, Harriet said, "By the way, Jocelyn asked me if two of her friends could leave their horses here for the blessing tonight. I said it was okay. They'll pick them up tomorrow."

"Who's going to take care of them?" Stanley objected irritably.

"Jocelyn."

"They should be here with their horses. I don't like the liability," he persisted.

"Oh, Stanley," Aleta said. "No one's going to ride them. They're going to stand in a stall."

"Well, I guess it'll be alright, especially since you already said yes."

Aleta looked up at her husband and saw a pleased look on his face. He was remembering the last half hour. He leaned down and kissed her.

"Next month we'll find out if it's a boy or a girl," she said.

"I'm not sure I want to know."

"I'm okay either way," Aleta said calmly.

"I like surprises," Stanley said.

You know I was hampered this year," Aleta said a tad apologetic, "No big surprises."

"This animal blessing thing is this year's surprise. Now let's get you ready to leave so I can help with the lights."

On the way over to Martha's, Harriet observed casually, "I gather Stanley has convinced you he's in this for the long haul."

Aleta was pensive. Harriet turned off the road leading to Martha's.

"Where are we going?" Aleta asked.

"To take the dogs home. They need to rest so they'll behave while they're being blessed."

"Stanley likes the celebration I planned," Aleta commented. "His mother is coming. He likes that she likes it."

"It is a great idea! And Jocelyn is absolutely thrilled she's been able to dig in and work on it. You're armlessness has given your sister a chance to come into her own."

"I'm not feeling very Pollyannaish right now."

"You wanted to give her a special gift for Christmas, Harriet said. "And that you've done."

"Stanley called it this year's surprise."

"I think more than the animals are going to be blessed tonight," Harriet said as she drove into the Tontine Lake subdivision. Immediately, all three Chessies woke up and began panting in anticipation.

Aleta waited in the car for longer than five minutes, but she couldn't go check on Harriet. She couldn't even honk to let her know she was worried.

The slings didn't prevent her from doing anything. It was the fact that she had no way to remove the tape that bound her wrists together so that one hand rested on the other. It was Stanley's invention. He knew the tape would remind her to obey. So she sat helpless wondering if something had happened to her grandmother, half of her knowing that there wasn't any emergency and half of her worrying that there just might be.

Harriet emerged from the house in a fresh outfit. She'd changed clothes.

"Thank you, Stanley," Aleta breathed before her grandmother opened the door and climbed in.

There were two police officers guarding Martha's house.

"Lyle thinks you're in danger?" Aleta asked as soon as she was seated in a chair in the small living room of Martha's modest two story frame house crowded onto a small lot two blocks from Main Street.

Martha cackled, "If Lyle thought I was in real danger, the house would be crawling with police."

The officers took up posts outside and Martha sent her housekeeper home as soon as the woman had finished setting up the lunch on the dining room table.

"We can eat and talk," Martha said.

And so the three gathered around the table, stood for a moment while Martha prayed, and then sat down.

Martha began the conversation.

In her high-pitched crackly voice she said. "They're connected, you know."

"Why do you say that?"

"Because both prophecies were given to you," Martha said. "Didn't that thought cross your mind?"

"Yes, and I puzzled over it, but I can't find any connection."

"You don't think on the whole of Chicago's North Shore there's not a single prophet?"

Her voice rose almost to a squeak.

"Well, I guess I hadn't thought about that."

"You've been chosen because the connection between your two visions is in our area."

"But it makes no sense," Aleta protested. "The targets are at the extreme ends of the social continuum."

"Which makes it all fascinating," Martha cackled.

"I was hoping that when Lyle rounded up the homeless men, that would be the end of it."

"It's only just begun" Martha predicted.

Aleta groaned and Harriet popped into the conversation.

"She's worried Stanley will decide she's not worth the turmoil."

"Stanley?" Martha chuckled. "Our Stanley?"

Harriet nodded. "She doesn't get it yet."

"My dear," Martha said kindly. "Stanley is happier than I've ever seen him. He finds you exciting, challenging and utterly delightful. Take a step back and take a look at him. It's written all over his face."

"Aleta," Harriet said, her rough voice a sharp contrast to Martha's thin voice. "Bertha can give you your bath and dress you, right?"

"Yes. She's an LVN. You know that."

"So why does Stanley do it whenever he's home?" The rough voice was almost accusatory.

"He likes…," Aleta blushed.

"Martha and I both had long happy marriages," Harriet responded. "And we still remember the honeymoon stage. It was full of fun and laughter and sex. From what we're able to gather that's what your life is like."

Aleta nodded, then protested, "But we've had some rough patches too."

"We had those too," Harriet said.

She looked at Martha.

"Do you have the picture?" Martha asked.

"Picture? What picture?" Aleta responded.

"Your grandmother is worried. Not about Stanley. Not about your marriage. But about you personally."

"Me?"

"I agree with her. You're near the breaking point," Martha said. Again her voice rose to squeak level. "So we've agreed to offer you an alternative. A choice, as it were."

"A choice? To disobey? I've already made that choice," Aleta said. "I could have just last night, but I can't."

"There is still an option," Martha said. "We can ask God to use us instead of you."

Harriet's rough voice took over.

"It would take the burden off your shoulders. With you as helpless as you are and feeling as constrained by your physical inabilities, this is perhaps just asking too much of you."

"Would God give me more than I can handle?"

"He might," Martha said, "if He wanted us to step up."

"Would God do that? Switch prophets mid-stream?"

"If He wanted to, He would," Martha said, her voice almost normal. "He has his own rules."

"We can always ask," Harriet put in. "There is nothing you can't ask."

"But won't He think I'm chicken?" Aleta said timidly.

"My stars, Aleta," Martha said, her voice soft, "Do you think He doesn't know how you feel?"

Aleta let a piece of a smile touch the corners of her mouth. "I guess I was hoping He wouldn't notice how badly I was handling this."

"You aren't handling anything badly," Harriet said, her rough tone also gentler, "You've been obeying. The fact that you don't want to do it has no relevance. Jesus didn't want to be crucified."

"But if God says no, I'll feel rejected," Aleta confessed.

It just came out--her deepest fear.

"Jesus asked to be spared," Martha said. "His Father said no, but it wasn't a rejection."

"So, how do we ask?" Aleta said tentatively.

Both women laughed.

"Aleta," Martha said, her voice almost soft. "God's been here listening to our whole conversation."

"And he's heard your agony," Harriet said. "We finish with Jesus' words. We'll wait for you to say them."

Aleta hesitated and the bowed her head and prayed silently. "I don't want these two to be hurt. Please say no if a yes would hurt either one."

The two elder women waited silently. And then it came.

"Thy will be done."

"Amen," the two chorused together.

"Now what?" Aleta said.

"Well, either you will continue to get the visions or one of us will," Martha said. "I have dessert planned."

Aleta smiled, "I need dessert."

"You aren't going to ask what it is?" Martha joked.

"Not now. I'm devoid of desire right now."

"You mean I could have served you stale donuts and you would have been okay with that?"

"I'd have eaten them and wondered why you did it when you had Beatrice bake a chocolate cake so you'd have something special to serve your great grandkids after tonight's celebration. They're coming over to help you hang your stocking. They're the ones who insisted you put up a tree so they have a place to put their gifts to you."

"My, my, my," Martha said. "Did you see anything else?"

"Someone is going to die tonight."

"I guess God wants you to keep going," Martha said. "Do you know who?"

"Peets' man, Don Wishnefsky," Aleta said. "There were three names. I fixated on his name."

"Peter French is the name of another man," Martha said suddenly. "He was shot in the back. He's West's right hand man."

"Rob Toccagino," Harriet added. "One of Milani's men. Evidently, it's going to be a bloody night."

"Did any of you see a time?" Aleta asked.

"Just before midnight," Martha replied.

"Lyle said the patrols were already set," Aleta said. "I guess God is going to let us share this prophecy."

"Who's going to call first?" Aleta asked.

"No calls," Martha said. "We're going to ask the three chiefs to come here. We need all three to understand there are three prophets involved now. We have no idea who may get the next vision."

"I want my cake while we wait."

"Let me tell the officer at the door what we want, and then I'll get our cake."

The three had just finished their chocolate cake when Chief Lyle West came through the door, followed by Chief Tom Milani and Chief Alan Peets.

"We had a joint vision," Martha announced. "We each got a piece. Three policemen are going to be killed tonight."

"It's going to be a bloody night," Aleta said.

"At midnight," Harriet added. "We don't know where but we do know who. Your man, Tom, is one. Rob Toccagino. He's going to be caught unawares and shot in the chest."

"Peter French, Lyle," Martha said. "He's going to be shot in the back."

"And Chief Peets," Aleta added. "Don Wishnefsky's gun is going to jam."

"Did you all get the same vision?" Peets asked. "Or did you decide to…?"

Martha interrupted him. "To what? Share the glory? What glory? Share the danger? At my age? Don't be silly. We asked God to take some of the burden from Aleta and He answered us by giving us a shared vision."

"So what do we do?" Peets asked.

"We take those men out of harm's way," West said.

"But won't someone else just get killed instead?" Peets asked.

"No!" chorused the women.

"God doesn't work that way," Aleta said. "He doesn't exchange lives."

"Where do we move them is the question," West mused. "We don't know if they were killed in the location we planned or a new location."

"On the streets is out," Milani put in.

"What's left?" Peets asked.

"The hospital," West offered. "We've got a guard on Mr. Mize now, so tonight we up it to three."

"They won't like it," Milani said. "Especially my man."

"Peter will chaff under the assignment as well," West said, "but he'll stay there if I order it."

"Considering the fact that I fire men who disobey orders," Peets said, "and it's the only thing my men are sure about, I think I can get Don to stay there."

"Rob's a hot head, but I'd hate to lose him," Milani said. "Can we put French in charge of the detail? Peter might be able to sit on him then."

"Okay by me," Peets said. "And Don will have a new gun.

"Okay, ladies," West said. "Anything else?"

"Martha believes the attack on the homeless is connected to the one on the CEO's," Aleta said.

"How?" West asked.

"No clue yet," Martha said.

"I've got a copy of today's Register in my car," West said. "Justin Conway has his own theory. And it's not half-bad. Only it doesn't connect the two events."

"May we see it?" Martha asked.

"I'll send it in," Lyle said. "If you get any ideas, let one of us know."

The three women poured over the news articles after the chiefs left, but nothing said in any of the articles spurred a new thought.

"Mr. Mize isn't in the same category as these three," Martha said. "He started his company and has headed it to now. He pays well and treats his employees fairly. The only thing he has in common with the others is that he's rich; but then so arc we."

"But why go after him now?" Aleta asked. "Why not wait until he surfaces and is back home."

"It has to have something to do with the will," Martha said. "He planned to sign it as soon as he got back."

"Someone has something against Mr. Mize leaving money to the homeless?" Aleta asked.

"I imagine his nieces would," Martha said. "The new will cuts them out."

"Maybe it's not our job to figure it out," Harriet suggested.

"Why is God interfering with these events with so much going on? Why is this so important?" Aleta asked.

Her question went unanswered.

Parked in the Arborville Town Library parking lot in the center of the town square, was Justin Conway, who'd followed Chief Peets when he'd left the station shortly after Justin had given him a copy of the Register. Justin realized as soon as Peets left the Oakwood border that something was going on.

When Peets didn't turn toward the Arborville Police Headquarters, but instead headed toward the center of town, Justin stayed on his trail.

When he was passed by Willow Glen Police Chief Milani, Justin was even more determined. Patrol cars at the entrance to Elm Court forced him to go straight and park in the library's small lot. The library itself was housed in an old Victorian mansion perched on a slight rise. It dominated the center of town. In front was a beautiful rose garden carefully tended by the Rose Society. In back, to accommodate the library's few patrons, was a small parking lot that accommodated ten cars.

Justin backed into a space near the end and had a perfect view of the entrance to Elm Court. He didn't have to wonder who lived there. He knew. Martha Cook. Next to her, separated by an empty lot containing a putting green built especially for Dr. Cook's wife Yancey, who hit the amateur circuit regularly, was the two story clapboard house of Dr. Wayne Cook who lived as modestly as his grandmother in a house built by his grandfather.

Justin saw no other police cars enter and he assumed that Chief West was already there.

The conference lasted about thirty minutes. West was the first to leave. Justin looked at the Register lying on the seat beside him and decided to beat Tom Milani back. He would state as his purpose for being at the Willow Glen Police Headquarters the hand delivery of the Register. He figured one of the other two would have mentioned his hand delivery and Milani would be expecting the same courtesy.

He met Chief Milani as he entered Willow Glen Police Headquarters and handed him the paper.

"Any comment?" he asked.

"I haven't even read it," Tom retorted, then brushed past him and told the dispatcher to call in Rob Toccagino. Justin sat down to wait. He watched Rob mount the stairs to the chief's office and he saw him stomp back down them ten minutes later.

Scowling Rob left the building. Justin followed him.

"Upsetting news?" Justin asked.

"None of your damned business!" Rob shouted back. He yanked open the car door and plopped into the driver's seat.

"Hate to be caught speeding by you now. You'd probably shoot me," Justin quipped, his hand on the door frame.

"Damn you! I'm not trigger happy. Get your hand off the door!"

"My story couldn't have done it," Justin said, removing his hand and stepping back. "Musta been Martha Cook. What's she got against you?"

Rob who'd slammed the door, rolled down the window.

"Martha Cook?"

"Sure. He just came from there," Justin said.

"He tell you that?" Rob asked cautiously.

"I saw him, West and Peets go into her house."

"He consulted a goddamn psychic?" Rob stormed. "He changes my assignment because some weird old lady tells him too?"

"It's a hellava way to run a police department," Justin said sympathetically.

"Guess what he's got me doing?"

Justin just raised an eyebrow. Words right now might give Rob pause. He was on a tear.

"He's got me guarding some sick old man in the hospital all night. All night! He said I'd get a bonus for the extra hours. Hell, I don't want the money! I want to be out in the field with everyone else, not standing guard in a hospital corridor all night. Do you have any idea how dead it is there at night?"

"Did he give a reason?" Justin ventured.

"None."

"So you've got to obey."

"You know what sticks in my craw the most," Rob went on. "The old man--the one in the hospital--he ain't on any of the lists of possible targets. There ain't no danger to him. Guarding him is a bogus assignment. That's what it is."

"Strange," Justin commented, hoping for more.

But Rob was done talking.

When Aleta arrived home, Stanley met her at the van. Between there and the house, which was twenty steps, she managed to convey all that had happened at Martha Cook's house. She talked non-stop at a rate that would have challenged a man not used to talking with excited children, who once they lost their reticence could chatter with the same speed they could run. He led her straight to the bedroom.

"What's going on?" she asked.

"We're taking a nap."

"I'm not tired," Aleta protested immediately.

"I am. And since I can't sleep with you loose in the house..."

Aleta interrupted him. "I'm not a puppy."

"You're worse," Stanley said, "so just stay penned up so I can sleep. I have a long evening and night in front of me."

"Oh you mean moving the trailer. Tell me Jocelyn hadn't seen it."

"She's been too busy helping Robert in the barn setting up for the blessing tonight. The trailer's well hidden behind the shed," Stanley said. "On top of that I'm in charge of clean-up. Bertha's leaving with Robert who's taking Jocelyn home so they can prepare their surprise for your grandmother."

"But I'm wide awake."

"I know," Stanley said, "but we're taking a nap."

Shortly after they climbed in bed, Aleta fell asleep. Stanley had discovered that visions wore Aleta out. When she told him about the latest one, he knew she needed to sleep.

While Aleta slept, miles away, in a modest house in Arborville, three brothers were pouring over the Tri City Register. While several years apart in age, they were all just shy of six feet, lean, with regular features.

"He wasn't CEO for five years!" Sam protested, with his customary ill-humor which had earned him the nickname Sour Sam. "He's only been there three years. Why can't reporters get their facts straight?"

"Bet it was a typo," Toby put in, trying to calm his elder brother. "The rest is accurate. This reporter's got his finger on the reason. That's better than we'd hoped. Now we don't have to leave a note."

"Where'd he get this information?" Fred burst in hastily, his defensive guard up. "I was careful with my investigation. I didn't leave any trails."

"The paper said yesterday their source was a psychic," Sour Sam responded.

The eldest of the three, he was one quarter away from graduating from college when his dad went broke.

The loss of their mother had hit the three hard, but their father's suicide had devastated them. Standing around his grave as the coffin was being lowered to the ground, the three vowed to revenge his death. They chose the following Christmas Eve which was his birthday. The killings would take place on that night.

There were two main targets.

"I don't believe this psychic shit," the youngest, Fred, said brushing back his mass of light brown curls that almost covered his eyes completely.

His mother had liked his long locks and he'd kept his hair long as she liked it after she died.

"Well, the faces of the homeless didn't come off a computer, Genius," Sour Sam retorted. "But so far it seems this psychic can only see victims, so our plan is good to go."

"Good?" Fred sputtered angrily.

The youngest of the three, he wasn't confident in his ability to carry out the shootings planned. Unlike his brothers he was less than a mediocre shot. Sam had assured him that it didn't matter. He just needed to shoot into the group. He and Toby would take out the targets.

"Look at the photos," Sour Sam said. "Our main target's not among them. And you and Toby marked him as well as the others. That's what you told me. So there are three of those you tagged still out there. One of them is our real target."

"What about Jackman?" Toby lisped.

Years of speech therapy hadn't helped. Toby elected to enter the field of electronics where his speech imperfection wouldn't matter. Fred had followed him into the field and surpassed him as a computer hack.

"Scratch him," Sour Sam decided. "We do the others."

"I could take out Cockman alone," Toby lisped.

"I'll take out Cockman," Sour Sam decided, yanking back the lead. "The prick is going to his party unprotected. You two take out Ludwig."

"There are two guards," Fred commented nervously, letting his hair fall over his eyes so his apprehension wouldn't be as apparent.

"Toby will take out Ludwig. You'll take out a guard. If you fire together, you'll surprise the other guard and maybe even panic him. If you don't, Toby will hit him."

"I could miss," Fred worried.

"Just shoot. You'll hit something."

"We can't leave Jackman," Toby objected, taking back the lead. "He's the one we want."

"Later," Sour Sam declared, again defending his status as the leader. "We take out that psychic first. She's too damned accurate."

"She?" Fred asked. "How do we know it's a 'she'?"

"The paper. The reporter slipped up third paragraph from the bottom," Sour Sam said.

"Can you find out who it is, Genius?" Toby asked Fred.

"Probably," Fred replied, "but not by tonight and I thought the plan was to do the whole job tonight."

"We started it on the date we set," Sour Sam said. "Dad wouldn't want us to get caught before we've finished. Still, we need someone to take Jackman's place. How about the names on the other list?"

Toby pulled up the secondary list on the computer.

Sam pointed to a name.

"Does she really live here in Arborville?"

"Where have you been?" Toby declared, happy to put his elder brother down. "Everybody knows she lives here."

"Cook is a common name," Sour Sam shot back. "I didn't know it was actually her."

"Nobody else lives close," Toby pointed out.

"It would work," Sour Sam pondered aloud. "After we hit a couple homeless areas, the police will be too focused on those areas to be patrolling the streets or answering calls."

"I could jam the switchboard," Toby offered.

An electronic whiz, Toby's expertise was one of the reasons they could be sure they were going to hit their targets in the dark.

"No. We don't want them to have a clue how we zeroed in on our targets," Sour Sam said. "We want them to think we relied on night scopes and dumb luck."

"How much research do we have on Martha Cook?" Sam asked Fred.

"She lives alone in a two story house an Elm Court, right hand side of the street, just before the empty lot. Her grandson lives in the house on the other side of the lot. She never goes out at night. And she almost never has visitors. And she never answers her door to anyone she's not expecting."

"We need to take a look at her place," Sam said.

Aleta woke with a start and looked over at the pillow beside hers. It was empty. "Stanley!" she yelled.

"I'm here," he replied from the bathroom.

Aleta heard the water running. Immediately he appeared half-lathered, razor in one hand.

"What's wrong?"

"Go ahead and finish," Aleta said. "Your empty pillow frightened me."

"I'm sorry. I thought you'd hear the water," Stanley said as he went back to finish his shave.

Aleta lay in bed thinking. Martha was the most vulnerable of the three of them. How did they find out? Or did they just guess? Or did someone spot all the patrol cars at her house and jump to the conclusion she was the prophet?

When Stanley emerged from the bathroom, Aleta said, "Can you get Lyle over here now?"

Stanley picked up the phone and punched a single digit. Lyle answered immediately.

"Aleta needs to see you now," he said.

"Milani's closer."

Aleta spoke up. "Tell Lyle to have Lauren and the kids come as planned. He'll meet them here."

Stanley relayed the message adding that he had no idea what was happening and that she specifically asked for him.

Aleta spoke again. "And tell him to wear his uniform. He's going to be dealing with Martha Cook officially after the celebration."

Lyle called in Peter French. "Handle things until I get back. But remember where I am putting you tonight. That doesn't change."

"Yes, Sir."

"You begin guard duty at the hospital at seven. Can I count on you?"

"Yes Sir."

"Something else has come up," Lyle said.

"I'll stick to the schedule, Sir," French promised.

Lyle, who was already in full dress, for his own protection, headed straight for the Praetzel house. Stanley, half-dressed, met him and escorted him into the bedroom. Aleta fully dressed was sitting in her wheelchair.

"I gather Martha's in danger," Lyle said. "Why did you have me come here?"

"It happens later tonight," Aleta said. "I got to thinking. Martha is so vulnerable and she hates being guarded. The best solution I could come up with was to sit a decoy at the dining room table, back to the glass. It can't be a person because I don't want anyone killed. Wayne can put his grandmother on one of the top floors of the hospital and put out any kind of press release he wants. We need her somewhere as safe as Stanley and I were until we can issue a press release saying she wasn't the psychic Justin alluded to in the paper."

"You think that's why she's in danger?" Lyle asked. "Can you think of another reason?"

"Frankly, no. I can't."

"We could guard her at her home."

"In my vision, I saw two policemen rush to her as she fell over. They were there!"

"I'll call French and have him move Mr. Mize to the next room over. Martha gets the one with the bulletproof glass. Then I'll get Wayne over here and we'll make detailed plans."

Lyle took both Peets and Milani aside when they arrived for the celebration and briefed them on the plan.

"The men at the hospital?" West asked.

"Don's one of my best," Peets said. "And he has a new gun."

"Rob was pretty upset about being put on guard duty," Milani said. "He was going to lead one of the patrols. This will make him happy."

"They aren't to know," West said. "I didn't even tell French. I'm not sure whether there's a leak or not; but on this one we take no chances. Her life depends on no one but us, Dr. Cook and the Praetzels. Wayne isn't even telling his wife. Mrs. Cook doesn't know yet either."

"Can we be gone when you tell her?" Tom asked hopefully.

"I want you to be gone," Lyle said firmly. "I will be leaving too. Again I don't know who's watching, but we have to pretend we don't know she's in danger."

"You're sure it doesn't happen here?" Peets asked.

"She's ambushed at home," Lyle said. "Much later tonight."

"Well, Aleta was right about Don's gun, so I'm convinced she still has the power," Peets said.

In the house, Stanley said to Aleta, "I wanted you to sleep, not have another vision."

"I did sleep," Aleta said. "And it's not as if I clicked on the TV or anything, so how is this my fault?"

"You're receptive," Stanley charged but there was no bite in the accusation.

"That's what women are supposed to be," Aleta shot back. "Or didn't you take anatomy?"

"How'd this get sexual?" Stanley snapped.

"You were hoping for a quiet evening where we could fool around, weren't you?"

"Quiet, yes, but that was all."

"You are so full of it!" Aleta laughed.

"What are we going to do to entertain Martha Cook after everyone else has gone?"

"You said Grams was going to help you move the trailer, so she'll be here."

"I'm not the world's most brilliant conversationalist."

"Then you do the dishes, and I'll do the conversing."

"About what?"

I want to know why she picked you for me."

"Explore the other choices?"

"Actually, I wanted to know what she saw in me that would guarantee that you'd like me."

"That's easy," Stanley quipped. "I've told you all that."

"Martha's a wise soul," Aleta countered. "I want to know what she thinks you like."

"I tell you that all the time."

"You can't be objective."

"Love isn't objective."

"I still want to know," Aleta persisted.

"Never mind." Stanley sighed. "Grill her. But no sex talk! "

"Aw…" Aleta smiled mischievously.

"Tonight is 'G' rated!" Stanley declared.

And Aleta let him have the last word.

The guests were still arriving when Stanley wheeled Aleta down the wide flat path to the barn. She was surprised at the beauty of the scene.

In front of the stalls holding Jocelyn's horse Yudi and their rescue horse, Sterling, and Jocelyn's friends' horses were tiny white Christmas lights illuminating the interior of the dark barn. On a straw-strewn floor, seats were arranged in a huge semi-circle with room for multiple animals in front and on the side of each group of chairs.

Aleta, with Scooby sitting in her lap, was wheeled to the far end near where the priest sat waiting. He was an older man with a wreath of white hair surrounding a balding pate. His eyes were sparkling and his smile warm. A man of ecumenical bent, this celebration was to his liking.

He leaned over and whispered to Aleta, "If I do a good job, will you invite me next year?"

"Put the date on your calendar," Aleta said. "Christmas Eve."

Softly playing in the background were strains of "O Come All Ye Faithful." Jocelyn had picked the sound level well. Aleta looked around and spotted the two visiting horses.

"What a pretty Appaloosa!" she exclaimed.

Jocelyn heard her. "The rescue group still has that Appaloosa if you're interested."

"It'll be months before I'm able to ride," Aleta replied. "Besides Stanley doesn't ride."

"You can ride with me."

"You have friends to ride with," Aleta said. "I'm afraid my riding days are behind me."

"You'd like the one at the rescue. He needs a home."

Aleta shook her head. "It's no go, Jocelyn. Once I've seen a beautiful Appy like this one, I'd be unhappy with less. We've got Sterling. He's all the horse we need right now."

"I think that brownish boy is pretty," Stanley said.

"It's a bay mare, Stanley, and she is nice," Aleta responded.

"Here comes Grams," Jocelyn said. "I promised her I'd hold one of the dogs unless you need me to hold Scooby."

"Stanley can…," Aleta started and then looked around.

He was gone. She spotted him out in the crowd directing people and setting up more chairs with Robert. Harriet stood off to one side, each of her dogs sitting beside her. Aleta knew they wouldn't move without permission so she told Jocelyn to help her with the puppy.

Aleta wondered where the refreshments were and asked Jocelyn who pointed to the stall behind her. She glanced back at the table covered with green cloth and saw two huge shiny coffee urns on each end of the table and guessed that they held hot cocoa and warm apple cider.

Christmas cookies of all sorts were on plates and trays under the covering. Bertha had been baking ever since Aleta first came up with the idea for the celebration.

As the strains of "O, Little Town of Bethlehem" began, the priest stepped up on the special wooden platform and not only began to sing but to sign. His voice was strong and true and the chorus in the background enhanced his solo. Stanley, by now seated beside Aleta, smiled at her. They didn't look at Lauren's eldest daughter Camay or at Lyle's brother, both of whom were deaf.

From the song, the priest went straight into telling the Christmas story as a wondrous tale. The children were enthralled. The words were familiar but they were spoken not read. The blessing ceremony was next. It took a while as the priest asked about each animal. The horses were last.

Jocelyn named them, Sterling whinnied when his name was called and the children laughed. It was a fitting conclusion.

The priest circulated after the ceremony, talking with the children. Aleta stayed where she was. When Martha came over to thank her, Aleta asked her if she would mind meeting her in the house after the other guests were gone. When Martha agreed, Lyle who was standing nearby gave Aleta a thumbs up.

Jocelyn went over to Chief Alan Peets' two children and asked them if they'd like to pet her horse. Both children looked apprehensive but Jocelyn was persuasive. They timidly watched her slip a bridle on Yudi. Then with a boost from Stanley, Jocelyn mounted and rode her horse bareback around the paddock.

Other children joined Alan Peets' two. The Cook twins begged for a ride. Stanley, after a nod of approval from their parents, lifted them one at a time onto the bare back of the horse in front of Jocelyn. She then clucked at Yudi who walked around the paddock with his strange load.

That Stanley engendered confidence surprised the onlookers, who while they knew he was a child advocate, had no idea how adept he was at calming a child's fears. Eventually, even the most timid decided to at least sit on the horse. A couple did no more than that, but since Yudi shifted his weight, they felt they had ridden him. After all, he had moved his feet.

Martha was in the house when Chief West wheeled Aleta inside.

"Something's up," Martha said. "I was wondering why you were in uniform."

"That was my idea," Aleta said. "I hoped it would tell you how serious this is."

"Aleta, my dear," the old woman said kindly, "I never question your visions. But why me?"

Distressed, Aleta shook her head.

"Don't fret, Child, I don't expect an answer."

"We have a plan," Chief West stated.

Then he sat down and outlined it.

"You expect me to spend Christmas Eve and Christmas in the hospital?" Martha spouted, her disapproval obvious.

"We need to put you somewhere we can protect you," West said calmly.

"Did Wayne go along with this deception?"

"Yes, he did."

"Well, I don't. I won't have my friends worrying needlessly. I won't condone a lie," Martha stated flatly, her voice almost at screech level.

Aleta was amazed Lyle didn't shrink from the obvious anger of the most powerful woman in his town.

She would've stepped back if she wasn't pinned to her wheelchair.

"I'm putting you in protective custody whether you like it or not."

"I'll stay away from the windows."

"Too risky."

"I'm willing to assume it."

"The plan we presented is the one we're going with," Chief West said firmly.

"I could have you removed from your position tomorrow," Martha warned.

Lyle smiled.

"Given that choice, I chose to save your life."

"You've always done as I asked," Martha sputtered.

"Yes, I have. But this time we're doing it my way."

"I won't…," Martha began.

Suddenly she stopped, a look of shock and dismay on her face.

It took Aleta only a few minutes to realize what was happening.

"Call for an ambulance," Aleta ordered, but Lyle was already talking into his radio. While he was still issuing commands, he went over to the couch and sat beside the old woman. He put his arm around her shoulder. Then he called Dr. Cook.

"Looks like a stroke," Chief West said.

Martha mumbled something.

Aleta responded soothingly. "Don't worry. Wayne will be at the hospital waiting for you. This is the fastest way, believe me."

Martha murmured again, her words so faint Lyle who was seated beside her could barely distinguish that she was speaking at all.

"I'm not sure He's not."

"Who's not doing what?" Lyle asked.

"She says God's punishing her for being a stubborn old woman. She said next time she'll take our advice without an argument."

"She didn't say all that!" Lyle protested, upset.

"Not so you could hear evidently," Aleta replied.

This time it was she who was calm.

Martha mumbled again.

"No, I'm not going with you," Aleta said. "Trust your grandson. He's the best doctor in the area. If you're having a stroke, fast action on his part could reverse the damage before it's permanent."

The siren could be heard coming up the road.

"Don't be afraid," Aleta said.

Harriet burst through the door. "What's wrong?"

"It's Martha," Aleta said. "I think she had a stroke."

"I'd like to go with her," Harriet said looking at Lyle for permission.

Somehow she knew he was in charge.

"Sorry," Lyle said. "Aleta, tell her what's going on. I need her to go home. I don't think anyone knows she's moved so I think that's the safest place for her."

The ambulance arrived at the door and Stanley came in right behind the paramedics. He knew the ambulance wasn't for Aleta. It was one of the options they had discussed for transporting Martha Cook to the hospital; however, the sirens worried him. That wasn't in any plan.

"I'll tell him," Aleta was saying as Martha was placed on the gurney. "I'll call later and I'll tell him. Now stop worrying."

At the hospital, Dr. Wayne Cook barreled through the parking lot and screeched to a halt in the closest space. He ran toward the emergency room entrance and called to the nurse on duty.

"An emergency stroke victim is only minutes behind me. Where's Brice?"

"He called in sick."

"Sick? With what?"

"It's a holiday," was all the nurse would say.

"Is there any doctor in the hospital?"

"Dr. Chesney has a woman in labor," the nurse reported.

"How far along?"

"First time mother. It'll be hours before she delivers."

"Get him down here!" Wayne ordered.

"For a stroke victim?"

"For my grandmother. I need another doctor now!"

"I can call a specialist."

"It's Christmas Eve! I'm not waiting. Besides he just went through this with his wife. He is an expert."

As the ambulance siren approached, the nurse called Dr. Chesney on his cell and told him Dr. Cook needed him in Emergency.

As the gurney rolled through the door, Wayne took his grandmother's hand and assured her he called in a specialist, an ob-gyn man. He saw her smile.

"The nurses are going to undress you and then you're going to have a CAT scan. Your doctor will be here by the time you're changed."

He left the room then. Dr. Chesney found Dr. Cook hunched over in a chair in the hall. He looked to Chief West for an answer.

"His grandmother is your patient. I think she's had a stroke. I think Dr. Cook ordered a CAT scan.

Dr. Chesney pushed through the door. The nurses were in the middle of undressing Martha.

He took her wrist and felt for her pulse.

"Well, you're still alive," he said cheerfully. "I want a CAT scan as soon as possible."

He patted Martha's hand, "Don't worry, I haven't lost a baby in weeks."

She managed a weak half-smile.

"I know your grandson may have his anatomy slightly mixed up, but I do plan on calling in the best neurologist in the area and your grandson will be looking over my shoulder every step of the way, so all you need to do is relax. And yes, I do understand how frustrated you must be not being able to speak and I'm sorry about that. I'll tell you what I'm going to do every step of the way, so there'll be no surprises."

As he left the examining room, Dr. Chesney heard Chief West telling Dr. Cook that Aleta had a message from his grandmother. Dr. Chesney told West to get hold of Aleta immediately.

"Tell me everything she said," Dr. Chesney told Aleta.

Then, anticipating Aleta's query, he added, "Dr. Cook needed a consult and I was the handiest doctor."

"And also one with recent personal experience with a stroke victim," Aleta responded. "I applaud his choice. Tell Martha, please."

As Dr. Chesney watched the nurses wheel his patient from the examination room, he listened to Aleta repeat the entire conversation she'd had with Martha Cook. Lyle, who'd waited for him, then told him which room he had prepared for her.

"She's a target," Chief West finished. "We have reason to believe someone will try to kill her tonight. I have officers standing by to guard her."

"I need her in ICU because we need to monitor her closely for the three hours after we start the TPA treatment," Dr. Chesney responded. "We'll move her to that room as soon as we can."

In the posh town of Winnetka, Joel Cockerton went down with a single round to the head as he was emerging from his car. He was handing the car keys to the parking valet when he fell. In the flurry of activity that followed, Sam Hepner snuck away.

Several miles west in a neighboring suburb, Toby and Fred waited in an upstairs bedroom across the street from the well-lit house where an open house was in progress. Toby had by-passed the electronic alarm system so no entry into the vacant house was recorded at all. Toby's first shot caught Charles Ludwig in the head. Fred's shot was wide and missed both guards and hit a parking attendant. Toby took out the guard who was looking around. They left the one leaning over Mr. Ludwig, pulled their rifles back inside the house and departed out the back.

The news of both hits electrified the three chiefs into action. It was happening as predicted. Their cities were next. Men were outfitted in riot gear and sent out in all three cities.

The chiefs had been told the assault would occur around midnight. It was only eight. Still they were nervous.

The report that two CEO's had been hit circulated through police ranks with the speed of a flash flood. It generated both excitement and fear in the men, but none were deterred by it.

On the fourth floor of the hospital the news came by way of a nurse who'd been called in to help with the expected onrush of patients. Rob had gone to the cafeteria to pick up sandwiches and coffee for the three stuck with guard duty. He got as many details as he could and came back with food and news.

"So the psychic called it," Don Wishnefsky observed.

"It appears so," Peter French agreed.

"Hell!" Rob Toccagino exploded. "You don't believe in that bullshit!

"How do you explain it?" Don challenged biting into his sandwich.

"Someone got a tip. And the cops in those towns didn't take it seriously," Rob Toccagino said. "Hey, don't it bother you guys none that there's gonna be action on the street and we're stuck up here?"

"Yeah, it does," Don Wishnefsky replied. "But when Peets tells you where to go, it's your job if you don't obey."

"Well," French said. "It wouldn't be my job, but West trusts me to do what he asks."

"Milani just gave me orders," Rob added. "But Justin Conway told me that the three chiefs had just left Martha Cook's house. Hell, she's just an old lady that tells West when someone in a nursing home is about to croak. Why stick three of us here?"

"West told me he needs me here," French said. "But your explanation means that the prophets are involved."

"All Peets did was tell me my gun would jam and give me a new piece," Don Wishnefsky reported.

"Did you test it?" Rob asked.

"No, I took his word for it," Don Wishnefsky said. "It's not like he left me without a gun. He gave me a new one. He had me take it to the firing range and check it out even."

Half an hour later, Rob Toccagino went into Mr. Mize's room and came out with Mize's coat and hat.

"What do you think you're doing?" Peter French asked.

"I tell you what I'm not doing. I'm not sitting on my thumbs no more," Rob declared.

He then exchanged his coat for Mize's long brown overcoat.

"Don't be a fool!" French argued. "You'll lose your job.

"And you could get killed," Wishnefsky added.

"You guys don't get it," Rob spouted. "That psychic saw three cops shot. We don't even know if we're the three cops."

"Then why pick us?" Peter French argued.

"Even if she did name us or describe us, it was cops that got killed."

"Homeless men too," Don Wishnefsky said.

"We got most of them squirreled away in that motel," Rob Toccagino argued. "I think I know where one of the others is."

"Tell Chief Milani," Peter advised.

"When I save the guy's life, Milani will be grateful. I bet I get a promotion out of this."

"No you won't. Milani won't take this kind of crap from you. He's the one who taught Peets, remember?" French said.

"Yeah!" Wishnefsky added. "If you don't find the guy, you're out on the street, out of uniform and away from your post. You're going to either be dead or in deep shit. It ain't worth it, Man."

"You two assholes can sit up here and guard two people no one cares about," Rob said. "Me, I'm gonna go be a real cop."

He plunked Mize's dark blue knit hood on his head and hurried toward the stairway.

"Should we call someone?" Don asked.

"Let's give him a chance to change his mind," Peter said.

"Last guy Peets put an guard duty, he fired," Don Wishnefsky related.

"What was the reason?"

"He left his post."

Peter grinned. "I guess we know who's going to hold it all night."

"You mean I can't?" Don asked, dismayed.

"I'll bring you a bedpan. They got lots of those here."

"I can't... you're kidding, aren't you?"

"Am I?" Peter questioned, poker-faced.

"And I just drank a whole thermos of coffee!" Don moaned.

The brothers met back at their house and regrouped. Toby picked up his tracking equipment. They handed Fred an assault rifle with instructions to shoot into the crowd only after one of them shot.

Then the three of them dressed in dark clothing with black knit ski hoods and left the house. They drove into Arborville and picked up a signal near the hospital.

"The man's running," Toby lisped. "Let's go for him first. If we're lucky, he's running from the police."

"Looks like he's heading for the abandoned warehouse near the tracks," Sam observed.

"I'm picking up a second signal," Toby hissed. "I say we park here and use the route we mapped out."

"What if we run into cops?" Fred asked, shoving the rest of his hair into the ski mask after Sam scowled at him.

"Just follow the plan," Sour Sam said. "If you want out, tell us now."

"Out? Me? No, I don't want out. Forget I said anything," Fred said, his manner replete with bravado. "I'm up for this. You can count on me. I ain't letting Dad down."

The area had several junk cars, behind which the Hepner brothers hid as they slowly moved toward their prey. There wasn't much else between them and the remains of a burned-out warehouse in front of which a few homeless men were gathered around a fire in a huge metal barrel. Wood from the building was the fuel the men used to keep warm.

Groups of homeless gathered on the outskirts of Arborville near the abandoned railroad tracks. Most of the group congregated near the old station house a quarter of a mile away from the few men the Hepners had targeted. Those homeless that dwelt here scattered whenever police came near and hid under what was left of the flooring of what was once a large wooden structure. The floor was not solid and the homeless soon learned that the cops weren't eager to break a leg navigating the rotten flooring, so those who called this home were pretty much left alone.

There were several men hovering around the fire when the newcomer arrived. One man immediately split off from the group. Toby ascertained that he was a target.

He located him in his sights and fired once. His man went down.

Sour Sam had the runner who had just joined the group in his sights. The man turned toward Toby immediately after the first shot. He looked as if he was reaching for a gun. Sam fired twice and the man dropped to the ground.

Fred began shooting and sprayed the entire area until everyone was lying down either because he was hit or because he didn't want to be hit. Hands covered heads and Fred took off.

Sirens from other areas converged on the shooting site as Fred scrambled over a small rise. When the searchlights from one police car began to sweep the area, Sam, who had made it to the getaway car first, started the engine and began moving.

Fred kept going between the beams from the lights, dropping each time the lights swung in his direction.

The car was long gone; but he knew the alternate pick-up location. He ran across yards not separated by fences and rounded the corner of a building and climbed into the dark car parked in the driveway of a house with a For Rent sign on its lawn.

Sam didn't turn on the lights for several blocks.

"I'm getting two signals," Toby announced.

"That can't be," Sour Sam snapped. "Only three men were unaccounted for and we just shot two of them."

"Suppose someone snuck out of the motel," Toby lisped. "You think the cops are going to announce that?"

"Which signal is closer?" Sour Sam asked.

"The one in Oakwood," Toby said. "It's in the middle of a neighborhood. Keep going straight."

After a couple miles, Toby announced, "It's in the middle of this street."

Sam cut the lights and drove down the street in the dark.

"We're in a residential neighborhood," Sam observed as he moved along.

"He's in there," Toby said pointing to an unlit house with a "For Sale" sign stuck on the front lawn.

Sour Sam kept moving slowly down the street. "We can't take him out the way we'd planned. In fact, I don't know if we can…"

He was stopped by Fred's shout.

"He's coming out!"

Sam glanced in the rear view mirror as Toby checked his tracking monitor.

"It's him alright."

"What's he doing in a house?" Sour Sam asked.

"Cheating," Fred deduced without much thought. "He's just pretending to be homeless and all the while he's got a place to roost in during the coldest part of the night."

Toby leaned out the window.

"Slow down," he hissed.

Sam glanced into his rear view mirror and saw the man walking toward the brightness of the streetlight. He eased to a gentle stop.

Toby fired twice in rapid succession. The first shot hit the base of the brain and the man fell like a puppet whose strings had been cut. The second shot sailed into the top of the skull of a dead man.

Sam hit the gas and wheeled around the corner before a single curious neighbor opened a blind to peek out.

He turned two corners down, flicked on his lights and slowed to a normal speed.

"We've got to go for the last one," Sour Sam decided.

"Should we hit Martha Cook on our way?" Fred asked, his spirit buoyed by their obvious success. The people in the dark were shadows, mere outlines of men, like silhouettes of ducks in a shooting gallery.

"Good idea," Sour Sam said. "Our last hit shouldn't be in our town. We'll hit Martha Cook next and then take out the man in Willow Glen."

The sound of sirens started up again as Oakwood responded to its single shooting.

"Elm Court is a dead end street," Fred informed his eldest brother. "Go down the next block and kill your lights."

"And do what?" Sour Sam asked annoyed that his youngest brother was vying for the lead.

"Pull up here," Fred ordered. "Toby can sneak around the garage on the other side of the empty lot. We'll have a clear shot at both the dining room window, the kitchen window and the bedroom windows upstairs."

"We should have two shooters," Toby lisped.

"I'll drive," Fred offered.

Sam turned into a driveway next to a dark house and parked in the deep shadow between the house and a tall hedgerow.

Sam and Toby opened the doors slowly and snuck out of the car. Faces covered by dark ski masks, rifles held upright, they crept along the hedge which in winter was little more than a mass of brambles. They both paused at the back corner of the garage before creeping along another hedge marking the back line of the property.

As they slipped through an opening in the thick hedge, the crack of a twig stopped them. Both held their breath. The sound of liquid hitting the dry leaves told them that around the corner, someone was peeing.

Sam reversed his rifle and holding the barrel, stepped out and swung. The cop was watching his flow. He never even saw the rifle butt. He sank to the ground causing the small branches to crack under his weight.

Sam and Toby stepped past him and eased up to the back of Wayne Cook's garage. There were lights on upstairs in the doctor's house, but the kitchen in back was dark.

Sam ran across the small expanse of grass to the rear of Wayne Cook's house. In the lighted dining room window, on the other side of the empty lot, he saw the back of the old woman who was seated at the table. Toby eased up beside him.

"Easy shot," Toby whispered.

Both men raised their rifles, aimed and fired. The body fell forward, the head landing on the table.

Something was wrong with the fall, Sam realized. Suddenly, lights went on flooding the empty lot and the side of the house. A huge beam swung toward them.

Without a word both dropped to the ground and quickly slithered toward the garage. Once there they ran hunched over to the bush wall and the car beyond.

Fred had turned the car around and opened the back doors. The two threw themselves in and Fred took off down the street away from the house.

Suddenly, he pulled into a driveway and stopped.

"What are you doing?" Sam asked.

"There's a chopper overhead searching the area for moving vehicles. We sit here until it moves on."

"Then what?" Sam hissed.

"We wait for the police car to go by."

"It was a set-up," Sam said. "We didn't hit a person. We hit a dummy!"

"Who knew?" Toby asked.

"That damn psychic!" Sour Sam responded.

"How are we gonna get her if she can predict every move we make?" Toby worried.

"She can be gotten to," Fred piped up. "Aleta Praetzel has been shot twice at least."

"Let's finish tonight's work," Sour Sam decided. "We'll do her after everyone has calmed down from tonight's attacks."

"What about Jackman?" Toby charged.

"First her, then him, then Martha Cook and then the rest on that list."

"Can we go now, Fred?" Toby whispered, his words slurring so only the tone was recognizable.

Fred started the car and took a circuitous route to Willow Glen. Toby watched his monitor. The activity was overwhelming when they passed the motel. Fred kept going and eventually Toby picked up a single signal separated from the rest.

Fred turned away from the place the scope indicted the man was.

"Cops!" Fred explained. "They've staked out the area."

"The man's moving," Toby announced. "Some of these guys hate cops."

"Any idea where he's going," Sour Sam asked, again taking the lead.

"I can only track him," Toby lisped.

"They're headed toward the school," Fred guessed. "Some used to bed down near the school. The cops came down on them hard and they gave it up, but tonight the cops are busy."

"They told you this?" Sour Sam questioned.

"Straight dope," Fred said. "You can't just plant those things without getting a bit chummy."

"You know, Fred, you're a great scout," Sam conceded reluctantly. "Go around to the staff parking lot in the back,"

"I've got a better place," Fred said, emboldened by the faint praise. "There's a drive leading from there to the front of the school that the utility vehicles use."

"Should we be so close?" Sour Sam worried.

"We won't be in the open," Fred remarked. "We'll be next to the building. Nobody will notice us."

"You sure about that?" Sam questioned.

"Trucks are parked here all the time," Fred said as he backed down the utility road. "The cops won't be anywhere around. This isn't a homeless hangout."

It took Fred only minutes to get there. Sheltered by the shadow of the school building, they left the safety of their car and watched five men cross the open school ground.

"Which one?" Sour Sam asked.

"One of the middle two," Toby lisped. "You take the one on the left."

"Fred, you ready?" Sam asked. "Sweep left to right."

Fred combed his hair out of his face with his hand, then said, "Go!"

Sam and Toby shot simultaneously. Both their targets dropped to the ground immediately.

Fred pulled the trigger on his assault gun and swept across the three still standing. All collapsed as the rounds found their mark.

The brothers climbed back in the car. Fred drove them home.

The siren and chopper activity told Aleta and Stanley that their worst fears had been realized. Her predictions had come true. How many died they didn't know. It had been difficult enough knowing what was about to happen.

Aleta was too upset to sleep and Stanley built a fire and they sat and watched it in silence, part of them wanting to know, part of them not wanting to know.

Toward midnight Aleta broke the long period of silence with a huge sigh.

"It's over."

"You're sure?" Stanley asked.

"Yes," Aleta said simply.

Stanley asked nothing more. For some reason Aleta felt responsible. He could feel her withdrawing from him.

She was going deep inside herself and he could think of no way to stop her withdrawal.

He excused himself and headed for the bedroom. Aleta scarcely acknowledged his departure. He picked up his cell phone from the nightstand and closed the bathroom door. He dialed Lyle directly. Lyle answered immediately.

"Aleta says it's over," Stanley began. "But I need help."

Lyle mouthed the words to the two chiefs standing in the hospital corridor as the last casualties were brought in.

Cook's interns were working madly trying to keep up. The morgue already had four bodies.

"What's going on?"

"I'm losing her, Lyle. I don't know what to say to her. Can you get Martha to speak with her?"

"She's in the ICU."

"Use your uniform," Stanley retorted. "You said it would get you in anywhere."

"Hang on," Lyle said. "Tell me what she's doing. I need something to go on."

"Do you know what catatonic is?"

"I know."

"She's practically catatonic. Her eyes are fixed and staring. She doesn't speak. She doesn't move. She's leaving this world."

"I'm in the elevator on my way to ICU," Lyle said. "I have no idea if I can do this."

"I'm moving back into the living room," Stanley said. "I feel it's a now or never proposition. Her mind is in a tangle."

"Have you watched the news at all?" Lyle asked.

"No, she couldn't."

"It's not all bad. The men in the motel were all spared. The two that stayed on the streets are both dead. So's one of Milani's men. It was one of those the three predicted would be killed. He was shot in the chest. But he wasn't on patrol. He took Mize's coat and went undercover. The last two men killed are mysteries. We have no idea why they became targets. Martha's house was hit. One of our men was discovered unconscious in the bushes. They got away."

"Thanks for the update," Stanley said. "So she saved two cops and seven homeless."

"And Martha," Lyle added. "I know she had a stroke, but if she'd gone home she'd be dead now. I'm here."

Dr. Chesney and Dr. Cook both looked up when Lyle walked in. "I have a call from Stanley. Aleta's losing it. He thinks Martha might be able to help."

"She can't speak," Wayne Cook said.

"Aleta can understand her," Lyle said. "Look, Aleta saved a lot of lives tonight. Please."

"Aleta?" Martha asked.

"Martha? How are you?" Aleta asked.

Lyle came on. "Can you understand her?"

"Of course, put her back on."

"Tell Wayne to go back to doctoring other people. His interns must be frantic by now," Martha ordered.

"I will, but tell me how you are," Aleta begged. "I'm so sorry I gave you a stroke."

"You didn't give me anything but my life back," Martha said. "The stroke would have happened anyway. And I would have been alone and the damage would have been permanent. Wayne says in three months I will probably be able to screech at everyone again."

"He didn't say that," Aleta charged. "He loves you too much to use so negative a term."

"You are so right. And he called in the nicest doctor. I'm falling in love. It's a delicious sensation. I thought I was past those feelings."

"With Dr. Chesney?"

"I know he's too young, but I'm enjoying myself, so tell Wayne to get back to work and let me have some time alone with my handsome ob-gyn man. Don't you think that's a kick?"

"Yes, it is," Aleta said. "We have a club you know. Most of us are pregnant, but since you're a patient, I guess you qualify."

"So where are you, dear?"

"Feeling like I ruined everyone's Christmas."

"You didn't ruin Wayne's. You saved me. That's the best Christmas gift in the world. And Don Wishnefsky's wife will open her Christmas present and thank a live husband. Whose Christmas did you ruin?" Martha questioned.

"I have this feeling..."

"Right now your feelings are lying to you," Martha said. "Talk to Stanley. Let him help. Give him that as your gift. He likes those kinds of gifts. They make his heart sing."

"Like my wedding vow, huh?"

"Just like that."

"Thanks, Martha. Close your eyes and Lyle will take back the phone."

"Are you done?" Lyle asked.

"I have a message for Wayne," Aleta said.

Lyle handed the phone to Dr. Cook.

"Your mother asked Aleta to tell you something," he said.

Wayne took the phone and listened intently. When he started to laugh, he saw his mother give him a wink.

"Bernard, take care of her. She says my interns are frantic and I should go help them. She wants time alone with you."

"Me?"

"She likes you," Wayne said and then left.

Lyle rushed after him.

"Is Aleta okay."

Wayne handed him his cell. "I believe she will be. Grams worked her magic on both of us."

The two entered the elevator together.

"How bad is the carnage?"

"We're at the end, but those coming in now are the worst. I think they meant to kill them all at the end."

Back in the Praetzel living room, Aleta lifted her face to Stanley.

"Kiss me," she whispered, "and I'll tell you what your Christmas gift is going to be."

"It's not Christmas," Stanley said.

"Look at the clock," Aleta returned, "and then give me my first Christmas kiss and I'll give you your first present on this our first Christmas together."

He kissed her gently. When she responded warmly, his kiss carried his deep love as well.

When he finished, he sat on the raised stone hearth and said, "I'm ready."

"It's another special word like 'pillow'. You get to pick the word. It's another promise. I promise whenever you ask me, rather than draw away, no matter how afraid of the consequences I might be, when you ask me to share my feelings. I will share them truthfully."

Stanley lifted Aleta from the wheelchair and gathered her close and kissed her.

When their lips parted, Aleta said, "You need to pick the word now."

"Midnight," Stanley said.

And Aleta began to tell him what she was feeling. She listened as he separated and clarified each of the sources that contributed to the feeling that she'd ruined everyone's Christmas.

Stanley started with Lyle.

He asked a simple question. "Did you see the joy in Camay's face when the priest began to sign as he sang?"

"But Lyle was pulled away from his family," Aleta said.

"It's part of his job. Did you see Josh's face when he walked into the celebration holding the hand of the Chief of Police, in full uniform? There are moments one remembers forever. Being proud of one's father ranks up there with the best of life's moments."

"Okay, what about Alan Peets."

"I was watching his face when his son overcame his fear and let me hand him up to Jocelyn. I know Yudi didn't do more than shuffle his feet, but when he ran to his father, he asked him if he'd seen him ride the horse. Alan's Christmas was complete in the joy he saw in his son's face. You made that possible. That was your contribution to his Christmas."

"And Milani?" Aleta asked.

"And Wayne Cook's family, too, right?" Stanley responded with a smile.

Aleta nodded.

"Their children got to ride a horse bareback. Christmas is always memorable; but there is nothing like your first time on a horse, and bareback. It's quite thrilling. You didn't take their fathers away from their families. Their jobs did that. What you did was gift them with a great memory."

"You're willing to talk about everyone, aren't you?"

"If that's what you need."

"What I need is to open the present Dr. Cook left for me. He told you, didn't he?"

"Well, yes. He told me," Stanley admitted reluctantly. "But maybe it should wait until morning when you're rested."

"It's Christmas Day!" Aleta declared. "I want it now."

"You're going to be adamant about this, aren't you?"

"Yes."

"Let's go to bed," Stanley suggested. "Your emotions have been on a roller coaster. I believe it would be best if you rest."

Suddenly, Aleta capitulated. "You win. I'll wait until the time is right."

Silently, Stanley helped her stand and walked her to the tree. She'd been staring at the gifts underneath. None were for her. He led her around to the rear of the tree where a huge box sat. The tag read "To You, From Me, with love."

She was about to say something when he put his fingers on her lips and led her to the bedroom.

As usual he turned on the stereo and the soft strains of Wagner floated around the room. He slowly, gently ministered to her bedtime needs.

She thought about hinting that some sexual activity would be welcome, but decided that the time wasn't right.

Brushing someone's teeth wasn't conducive to romance, she thought.

She looked at her husband fondly. Just having him next to her was a singular blessing.

After he undressed her, he gently lowered her into bed. A few minutes later, he joined her. He leaned over, kissed her gently and whispered, "Sweet dreams."

She let her wish go unspoken and closed her eyes. The next kiss was just above her breast and she kept her eyes closed and relaxed into his ministrations.

She wasn't sure how much time went by so wrapped up was she in the pleasant sensations that were washing over her when she heard his voice quietly say, "The time is right."

Their subsequent coupling, despite its restrained passion, was ultimately satisfying.

Afterward, she inquired timidly, "That was Dr. Cook's gift?"

"Hardly," Stanley said. "That was mine."

"But you said…" she began.

"Tomorrow," he whispered.

And Aleta closed her eyes and slept.

At the Tri City Hospital, Martha waited while Dr. Chesney examined the latest readout from the trans-cranial Doppler.

"It looks good to me," Dr. Chesney smiled. "The TPA appears to be dissolving the clot. There's blood flowing through the affected blood vessel. Still, I'm not a neurologist. And while the classes we all attended taught us all how to use this contraption you bought us, a second opinion wouldn't hurt."

Martha nodded.

"I can see you are leaving it up to me to pick the consultant," Dr. Chesney said with a woeful expression. "Do you have any idea what a pickle that puts me in? Any one of them would come running if I mentioned your name. And everyone would want to know why he wasn't called first."

Martha managed a half-smile.

"Stop enjoying this," he quipped.

He thought for a few minutes. "On the other hand, let's us both have some fun. How about I just call you one of Wayne's special patients?"

She furrowed one brow.

"Don't worry. He calls them all special when he's asking for help," Chesney explained. "I will be honest and you can listen to me and I'll repeat their answers. Would you enjoy that? "

Martha nodded and her eyes twinkled.

"Let me start with the ones I know will say no, otherwise this won't be any fun," Dr. Chesney said as he took out his notebook, looked up a number and made his first call.

"Dr. Lemmon, this is Bernard Chesney. I'm monitoring a stroke patient for Dr. Cook and I need a consult... Yes, it's one of his special patients... No, she's not insured... Yes, I'm here because I have a patient in labor... Yes, I know what time it is... Day after tomorrow?"

Martha shook her head.

"Sorry, I need someone now."

He hung up. "What you didn't hear was that while he was willing to consult with Wayne, he'd do it only at a convenient time."

He grinned at her. "One pompous ass down, at least three more to go."

"Dr. Trattner," Chesney began and explained how he came to be monitoring a stroke patient for Dr. Cook. There were no questions and he hung up.

"Ah, Mrs. Cook, he said he wouldn't come out in the middle of the night for his own grandmother, let alone one of Dr. Cook's special patients!

"Jackass!" Dr. Chesney said. "If this is depressing you, I'll stop, but I have one more puffed-up neurologist to go.

I'm rather enjoying this. These guys aren't use to night calls."

Martha smiled. It was only a slight twitch but Chesney caught it.

"We keep going."

He dialed the next number.

"Dr. Dunlap, Dr. Bernard Chesney here... Yes, I know what time it is... I'm monitoring a stroke patient for Dr. Cook who's busy in the ER and I need a consult... Yes, at this hour. I'm in the middle of monitoring the effects of the TPA and... Yes, it's one of Dr. Cook's special patients... Oh, really."

He hung up and said, "He said Wayne had used up all his favors and I shouldn't worry about the test results. In this case, it wasn't important."

Martha frowned.

Dr. Chesney made another call and reported Dr. Nokes' reply.

"He said, 'We all have to die sometime. If the TPA doesn't work, it's her time.'"

Martha expression was unreadable.

"Cold," Chesney commented.

Dr. Patten stated brusquely he didn't take night calls.

"This can't wait," Dr. Chesney said.

"Find someone else," he'd replied and hung up.

"He's a doctor at his convenience," Chesney said. "I'll bet he times his patient's visits. Ten minutes and you're out of there."

Martha's worried look gave Chesney pause.

"Let's try one of the real doctors on staff," he said. "We have them, you know."

Martha's worried look faded. Dr. Chesney made another call.

"Dr. Kurland, I have a 90-year--old woman, a special patient of Dr. Cook's. She's suffered a stroke... Yes, he did a CAT scan... Ischemic type... That's what I'm in the middle of, but I could use a consult… No, no history of stroke… Yes, I'm a bit out of my territory, but I happened to be in the hospital and… Yes, good…"

He turned smiling. "He's bringing his partner, Dr. Hughes."

Martha's face still held a question.

"No, they aren't youngsters. They are two of our best. Kurland said he wanted to meet a 90-year-old who hadn't had a stroke until now. You're an anomaly," Dr. Chesney said. "Isn't that great? I'm taking care of a patient who's an anomaly. And yes, doctors like the rare and interesting cases. Of course, I like you. You remind me of Aleta. Did I ever tell you what she did for my wife?"

Martha's mouth twitched.

"Yes, we have the time. We've got to let them get their pants on. Obstetricians are like firemen. When we get out of bed, our pants are standing there waiting."

Martha's eyes twinkled. This was a special man. When she could talk again, she'd tell Wayne about tonight.

Not too far away the three Hepner brothers reentered their house and collapsed in three chairs around a fireplace whose burned out logs had gathered dust as time had passed without use. A spider had spun a web in the back and now hung down on a single thread in the center.

The TV set, which sat next to the fireplace, was switched on and Fred brought in a six-pack. The three lay back and watched their handiwork on TV.

A clever TV newsman unearthed Simon Jackman in a posh hotel in downtown Chicago, pushed a microphone in his face and asked him how he felt about escaping death.

"Those others targeted should have taken the threat seriously," he announced coldly.

"What about the Tri City Register headline calling you a 'Snake Oil Specialist?' Should we take that seriously?"

The brothers sat forward.

"I guess some people don't understand the corporate world. We're hired to do a job. Firing people is never easy; but sometimes for the company to survive it must be done."

"Bullshit!" Sam spit out.

"But you leave the companies in worse straits than…"

Jackman interrupted. "The companies were in a financial downfall. Every doctor doesn't save every patient."

"Still, you left a rich man," the reporter finished.

"The doctor gets paid even when the patient dies," Jackman retorted smugly.

"Aren't you just a quack, selling something that has no chance of doing any good?"

Sam pounded his fist on the chair. "You got him there! Let's see how he deals with that!"

"Yeah!" Fred exclaimed.

"The poor are always jealous of the rich. People get what they deserve in life," Jackman replied.

The interview ended there.

Toby said, "He doesn't deserve to live, but do you know what he deserves more?"

"What?" Sam and Fred asked simultaneously.

"To be poor."

"He could never be poor," Sour Sam said. "He's too rich."

"We got time while we hunt down the psychic and take care of her," Toby suggested. "Let's make him poor. How about it Fred?"

"I can move money between bank accounts, but he's got all sorts of investments. It'd only be a pinprick."

"We can't sue," Sour Sam said. "We'd give ourselves away."

"We got to do something," Toby declared. "The man's too full of himself. He needs to come down."

"We've got all day," Fred said.

"Let's start with what we can do," Tony suggested.

"I can gut his bank accounts," Fred said. "Where do you want the money to go?"

"Anonymous donation to the food banks in the city," Toby said.

"I've got a better idea," Sam said. "Can you hack into the power company billing computer?"

"Probably," Fred said.

"What would you do with a two hundred thousand dollar light bill and a third notice to pay?" Sour Sam said.

"How much do you want to bet he pays his bills automatically?" Fred came back.

"If that's so, make the amount just a little under what's on hand," Sam said.

"That'll hurt!" Toby snickered. "What else?"

"Later," Sour Sam said, upset because Toby and Fred were deviating from their main plan. "Let's watch the news from our area and see if we got our man."

Chapter 5

Aleta woke with a start. Stanley was not in the room. The house was eerily quiet. Then she heard a voice outside calling to Scooby to come and she relaxed.

She saw the cell phone on the nightstand next to the bed. She had this urge to call Martha; but she had no idea if she had a phone in her room. She couldn't speak after all.

Wayne would be there, she knew. His number was programmed into the cell.

How much harm would it do to reach over and grab the phone? It wasn't heavy. She lifted her arms every day when she was being dressed. Surely she could reach that far without injuring herself.

Stanley had said she was like a puppy, she recalled, a naughty puppy, one who got into mischief the minute she was left alone.

"I'm not a puppy," she muttered. "And I can make reasonable decisions as to what I can and can't do."

And this is important, she reasoned. Abruptly, she remembered her promise to obey all the constraints placed on her by Dr. Cook. She was about to destroy his trust with one phone call. What was she thinking?

She looked out the window at that moment and saw Stanley holding Scooby up and waving his paw at her. Minutes later Scobby was plopped in bed with her and Stanley disappeared into the bathroom, He turned on the water in the tub.

The pup crawled all over the bed, stopping occasionally to lick her face.

"Oof!" she breathed when he bounced on her chest. Stanley plucked him off the bed and put him in his pen.

"You can help us open presents in a few minutes," he told Scooby.

"I need to call Martha," Aleta said.

He spotted the phone on the nightstand. "You were tempted, weren't you?"

"Very," she replied.

He turned off the faucet and dialed Wayne's number. "How's Martha?"

He waited for the response then said, "That's good news."

Aleta held up her hand.

"Aleta wants to speak with her," Stanley said. "Then I imagine she'll want to talk with you."

Aleta heard a mumble. "Yes, Martha, it's me... I'm fine. Really I am. I took your advice. It made all the difference... Yes, I'll tell him. Merry Christmas to you too."

Wayne came back on the line. "You have a message for me?"

"Your grandmother wants you to videotape your Christmas morning for her. And her gifts for your children are in the cupboard next to her tree. She says to go home and come back later. Dr. Chesney promised to spend the morning with her."

"Whatever for?" Wayne asked.

"Because he likes her company. Besides, they have some sort of scheme going and it's going to unfold this morning. She wants you gone."

"What in the world are you talking about? What scheme?"

"If you want details, talk to Chesney," Aleta said. "But remember, she wants you gone."

"You said that," he retorted, annoyed.

"Well, remember it! It's Christmas. Let her have a bit of fun," Aleta ordered.

When Aleta finished, Stanley laid out her clothes and then helped her into the bathroom.

"You put out my jeans," Aleta said, as Stanley lowered her into the tub. "I want to dress up for Christmas."

"When your family gets here, we're going to go out to the barn to present Jocelyn with her gift. I thought you'd want to walk."

Aleta was silent for several minutes. The walk to the barn was not one where she'd get dirty; but it was Christmas. Why not let Stanley decide? Her family wouldn't care. And she could have Stanley help her change later when it was time to eat and his parents came.

"We'll do it your way," she said.

A honking horn startled them both.

"Who's that?" Aleta asked.

"I'll see," he said rushing out.

She realized for the first time that Stanley was fully dressed. And he was wearing jeans.

"It's your dad!" he called back. "He's got a new truck!"

Aleta heard the sound of voices and realized the bedroom door was half-opened. A few moments later she heard it close.

"Are they early?" she said.

"Yes, we are Ma'am," Bertha said, entering the bathroom. "I told Mr. Praetzel I'd finish helping you dress. Are you ready to be dried?"

"Bertha, it's your day off. You're supposed to be a member of the family today."

"Then, Aleta, let's get you out of that tub and into some clothes, so we can get our Christmas day started."

"Dad got a truck?" Aleta asked, stepping out of the tub with Bertha's help.

"His mother surprised him with it. He's always wanted a truck."

"I never put my dad together with a truck," Aleta said as Bertha toweled her dry. "But then I never thought I'd hear him honk up a driveway."

"He was thrilled," Bertha said. "He insisted Stanley and Mr. Praetzel look at it."

"The Praetzels are here?"

"You weren't expecting them?"

"For dinner, yes, but it's early."

"They wanted to see Jocelyn get her gift," Bertha explained as she helped Aleta sit down on the bed.

"Stanley set out my jeans," Aleta said. "I think that's a bit too casual."

"I'd say that today is a good day to do as your husband wishes," Bertha said as she slipped a blouse up Aleta's outstretched arms. A sweater was next. Then the arms were put into their slings.

Stanley poked his head in. "Are we almost done? Jocelyn can't wait any longer."

"Is the turkey in the oven?" Bertha asked.

"Mother saw to it. And there are warm rolls waiting."

Bertha slipped the jeans up Aleta's legs and fastened them. "You're going to need new jeans pretty soon," she commented.

Stanley spoke up.

"Bertha, I'll take care of picking up in here. You just take Aleta out and get some hot coffee into her. It's cold outside."

"Close the door," Aleta whispered to Bertha.

She nodded at her dad. Robert signaled Hubert and Jocelyn and they followed them into the section under construction. Between the three of them, they wrangled the recliner through the half-finished doorways and sat it in the space next to the tree that Harriet, Lydia and Bertha had cleared.

"I'll bet he doesn't even notice," Stanley's mother said.

Harriet smiled. "I'm not betting against you."

Stanley emerged from the bedroom to a circle of smiling faces.

"Aleta wants you to open her present first," Robert said. "It's that small green box tucked way under the tree. You may have to sit in the chair to reach it."

Stanley sat down and looked under the tree. "I see it."

He reached under the tree and snagged the green box. "This chair swivels," he said. "I like that."

"You noticed!" his mother wailed.

"You wouldn't notice if someone put an elephant in your living room?"

"We were betting you'd be oblivious to its presence," Harriet commented.

"Anyone take your bet?" Stanley grinned, then paused as he looked around. "Too bad. They'd have cleaned up."

"So what's in the green box? Or was it just a ruse?"

"Open it and see," Aleta said eagerly.

Stanley opened the box. "It's a piece of paper."

"Open it," everyone urged.

"A drawing of a study," Stanley said. "A beautiful study." He held up the paper.

"That's the rest of your gift," Aleta said. "Every home needs a study. It was my favorite room when I grew up. It was my father's special room. Do you like it?"

"I didn't think you could surprise me, Aleta, but you did," Stanley said, then his voice wavered. "It's a wonderful gift. A really wonderful gift."

"I think we should have some rolls and coffee to celebrate," Bertha said. "Moments like these shouldn't be rushed. You are going to let us all try out your chair, aren't you?"

While Bertha poured the coffee into mugs and set out the rolls, Aleta announced that she'd just talked with Dr. Cook and the news was good.

"For those of you that didn't know Martha Cook had a stroke last night after the celebration. But they gave her that new TPA treatment and believe the effects won't be permanent. It'll be three months before the doctors know for sure if all the damage will be reversed. Right now she can't talk."

"Who's her doctor?" Lydia asked.

"Dr. Chesney."

"Isn't he an obstetrician?" Lydia asked surprised.

Aleta smiled. "I guess Wayne thought she needed one."

"You're kidding," Lydia said.

"She's thrilled with him and he sat with her for hours. I think he took time out to deliver a baby; but they had a date this morning. I had to tell Wayne to go home."

"She has two neurologists on the case," Stanley added. "Dr. Chesney called them in."

"Lemmon or Trattner?" Lydia asked.

"Guess again."

"Nokes and Patten."

"Dunlap turned her down too," Stanley said, and turning to Aleta he explained, "Dr. Chesney called me."

"They turned down Martha Cook?" Lydia gasped. "I don't believe it."

"Chesney told them he needed a consult on one of Wayne's special patients. I guess he and Martha were having some fun."

"So who came out?" Lydia persisted. "Surely he got someone."

"Kurland not only rushed over, but he brought Hughes with him. They were shocked when they discovered whom they were treating."

"Are they good?"

"According to Chesney, they're the best," Stanley said.

"Now can we go out to the barn so I can get my Christmas presents?" Jocelyn said, gathering cups so no one would have seconds.

"Are you walking, Aleta?" her dad asked. "I can walk you past my truck."

"You're really happy with it, aren't you?"

"Always hankered for one. Somehow it never fit my lifestyle before."

"Show it to me," Aleta said gaily. They were the first out the door, but the last ones to reach the barn. When they arrived, it was Aleta who was greeted by a circle of smiling faces.

"I didn't wrap your gift," Stanley said. "It wouldn't stand still. His name's Stacey's Shadow but he goes by Shadow."

"The Appaloosa is mine? You bought me a horse!!"

"Merry Christmas," Stanley said. "Do you like him?"

"I love him. He's gorgeous!"

"The brown one is nice too," Stanley offered. "You can choose. I rather like the brown one."

"It's a bay and I love the one you chose for me," Aleta said.

She walked over to the stall and gasped.

"He's saddled!"

"Thought you might like to try him out," Stanley said.

"Oh, would I! Could I? Will Dr. Cook let me do that?" Aleta asked, her excitement rising.

"Dr. Cook said you can sit on him," Stanley said.

Jocelyn led the Appaloosa out of the stall over to the platform the priest had stood on the night before. Her father held her as she put one foot in the stirrup and supported her as she threw her other leg over the back of the horse. She settled in the saddle.

"This feels as good as my old saddle," she said.

Harriet smiled. "That's because it is."

Her dad looked at Aleta. "How do you like him?"

"Isn't he beautiful!" she said again. "Where's Stanley?"

Jocelyn walked Shadow around so he was facing the stall where the bay mare was being saddled.

"Where'd you learn to saddle a horse?" Aleta asked.

"Someone's going to have to do it until both your arms are well."

"Who's riding the bay?" Aleta said looking around.

"I am," Stanley said simply as he checked the cinch.

"You don't ride," Aleta blurted out.

"How hard can it be?" Stanley asked. "You just put a foot in the stirrup and climb on."

Having said that he slipped his foot in the stirrup and swung his leg over the saddle with a smoothness that bespoke of practice.

Aleta's mouth dropped open.

He moved Minx out of the stall and taking hold of Shadow's rein, clucked, and Minx moved out of the barn. Shadow followed.

"Are you ready for a fast walk?" Stanley asked.

"You can ride!" Aleta exclaimed.

He turned and smiled. "Merry Christmas, Aleta."

He nudged Minx to move faster than the slow walk she had settled into. Shadow stayed with Minx as she quickened her pace. The two moved around the entire circumference of the wheat field twice before Stanley brought them to a halt near the barn.

"Now it's Jocelyn's turn to be surprised," Stanley announced. "We'll watch from here. Aleta will want another ride after Jocelyn opens her present."

"My present?" Jocelyn said. "I thought that was just a pretend thing to get Aleta out to the barn."

"There are three red bows. Each one is attached to a present for you."

"There's one on that post," Jocelyn said. "I don't understand."

"Read the card," her father urged.

Jocelyn opened the card. "The first part of your new practice ring," she read. "A ring? I'm going to have my own practice ring? Where?"

"Here," Aleta said. "In the field behind me or in the field in front of the house. You can choose."

"Wow!"

"There's another bow waiting," her grandmother urged.

Jocelyn looked around. "There's one on top of the tarp."

"Look underneath," her father prompted.

Jocelyn pulled off the tarp.

"Jumps!" she exclaimed. "I have practice jumps!"

"There will be more by the time the ring is ready."

She looked at them carefully. "These are handmade, aren't they? You did them, Dad, didn't you?"

"You like them?"

"They're wonderful!"

"I see another ribbon over there," her father said. Jocelyn tore it open and gasped. "A trainer! I'm going to have a trainer! Oh, Grams, thank you!"

"Our gift is out behind the barn," Stanley said. "I didn't have time to wrap it."

Jocelyn danced through the back door and called back. "I don't see it."

"I'm sure it's still there," Stanley said. "But we'll come around and check."

With that Stanley deftly moved both horses around the outside of the barn to the back of the trailer. Everyone else moved to the back door of the barn and stood smiling.

Jocelyn looked around. Everyone was smiling.

"Dare to think big, honey," her father said gently.

She looked at the trailer.

"It can't be!" she gasped.

"Merry Christmas!" everyone chorused.

Stanley turned the horses and rode off with Aleta.

Hubert Praetzel put his arm around his wife's waist. "Ever think we'd see our boy on a horse?"

"He looks so comfortable on that horse," Lydia said, rendered almost speechless.

"Knowing him, I'd say he's been practicing with this day in mind."

"And practicing a lot," Harriet said, coming up from behind. "But he does sit well. That's natural."

"Aleta was thrilled with her horse," Lydia said.

"She's more thrilled with him on a horse riding with her," Harriet commented. "Those two put a new spin on the word 'gift'."

Lydia stared at the two riding to the farthest reaches of Stanley's acreage. "He'd be devastated if anything happened to her."

"That's true for her as well," Harriet said. "Well, Lydia, shall we go in and help Bertha?"

Hubert looked at his wife, surprised.

"She's not working today. Today she's family," Lydia explained.

"But you don't cook!" he said.

"I can peel potatoes," Lydia retorted. "Harriet doesn't cook either. Today we're scullery maids. It was Stanley's idea. Aleta wanted a family gathering here."

Hubert smiled. "Aleta's contagious."

"I think you hit on the right word," Lydia responded gaily. "And Stanley has caught whatever it is she's got."

"I can't get over the planning involved in his gift," Hubert said.

Outside the front fenced portion of the field, in a car parked on the rise in the road from which they could view the Praetzel property, Fred Hepner, now the designated driver of the group had pulled over and stopped.

It was Sour Sam who exclaimed, "She's on a horse!"

"Are you sure that's her?" Toby lisped. "She doesn't look injured to me."

"The paper said she broke a collar bone in that explosion," Fred inserted.

"We can't see anything with that cape covering her so completely. She could have one arm in a cast," Sam put in. "They're riding close together," Toby noted.

"So?" Fred said.

"It's just different."

As they came to the front corner, Toby raised his binoculars.

"He's leading her. She's riding without her hands."

"She's got them on the saddle," Sam said.

The wind parted the cape slightly.

"One arm is in a sling," Toby announced.

The horses stopped. Stanley moved up to his wife, leaned over and kissed her. Her hands never left the inside of her cape.

Toby kept the binoculars trained on her. "Where is her other hand?" he muttered. "She can't be without both."

"It's cold out," Sour Sam said.

"Why's he leading her horse if she's got a free hand," Toby persisted.

"Because she's a beginner," Sour Sam replied.

"I don't buy it," Toby lisped as the two on horseback started up again. "She's not holding on!"

"A woman riding a horse should be an easy target," Fred interposed desperate to contribute something.

"Better than that," Toby lisped excitedly. "A woman without arms can't stay on a horse that's been spooked."

"An accident," Sour Sam ruminated aloud. "I like that."

"Those people walking toward the house," Fred interjected. "You know that one of the psychics is her grandmother. It's Christmas. Toby, is there an older woman in the group?"

"There are three," Toby replied focusing on the three women. "Sam, zoom in and take a picture.

"Already on it."

"And you got the pair on the horse?" Toby lisped.

"Didn't you hear the camera click?" Sour Sam snapped.

"No cops anywhere," Fred said. "Whoa! Look at the dogs!"

"How many are there?" Toby said trying to find them in his binoculars.

"Three big ones. Two puppies," Fred reported. This time Toby heard the camera's click.

"That changes things," Sour Sam said.

"Why?" Fred asked.

"Dogs have these great noses. If we try to hide too close, the dogs will know we're there."

"Maybe they aren't her dogs."

"People don't bring their dogs when they visit," Sour Sam declared. "Let's go. I need to think."

Stanley and Aleta took one more complete turn before they stopped at the same corner they had before.

"What did you see?" Aleta said noting that Stanley had looked around slowly. She knew he was rechecking the area.

"Just nerves, I guess," Stanley said.

"Why are you lying to me?" she probed. "You saw the same car I did and it worried you. Why?"

"People don't usually stop in that spot," he said.

"They were probably watching us ride," she said. "We did look good riding in sync like that."

Stanley smiled, "I've never been stared at because I looked good."

"A horse becomes you," Aleta said. "I'll have to keep an eye on you when you're in the saddle."

Stanley turned their horses and they began to walk back. "You said last night that it was over. Did you mean it was over last night or over for good?"

"More is coming," Aleta said. "It's possible we won't even be involved."

"I like the sound of that," Stanley responded. "Did you have any idea what your Christmas present might be? I thought maybe seeing two horses in our barn Christmas Eve might have started your brain going."

"It would have if you hadn't sounded so upset when Harriet mentioned that Jocelyn wanted to bring her friends' horses over," she replied. "That was clever."

"I was so worried you wouldn't like Shadow."

"What's not to like?"

"I was depending on Jocelyn."

"She knows my taste in horses," Aleta said. "This was a wonderful gift--the whole package. It is grand to be up on a horse again."

"I hired a horseman," Stanley said. "I think that's what you call them."

"Can we afford another hired hand?"

"If you stop taking charity cases we can."

"I'm not taking any cases," Aleta protested.

"Well, when you take cases again--paying clients only."

"Bessie Dobbins paid us."

"With a painting."

"Which is worth a fortune now and still appreciating."

"The answer, seriously, is yes, we can afford a man to help with the horses."

"I was hoping to hire a nanny when the baby came."

"You have no idea how rich I am, do you?" Stanley said.

"No, but I don't want to tax your generosity."

"I'm not a generous man."

"This gift belies that."

"Let's say I'm ordinarily not a generous man."

"You are not a parsimonious man," Aleta said. "Judicious is what you are. More judicious than I am and that's good."

Stanley stopped both horses, leaned over and kissed her.

"You do come up with the nicest words."

"You know kissing on horseback isn't the safest idea," she cautioned.

"You're saying that because you think my parents are watching.

"I'm saying that because my hands are still taped," Aleta countered.

"In two weeks the tape comes off."

"And the sling?"

"Both stay on for at least another month. Dr. Cook wants to ease you back into using your hands and arms."

"That doesn't give me much usage," Aleta complained.

"It's better than another six weeks like this. Those shoulders have to heal all the way."

"Who is that old man?" Aleta asked as they neared the barn.

"Our new groom," Stanley said. "He was anxious to meet you and look over the horses."

"He's so old."

"His former employer didn't pay the Social Security tax on his earnings. Then she decided he no longer moved fast enough for her, so she planned to kick him out."

"We can do something, can't we?"

"Kurtz West already did. He called me. We settled with the lady out of court. We secured his room in the barn for as long as he wanted it; but she refused to let him touch any horse but one old mare. When she threatened to put Jezebel down, he came to me. He needed a place to go what would take him and Jezebel."

"Tell me we're paying him," Aleta said.

"Room, board, a salary and a stall for Jezebel plus free vet care."

"Room? I heard you say room."

"He wants to see if he can turn that back storage space in the barn into a room."

"He can't stay in our barn! There's no heat!"

Stanley smiled. "So you've noticed."

He dropped Aleta's reins into the old man's gnarled hand, "Aleta, meet Hubbs."

Then he dismounted and led Minx into the barn and put her in her stall. He took off the saddle and set it on the rail.

"Stanley!" she said, a bit tersely.

"Wait," he replied evenly.

Aleta smiled down at Hubbs. "He knows I love it up here. We can move into the barn if you're cold."

"Do you want to dismount?" he asked.

Aleta called into the barn.

"Stanley, didn't you tell Hubbs anything?"

"Not about you," Stanley called back. "He was more interested in the horses."

"I'll wait until Stanley is free," she told the old man. "Tell me, do you like our horses?"

"I like horses," Hubbs replied. "You got a nice bunch. You planning on fencing off pastureland for them come summer? A horse shouldn't ought to live in a barn when there's grass growin'.."

"Stanley, are we going to make a pasture for the horses?"

"Whatever you and Hubbs decide."

She smiled down at the old man. "I guess the answer is yes."

"Jezebel likes grass," Hubbs commented.

Aleta saw her father leave the house and hurry toward her. Jocelyn rushed out of the house and ran after him.

"Aleta," he said when he was near. "Do you need a hand?"

"Stanley told me to wait," Aleta said as her sister caught up.

"He's not your boss!" Jocelyn declared vehemently.

Robert Locke turned on his youngest. "Hush, child. When you're older I'll explain it to you."

"I'm not a child!" Jocelyn protested. "And this is dumb! When does she get to come down? When Stanley says so?"

"Yes," Aleta replied. "Now do you have any questions about Mr. Hubbs' responsibilities?"

"Who's he here for?"

"All the horses," Aleta said. "Only we expect you to rub Yudi down after a ride."

"Cool!"

"Hubbs is a horseman, Jocelyn. You will pay attention to everything he tells you. And you will do what he says or you'll answer to me."

"Not Stanley?" Jocelyn quipped her tone dripping with sarcasm.

"Get over that attitude!" Aleta said. "Giving a man the respect he deserves doesn't lessen the giver."

"I'll take it," Hubbs said abruptly.

"Take what?" Aleta asked.

"The job," he said. "On Mr. Praetzel's terms."

"What terms are those?"

"To deal with you in all horse matters. I wasn't sure I could take orders from a lady again."

"Well, for starters I don't want you to live in an unheated barn," Aleta said.

"Mr. Praetzel said you'd object to that. It really won't bother me none. I like to be near horses. And with five of them the barn won't be as cold as the outside."

"Dad, see if that back room in the barn can be made into livable quarters," Aleta ordered. "Hubbs, let Jocelyn hold Shadow's reins and go look at the room. See if it'd be suitable. I expect an honest answer."

"That's what you'll get, Ma'am."

Jocelyn took the reins unwillingly.

"Stop pouting," Aleta ordered. "My relationship with Stanley is my business. Respect it."

"He's got you under his thumb," Jocelyn muttered. "You used to be so independent."

Aleta smiled broadly. "Boy, you are so right."

"So why did you stop?"

"I found a better way."

"I don't get it."

"You will someday. Meanwhile, sit on that attitude around here."

"And if I don't?" Jocelyn challenged.

"I'll go back to treating you like a recalcitrant child."

"What's that?" Jocelyn asked.

"Look it up."

"Dad!" Jocelyn cried, dropping the reins and running into the barn. "She called me a name."

Robert popped his head out of the room. "You dropped the reins!"

Aleta clucked at Shadow, gave him a nudge with her knees and the horse moved into the barn.

"Whoa," she said softly, and Shadow stopped.

Stanley emerged from Minx's stall, stepped up on the platform, put his hands an Aleta's waist and helped her dismount.

Hubbs emerged from the room in time to see him do this. Not once did her arms come out from under that cape.

What was wrong with her arms, he wondered.

He heard Stanley say, "Your dad can help you back to the house or you can wait for me. It's your choice."

"I'll wait," Aleta said. "I wish I could help."

"I know," Stanley replied. "That day will come."

"Do you need a chair?" her father asked.

"Standing feels good," Aleta said. "Almost as good as riding. Tell me, Hubbs, do you ride?"

"Not no more," Hubbs said. "But it's a good feeling alright. Ain't none better."

"What stall do you want for Jezebel?"

"She'd do best next to the Morgan."

"Sterling? Why?"

"The others are gonna be ridden," Hubbs replied. "Horses are sensitive to who gets how much attention. They wanna feel special, just like folks."

"Put her in Shadow's stall. He can move to the other side of Minx. We'll do it now."

"Aleta, the stall's not ready," Stanley pointed out.

"I can do that," Hubbs said. "And I can rub down Shadow for you too. You've got guests up at the house and I'm free."

"My dad's getting the hitch on his truck next week…"

"Monday," Robert Locke said. "I'll come here sometime around noon and we can hitch up the trailer and get your things. I'll drive you home tonight so you can pack."

"Where's he sleeping?" Stanley asked.

"Excuse me, Ma'am," Hubbs said with considerable deference. "I got me a bed and stuff. And that room in back just needs a bit of cleaning's all. I can do that this afternoon after I take care of Shadow. I got a right good sleeping bag that works better'n any heater and it don't stink none either."

"Is that what you want?"

"Would suit me just perfect."

"Then that's settled," Aleta said. "Jocelyn will fetch you when dinner's ready."

"Ma'am, I'd rather not," Hubbs said politely.

"Bertha's a great cook," Aleta responded, knowing that wasn't the problem.

"That's the truth," Robert Locke said picking up the opening to explain Bertha's role. "During the week she has charge of the house and she doesn't eat with the family. But we're engaged. So the rest of the time, including today, she's family. And Aleta is asking you to join us for Christmas dinner as a guest. You need to get to know us a little. We're a tight knit group and all the usual rules don't apply. Bertha will fill you in."

Hubbs turned to Aleta. "Thanks, Ma'am. I'll be pleased to eat with you folks."

Shortly afterward, as they were walking back to the house, Aleta asked, "Is that big box under the tree there to fool me?"

"No, it has a small gift inside," Stanley said.

"You thought of everything, didn't you?" Aleta smiled. "Boy, you are one great guy!"

"You did me proud today," Stanley returned. "You are one great gal."

They stopped and Stanley turned her toward him and kissed her. She closed her eyes and let herself return the passion.

"I don't understand her at all," she heard Jocelyn say as she and her father passed them.

Aleta smiled inwardly. She didn't want to be understood by a sixteen-year-old. It was a delicious moment.

Robert Locke's voice interrupted them.

"Stanley, take Aleta back to the barn NOW!"

Without asking why, Stanley turned Aleta around. "Can you run?" he asked.

"Yes," came the reply.

Together the two broke into a trot and then a run. Hubbs was fixing the stall for Shadow who stood tethered to a nearby post.

"Quick," Stanley called to Hubbs. "Saddle Minx."

He grabbed Shadow's lead and moved him to the platform where Aleta stood waiting.

By the time Aleta was settled in the saddle, Hubbs had the saddle on Minx.

"Hand me the reins," Aleta said. "I'll go out the back and wait."

Stanley took two steps and looked down toward the house. Several cars had pulled up around the front door.

"Are you sure?" he asked.

"Trust me," she said. "I won't use my arms."

Stanley not only gave her the reins, he untaped her wrists. She clucked softly and nudged Shadow with her heels. He moved forward toward the door at the rear of the barn.

Quickly, Stanley mounted Minx.

"Close the door behind me," he told Hubbs. "Don't answer any questions."

"Yes Sir," Hubbs replied, following in the horse's wake.

Stanley headed for the gate at the back of the field.

Hubbs watched Aleta ride. He recalled her promising not to use her arms. How could she use her hands and not her arms?

It was a puzzle. This whole thing was a puzzle. He slid the old barn door in the back shut. He had no time for puzzles. He had to clean two stalls and get one ready.

Chapter 6

Stanley dismounted at the gate in the rear fence and Aleta looked back toward the house. Through the branches of the scrub trees around the shed she could see the tops of two white vans with satellite dishes mounted on their roofs. She saw two cars as well. One had a police light bar on it. That puzzled her. None of their friends would show up with a TV crew unannounced.

Stanley held the gate open and she moved Shadow through it. He closed the gate and mounted Minx.

"There are TV reporters at the house," he said. "I figured your dad spotted something that spelled trouble. Let's go."

"Where?"

"Wherever this path leads," he said lightly.

They started at a walk and the horses who'd already trotted a bit were happy to be walking. Aleta caught up to Stanley and rode beside him.

"Who called them?"

"No idea."

"There was a police car."

"Well, we know who it wasn't," Stanley replied calmly.

Suddenly, Aleta's doubts vanished. "You're absolutely right. It's not their style. It's someone whose back is against the wall."

"It was going to happen once you spread your wings," Stanley remarked.

"Wings?" Aleta laughed. "What wings? Mine are clipped."

"Your prophetic wings."

"Oh, those," she murmured.

"Some reporter did his homework and tipped off a detective--a quid pro quo thing."

"We left our poor family to cope," Aleta worried.

"Our poor family!" Stanley gasped, then chuckled. "Aleta, my mother's a judge, both our fathers are lawyers, and your grandmother can shoot the eye out of an eagle at a hundred yards. Talk about coping skills!"

"Okay, so maybe they can handle it," Aleta conceded. "Where are we going?"

"We could stop off at my parents' house and I could show you my old bedroom. You've never seen it, you know."

"I know what's on your mind."

"You are so right."

"Where would we put the horses? You can't just park them like cars."

"Cowboys did it when they went into a saloon."

"What do we do---tie them to one of your mother's prize rose bushes?"

"So I guess, that's a no," Stanley lamented. "I just get permission to have real sex with my wife again and you cut off the first golden opportunity that comes along."

"And what was last night--lead?"

Stanley smiled. "I'd like seconds."

"If you don't get serious, I'm going to drop back and not talk to you at all."

"Don't say anything," Stanley said. "That's my advice."

"Advice? What was the question?"

"What you should do about the reporters."

"But I haven't done anything wrong."

"Even Jesus didn't like publicity. He told those he healed to say nothing."

"I thought that was a subterfuge to… My stars, I thought He was using psychology to prompt people to share. Psychologically, nothing is more compelling to spread around than a secret, but Jesus wouldn't use trickery."

"I'd say he was faced with what you're faced with now. Disbelievers trying to trip you up. Or if not that, to ridicule you."

"But He answered them."

"Sometimes he did. Sometimes he didn't."

Aleta capitulated.

"You have a better handle on this than I do. As far as I'm concerned you're in charge."

"Let's ride."

Meanwhile, back at the house, Robert and Jocelyn made it inside just as the cars and vans rolled in.

"Company," Robert announced. "I sent Aleta and Stanley off. Hubert, as the family lawyer, you want to handle this?"

Hubert got up from the recliner which was facing the window. He'd seen Stanley and Aleta head back to the barn on a run. If he knew his son, he wouldn't be there long.

He went to the door at the first knock. The man standing there was holding a copy of a news clipping announcing Stanley and Aleta's wedding. Hubert's son bore a striking resemblance to his father.

Detective Dale Sykora, a thin man with a pockmarked face showed Hubert Praetzel his badge and folding the paper, stuffed it in his coat pocket. His partner, Louis Ross, joined him as he spoke.

"Mr. Praetzel?" he asked.

"Yes," Hubert said. "What can I do for you?"

"We want to question your wife with regard to the prediction of the Charles Ludwig killing."

"Sweetheart," Hubert called back. "There are two officers who want to question you about the death of one of the CEO's."

"Take care of it. I'm busy," Lydia called back grasping at once the mistake the police officer had made which Hubert for some reason didn't want them to straighten out just yet.

Her reply rankled Detective Sykora.

"Either she answers questions here and now or she answers them at police headquarters," he growled.

"Don't be stupid," Hubert Praetzel said. "You have no reason to question my wife."

"Did she predict the deaths of three CEO's?"

"No, she did not."

"That's a lie!" shouted one of the newsmen standing behind the detective.

"Now you people will leave this property or I will call the police." Hubert Praetzel said calmly.

Detective Sykora's mouth dropped open.

"We are the police," he snapped.

"Not the local police," Hubert retorted. "And according to the paper you fumbled the ball on this one. You have a dead CEO as a result."

He turned, "Harriet, call Chief Milani and tell him we have trespassers."

"You want to play hardball," Sykora spit out. "Well, I came prepared. I have a warrant for your wife's arrest."

"On what grounds?"

"Obstruction of justice."

"My wife?" Hubert laughed. "You're out of your head."

He slapped the warrant in Hubert Praetzel's hand.

"They have a warrant, Dear."

Lydia emerged from the kitchen and Hubert handed it to her.

Sykora stared at the woman wishing he could remember the face in the news article. What he did know was that this woman wasn't her.

Lydia handed it back. "This doesn't have my name on it."

"Are you Mrs. Praetzel?" Sykora asked, upset that these people were toying with him.

"Well, I am, but I go by my maiden name when I'm on the bench, Lydia Davis. You want Aleta Praetzel, my son's wife."

Sykora's face turned red.

"You played me!" he shouted. "Now get the hell out of my way or I'll arrest you."

"Judge Lydia Davis," Lydia said, reintroducing herself. "Aleta Praetzel is not here. Why weren't you specific in your query? Are you usually this careless in your police investigations?"

"Produce Aleta Praetzel," Sykora snapped. "Is that specific enough for you?"

"She's not here," Lydia replied.

"Well, where is she?"

"I don't know," Lydia responded.

"I want to search the house."

A police siren could be heard coming down the road. "You called the police?" Sykora asked, shocked.

"We asked you to leave," Hubert replied. "I'm asking again."

"You aren't Stanley Praetzel."

"I never said I was."

"This is his property."

"I'm his lawyer."

Milani's car rolled up and Tom hopped out. Two more squads roared in after him.

Tom went to the door. "What's the problem?"

Sykora flashed his badge. "I'm here for the psychic."

"Which one?"

"The one that predicted the Charles Ludwig killing."

"Which you didn't pay attention to," Chief Milani said. "In fact, your chief was unbearably rude to me when I called. And now that you discover she was right, you intend to blame her for your error in judgment."

Sykora waved the warrant.

"Judge Davis," Chief Milani asked, "Is Mrs. Aleta Praetzel in this house?"

"No, Chief, she's not."

"Do you know where she is?"

"No."

"Do you know when she'll return?"

"No."

"Well, Detective, you can't enter the house."

"I'm looking in the barn," Sykora said.

"Gary, go with him," Milani ordered. "The warrant only covers the arrest of Mrs. Praetzel. He is to remove nothing from the premises."

"What the hell!" Sykora exploded. "This isn't very courteous."

"You set the tone when you barged into my town without so much as a call," Milani answered coldly. "This is a bogus fishing expedition. You know it and I know it."

When Sykora stormed off, Chief Milani ordered the TV crews to leave the property. Then he went inside.

"I don't want to know where Aleta is right now," he said. "But I'm wondering if one of you can get the warrant rescinded or overturned or whatever. I can't see any basis for it. The chief probably feels that if they corral Aleta, they'll be able to divert questions about their investigation until the media turns its attention elsewhere."

I'll take care of it," Lydia said. "Give me a few moments alone in the bedroom."

"They can look around on the property," Milani said. "I can't stop that."

"I think they're elsewhere," Hubert said.

"His car's here," Milani said. "And her wheelchair is sitting by the door."

"You said you didn't want to know," Hubert observed.

"I don't want to be embarrassed."

"You weren't lied to," Hubert said. "There's another explanation. There usually is."

Tom grew thoughtful. He pulled out his cell.

"Lyle, I need to talk to you... Well, where are you...? I'll come there as soon as I'm finished here."

Lydia emerged from the bedroom. "Judge Terrance wants to talk with you."

"Yes, Sir. That's true... Absolutely... Thank you, Sir."

He handed the phone back to Lydia. "Thank you. Now before anyone else does anything, I'm placing Aleta, and you too, Harriet, in protective custody."

"So your men are staying?" Harriet asked.

"There's another chief out there that might try the same ploy. I don't want anyone carting Aleta off somewhere they might not treat her well."

"Thanks," Harriet said. "And I'm sorry about your man."

Chief Milani acknowledged her statement with a nod and then said, "Give me a chance to get rid of these two detectives before you call Stanley and tell him he can bring Aleta home."

Tom paused at the door. "Warn him there may be TV crews parked on the road in front of the house."

He waited another second, then asked, "Are you going to tell me how they did it, so I can go back to concentrating on the shootings?"

Hubert smiled. "Stanley bought Aleta a horse for Christmas."

"A horse? She can't ride."

"Bought himself one too."

"I thought he didn't know how to ride."

"Evidently, he learned."

"Horses," Tom murmured as he left. "I never would have guessed."

Chapter 7

After about twenty minutes, Stanley called his father on his cell.

"When's dinner?" he asked.

"Forty minutes," Hubert replied. "TV trucks are on the road in front. The cops that are here now are Milani's. He put Aleta and Harriet under protective custody."

"We'll start back right away. Thanks, Dad."

"What's that?" Aleta asked pointing to a grove of trees.

"The Forest Preserves."

"What are those?"

"Just what the name says. A place where the forest has been preserved. Illinois is not a state with a lot of forests. We save those we have."

"Can we take a peek?"

"Sure, why not? Dinner isn't for forty minutes."

It was quite by accident that the Hepner brothers spotted them.

After they had watched the two ride around the Praetzel acreage, they went out for breakfast. They were using a little known back road which Fred wanted to scout out to see if it would make a good escape route.

"She's riding by herself," Toby lisped.

"Looks like they're headed for the Forest Preserves," Fred observed aloud.

"Yeah," Sam agreed. "Everyone's at home. It's Christmas."

"We wouldn't be seen," Toby noted suggestively.

"Except by them," Sour Sam pointed out, peeved that Toby was leading the way again.

"We can catch them just after they cross the road," Toby pushed on. "They won't be looking our way at all. And afterward, he'll be too busy picking his wife up off the ground to see us. I say we'll never find a better time or place. No traffic. No neighbors. Nothing."

"How do you want to do this?" Fred asked and, by his query, accepting Toby's plan.

"You drive," Sam growled, then lightened up as he realized he was back to being the planner. "Toby and I will shoot. Then you get us out of here fast and quiet."

In the stillness of the forest, Aleta didn't say a word. The horses plodded along on fallen leaves, soggy from a recent rain because they were sheltered from the sun that would have dried them. The musty smell coupled with the strong scent of pine and fir refreshed her spirit even further. The fear of being cornered by the media and strange policemen who would scoff at her gift began to fade after Stanley's call, but not until the forest's calm did she find peace.

After about ten minutes Stanley said softly, "Time to go back."

He opened his cell. "Dad, have Hubbs open the back gate. We'll be there shortly."

"Why'd you do that?" Aleta asked.

"Just seemed like a good idea," Stanley said.

"Hubbs will have a long walk through a rough field," Aleta pointed out.

"You want me to call Dad back?"

Aleta suddenly remembered that she'd agreed they'd do things Stanley's way. That the thought came back at that moment surprised her. Why did she argue with every decision he made?

"Don't call. Let's ask Hubbs when we get home if it's too hard for him."

"He'll say no," Stanley predicted.

"Let it go. You gave him plenty of time and he's probably finished with the stalls."

"And working on his room."

"Without you?"

"Well, we'll find out how orderly he is," Stanley said. "That'd be good to know."

"You're right," Aleta said as they left the preserve and crossed the road to the trail alongside the bare fields. They walked side by side.

Toby cussed softly.

"We shoot when he gets ahead of her," Sam hissed. "Remember, just nick the horse. We want them bullets buried in the dirt.

"There!" Toby whispered. "It's happening."

The shots came one after the other. One grazed Shadow's rear just above the tail. The second nicked him just above the hock.

When Shadow felt the sting, he reared onto his hind legs, whinnying his protest.

Aleta, startled by the sudden rise of her horse onto his hind legs, automatically leaned forward and gripped the horse's sides with her legs. When Shadow came down, she fell forward and her hands hit the saddle horn so hard. The pain forced her fingers to loosen their grip on the reins. They slipped from her hands.

Aleta reached out and grabbed Shadow's mane just in time to stay her fall backwards as he took off. The resulting jerk from the sudden move forward produced sharp pains in both shoulders. She inadvertently screamed when the pain hit. The yell prompted Shadow to panic further. He not only increased his speed, he left the path for a more direct route back to his stall and safety.

Aleta gritted her teeth and hung on. A fall would be disastrous she knew.

The pain shot across her back on one side and down her chest and arm on the other. She wished she could keep the small yelps and groans from escaping as each landing of the front feet jarred her shoulders. Stabs of pain shot down her arms, still she hung on.

Shadow left the twists in the path to cut through a field. Aleta saw wire fencing ahead.

He doesn't see it she realized.

He'll run right into it and break his legs.

She gripped his mane tighter and stifled her utterances of pain. The thought of being thrown from the saddle by the sudden stop when Shadow's legs hit the wire and flying through the air head first terrified her.

The first alternative that flashed into her mind was to stay on the horse. Immediately, she realized that if she went down with him, she could wind up beneath him and be crushed. She might survive but the baby wouldn't.

He might see the fence in a second, she thought. He had to see it or he'd never jump.

Did he even know how to jump? she wondered.

At that moment, the sun broke through the clouds and the metal wires reflected its light.

Aleta leaned forward and urged the horse to speed up. At the precise moment when he should take off, her whole body reacted with the movement of an experienced horsewoman.

Shadow recognized the authority in the voice and body movement and thrust his hind legs down as he raised his front legs.

Behind her, still on the trail, Stanley was yelling at her to turn the horse. He stopped shouting when he saw Shadow leap into the air. He gasped and then didn't breathe as he watched Shadow sail through the air, his wife hanging onto the mane all the while leaning into the jump.

The landing jarred Aleta and Stanley heard another loud scream.

She's re-broken that shoulder, he thought.

He couldn't believe she was still hanging an.

The jump seemed to startle Shadow into a slightly slower pace. Stanley saw Aleta lean forward.

The gallop smoothed out. Aleta, the reins out of reach, used her legs to signal Shadow to turn. That he obeyed the pressure surprised her, but his obedience sent them along the second fence to an opening just off to one side. She hoped that she could reach the trail by going through it. Shadow spotted the opening and headed straight toward it. He didn't want to tackle another jump either.

When they reached the opening, Aleta chanced a lean to one side and Shadow turned onto the path that led home. His panic lessened enough to keep him on the trail, but not enough to get him to slow to a canter. The twists and turns in the path while barely noticeable when walking were major jarrings insofar as Aleta's shoulders were concerned.

Each wrenching brought a new shot of pain and an accompanying yelp. Shadow's panic was fueled by each screech. Aleta saw the straight stretch around the next bend. It was the last before they were home.

If the gate wasn't open, they were in trouble. She began to urge Shadow to slow down, keeping her voice as even as possible. Shadow, however, still afraid, took the last turn at full gallop and Aleta saw Hubbs hobbling toward the closed gate. When he spotted the runaway horse, he broke into a faster gait.

Aleta could tell he wasn't going to make it. She leaned forward.

"Once more, boy. Once more. Let's give it all we've got.

The gate was made of wood and Shadow saw it. With one final thrust of powerful rear legs he leaped into the air with Aleta astride his back.

Her father, who'd come to the barn to help her dismount, saw Shadow fly through the air, Aleta clinging to his mane. The shock of seeing his injured daughter astride a horse flying across a gate nailed him to the spot. Hubert who had tagged along to help was equally stunned.

When the horse landed, Aleta hung on, her final scream of agony electrifying everyone into action.

Stanley came around the corner and saw the closed gate and knew what Aleta had done a second time during what to her must have been not only a harrowing, but torturous ride.

Hubbs had the gate open by the time Stanley arrived. Minx cantered through the gate. Stanley heard Aleta yelling at the two men to get out of the way.

Shadow went straight into the barn and stopped in front of his stall. The gate was closed. He waited for someone to open it.

Both fathers rushed into the barn. Aleta asked them to wait for Hubbs to come and gentle the horse.

"He's too spooked to stand still just yet."

Both men noticed the heavy heaving of the exhausted horse and saw his wide-eyed look.

"Relax," Aleta said. "We bonded. My shoulders are probably ruined, but, Dad, he minds me. We took two jumps. This is a hellava horse."

"What made him run?"

"Someone shot him," Aleta said simply.

Stanley rode up and dismounted.

"She says to wait for Hubbs," Aleta's father said.

"She's injured," Stanley protested.

"The horse could still throw her," Hubert said. "It's not really calm yet."

Stanley got back on his horse and rode off.

"Where's he going?" Robert asked.

"To get Hubbs," Aleta said.

A few moments later, Hubbs rode in on Minx. He dismounted and handed the reins to Hubert who didn't quite know what to do.

Aleta saw the bewildered look on her father-in-law's face. She smiled.

"Just be a post," she said.

"Quite a ride you had, Ma'am," Hubbs said.

"Someone shot him," Aleta said. "Actually there were two men I think. The guns sounded different."

"Well there's a bit of blood on the hock," Hubbs said. "But let's get him calm. I'm not sure moving his home today would be a good idea."

"Let's not do it then," Aleta said.

"Yes, Ma'am," he said as he opened the stall door. Shadow trotted in and waited for Aleta to dismount.

Hubbs saw the slings for the first time. "How much use you got in those arms?"

"Almost none right now. If I move either one, I know I'll scream."

"We'll wait," Hubbs said, petting Shadow's muzzle.

"I can't pet him," Aleta said. "Can you stroke his neck while I tell him what a good boy he is."

Hubbs moved one hand to Shadow's neck; the other held the reins. Aleta began talking to her horse in soft soothing tones.

"I'm sorry I yelled, but I wasn't yelling at you. You are such a good horse. You turned when I told you to even though I didn't have the reins in my hand. And those jumps!"

Aleta gushed. "You sailed over them. What a magnificent jumper you are! What a prize horse. I love you so much."

Stanley walked in as Aleta was speaking.

"Well, I'm glad he's not in the dog house with me."

Aleta looked over. "You aren't in the doghouse. You didn't shoot the horse. Let's put the blame where it belongs. What you did was give me a great horse!"

"Why are you still up there?"

"We can't move the platform to the horse or the horse to the platform," Robert Locke said. "The horse hasn't settled yet.

"And she's too high to reach and lift down," Hubert added.

"Standing on the ground," Robert finished.

"I've got an idea," Stanley said. "I'll be the platform. Then, Robert, you can help her down, can't you?"

"You can't!" Aleta protested. "Shadow could kick you or step on a hand."

"You have got to come down off that horse," Stanley determined.

Having said that, he walked into the stall, his hand running along the horse's flank. Hubbs stroked him as well and talked to him in low tones.

Robert slid along the side of the stall behind Stanley who dropped on all fours. Robert reached up and urged his daughter to trust him to catch her. He put a hand on her thigh to steady her as she swung her leg over the back of the horse and let it drop alongside the horse. Her father guided her down onto Stanley's back. Then putting his hands on her waist lifted her down to the ground.

One of her legs buckled under her as her feet hit the ground, but her father had a good hold on her. Hubert rushed to unfold one of the chairs rented for the Christmas Eve festivities and Robert lowered her onto it.

Robert opened another chair. Stanley, rising slowly and backing out of the stall, brushed himself off and sat beside Aleta, took her hands in his and held them.

"Those were magnificent jumps," he said softly. "They must have hurt like hell!"

Aleta smiled wanly.

Hubert and Robert moved away. Robert put in a call to the house and told Jocelyn to come to the barn; Hubert called Chief Milani and told him that Aleta had been shot at while on her horse and that he needed an ambulance as she'd been injured. He told him that the paramedics should drive up to the barn.

Aleta heard the last part of the call and protested that she hadn't had dinner yet.

Stanley squeezed her hand lightly. "We'll hold it for you."

"No, I don't want that!" Aleta declared. "I want you to eat it and rejoice because I wasn't thrown on my head and I didn't die. Promise me you'll do that."

"I'm going to the hospital with you," Stanley said.

"Then everyone will come with you. Let Dr. Cook do the MRI. That'll take an hour. Then everyone can come and pace in the waiting room."

"I don't want you to be alone."

"Dr. Cook's a friend. I won't be alone."

Jocelyn burst into the barn announcing that dinner would be ready in ten minutes. Her father told her to unsaddle and rub down Minx. She saw Stanley sitting beside Aleta. She noticed her pale face and furrowed brow and realized she'd been injured somehow. Without another word, she went to work.

"I can do that, Sir," Hubbs was quick to say.

Robert thanked him and told him, he was hoping this way that both of them would be to dinner on time. "My mother always adds ten minutes on because she knows I'll arrive ten minutes after she calls."

Five minutes later the wail of the siren brought everyone out of the house on a run. Dr. Cook had already promised to meet Aleta at the Hospital. Stanley had also called Lyle who told Stanley to wait for Tom.

It was with great reluctance the family agreed to Aleta's plan. Dinner was the furthest thing from everyone's mind.

"We'll have to wait at least an hour at the hospital," Bertha mentioned. "And we're all hungry."

The ambulance left and Stanley told Tom Milani what had happened and where. Tom sent out a crew under their forensic expert, Hawkins Monroe, with metal detectors to find the bullets and search the crime scene. If the shooter left anything behind, Hawk would find it.

Stanley and Tom leaned over the stall rail while Hubbs showed them the two wounds and told them that he had some ointment back at his place that'd do the trick. Stanley called the vet anyway. He couldn't take any chances with Aleta's horse.

"Could one man with one rifle do this?" Tom asked.

"Angles different," Hubbs said. "But possible."

"The shots were almost simultaneous," Stanley reiterated. "Then I was worrying about controlling Minx while I watched Aleta's horse rear. It was a miracle she wasn't thrown. Then when Shadow took off, she wound up leaning so far back, she would have fallen off the back of the horse if she hadn't caught hold of the mane. I heard a car drive away, but that's all. There had been an old brown car on the road earlier that waited for us to pass. It had three people in it. All men I think. The license plate was covered with mud except for the last letter which was a four.

"Did you hear the car start?" Tom asked.

Stanley looked surprised. "No, as a matter of fact, I didn't. I just heard it speed away."

"Two shooters and a driver."

"I've seen the car before," Stanley remarked, "which is why I remember it."

"Where?"

"On the rise in the road, earlier when Aleta and I were riding around the property. Aleta said they were watching us because the horses were trotting like a matched pair."

"How many were in the car?"

"Two on my side and probably a driver although I didn't see him."

Stanley's cell rang.

"Milani there?" Chief Lyle West asked.

"How's Aleta?" Stanley inquired.

"Wayne took her in to do an MRI. Her body's in shock. They've got her wrapped up like a mummy. She said the horse jumped. You didn't tell me that part."

"Here's Milani," Stanley said.

"Two hits," Tom said. "Different locations. Different angles. Stanley said he thinks it was the same bunch that was spying on them earlier. Only one number on the license plate. Last digit was a four. Car is old and brown. A sedan. Square grill on the front."

After a brief conversation, Milani handed the phone back to Stanley.

Lyle passed his idea by for approval. "I'm going to ask Martha if I can put Aleta in with her."

"So Cook is going to make her stay overnight?"

"At least," Lyle replied, then asked, "She jumped a horse? How high?"

"Two four footers," Stanley said, then added with obvious pride. "You should have seen her. She was magnificent!"

"You bought her a jumper?"

"I bought... I adopted a pretty Appaloosa from our local Horse Rescue Group... Background unknown. Rideable was all I was told."

"For a donation," Lyle added.

"A sizeable one," Stanley confided. "And I promised another if Aleta liked him. Well, Aleta loves him."

"I guess you're going to make another sizeable donation," Lyle concluded.

"Immediately. If Aleta ever finds out the deal, she'd make me double it."

"How many horses do you plan on rescuing?"

"This is it," Stanley said, "except, of course, for Jezebel."

"Who's Jezebel?"

"She's Hubbs' old mare."

"Oh, Man! Three rescue horses.

"Four. My horse is a rescue too," Stanley said. "Minx was too nice to leave there. But Minx is the last."

"Aleta asked me if you'd called a vet."

"He's coming in a few hours. Hubbs says Shadow wasn't badly hurt."

"I'll tell her," Lyle said. "I think you should consider leaving her here for a while."

"Aleta won't go for that."

"Just think about it."

Two hours later Aleta was settled in the bed next to Martha Cook. Before she had a chance to say much, Dr. Chesney entered the room.

He greeted Martha first. "We had fun this morning didn't we? I'm going to let you tell Aleta all about it in a few minutes. First I want to check on that baby of hers. I hear he rode on a horse that took a couple fences today."

He drew the curtain and began asking Aleta questions.

"Dr. Cook said the baby was okay," Aleta insisted the minute the query stopped.

Dr. Chesney smiled, "He also asked me to make sure he didn't miss anything."

A few minutes later, a worried Aleta asked, "Did he miss anything?"

"Not this time," Dr. Chesney said as he opened the curtain. "He rarely does, but he said he never had a pregnant woman jump a horse before."

"It wasn't by choice. I was going over that fence with or without the horse. I chose not to fly over alone."

Chesney smiled. "Good choice. See you ladies later."

"Later?" Aleta asked.

"I'll bring chocolates," he said.

"Then do come!" Aleta exclaimed.

Martha mumbled something and Aleta added, "She wants some too."

"Of course," he chuckled. "I wouldn't neglect my favorite patient."

When he left, Martha began to talk. "I owe you an apology."

"Me? What on earth for?"

"I had this vision of you on a horse that reared, but I knew you didn't own a horse and you told your sister it'd be a long time before you could ride, so I dismissed my vision as just being a fanciful imagining resulting from being at your place for the animal blessing."

"Did you only get one vision?"

"No, I got two. In the first, Stanley handed you the reins and your wrists were taped together. That made no sense at all. I couldn't see Stanley doing that. I just couldn't. I'm so sorry."

"How were you supposed to tell me?" Aleta said.

"I never got to that part," Martha confessed. "It seemed so unreal. I was sure my mind was playing tricks on me."

"Maybe God didn't want you to tell me," Aleta said. "Maybe he just wanted you to trust your mind."

"I'm sure I was supposed to tell you."

"Maybe. Maybe not. But my guess is that that's why I'm here," Aleta said. "I think you've been promoted."

Martha laughed. It came out as a gurgle, but Aleta recognized it for what it was.

"Full-time prophet," Aleta tittered. "What you always wanted, right?"

"For heaven's sake, no! I never... You're joshing aren't you?

"We asked God to distribute the load, remember?"

"But I didn't really think He'd do it."

"That'll teach you to ask for what you don't really want."

"You mean like asking for patience and He gives you trials that demand patience," she mused silently.

Aleta read the thought as if it was spoken.

"Exactly," she responded.

"But I can't speak," Martha said.

"I have no idea how that fits, but it does somehow."

"You're sure?"

"Nope. But tell me about your other vision."

"How'd you know?"

"I just did."

"Her name's Enid Bernstein. She's head of an advertising agency in Chicago. I forget the name. The woman has never impressed me. She's hard and pushy."

"How do you know her?"

"We sit on two boards together. She's on the Tri City Hospital board. She thinks I simply inherited a going business from my husband and that it grew despite me, not as a result of my leadership, so she dismisses my opinions. She'll never listen to me."

Aleta urged her to continue when a paunchy white-haired doctor entered the room. He startled Aleta.

"Who are you?" Aleta asked.

The fat man ignored her. He addressed Martha directly.

"Mrs. Cook, I am so sorry Dr. Chesney didn't tell me it was you."

Martha began to mumble.

The doctor began to guess at what she was saying, "I know how difficult it must be not to be able to speak. If you'd like, I'll be happy to consult with…"

"Dr. Dunlap," Aleta broke in. "She doesn't want your help."

The fat man scowled at Aleta. "Stay the hell out of this, young lady! I don't need some stupid woman's opinion on a matter as serious as this one."

"Watch it!" Aleta charged angrily.

Martha mumbled and Aleta smiled. "Really?"

"Don't pretend you understand her," Dr. Dunlap charged.

"How'd I know your name? You didn't introduce yourself."

"I'm well-known."

"As a snob," Aleta said. "You think poor people aren't worth your time."

"They aren't," he responded tartly, then turned attention to Mrs. Cook. "I'll move you to a private room. I can't imagine what Dr. Chesney was thinking of."

"Her safety," Aleta said. "Someone attempted to kill Mrs. Cook last night. This room is the only room with bulletproof glass."

To his credit, Dr. Dunlap recovered instantly.

"Well, then I'll move this chatterbox to another room, and make this room a private one."

"I was shot at this morning," Aleta said.

"I'm sure arrangements can be made to protect you elsewhere.

"I was invited to share this room by Martha. We're friends."

"Everyone is always trying to coddle up to Mrs. Cook to con her out of something."

"As you're doing now?"

"I'm not trying to get anything from her.

"I'd be careful of this young lady," Dr. Dunlap said. "She wants something. Whose patient are you anyway?"

He picked up the chart. "Dr. Cook. You're one of his patients?"

"Yes."

"You're pretty beat up, aren't you?" Dr. Dunlap said.

"Yes."

Dr. Chesney walked in as Dr. Dunlap was reading Aleta's chart.

"She doesn't need a neurologist," Dr. Chesney said matter-of-factly. "She's pregnant."

"She's not here for that," Dr. Dunlap said. "And I'm not happy with the trick you played on me last night."

"I told you the truth. Martha Cook is one of Dr. Cook's special patients. She doesn't have a family physician. She's 90 plus. She was having a stroke. What did I leave out that was important?"

"That she was Martha Cook."

"Aleta," Dr. Chesney asked. "Does he know who you are?"

"He knows I'm one of Dr. Cook's patients."

"So he's treating you poorly?"

"That's the gist of it."

"Well, Aleta, Dr. Hughes wants to consult on your case," Dr. Chesney said. "He's fascinated by a woman your age having a stroke and the ability it's left you with. Martha will tell you he's nice. She met him last night. He says he won't charge you a red cent."

"As if he could collect if he did."

"I pay my bills," Aleta quipped. "Well, actually, my husband pays my bills. I need to get well before I can generate any income on my own."

"What does your husband do?" Dr. Dunlap asked pointedly. He was beginning to suspect he was missing something.

"He works with children," Aleta replied.

Martha mumbled something.

Aleta began to speak when Dr. Chesney stopped her.

"Please let Dr. Hughes listen to this exchange."

Martha nodded and so did Aleta.

Dr. Chesney rushed to the door and waved in a mature dark-haired doctor with gold-rimmed glasses and a decided limp. Dr. Hughes leaned on his cane and thanked both women warmly.

"Do you want Dr. Dunlap to leave?" Dr. Chesney asked.

"No," Aleta said. "Martha wants him to give his sister a message."

"Can you translate what she says as if she's speaking?" Dr. Hughes asked, pulling out a tape recorder.

"Come closer," Aleta said. "You can't afford to miss anything she says."

Dr. Hughes moved between the two women.

Martha mumbled for a few seconds.

"Dr. Dunlap, your sister Enid Bernstein is in grave danger. Tomorrow morning when she climbs into her car to leave for work, she's going to be shot in the head."

"This is garbage!" Dr. Dunlap blustered.

"She'll die if she goes to work tomorrow. Tell her to take a week off. She can afford it." Aleta went on translating what Martha was saying.

"I will like hell," Dunlap said. "This is a con. I don't know what you're after, but I'm not telling her a goddamn thing. I'm not even telling her I had this conversation."

"I'd believe these two if I were you," Dr. Chesney said. "They've proven themselves as prophets."

"You played your one and only trick on me last night. I'm not falling for another one," Dunlap snapped.

"Check it out," Dr. Chesney said. "Chief Lyle West…"

Dunlap cut him off.

"I'm no fool."

"Actually, you are!" Aleta said.

Dunlap stormed out of the room.

"That went well," Aleta remarked.

The two doctors laughed.

"Now what?" Dr. Chesney asked.

"We need Chief West," Aleta said. "And no more stupid doctors."

"Martha and I took care of the rest this morning," Dr. Chesney said. "Dunlap was the last one."

"Good!" Aleta said. "He wore me out!"

Dr. Hughes came over and took her pulse. Then he took Martha's. He indicated to Dr. Chesney that he should do the same. Dr. Chesney called the nurse.

Within minutes both doctors were taking the blood pressure of the two women in the beds. Both noted their readings on the charts.

"In ten minutes we take it again," Dr. Chesney said. He rang for the nurse and quietly gave her orders.

Martha mumbled something and Aleta told Dr. Hughes to fetch Chief West immediately. When he hesitated, she coached him.

"Those are his men standing guard. Tell one of them I want to see him."

Dr. Hughes leaned out through the doorway and passed along the message just as the hospital PA system began paging Dr. Cook.

Chief West, however, came through the door first. Both doctors were again taking blood pressure readings. Lyle tried not to reflect the concerned look on their faces.

He smiled at Aleta, "You called?"

"Martha has a prediction," Aleta said. "Dr. Dunlap refuses to warn his sister."

"And that upset both of you?" Lyle queried quietly.

Both women nodded.

"You've got to stop trying to warn people directly unless you know they'll believe you," Lyle counseled. "Such encounters are apt to send your blood pressure through the roof."

Martha mumbled a reply which Aleta translated with an impish grin. "We should let your blood pressure soar?"

"Not mine. I've gotten used to this stuff. Tom's is apt to rival yours, however."

"I don't want to do that to him," Aleta said.

"We've divided your group up," Lyle responded. "Martha's mine. You and Harriet are his. Only when you're under my protection in the hospital, you're mine."

Martha mumbled angrily and Aleta translated her words exactly.

"I don't like the division! Aleta should be allowed to call whomever she feels comfortable calling."

"Aleta," Lyle said gently, "you may call me anytime you want; however, if the problem is in Tom's jurisdiction, I'll call him. I'll tell him that you're worried about his blood pressure. That'll really ruffle his tail feathers."

"Don't tell him," Aleta begged. "He's doing a good job. I don't want to hurt him."

"Okay, so who's the target this time?" Lyle asked.

"Enid Bernstein," Aleta said.

"What about Enid?" Dr. Cook said entering the room. "And why are you two taking blood pressure readings simultaneously. And why is Lyle here? Someone tell me what's going on."

Aleta replied immediately.

"Dr. Hughes is trying to figure out what caused my stroke. Dr. Chesney is trying to figure out why Martha's blood pressure is climbing. Lyle is here to calm us down."

"And how is he doing that?"

"By believing us," Aleta stated flatly.

The two doctors recorded their readings on the charts and then handed the charts to Dr. Cook.

"I guess Lyle is doing his job," Dr. Cook commented. "Who riled these two?"

"Dunlap," Chesney responded. "Let me fill you in. While the doctors were conferring, Lyle asked Martha if she knew where Enid Bernstein lived."

"Willow Glen."

"Tom's bailiwick," Lyle remarked. "Tell me as much as you can."

Aleta translated every word Martha uttered without any comment.

Shortly thereafter, Dr. Cook returned to Aleta's bedside. "I want you to stay a few days. Lyle wants you here too."

Martha murmured something and Aleta immediately announced, "I'll stay."

Cook and West exchanged glances. Aleta was being too easy. There had to be a catch.

"Don't look a gift horse in the mouth," Cook said after a moment's reflection. "Lyle, I want only the four doctors that are attending these two to enter this room. No others."

"Done," Lyle said.

He turned to Aleta, "If you need me, just call 'Guard!' and one of my men will enter. They can call me on their radio anytime day or night. Now I have to go tell Tom he's got a target to protect."

Dr. Cook motioned to the other doctors to follow him out. "These ladies need to rest."

Once out of earshot, Dr. Cook consulted with the other two on the best course of treatment.

"Both reacted to Dunlap with the same extreme rise in blood pressure," Dr. Hughes noted. "Why?"

"Stop me if I'm wrong, Wayne," Dr. Chesney said, "but both Aleta and Martha are strong, reasonable women."

"Agreed," Cook said.

"So what happens when they receive a prophetic vision?" Chesney asked.

"They are viewed as unreasonable," Cook concluded.

"They are also both honest women," Chesney said.

"And their veracity is questioned," Cook responded.

"But most important," Dr. Chesney concluded, "they are showered with contempt. These are not women who handle that easily, especially when they are acting to save a life. Can you imagine the pressure?"

"Chief West said something early on," Dr. Hughes reported. "He told them to stop reporting their visions to unbelievers. He may have a point."

"What point?"

"If Chief West, for example, tells someone a psychic told him something and that person rejects it, West doesn't take it personally," Dr. Hughes explained.

"Wayne, I think our colleague has solved the puzzle," Dr. Chesney said. "So let's make a plan."

"We aren't going to tell them, are we?" Dr. Hughes asked.

"There's no other way to deal with my grandmother," Wayne Cook said. "And Aleta's cut from the same cloth."

"It's just a matter of how we tell them," Bernard Chesney explained.

Chapter 8

Stanley turned to the group still gathered at his house waiting for word on when Aleta could have visitors.

"Dr. Cook says there was a setback," Stanley reported.

"I thought she was out of ICU," his mother commented.

"She is. Evidently, a visit from Dr. Dunlap sent both hers and Martha's blood pressures soaring. He said Dr. Chesney and Dr. Hughes were there at the time. They're keeping a close watch on both. No visitors until four. Then it's me only. Harriet, however, has been invited to visit Martha at the same time."

"That's weird," Harriet said. "Something's going on."

"It gets even stranger," Stanley said. "Dr. Cook asked Aleta to stay a few days and she agreed."

"Aleta agreed to stay in the hospital voluntarily?" her father exclaimed. "Not in a million years!"

"You ready for the topper?" Stanley asked.

"There's more?" Robert asked.

"Dr. Cook won't be available to talk with us at four," Stanley said. "Dr. Chesney and Dr. Hughes are supervising

Aleta and Martha until eight. They've ordered a private duty nurse. They insisted Wayne get some sleep. He was up all last night handling the shooting victims as well as his grandmother. It seems Dr. King, who was supposed to be on, called in sick."

"Brice King?" Lydia said. "Wasn't he at Whitworth's open house last night?"

"I know he was," Hubert said. "He singled me out to chat with. Seemed fine to me."

Chief Lyle West picked up the Christmas edition of the Tri City Register on his way to Tom Milani's office to discuss the latest threat to a citizen in the Tri City area. He scanned it quickly before heading out. As he drove he called Ed Ornstein on his cell.

"I need your help," he said. "I know it's Christmas; but…"

"Tell me what you want and I'll do it."

"Read Justin Conway's stuff in today's paper. I'll be at your office in an hour."

"I'll be waiting."

When Lyle West walked into Tom Milani's office, he saw Alan Peets. He smiled.

"Boy, am I glad he called you."

Alan Peets grinned. "He likes to share the misery."

"Yeah," Lyle agreed. "All of us are going to have to do a lot of making up with our wives. You'd think the criminals would have a little consideration and wait until after Christmas to kill people."

"Is this something that couldn't be handled over the phone?" Milani asked as a prompt to move Lyle back to his reason for hauling him back to the office when he was in the middle of an investigation.

"Martha and Aleta both had a serious setback. The doctors need our help."

"Our help?" Peets asked.

"Let me tell you what happened," Lyle said and then did so.

"Sickness makes one vulnerable," Milani said. "I would think a doctor would know that."

"Some do. Evidently Dr. Dunlap is not one of those," West responded. "I told Aleta she could call any of us with any predictions and we would sort out whose responsibility it would be to take care of it."

"That makes sense," Peets said. "Of course, I'm pretty much out of it. Nobody of significant wealth lives in Oakwood."

The red light on Milani's phone flashed.

"I told you no calls," Tom barked. "Oh… that's different… Peets, it's a call for you from Harriet Locke."

"Out of it, huh?" Lyle chuckled.

"Peets, here," Alan said, scowling at the two grinning countenances.

When he hung up, Peets reported Harriet's take on the distribution of their work. "It seems that Tom is busy investigating this morning's incident and Lyle is busy with the attack on Martha Cook and I have nothing much to do which is why she called me."

"An out of towner?" Lyle guessed.

"River Forest," Peets replied.

"Nothing like breaking new ground," Milani said. "I think maybe I'd rather have my prediction to deal with."

"Name's Rodney Aiken," Peets said. "Either of you know him?"

"Even if I did," Lyle said, "you're not handing off that hot potato to me."

"What was all that talk about sharing?"

"We are sharing," Lyle said. "Milani has Enid Bernstein and you've got Rodney Aiken."

"And what have you got?"

"Time to work with Ed Ornstein on a theory I've got."

"Ed? Why him? We all have computer people," Peets said.

"Because I'm going a bit far afield."

Milani sat forward. "Lyle, if you step over the line, we can't use it later."

Hawk burst into the room, his eyes alight with excitement. Only Lyle West raised an eyebrow. Milani and Peets were accustomed to Hawk's unbridled enthusiasm that overrode all protocol.

"You still burst into meetings," Lyle commented.

"Yeah," he said excitedly, brushing his long blonde hair out of his eyes. "You're all gonna want to hear this. I know how the shooters could find their targets in the middle of the night."

He plunked a tiny metal chip on the desk.

"What is it?"

"A transmitter."

West picked it up. "It's so small."

"Top of the line. Someone has access to some really sophisticated equipment.

"Where was it?"

"Under the collar in the coat Rob wore, the one Foster Mize arrived at the hospital in. The shooters didn't recognize the coat, they homed in on the signal," Hawk explained. "I didn't spot it first time I went over the coat. It was buried in the fabric."

"Can we pick up the signal?" Lyle asked.

"I can rig up a receiver," Hawk said. "Why?"

"We need to find the rest of those chips. The shooters are still out there."

"And they don't know Mize is in the hospital," Milani added.

"So they'll be back," Peets said.

"Can you fix up three receivers?" Lyle asked.

"I'll get right on it," Hawk said rushing out as fast as he'd come in.

"Now," Milani said. "Share your theory."

"Did either of you read Justin Conway's articles in the paper today?"

Both men shook their heads.

"Well, it wasn't actually in today's articles but in the focus of the next article in this series--the people who hired these CEO's."

"CEO's are at the top," Peets said. "Who does hire them anyway?

"The Board of Trustees," West said. "And Martha Cook is a member of one of those boards as is Foster Mize and Enid Bernstein."

"How do you know this?" Tom Milani asked.

"Mostly from Martha Cook who was steamed when Enid railroaded her candidate--the nefarious Simon Jackman--over several Martha wanted to consider. Enid never investigated Jackman. She didn't have the time, but she didn't want Martha's voice to prevail, so she fought hard for his hiring and the other Board members didn't want to get into a cat fight so they just picked the most obnoxious woman and voted with her. It was six to two. Only Mize voted with Martha."

"How does Rodney Aiken fit in?" Peets asked.

"He doesn't," West said. "But the timing is interesting. Martha got her vision about Enid this morning. Harriet got hers after the paper came out. It would seem, Gentlemen, that our perps are literate."

"Are you saying they're going to kill so we won't guess who the real target is?" Peets asked.

"That's my guess," Lyle responded.

"That means Justin has his finger on a piece of the puzzle," Peets noted.

"So what kind of research is Ed doing?" Tom asked.

"I want to know what happened to the men Jackman axed."

"So you don't think someone tried to kill Martha because she's a prophet?" Peets asked.

"No."

"Why not?"

"Because no one has gone after Harriet," West replied. "If whoever it was knew about the meeting at Martha's house, why go after only Aleta and Martha?"

"Good point," Milani said.

"So they think we only have one prophet in the area—Aleta Praetzel," Peets concluded. "So they don't know everything."

"Should we talk to Justin Conway?" Milani asked.

"Definitely," Lyle said. "We have to get the predictions out. Justin has TV connections."

"I'll call him," Milani said. "I'm sure Enid will be as stubborn as her brother and then he'll blame me if she dies. I can suggest that Justin interview Dr. Dunlap as well as Enid. That should make great copy. And just maybe scare them into cooperating.

"What about Rodney Aiken?" Peets said. "He's not local."

"The only reason television picked up the predictions last time is because they weren't local," Lyle said. "We're still hot news. Give Justin everything."

"Won't we be putting our ladies in jeopardy?" Peets asked.

"Suppose you were our perps and you found out there are three prophets out there protecting each other," Lyle said.

"I think I'd steer clear of them," Peets said.

Not far away, in a small house in Willow Glen, Sam and Toby were hovering near Fred who was busy on his computer.

"We've got to have someone from Ludwig's Board," Sour Sam said for the third time.

"Why not another from Cockerton's Board?" Fred said. "I've got that whole list."

"Toby what do you think?" Sam asked.

"Two from Cockerton's Board might cause the police to focus their attention onto that group," Toby said. "They don't know we're after Mize. So that would even things up."

"That sounds reasonable. Who looks good?"

"Harold Moshansky."

"He lives in Evanston. We haven't been there before."

"Okay, Fred, let's concentrate on these two and make a plan," Sam said

Just before four as Harriet Locke was entering Tri City Hospital, she stopped and told Stanley to go on because she had a phone call to make.

"I'll wait," he said.

She dialed Chief Alan Peets' number.

"I have another one for you," she said, knowing he'd recognize her rough voice. "Harold Moshansky, entering some Country Club tomorrow afternoon. Tell him to cancel his racquetball date. And that last one I gave you, Rodney Aiken, tell him not to go to work. That appointment isn't worth his life."

"What country club?" Peets asked.

"No idea," Harriet said. "Name's not that common though. Guess you'll have to do same detective work."

"Yes, Ma'am," Peets said. "And thank you."

Harriet wore a puzzled frown as she clicked her cell closed. Stanley walked quietly beside her toward the hospital.

"He thanked me," Harriet said. "He hasn't done that before."

When the two exited the elevator on the fourth floor, Dr. Chesney and Dr. Hughes took them aside and told them all that had happened.

"That explains a lot," Harriet said.

The doctors glanced at Stanley who shrugged.

Harriet entered the room first and announced, "Good news, you two. God has given you a reprieve. I'm getting all the prophecies now."

"What are you talking about?"

"Have either of you had a vision or anything since Enid Bernstein?"

Aleta looked at Martha who shook her head.

"Me neither," Aleta said as Stanley walked in.

"Well, I've gotten two."

"Oh, Grams!" Aleta wailed.

"And our dear Chief Peets actually thanked me when I called him the second time," Harriet smiled as she pulled up a chair beside Martha's bedside. She took her hand and murmured. "I can scarcely imagine how frustrating this must be for you, but since you can nod, we can communicate."

Stanley reached under the cover and took his wife's hand. "Your grandmother's fine, Aleta. She's pleased to be a bigger part of this."

He leaned over and kissed her gently and then sat beside her. "You chose not to come home. Is there a reason?"

"I could say it was because Dr. Cook asked or because Lyle asked or because Martha asked, but it was something else," Aleta said. "I just don't feel good."

"For how long?"

"Since the ride this morning."

"Why didn't you say something?"

"I thought I'd feel better. In fact, I did feel better when Lyle was here."

Aleta began to cry. "Stanley, I'm so scared. Please, please, don't leave me tonight."

Stanley rose and whispered, "I'm only going as far as the door. Okay?"

He spoke quietly with the guard at the door and the guard nodded. "Chief West told us to do anything you asked, so we'll take care of it."

"Thank you," Stanley said. He then returned to Aleta's side.

"Tell me what you're afraid of."

"If anything happens to me, promise me you won't blame Shadow."

"Aleta, what's wrong?" Stanley pressed.

Aleta avoided answering.

"Talk to me about Shadow," she begged.

"The vet says the wounds were superficial. He put some antibiotic on them and said he'll be good as new in a couple of days."

"Is he still upset?"

"Hubbs says he shouldn't be alone so he's sleeping in our barn tonight. And don't worry. I gave Hubbs my warmest sleeping bag."

"Hubbs was a good choice," Aleta murmured.

"Aleta, will you please tell me what's going on," Stanley begged.

"He was the perfect Christmas gift. Everything you did made it perfect."

Her voice trailed off, but her grip on his hand remained tight.

Dr. Cook walked in followed by Dr. Chesney and Dr. Hughes. He drew the curtain. Both grandmothers looked startled. Neither protested. Instead Harriet clasped her friend's hand and whispered, "Let's pray."

They prayed silently so as to disturb no one.

"So bring me up to date," Dr. Cook asked Stanley.

"She's scared out of her wits," Stanley said, "because something is happening that she's been through before."

"Aleta," Dr. Cook said gently. "Tell me what's wrong?"

Aleta opened her eyes. "Where's Stanley?"

"Still holding your hand," Stanley said.

"Why is everything so blurry?" Aleta asked. "Stanley, tell me I'm not going to die."

The last was a cry that sent a chill down the spines of everyone in the room. Her fear enveloped them all. This was a woman who could predict the future. Her words could not be dismissed as a normal expression of fear that comes when illness strikes.

Dr. Cook was the first to recover. "We need an MRI."

"I need to stay with her," Stanley said.

"You know the rules," Dr. Cook said.

"She's under police protection," Stanley replied evenly. "Give Lyle time to get here."

"So he can do what?" Lyle asked walking around the curtain.

"Deputize me," Stanley said. "So I can stay with Aleta."

"I can't do that," Lyle declared firmly. "Much as I might sympathize with your need and Aleta's, I can't do that."

"You need me," Stanley argued. "Your force is overwhelmed right now trying to round up the homeless men you let go this morning. I'll make a good deputy. I know the law. I'm an expert with a gun. I'm trustworthy. And I'm willing to take orders."

"You're emotionally involved," Lyle countered.

"I'm in control," Stanley said. "And you know it."

From the other side of the curtain, the well-recognized high-pitched voice of Martha Cook shouted, "Lyle, do it!"

Dr. Cook pushed back the curtain. "Grams, you spoke!"

"Praise God!" she exclaimed, her words almost slurred beyond recognition. The rest of her sentence was lost.

Dr. Cook patted her hand. "The rest will come!"

Lyle smiled and, looking at Stanley, said, "Raise your right hand."

After Stanley was sworn in, Lyle called in one of the guards on the door and told him to loan Stanley his gun, holster and vest.

"Does he know how to…" the officer began as Stanley opened the gun and inspected it.

"Very clean," Stanley commented, laying it down as he donned the vest and holster.

"Your handcuffs and hand set too," Lyle ordered. "Go back to the station and get replacements. I'll take your watch until you return."

"He needs a badge," the officer said.

"You need yours," Lyle said. "I'll loan him mine."

As he pinned his chief's badge on Stanley's vest, he quipped, "Don't do anything I wouldn't do."

Stanley took his friend's hand. "Thank you."

"Just remember your first priority is to protect her."

"I won't forget."

"No strangers get to approach her. That's what the handcuffs and radio are for," Lyle said. "The perps want her dead. Don't for a second forget that."

"I won't leave her no matter what."

"That's what I'm counting on. That's why I deputized you."

"Those orders I can follow."

He walked over to Aleta and she opened her eyes. "You're all dressed up. You going to a party?"

"Yep. Yours," Stanley said. "First we take a trip to get you an MRI and then we decide what room you're going to after that."

"It'll be the operating room," Aleta predicted.

"Is that a prophecy or a guess?"

"I'm a good guesser. I remember the symptoms from last time," Aleta said. "I need you with me all the way. I don't know why I'm so scared. I've been through this all before."

"Don't fret about your feelings," Stanley said. "Just let me know what they are."

"I'm not very proud of myself right now," Aleta confessed.

"But I am," Stanley said. "A man who is unafraid is a fool. A man who acts despite his fear is brave."

"You always put a good spin on things."

"Not always. But now it's easy. I saw you ride this morning. Remember? As scared as I was, I wasn't too scared to appreciate the magnificence of that ride. Aleta, you will always be the woman who hung on to a runaway horse and used his energy to get him home safely. You have no idea how awed I was at what you did and how the remembrance of it still thrills me. You have got to be the world's most exciting and beautiful woman. And all those feelings you had during that ride are bound to tumble out now that it's over. And now you have new feelings of apprehension and fear. It's no wonder you're having trouble dispatching them. You must be overwhelmed."

"I love you," Aleta whispered.

"I know."

Back in a small house in the low income section of Arborville, Toby was watching the five o'clock news and was the first of the brothers to find out that all three of their targets on the morrow made the broadcast as the unknown Willow Glen's psychic's newest predictions.

He called his brothers in and they flipped from channel to channel trying to find out what kind of action the police planned.

This time the television stations sent reporters to interview the targets and one channel presented an interview with Rodney Aiken whom the reporter had caught at his office.

His first reaction was shock, followed by anger. After he rambled on about the supposed vendetta against honest businessmen, the reporter broke in.

"Aren't you a member of the Board of Trustees of the McDeere Corporation?"

"That and several other boards," Aiken replied.

"Didn't you vote to hire the late Joel Cockerton?"

"His resume was impressive."

"He ran the McDeere Corporation into the ground."

"It was in trouble when we hired him," Aiken said. "We needed someone to cut costs. And he did that."

"He fired people."

"Yes. That was his approach."

"He fired the highest paid people."

"They were expendable. The cost saving was immediate."

"They were the most knowledgeable. He left the work in the hands of people less knowledgeable."

"That points to the failure of the men at the top. They didn't groom those below them."

"So you feel his approach was the correct one?"

"I do."

"Do you plan to go to work tomorrow?"

"I will leave the house at eight as I always do. This crazy prediction is not going to deter me."

"Isn't that risky?"

"Not particularly. The police will escort me to my office at eight. I think the shooter, whoever he is, will think twice."

"The psychic said you should stay home.

"No crazy woman is going to dictate my actions," Aiken declared. "I'm not giving her that power."

When the interview ended, Sour Sam turned to his baby brother Fred, "He made a point of saying he left the house at eight. Are we sure about the six o'clock time?"

Toby answered before Fred did. "He said it twice. He wanted us to lock in on eight o'clock. It's a subterfuge."

"The meeting's a secret one," Fred said. "He doesn't want anyone to know. That's why it's being held before the office opens."

"That Aleta Praetzel is a pain in the butt," Sour Sam declared angrily. "We'll monitor the news, Fred. You do a computer search and see if she's still a patient."

The helicopter carrying Dr. Michael Taekman landed on the roof of Tri City Hospital at six Christmas evening. Stanley was in the pre-op area holding Aleta's hand when the neurosurgeon strolled in.

"You've changed professions?" he asked Stanley.

"You turned me into a hybrid lawyer-cop," Stanley said. "You don't get another shot at me. Aleta, however, so enjoyed your last visit she invited you back."

"Aleta, you do know it's Christmas?"

"I got a horse," Aleta said. "He got shot. He got scared. I had a bumpy ride home."

"It would be a good idea to keep your horse off the gun range," Dr. Taekman commented. "Are you ready for this?"

"You're going to shave my head again, aren't you?"

"I'm afraid so," he said sympathetically.

"Good! Stanley won't have anything to measure for at least a month," Aleta quipped.

Dr. Taekman grew serious. "We're going into the area bruised by the explosion. You're wondering if you should ever ride again. The answer is yes."

"But the jarring?" Stanley asked.

"Wasn't good, I'll admit; but the vessel was already weakened. If it wasn't the horse, it would have been something else. It's not uncommon for such bleeds to occur as long as three months after the original trauma."

"But it didn't show up on the MRI taken this morning."

"My guess is that the encounter with Dr. Dunlap that caused your blood pressure to skyrocket may have been the proverbial straw that broke the camel's back."

"I'm glad it wasn't a stroke," Aleta murmured. "I was so afraid it was."

"The prognosis is good. Subdural this time. We won't need to go as deep."

"I'll be with you all the way," Stanley said.

"Are you sure?" Dr. Taekman asked. "Have you ever seen an operation?"

"No. But I'll handle it," Stanley stated unequivocally.

Dr. Taekman believed him.

The six thirty news carried Justin Conway's interview with both Enid Bernstein and her brother Dr. Roy Dunlap.

Toby was the only one watching at the time, but his yell brought the two brothers into the room in time to hear Enid proudly claim that Simon Jackman was her choice.

"Martha Cook opposed me all the way," she gloated, "but I won. And Jackman did a thorough housecleaning and brought Vision Research Company into the black for the first time in almost a decade."

"It filed for bankruptcy shortly after Jackman left," Justin pointed out.

"We don't always succeed," she stated.

"He insisted the pension funds be invested in the company and when it went bankrupt people lost their pensions."

"It was an incentive program," Enid explained. "The workers didn't try hard enough."

"You don't believe it was a mistake to replace knowledgeable people with people who would vote his way."

"A company can't move forward without a solid core at the top. Dissension doesn't foster growth."

"It would appear that unanimity doesn't either," Justin commented before asking what steps were being taken to protect her from those who had targeted her.

"Chief Milani was here to discuss measures he was prepared to take; however, this is foolishness. I'm not in any real danger. My brother told me that the woman who predicted my demise was Martha Cook. That's right the same woman who fought me on hiring Jackman. She's just using the deaths of a couple of CEO's to take revenge on me. She wants me to have a bad night."

"So, you're doing nothing?"

"Chief Milani has set up guards around my house, but I won't permit him to follow me into Chicago."

The next interview followed immediately.

The brothers sat on the edge of their chairs as Dr. Dunlap mentioned both Aleta Praetzel and Martha Cook in his first sentence.

"Martha has had a severe stroke. She can't speak," Dr. Dunlap reported. "Aleta Praetzel was put in her room. Mrs. Praetzel claims to be able to understand the garbled gibberish the old lady is spouting which is an impossibility. The psychic predictions are hogwash. They wanted me to tell Enid about them, but I refused. Evidently, Chief Milani is ready to believe anything a rich person tells him, no matter how crazy that person is."

"These psychics appear to have correctly predicted the events of Christmas Eve. How do you explain that?" Justin asked.

"I only know what I saw in that hospital room. One old lady suffering from a stroke she will probably never recover from and one young lady who lost control of her horse and claims someone shot at it. Now I ask you--who goes out hunting on Christmas Day and mistakes a horse with a rider for a deer, and within the city limits no less."

"The police believe her," Justin observed.

"Our police chief isn't too bright. A big city chief wouldn't be so gullible."

"They saved lives last night," Justin said.

"Put a bunch of homeless men put up in a motel at taxpayers' expense and claimed they saved them. How do we even know they were targets? Maybe the only targets out there were the ones that were shot. On top of that, the police haven't a clue as to who did it. Not very good police work if you ask me."

"What could Aleta Praetzel hope to gain by making such predictions?"

"She's new in town. Maybe she just wants to be noticed."

"There are reports that there is a third prophet--that's the term the ladies use to describe themselves. What's your take on that?"

"If this publicity keeps up, next week there'll be ten--all fake!"

The end of the interview left the three brothers satisfied.

"Two of our targets are set," Sam said. "But after we hit them, the whole world will begin to take Aleta Praetzel seriously. If we don't take her out..."

Toby interrupted.

"What about the other two prophets?"

"What other two?" Sour Sam countered testily. "We're being made to believe that there's more than one so we won't go after Aleta Praetzel."

He got up and signaled Fred to follow him. Toby stayed by the TV. If he hadn't, he wouldn't have seen the news flash banner appear at the bottom of the screen.

"Hey, you guys!" he shouted. "Come back."

Fortunately the banner rolled across the screen several more times. "News flash! Prophet Aleta Praetzel is undergoing brain surgery. Renown Cook County Hospital neurosurgeon Dr. Michael Taekman arrived at Tri City Hospital at 6 PM."

"What are we supposed to do?" Sour Sam asked, annoyed.

"Brain Operations take hours," Toby lisped. "And doctors need light."

"Hospitals have back-up generators," Sour Sam said, closing the discussion with his tone.

Toby ignored his obvious ill humor.

"Fred's always saying he could plunge the whole town into darkness if he wanted to. So, Fred, can you shut down the hospital?"

"Yeah, I can do that. What about the back-up generator?"

"I'll take care of that beforehand," Toby declared. "It's Christmas Day. The basement will be deserted. The cops will be upstairs guarding Mrs. Cook."

"There'll be one guarding Aleta in the operating room in the basement," Sour Sam put in, disgruntled because Toby had taken over the lead again.

"Fred, pull up a schematic of the hospital, Toby ordered. "I know that's what you've been working on. I need to know precisely where the generator is."

"What are you going to do?" Sour Sam asked, suddenly more curious than vexed.

"Disable it," Toby replied, then added, "After I get back, then we'll shut down the power from here. They should be at a critical juncture in the Operation then."

"They could move her," Sour Sam suggested, his annoyance at Toby's leadership resurfacing.

"With her brain exposed?" Toby snapped.

"You can't just walk in," Sour Sam proclaimed crossly.

"I don't intend to be seen," Toby lisped. "There's a tunnel connecting the new wing to the hospital basement. I'll use it."

"Suppose you're spotted?" Sam asked.

"Let's hope I'm not."

"I got it!" Fred exclaimed pointing it the schematic on the screen. "Generator's in the far right corner from the tunnel entrance. The lab's on your left as you come in. The operating theatres are in the basement. There could be a guard posted outside the one she's in. You need to take this corridor here and avoid this section."

His finger subbed for words.

Toby followed the finger on the schematic. He left immediately.

Chapter 9

Aleta was wheeled into the operating room holding Stanley's hand. He bade her release it as soon as they were in the room.

"This is as far as I go," he said. "But I'll be here until you're done and I'll be with you when you wake up."

"I'll hold you to that promise," Aleta said.

The anesthesiologist held the mask close to her face.

"Start counting backwards from ninety-nine," he said as he put the mask in place.

Aleta got as far as ninety-five.

"Scalpel," Dr. Taekman said.

The first cut would be the hardest Stanley had been told. He looked away momentarily. Then he took a deep breath and began to watch.

He wasn't certain how long he'd been watching when he heard Lyle's voice in his ear. Just before they left for the operating room, Lyle came down and replaced his hand set with a head set.

"Stanley where are they?" Lyle asked.

"They've just folded back the skin and Dr. Taekman is drilling the holes in the skull."

"Oh, for heaven's sake, Stanley," Lyle exploded. "Don't give me details. So, they've just begun; right?"

"Correct."

"And this is a long operation, isn't it?"

"They have to drill six holes. They're only on the second one. Then they have to saw between. .

"I told you not to do that!" Lyle shouted.

"Why did you call?"

"Aleta made the seven o'clock news. Not from here. Dr. Taekman's host at the party wanted to know what was up. Taekman told him. He called Aleta a prophet. Seems the man is a TV exec and he gave his news team a heads-up."

"You expect trouble?"

"I'm putting a man outside the door. He will be wearing a gas mask. Be alert."

"Hard to fall asleep when two doctors are drilling holes in one's wife's skull."

"Stanley!"

"They haven't even got to the sawing part yet. And when they fold back the skull…"

"Shit!" Lyle interjected. "You're hopeless."

Stanley smiled as he went back to watching the doctors. They began talking casually and Stanley decided he could ask a question.

"Is the light the most important external element contributing to this operation?"

Dr. Taekman chuckled. "Leave it to a lawyer to use long words to ask a simple question."

"Could you operate without the light?" Stanley asked.

"No," Dr. Taekman said.

"The hospital has a back-up generator," Dr. Cook added, "so we'd only be without power for a few minutes."

"Other things run on power, don't they?" Stanley asked.

"Air conditioning," Dr. Taekman said. "I'd hate to be five hours in a windowless room with no air."

"Stanley, stop worrying," Dr. Cook said.

But Stanley spoke into his mike. "Lyle, you there?"

"So long as you aren't going to treat me to another graphic description."

"Not this time," Stanley said. "The hospital has a back-up generator.

"So?"

"We know that one of our group is an electronic whiz. What if somehow they took out the electrical power and the generator?"

"How are they going to take out the power?"

"I don't know. But if our generator is down, we'd be screwed."

"It's Christmas Day. Where am I going to find a technician?"

"That's the point. It's Christmas. Someone could disable the generator and no one would know."

"As usual, you make a good argument. I'll get someone to check out the generator."

When Stanley looked back at the group of doctors, he saw the anesthesiologist staring at him.

"Is there the possibility that we could lose power?"

"Chief West is checking that out now."

"It's my job to be prepared," came the answer. "Call your chief. Tell him we have standing lights that operate on batteries in the storeroom. Have them moved outside our door just in case. There is also a cabinet in the storeroom that's stocked with things I'll need if we lose power."

Stanley relayed the anesthesiologist's request and Lyle said he'd take care of it.

Fifteen minutes later Dr. Hughes walked through the door. A nurse followed. First she gloved him and then she tore open a sealed packet and put the headgear with the light on his head.

"I will stand in for each of you while you're prepared," Dr. Hughes said. "You first."

The anesthesiologist stepped out asking, "So it's going to happen?"

"The generator's been tampered with," Dr. Hughes replied as he took his place. A few minutes later he replaced Dr. Cook. Dr. Taekman never skipped a beat. He was working with a light already.

"Do we move the lights in?" Stanley asked.

"You receive the lights from the men outside," Dr. Hughes said. "I'm sterile. The orderly will have removed the plastic cover and I will show you where to place each one.t

"I want the cabinet inside right away," the anesthesiologist said.

Nothing made it through the door before the lights went out.

Plunged into darkness only the lights on the heads of the doctors lit up pieces of the operating field.

Stanley opened the door and wheeled in the first large light. He turned it toward the wall and flicked the switch. The room immediately had light.

The cabinet was rolled in next followed by three more lights. The surgeons waited. Stanley worked quickly and Dr. Taekman returned to his task after the second light was adjusted.

Lyle called. "Do you need anything else?"

"The air conditioning. This room is heating up fast with these lights. The doctors are beginning to sweat," Stanley reported.

"The tech said there's no way he can fix the generator," Lyle responded. "He needs parts. Whoever did this knew exactly how to cripple it permanently."

"How'd they take out the power?"

"Computer," Lyle replied.

"Can Ed do anything?" Stanley asked hopefully.

"He's working on it."

"The outage couldn't have come at a worse time. This is the trickiest part of the operation," Stanley moaned softly. He watched two nurses moving from doctor to doctor wiping brows and offering each his own water. Dr. Cook and Dr. Hughes alternated assisting and thus had brief respites away from the additional heat of the lights. Even so, Stanley could see they were having a hard time as the temperature in the room rose. More and more Dr. Taekman stepped away from the table and Stanley feared the doctors might not be able to finish.

One of the nurses fainted and no one had the strength to carry her out, so she lay on the floor where she fell. Another nurse put a wet cloth on her head, but then hurried back to tend to the doctors.

Stanley called Lyle. "We need air in here. How close is Ed?"

"Sorry, it's not going to happen soon."

"I'm not sure they can complete the operation," Stanley commented, a touch of apprehension in his tone.

"We may have to fly her to another hospital."

"Lyle, they have her head open," Stanley hissed. "They can't close it up now. That'd kill her. Even if they could, the trip itself would kill her."

"I don't know what to say."

"We need another source of power," Stanley said.

"There's not any source that could supply the power needed by this hospital."

"All we need in here is air," Stanley said. "Is the technician still there?"

"Yes, he is."

"Ask him if the generator in the new physical therapy wing could be hooked up to the air conditioner."

After a brief moment, Lyle came back on, his tone considerably brighter.

"Yes, it's possible," he reported. "All we need to do is lay some cable. He says there's a whole roll in the new wing."

"Hurry," Stanley said looking back at the group around the operating table.

The anesthesiologist was staring at him.

"Yes, they're going to string cable from the generator in the new physical therapy wing to get us some air."

"And lights?"

"No, just air," Stanley reported. "It's not as big a generator and it will have to pump air to the entire hospital."

"Right now, air is what we need," Dr. Cook said. "Thanks."

Twenty minutes later, the first whiff of cool air hit the operating team. An hour after that, the power was restored. An hour and a half after that, the operation was over.

Stanley accompanied Aleta to the recovery room. What he didn't understand was why neither Harriet nor Martha prophesied the danger. If they had, he would have had Aleta flown to another hospital.

He scolded himself for thinking any of the three women could conjure up a prophesy at will. The visions were given. They weren't created by the recipients. They were merely received.

Both Martha and Harriet loved Aleta. They would have shared even the faintest hint of danger.

As he held Aleta's hand, his worry moved to the fact that while the job was done, the conditions had been anything but ideal.

Dr. Cook and Dr. Taekman came in together after Stanley had gone over every scrap of conversation between the doctors during the operation, every bleeder that was caught, every order that was given, every caution. His worry nagged at him.

"Sorry, we took so long," Dr. Taekman said when the two entered.

"You weren't gone long. She's not even awake yet."

"I meant with the operation," Dr. Taekman said. "The conditions were so bad, we double checked after each step. Nothing went wrong; but we had to be sure we didn't miss anything."

"You showed a lot of grit, Stanley," Wayne Cook said. "I'm surprised your brain could even function under the circumstances. Your solution may well have saved her life."

Aleta opened her eyes. "How?"

"How what?" Dr. Taekman asked.

"How did he save my life?"

"Brilliantly ," Dr. Taekman smiled. "How are you feeling?"

"You're not blurry anymore," Aleta observed. "I'd watch that if I were you. A doctor should present a sharp image."

"I see your brain is working."

"Do I get a reward?"

"Aleta!" Stanley gasped, his tone carrying a reprimand.

"I provided two doctors…"

"Three," Stanley said. "Dr. Hughes joined the team."

"Wanted practice, did he?"

"That wasn't it at all," Stanley protested.

"As I was saying, I provided three doctors with an exciting evening and I should get a reward."

"Your life doesn't count?" Taekman inquired, his eyes twinkling. He loved this Aleta.

"That's your reward. I want one all my own."

"Aleta, you're…" Stanley began.

Dr. Cook interrupted, "And what reward do you want?"

Aleta grinned. "I thought you'd never ask. You doctors are so dense sometimes. Can't you guess? "

Dr. Cook couldn't help but smile, but his words weren't lightly given. "The slings stay."

"Wasn't I good during the operation?" Aleta asked, still intent on getting her way.

"You were wonderful," Dr. Taekman said. "But your reward is you have doctors who are determined to restore you to complete health."

Aleta sighed, "Ah, well, there is that."

"Aleta, you're alive!" Stanley exclaimed. "Earlier that's all you wanted."

"I was a basket case wasn't I?"

"That probably saved your life," Dr. Taekman said. "Your husband's presence proved to be the key to our success."

"We'll let Stanley tell you that story," Dr. Cook said.*"I need to assure our grandmothers their prayers were answered in the way they hoped."

Chapter 10

Back in Martha's room, after Wayne had given the two ladies the good news, Harriet said, "We can't find the remote. We'd like to watch the news."

Dr. Cook opened the nightstand drawer, pulled out the box of chocolates, reached way back and extracted the remote. Martha pointed to the chocolates.

"Yes, Grams, I know Dr. Chesney snuck in a box. They won't hurt you any."

"Not much gets by you, does it?" Harriet said.

"Just go on thinking that way," Wayne replied, handing Harriet the remote. "I need to check an Aleta. Stay with Martha a while longer, will you, Harriet?"

"My pleasure," Harriet replied.

She clicked on the television.

"News," Martha mumbled and Harriet flicked through the channels until she found a newscast.

"Who's that?" Harriet asked.

"Yours," Martha mumbled.

"Rodney Aiken?"

Martha shook her head.

"Harold Moshansky?" Harriet posed.

Martha affirmed the guess.

Apparently, the interview was half over.

"Are you planning to change your plans for tomorrow?" came the question.

"My attitude is the same as Rodney Aiken with regards to that as well. I'm on vacation and I intend to enjoy myself."

"So you're going to keep your racket ball date?"

"Come along and film nothing happening," Moshansky suggested. "I don't know what this so-called psychic is up to, but I'm not buying into the con."

"Wonder what Aiken said," Harriet mused aloud. She didn't have long to wait. Aiken's interview was aired next followed by Enid Bernstein's and her brother's.

"How dare he say that!" Martha exploded.

"Martha, take care. Calm down," Harriet said pushing the button for the nurse as she tried to turn off the television.

"Call Dr. Cook. And how do you turn this damn thing off?"

"I'm aw rite," Martha mumbled shooing the nurse aside so she could watch the rest of the interview.

The nurse took the remote, turned it around and the television screen went dark. She then hurried to call Dr. Cook.

"He's wrong, you know," Harriet said. "You are already regaining the ability to speak. He is such a puffer fish, isn't he?"

"My company," Martha murmured.

"It'll be there when you're well," Harriet said.

"Take over," Martha said.

Dr. Cook rushed in. "Grams, what happened?"

Harriet answered his query. "Dr. Dunlap was on the news. He said Martha had had a stroke, couldn't speak, would probably not recover and was crazy."

"Oh, my God!" Wayne exclaimed. "And don't lecture me, Grams. This is that kind of situation. Did you believe any of that garbage?"

From Martha there was no head shake, no scowl, no mumbled denial. Wayne read her lack of response as an affirmation that she had indeed believed him.

His righteous indignation spilled out, "How could you? I'm a better doctor than he is. I've never lied to you. I would tell you if you were dying. I would tell you if you weren't going to get better."

Martha bowed her head like a naughty child. Wayne sat down and gathered her into his arms. "Grams, you mean the world to me. And when you face death, I'll face it with you. It's going to happen. I know that, but not today. Dr. Chesney and Dr. Kurland and I are not liars. Dr. Chesney sat beside his wife until her last breath and he never tried to tell her it wasn't the end. You like him because he won't abandon you at the end. Neither will I."

He leaned back. "As for you being crazy. Well, you've always been that. I've always considered that one of your more interesting character traits."

Martha patted his cheek with her hand.

"I love you too, Grams," he said leaning over and kissing her on the cheek. "I'm bringing Aleta back to the room in a few minutes. She's doing well. Stanley insists on remaining a deputy. He says I can't tell him when to go home."

"Smart boy!" Harriet chuckled.

"What he doesn't know is that I can insist he guard Aleta from outside the room."

"He'd hate that," Harriet said. "But you do know he'd do it.

"It's going to be up to you, Grams," Wayne said.

"I like him," Martha mumbled.

"I almost understood you, Grams," Wayne joshed. "I'd swear you said you liked him."

He left her smiling.

Harriet went back to the words Martha spoke before Wayne burst in. "Martha, you said you were worried about a takeover of your company."

Martha nodded.

"How fast would the group you fear move?"

Martha waved her hand.

"That fast, huh?" Harriet said.

Martha nodded.

"When Stanley gets here, we can ask him what to do." Martha nodded.

"But he won't give you a word of advice until he reads your corporation documents," Harriet said. "Are they at your house?"

Martha nodded.

"Do you want me to fetch them and give them to him?" Martha's nod was vigorous.

Harriet went over to the closet and took out Martha's purse. She extracted the keys and held them out.

Martha pointed to two.

"Side door? File cabinet?" Harriet guessed. Martha's response told her she was correct.

"Will I be able to recognize the papers I need."

Martha nodded.

"Will you be okay until I get back?"

"Aleta," Martha managed.

"That's right," Harriet said. "She'll be coming down."

With that Harriet donned her coat, waved goodbye and left. Martha didn't have long to wait.

Aleta was rolled in and settled in bed. Stanley was stopped at the door. Martha heard one of the guards tell Stanley that Chief West needed him to take his place at the door.

"He wants two out here," the guard said. "He's one man short on the street.

"Give me five minutes with my wife and then I'll be out."

Stanley told Aleta that he would be standing guard outside the room. She didn't argue with him. He'd been with her through the rough part. She could let him go now.

"Do me a favor," she said. "Take off this hospital gown. I want to sleep in the nude."

Stanley rose quickly and drew the curtain asking Martha to excuse them. He had some things to say to his wife.

Martha nodded and smiled. As if she wouldn't hear every word.

"Aleta," he whispered. "You can't sleep nude here."

"Why not?"

"Because it's inappropriate to walk around nude in a hospital.

"I won't comment on how little these gowns cover," Aleta quipped. "But your point is moot. I have no intention of walking around naked. Come morning, the nurse can dress me after my bath--gown, slings, the works--but tonight I want to sleep nude and unrestrained."

"You need the IV," Stanley pointed out. "You won't be completely unrestrained."

"I can live with that," Aleta said, "if the rest of me is free."

"You're making no sense."

"It's a small request, Stanley," Aleta said. "Please."

"Can't you wait until you come home?"

"No."

"What will Dr. Cook say?"

"Do we care?"

"Oh, Aleta, can't you be appropriate just this once?"

"I need to be in control of something," Aleta said. "Please."

"I can't undo your IV," Stanley argued weakly.

He'd given in. Silly as the request was, it wouldn't hurt anyone and he understood Aleta's urge to declare that she was still in control.

Aleta smiled. "Just unhook the bag. Slip off the gown and then hang the bag up again. And don't tell me you didn't know that."

Stanley reached behind her neck and untied the tie. He kissed her lightly on the mouth as he did so.

"That's the only kiss you get tonight," he warned her. "You're far too tempting nude."

He removed her gown quickly.

"Say goodnight to your son," Aleta said. "He's been through an ordeal too."

He kissed her on the lips again.

"Pass it along," he whispered as he tucked the sheet around her. "I can't believe you're trying to seduce me here and now."

Aleta giggled. "You're blushing."

"Go to sleep," He said, pulling open the curtain.

"Goodnight, Mrs. Cook."

Aleta giggled again and Stanley left abruptly.

"Feel better?" Martha asked.

"Yep!"

Dr. Cook came down the hall shortly afterward. He smiled at Stanley. "Lyle's not going to let you off the hook, is he?"

"I owe him," Stanley said tersely.

"Harriet in there?"

"She's coming back Martha said."

"When she does, she has five minutes," Dr. Cook said, "I want those two ladies to sleep tonight."

"Yes, Dr. Cook," said the other guard as Dr. Cook went in to check on Aleta.

Stanley waited to hear some exclamation from Dr. Cook but he only heard faint mumblings.

Dr. Cook emerged grinning. "She is full of surprises, isn't she, Stanley?"

"You could say that," Stanley said dourly.

"You perked her up by complying," Dr. Cook said. "You're a real asset."

"I wish her requests were a little less... er... extraordinary," Stanley stumbled.

"No, you don't!" Dr. Cook commented and then walked away.

Harriet came down the hall and was stopped by Dr. Cook. She continued on after a few minutes of conversation.

She handed Stanley a packet and told him Martha needed legal help. She was afraid someone would try to take over her company because Dr. Dunlap stated on television that she wasn't going to recover.

Stanley's jaw dropped at that piece of news and he took the packet.

"I'll read this before I leave here and I'll wake her to talk before morning. Tell her that. Then she'll sleep."

Harriet passed along his message and Martha relaxed. Harriet then went over to say goodnight to Aleta and spotted the hospital gown thrown over the chair.

"Did you make Stanley do that?"

Aleta nodded.

"How?"

"I won the argument."

Harriet leaned over and kissed her. "This act is going to persuade your father you're alright. He would expect something like this from you. It's a bit more creative then he would have envisioned, but he's going to love it."

"That's not why I did it."

"I know that. Have a good sleep. You'll never know how happy I am that you made it out of that operating room alive. I think Stanley feels the same way. He wouldn't have complied otherwise."

"I know," Aleta murmured. "I feel so good right now." She was asleep before Harriet walked out the door.

Chapter 11

Not a hint of dawn was evident when Fred Hepner drove his brown sedan past the River Forest home of Rodney Aiken. Sam and Toby had been silent for the last ten minutes. Fred had already assured them both several times that Aiken had planted the eight o'clock time to throw off the assassins. He would be leaving at six.

As they passed the house, they saw a light go on in what they assumed was an upstairs bedroom. A second light followed. The occupants were up. Fred had read the situation correctly.

They drove up and down the nearby streets until they were familiar with the surrounding area. At a quarter to six Fred pulled past the house on the far side of the street parked and cut his lights.

The brothers' plan was a simple one.

At a few minutes before six Sam and Toby left the car and positioned themselves behind parkway trees half a block from the front door of the house. Both had scopes on their rifles.

The light above the front door went on. The door opened. The two men looked through the telescopic sights on their rifles and readied their fingers on the triggers.

A maid came out the door and walked out to the car and looked all around. She was decidedly nervous. She shook her head and Rodney Aiken poked his head out the door and surveyed the area himself. Then, apparently satisfied, he stepped out of the house. The maid ran past him back into the house.

Rodney straightened up and strode confidently toward his car. Both shots hit him in the head. He dropped like a rock and the two brothers heard the maid screaming inside the house.

They ran to the car and slipped in through the open doors and Fred drove slowly down the street and turned the corner. He turned on the lights after a third turn and they drove straight toward Oak Park and then turned north toward Willow Glen.

Aleta was awakened, bathed and dressed in preparation for breakfast. She heard voices on the other side of the drawn curtain. She was certain one voice was Stanley's but couldn't fathom why he would be talking with Martha Cook so early in the morning.

When the curtain was pulled back, the man was gone.

"Was that Stanley?" she asked.

Martha nodded.

"He didn't say hello," Aleta murmured.

"Busy," Martha mumbled.

"Still, he could have…," she started. "No, he wouldn't have."

"Be back," Martha uttered.

"How long do you suppose he was on duty?"

Chief West walked in. "All night. He went home to change. So how are you two this morning?"

"Better," Aleta said. "We're both better."

"The shooters took out Rodney Aiken at exactly six o'clock just as Harriet predicted."

"Weren't the police there?"

"Aiken said he wasn't leaving the house until eight. He lied to them. Had same sort of secret meeting scheduled. Can't figure out how the shooters knew that. No one else did."

"Enid?" Martha asked.

"Milani is over there now trying to talk her into staying home. He's got squads on the streets nearby looking for the brown car Stanley saw."

"The guy who shut down the power last night," Aleta mused, "was a computer expert. Suppose he hacked into Aiken's email?"

"That might explain how they knew Aiken was leaving at six," West said, "but it doesn't put us any closer to our group "

"Why can't you find the car?"

"You do the math."

"One in every ten license plates ends in four," Aleta said. "That's one thousand cars in every ten thousand. And figure two cars per family; that amounts to several thousand cars... I'm getting the picture. Doesn't the color help?"

"Color isn't noted on the registration, just make and year. Stanley narrowed it down some, but not enough."

"You're looking at the general population," Aleta said thoughtfully. "Why not look at a specific group?"

"What group?"

"Any of the three companies whose CEO's were targeted," Aleta said. "Bet they give out employee parking stickers and keep records of license plate numbers."

"And then narrow it down to someone in our area," West said picking up on her idea and taking it one step further.

"Just keep thinking, "West said as he headed for the door. "You can be my personal think tank. What else have you got to do?"

"That's my line," Aleta called to his back. "And it's reserved for police chiefs."

"And their chief assistants," West shot back. "I'll be back."

Aleta smiled, then turned to Martha.

"If you wanted to kill someone and the area was swarming with cops, what would you do?"

"Give up," Martha stated, her voice clearer each time she spoke. Wisely, she confined her speech to brief phrases.

"Why wouldn't someone give up when the odds were stacked against him."

"Personal."

"Strong personal reason," Aleta said. "I agree. These men are strongly motivated. And as far as I can tell no money or power is involved. That leaves revenge. What would push a man to murder?"

"Death."

"These CEO's were responsible for someone's death or, if not death, a tragedy of equal magnitude."

"More," Martha said.

"Death plus other loss?" Aleta asked.

Martha nodded. "Turn around."

"Loss followed by death?" Aleta queried.

Martha's nod was more vigorous.

When Martha held up her hand, Aleta asked, "A new puzzle?"

Knowing Aleta could understand her, Martha explained her dilemma. She had seven department heads, all ambitious men, five of whom were qualified to take over Cook Construction. Stanley had told her she needed to put in an interim head. It was the only way to head off a take-over, but it had to be someone capable of doing her job or the person would be trampled as the heads vied for her job. It was a small loophole that the contenders would figure she couldn't do in her state. So he told her to sort through her people and pick one now.

"And I can't do it," she declared.

"Sure you can," Aleta said. "Take the five and decide which you wouldn't want to take over. Who are your top four?"

Martha rattled off four names, "Les, Mike, David and Matt."

"Which of those do you personally like to work with?"

"David Hansaard."

"Who's the smartest?"

"Matt Blair."

"Who knows the company best?"

"Les Swekla and Mike Carlson."

"Who's the strongest leader?"

"Mike."

"Who has the most integrity?"

"Les and David."

"Most creative?"

"Matt Blair."

"What does your company need right now?"

"Me!"

"What's your worst fear?"

"That whoever takes over will sully the Cook name."

"Good, that narrows your choice to two. Les Swekla and David Hansaard," Aleta said, then asked, "Which one could handle Mike Carlson the best?"

"I have no idea," Martha said. "I've always arbitrated disputes."

"You need a fresh eye," Aleta said. "Someone who isn't interested in taking over ever."

"Someone sharp and tough," Martha said.

"Too bad I'm unavailable," Aleta joked. "I'm busy being Chief West's chief assistant. How about my grandmother?"

"Harriet?" Martha repeated thoughtfully.

"She could go in telling them you can't decide which of the seven to promote, that you don't want to go outside. She can interview each and get the group's input on who should take over. Why not let them help?"

"That's a superb idea," Martha said.

"Let's hope the shooters don't find out she's the current prophet," Aleta said.

"What's our next problem?" Martha said.

"How they are going to kill Enid?" Aleta asked.

"What's been their method so far?"

"Shooting from a distance," Aleta said. "At least two sharpshooters."

"Two," Martha mused.

"You think there's a competition?" Aleta asked.

"Don't you?"

"It's natural," Aleta said, "but how does that help us?"

"What does a competition mean?"

"They'd want to challenge one another. Make the target more difficult."

"Make it smaller," Aleta said. "Or shoot from farther away."

"Guard!" Aleta called.

When a head was poked into the room, she said, "Please call Chief West. We have something important to tell him."

"Is it something I can transmit?" the guard asked politely.

"Sorry," Aleta said.

She heard him call the chief on the radio. In a couple of seconds he reported that the chief was on his way.

Dr. Cook walked in as the guard was passing along the message. "Don't you two ever rest?"

"We're resting," Aleta declared. "That is our bodies are resting. Our minds need exercise."

"Grams, you're looking better," Wayne Cook said putting his fingers lightly on her wrist. "How's your speech?"

"Getting better," Martha said, her words still slurred but understandable. "Aleta can understand me."

Wayne Cook guessed at what she said. All he understood was Aleta's name.

"Soon we'll all be able to understand you," he ventured.

Her crooked smile told him he'd guessed correctly. He picked up her chart and read it.

"Good progress," he said. "But no, you aren't going home for at least a week. And if it helps any, Aleta is staying that long as well."

"Okay!" Martha said.

Dr. Cook turned to Aleta. "What am I missing?"

Aleta grinned. "Lyle made us his think tank. We're solving problems."

"Not psychic stuff?"

"Reasoning stuff."

"I can't fault that," Dr. Cook said taking Aleta's pulse. "You're looking much better today."

"Shaved head and all?" Aleta joshed. "I must have looked like dirty underwear yesterday."

"Aleta, you were sick, not disgusting," Dr. Cook said. "Dr. Taekman called to see how you fared the night, so I told him all."

Aleta blushed. "You didn't!"

"He deserved a bonus. It was Christmas Day after all."

"What happened to privilege?"

"Between two doctors on the same case?"

"Never mind. Next time I'll appeal to your sense of decency."

Chief Lyle West walked in.

"I've a bone to pick with you, Wayne. You didn't tell me you ordered a bath for her before breakfast."

Aleta gasped. "He's not a doctor on the case!"

"I didn't want him walking in on you," Wayne said straight-faced.

"He didn't tell me," West corrected.

"Stanley wouldn't."

"My men are required to make reports," West said. "Last night Stanley was my deputy."

"He worked all night!" Aleta declared. "That was too long!"

"I knew he'd guard you well. I needed a night's sleep."

"You took advantage!"

"Yes, I did," Lyle smiled. "Now, why am I here?"

"Martha and I have come up with the motive and the method," she said and then proceeded to summarize their take.

"You two are gold!" Lyle exclaimed hurrying off. They heard him call Tom on his radio. "Meet me at Enid Bernstein's house."

"Wayne," Martha said, turning to Dr. Cook.

Without stopping she began a rapid mumbling which Aleta began interpreting as she was speaking. "I want Harriet to stand in for me, interview my department heads and help me select a successor. Stanley studied my corporate documents last night and said if I do that today, I might supersede any takeover attempt."

"But you won't retire, and they'll know it."

"Oh but I will. In three months I will hand the reins over to my successor."

"Nobody will believe it."

"I've never been seriously ill before. They'll believe it. Dr. Dunlap may have done me a favor. But I want to depart on my terms. Stanley said the element of surprise would catch them off-guard. "

"Grams, if I can help, I will."

"You may need to later."

"You do know some will discount my saying you're capable of making decisions," Wayne said. "They'll say I'm putting a positive on this because you're my grandmother."

"And Drs. Chesney, Hughes, and Kurland?"

Wayne grinned. "That should do it!"

"Can you get those three doctors to attest that Martha is lucid today?" Aleta asked. "Martha needs Harriet to start today.

"Sure. They're probably all doing rounds and should be stopping in to check on you two."

"Me?" Aleta said.

Chesney thinks of you as his patient. Hughes wants to keep tabs on you and Kurland will   want to meet you."

"I guess it's a good thing I dressed up this morning," Aleta snickered.

"Is Stanley preparing the paperwork for the doctors to sign?" Dr. Cook asked.

"No," Aleta said. "He's sleeping."

"Yes," Martha contradicted her. "I expect to see him any moment."

Aleta translated her response with a surprised voice.

"My dear," Martha said to Aleta. "He is still wearing his badge. He'll be back. I think he's planning to be here as much as possible."

"He has to take that badge off or Lyle will put him to work again."

"He's a grown man," Dr. Cook remarked. "He can always refuse."

"But he won't!"

"You can't do it for him," Dr. Cook counseled. "That would be disrespectful."

Aleta sank back onto her pillow.

"That's better," Dr. Cook said. "Are you still under orders to obey me?"

"Yes," Aleta murmured. She knew what was coming.

"Then I order you to stop worrying about Stanley and relax," Dr. Cook said. "Now tell me, have I crossed over the line?"

"No," Aleta replied. "I'll do it. Worrying isn't doing anything but making me tense."

"Go back to catching the crooks. Then we'll all get some sleep."

The two chiefs had been standing on the front step of Enid Bernstein's house, surveying the neighboring houses from which a shot could come while on the second floor of one of those houses Sam and Toby Hepner watched them. The occupants were on a skiing vacation and the house was on the police watch list. Toby had bypassed the alarm system and the two had entered undetected. They'd set up in a bedroom that overlooked Enid Bernstein's front door which was partially blocked by a huge tree. Most of the leaves were gone but the myriad of branches made the chiefs dismiss the windows they could scarcely make out as an unlikely spot for a sniper.

Fred, after dropping his brothers off, parked the brown car in their garage. When they had entered Willow Glen, they had picked up the police band and discovered their car would be stopped as soon as it was light enough to distinguish its color.

They would need to use their other car. It was newer and white but Fred liked his brown car because it was an eight. The white was a six.

That night they would abandon the brown car which the police computer files would show had been reported stolen two days before Christmas. Fred would be inserting that line of information into the police record while he waited for his brothers to call.

Upstairs in the two-story house, Sam and Toby each selected an opening between the branches. They used the heads of the two chiefs to line up their shots.

They thought they were ready when the front door opened. The chiefs had moved away, so there was nobody to block their shots. They eyed a head emerging from the house through their sights.

"It's a cop," Sam said. "And he's shielding her completely."

"There are two," Toby lisped.

"Shoot him in the leg," Sour Sam ordered.

Toby's finger squeezed off a round. The shot hit the man in his knee. The leg collapsed automatically and the cop went down.

Sam's shot hit Enid Bernstein between her eyebrows which had shot up in complete shock. She fell on top of the police officer.

The remaining cop looked straight toward the house where the shots came from. Toby's second shot took him down as well.

The rifles were quickly withdrawn and the windows closed. Both men moved quickly. They picked up their shells, tucked the guns into special harnesses under their overcoats and hurried down the stairs. Within seconds of the shots, they were walking down the street toward a white car parked a short distance away.

The car turned several times to avoid patrol cars and slowly proceeded toward the outskirts of town. Fred drove to a diner ten miles outside of town where, after Sam and Toby put their guns wrapped inside their coats in the trunk, the three brothers went inside and ate a hearty breakfast.

The news hit the air via live feed at the start of the nine o'clock news. The stations were ready to show Enid being safely escorted to her car. What they got was the shooting, every second of it. It was stunning coverage. Every newscast showed it the rest of the day.

Justin Conway was there with the camera crew and he had just announced the names of two men guarding Mrs. Bernstein when the shooting began. He kept up with the events as they unfolded naming each person who rushed in to help.

Justin took his television crew past the fallen men toward the house where the maid stood in the open doorway sobbing.

He stuck a microphone in front of her and asked, "Why did the police let her come out of the house?"

"She said they weren't going to stop her," the maid told Justin. "She said she'd sue if they tried."

"Didn't she believe them when they told her there was danger?"

"She said her brother was smarter, and he said nothing would happen. He's always so sure he's right. This time he wasn't and his sister's dead."

"What about Mr. Bernstein?"

"He tried to get her to stay home, but she always listened to her brother."

The woman was pulled inside and the door slammed shut.

Justin led the crew back to the fallen officers. Both were sitting up as the paramedics worked on them. One was pointing at a house and Justin had the cameraman follow the pointing finger.

The body of Enid Bernstein had already been covered with a sheet and it was the last image in that segment of the report.

Justin headed for the hospital.

Stanley was in Aleta's room when he heard a racket out in the hall. He was still wearing his vest and badge and he stepped out to see what was happening.

Dr. Dunlap was storming down the hall, Justin Conway and his TV cameraman were close on the doctor's heels.

Stanley said to the two guards, "Under no circumstances let that doctor enter this room."

The new man on the door spotted the badge on Stanley's chest that said "chief" and he recognized at once that this man was special. One obeyed the badge if nothing else.

"Yes Sir," came the crisp response.

Stanley walked toward the group. "Please turn around and leave. This area is off limits."

"Not to doctors it isn't," Dunlap declared with pomposity.

"None of the patients at this end are yours."

"I'm a consulting neurologist," he sputtered, unused to his authority being questioned. "Now, step aside."

Stanley blocked his way. "If you try to go further, I will have to arrest you."

"Don't be stupid!" Dunlap spat out as he pushed past Stanley.

He was completely unprepared for the swiftness with which Stanley caught his arm, spun him around and cuffed him. The guards who were watching were impressed by Stanley's deftness.

Then to their surprise Stanley arrested the man, quoting the laws he'd violated by ignoring an order from a man wearing a police badge, read him his Miranda rights and then motioned to one of the men at the door.

"Book him."

At the last order, Dunlap found his voice. "You can't do this. I'm a respected doctor in this hospital."

Stanley used his handheld radio to call Lyle. "We need another man up here. The TV crews have found the room. Our first arrest is corning in."

"Arrest?" Lyle questioned surprised. "Who?"

"Some fat doctor," Stanley said. "George is bringing him in. I don't have a police car yet."

"Dunlap," the doctor yelled. "Tell him who I am."

"And I want my handcuffs back," Stanley said over the radio.

"You can't do this," the doctor screamed. "I'll have your badge."

"What did he actually do?" Lyle asked over the radio. He didn't care if his men heard the exchange.

"Tried to confront Martha and Aleta. He was mad as hell."

"I'll see he doesn't get out of here without a restraining order," Lyle said. "You are on duty outside until I get another man over there."

"Yes, Chief," Stanley said.

Ten minutes later when Dr. Chesney arrived, he smiled at Stanley. "Aren't you on the wrong side of the door?"

"Not at the moment," Stanley replied politely. "Mrs. Locke has a document for you to sign. Mrs. Cook will explain."

"What's Stanley doing on the door?" Dr. Chesney asked the two women.

"He just arrested Dr. Dunlap," Aleta responded. "We heard it from in here. It was delicious!"

"Whatever for?"

"For not obeying a police directive," Aleta rejoined. "The guards are there for a reason."

"They let me through." Dr. Chesney remarked slightly puzzled.

"You're on the list," Aleta said. "I think it's because you bring chocolates."

"And I'm your doctor."

"Oh, yeah. That too."

"He's taking that job seriously."

"Lyle wouldn't have deputized Stanley if he didn't think he would."

"You're looking better this morning. How are you feeling?"

"I'll tell you when you tell me the operation didn't hurt the baby."

Dr. Chesney drew the curtain.

Chapter 12

The Tuesday following the Monday holiday, Harriet Locke walked into Martha Cook's office at eleven o'clock. Martha's secretary, a slender, older woman, Violet Andrews, hurried after her, politely informing the obviously professional lady that Mrs. Cook was not in the office.

Harriet introduced herself and asked Violet to inform all department heads that there was a mandatory emergency meeting in half an hour. She emphasized the fact that it was mandatory. It was a term Martha Cook liked to use and Martha had said if anyone failed to show, the censure was to be immediate and final.

Fifteen minutes later, Violet reported that she'd personally told every head about the meeting. Martha had always insisted she not go through a man's secretary when she called a mandatory meeting. Nothing took precedence.

At exactly eleven thirty, Harriet walked through the door to the conference room. Six men were seated around the table. In front of each man, as requested, sat his nameplate. Harriet carefully read each nameplate aloud and then acknowledged the man with a brief comment.

"Les Swekla, Martha says you are one of the most experienced men in the company. She respects your knowledge and integrity."

The lean, well-tanned man, who spent a great deal of time on site, beamed.

"Matthew Blair, I hear you are a creative genius. Martha says your intellectual prowess is a resource this company hasn't even begun to tap."

Blair, a chubby, balding man in his late forties warmed to the woman who recognized his particular talent.

"David Hansaard, I understand you have the capacity to get the best out of the people working for you--a most valuable trait in a leader."

Harriet continued through the group, Vincent Garrett, Bill Clay and Russ Wolcott all received praise for the qualities that Martha appreciated in them.

When Harriet finished, she remarked, "Mr. Mike Carlson has elected not to attend this meeting, I gather. Ms. Andrews, did Mr. Carlson inform you he might be detained?"

Violet shook her head. "No, Ma'am."

"Well, I will explain the purpose of this meeting at the end of which if Mr. Carlson has not shown, he will be removed from consideration for the top position in this company. And yes, Gentlemen, that is why I am here.

"In three months' time, Mrs. Cook is officially retiring and she is choosing her replacement from the group assembled here."

Harriet noticed three men surreptitiously paging someone. She guessed it was Mike Carlson. She noted who the three were.

"Mrs. Cook has had a stroke, of which I am sure you are all aware. Her doctor has allowed only one visitor--me--which may sound strange but her doctor is her grandson and so he represents the family. I'm a longtime friend."

Harriet noted that a tall, gray-haired man slipped through the door and into the nearest empty seat.

"Ah, I see Mr. Mike Carlson has decided to join us.

"Obviously, one of the pages was persuasive. You may thank Mr. Garrett, Mr. Clay and Mr. Wolcott for their effort on your behalf," Harriet told him. "I personally wouldn't have paged you. You are the top competitor for the opening that Mrs. Cook's departure will create. I personally would have let you eat the fruit of your defiance."

A couple men coughed and Harriet continued.

"But I agreed that if you made it before I finished speaking you would still be employed by the end of the meeting. And, yes, Gentlemen, I have the legal authority--oh, did I forget to mention that Mrs. Cook's personal attorney has filed the necessary paperwork with the court. I am, Gentlemen, your interim CEO with all the power of that office. Now I will take your questions."

"I heard Martha can't speak," Matt Blair said. "Yet, she seemed to be able to communicate. How is she doing this?"

"She has an interpreter."

"And interpreter? She speaks English."

"Not very well at the moment. Only one person can understand her. Her speech, however, is returning and should be back to normal in three months or less."

"Why are you here?" Mike Carlson asked. "What do you know about the construction business? What's your background?"

"Ah, Mr. Carlson, it didn't take you long to challenge me. Martha said you'd be the first, but Mr. Blair's intellectual curiosity was more demanding. Let me answer you honestly. First, I'm here to help Martha decide who is the best man for the job. Second, I'm retired and have no intention of reentering the work force, so no one need fear me as a competitor."

"Excuse, me, Ma'am," Mike interrupted, "but if you think we are gullible enough to believe that you aren't sitting in as interim CEO with the idea of slipping into the position as permanent, you are mistaken. This is a huge company. There is no way you don't want that chair to be permanent."

"Mr. Blair, tell Mr. Carlson why he is mistaken," Harriet directed. "You had almost twenty minutes before the meeting. You looked me up, didn't you?"

"Er… Yes, I did," Matt admitted. "I like to be prepared."

"An admirable quality," Harriet said. "Did anyone else bother to do that?"

Les spoke up, "I didn't do it myself. I asked Matt what he'd discovered."

"Another admirable quality. Using a valuable resource," Harriet remarked. "So, Mr. Blair tell Mr. Carlson what you discovered."

Matt cleared his throat, "Mrs. Locke was Vice President in the Trust Department at Atherton Bank in Oakland, California."

"That doesn't qualify her to run this company," Mike Carlson sneered. "She knows nothing about our business."

"Which is why I'm not in the running for the position I am temporarily holding."

"You shouldn't even be there," Mike said. "One of us should be there."

"One of you will be," Harriet said. "Before three months if I do my job well."

"That's not all," Matt Blair interjected. "Mike, shut up until I'm done. I know you think the job is yours, but it won't be if you keep sticking your foot in your mouth."

"What else is there?" Mike countered derisively, "So the lady rose to second chair. Bet the bank president was a man."

"Was is the operative term," Matt Blair said. "I didn't have time to investigate that, but Mrs. Locke was in charge of a fund whose assets tripled from millions into over a billion in assets. She is one of the principal partners in the Tontine Group whose money she was solely responsible for investing. She doesn't need to work. Five of our new projects are from her Tontine Group. She is one of our major clients, Mike. She may not know construction, but she knows how to make money."

"I still don't think she knows who'd run this outfit the best," Mike remarked.

"Excuse me, Mr. Carlson," Harriet said, "but Matt isn't done."

"I'm done," Matt declared.

"Mr. Carlson asked about my background. He deserves to know all you know."

"I'd rather not, Mrs. Locke," Matt said. "Besides it shouldn't enter in here."

"Ah, Matt, how naive you are. It is perhaps the most important fact."

David Hansard spoke up, "Share it Matt. She gave you permission. If you found it in your computer search, it's okay. That's not the same as a secret someone confided to you."

Matt cleared his throat again. He looked into the clear blue eyes of the blonde moustached man sitting across from him and found them curious only.

"Mrs. Locke's father was a Negro educator in Elyria, Ohio."

"He educated Negros," Mike retorted. "So what?"

David chose to explain. "He not only educated them, he was one. Mrs. Locke is bi-racial."

"She's a Negro?" Mike blurted out. "That tears it!"

"Leave it to Mrs. Cook," Les said. "If you thought you were going to bully your way into her chair, Mike, you don't know the lady. She is always one step ahead of us. Frankly, Mrs. Locke, you might well be the only one in the room capable of handling this bunch."

"Are you kissing my ass, Mr. Swekle?"

"I would if it'd do any good," Les grinned. "No, I'm not, but I've worked for Mrs. Cook tor over thirty-five years and I've learned to respect her singular abilities to keep this crew corralled and focused. Mrs. Locke, you passed out compliments at the beginning of the meeting, which Mike would have enjoyed had he been here; now allow me to pay you one. Mrs. Cook has a friend of equal strength and astuteness. You would fill her shoes the best. Each of the rest of us would do it in a different fashion. I'm assuming she is looking for specific qualities in her successor. What exactly are those qualities?"

"Integrity tops the list," Harriet said. "While Martha has been arbitrary in her demands, she has never been devious."

"What else?" Les urged.

"I'm not sure," Harriet said. "That will come out in the interviews because, Gentlemen, it will become your company and what you want will mold the future of Cook Construction."

Having said that Harriet abruptly left the conference room.

Violet handed out a schedule of interview times. "You may change your times if you have a conflict. You may choose not to participate."

"As if we have a choice," Mike sneered.

David put his hand on Mike's shoulder, "You're still in the game, Mike. Pull yourself together."

"So who do you think she has her eye on?" Mike asked.

"You, for one. You went toe to toe with her. That might be perceived as positive. I don't know the woman," David replied.

"What about Les?"

"I think he's your main competition."

"And you?"

"A remote possibility."

When Violet returned to the office, Harriet called her in.

"Any changes?" Harriet asked. "No, Ma'am."

"Any refusals?"

"None yet."

"What did Mike say?"

"He asked who his competition was."

"Who answered?"

"David Hansaard. He said you might like a man that would dare to challenge you. He said Les was Mike's competition."

"What about himself?"

"He said that was a remote possibility."

"I see the field has already been narrowed down for me," Harriet said. "Change the schedule. I want to talk with David first."

Violet turned to go.

"Wait," Harriet said. "Don't change it. That'll upset Matt. Instead ask Mr. Hansaard if he would lunch with me in my office and send out for whatever Martha usually gets when she does this."

Violet smiled. "You truly are much alike."

"Do you know why we do it this way, Violet?"

"No, Ma'am."

"Because then the gentleman has been treated to lunch; however, the woman has not picked up the check in public."

David Hansaard was surprised at the invitation. He accepted with pleasure and showed up promptly at twelve thirty.

"Lunch will be here shortly," Harriet said. "I don't drink except for a glass of wine at dinner; however, I do believe Martha may have a fully stocked bar, so help yourself."

"Martha has every imaginable soft drink," David said, slipping into the role of host. "Perhaps you'd like a fruit flavored sparkling water or a soda or iced tea? Raspberry ice tea is Martha's favorite."

"I'll try that," Harriet said watching David relax as he poured two drinks.

"Tell me why you think your chance of being CEO is remote."

"I'm good at smoothing over roughened feelings. I'm not a leader. I encourage people to fulfill their potential. It's a good quality, but it's not leadership."

"What about Matt Blair?"

"Probably the sharpest man on staff; which you already pointed out. I guess that pretty much sums up Matt."

"So, you think it's between Mike and Les?"

"Don't you?"

"They're on the short list."

"So Martha has already narrowed it down. I couldn't believe she hadn't."

"You're on it."

"She and I work well together, but I'm not her."

"What's Mike's strongest attribute?"

"He's a strong leader. Half the heads already look to him for leadership."

"And his weakest trait?"

"He's opinionated."

"Aren't most leaders?"

"I guess so."

"What's Les' strongest attribute?"

"He knows the company inside and out. The men love him and respect him."

"His weakest trait?"

"He doesn't do as well in the board room," David offered, almost apologetically.

"What's your strongest attribute?"

"I understand people."

"And your weakness?"

"Same thing. I understand where they're coming from and I have trouble being arbitrary."

"The food's here. Let's eat," Harriet said.

To David's astonishment, there was no more talk of work, just pleasant conversation about hobbies and children. At precisely one o'clock, David rose to leave.

"There's a mandatory meeting in an hour, at two," Harriet said. "Please send Violet in."

After sending Violet off to deliver the message, Harriet picked up Martha's private line and got hold of Wayne Cook. She spoke for a few minutes and then put down the phone and walked out the door. To her relief, no one was in the outer office. She pulled the plug on Violet's phone and then went back into Martha's office.

She only had a few more minutes to wait until she heard Martha's mumble.

"I've got your successor," Harriet announced boldly.

"You sure?" Martha asked.

"Absolutely," Harriet said. "You want to hear my reasons now or will you wait until I see you?"

"So quick?"

"They sorted themselves out," Harriet said. "It came down to your top three. I'm holding a mandatory meeting at two and I'm going to announce my recommendation and the reasons."

"Do it!" Martha said.

"See you soon."

Wayne took the phone. "Okay, tell me. And give me the reason."

And Harriet did so.

"I've always liked him. You've got my vote."

At two Harriet entered the conference room and saw the same six men she had that morning. Mike Carlson was missing again.

Harriet went around the room and asked the men one by one what they would do about his absence.

Several wanted to call and remind him. Others wanted to impose a censure of some sort. When they got to David, he said, "I know what Martha would do, but I'm not her. I guess I'd warn him not to do it again."

Les was last.

"Have the rules changed in the last couple of hours?" he asked. "Missing a mandatory meeting is grounds for dismissal."

"Would you do it?" Harriet asked.

"This is the second one he's missed," Les said. "Yes, I would."

There were murmurs of dissent. Bill Clay argued that perhaps Mike didn't think Harriet knew how rare mandatory meetings were and that Mike just assumed she was using the term for a regular meeting which was always voluntary. Vincent Garrett argued that perhaps he was caught in a situation he couldn't extricate himself from without hurting a relationship with a client. Russ Wolcott suggested that he didn't hear the time right or perhaps thought it was tomorrow.

Matt Blair remained silent. If Mike wasn't fired, and even if he was, he didn't want a hand in either choice. He was still upset that his interview had been cancelled. He had things he wanted to say that had nothing to do with this political game they were all playing.

"We're all here," Les Swekla said. "The last time Mrs. Locke called a mandatory meeting it was to tell us Mrs. Cook was retiring and looking for a successor. Mrs. Locke cancelled the interviews and as she called the hospital, I'm assuming she wants to give us on update on Martha Cook's condition.

Harriet looked at him. "I thought I unplugged the right phone."

"You did. It upset Violet. She came to me and I plugged it in and pushed the redial button and got the hospital."

"Did you tell anyone?"

"I figured that was the reason for the meeting."

"You are correct," Harriet said smiling. "Martha has told me to pass along the job of interim CEO to her successor. The job will be permanent once the Board of Trustees meets."

"You've decided?" Matt blurted out. "But you didn't talk to any of us."

"Oh, yes, she did," David said. "She talked with me. Only I didn't know until this minute she'd made her decision."

"You actually used the key phrase, David. Who did you say was loved and respected by the men in the field?"

All eyes turned to Les Swekla.

"That's the phrase that was used in Mr. Cook's obituary. That and the word integrity," Harriet said. "Martha Cook doesn't want another person like herself to take over. She wants a person like her husband. She's always said it was his company. She had her own style of leadership but she held fast to his principals."

Les Swekla sat with his mouth agape.

David Hansaard was the first to rise and congratulate him. "From what Martha has told me about her husband, you are very much like him. And we're all proud of the honesty and integrity of Cook Construction and the fair way it treats the men in the field. You'll keep that tradition alive."

Matt Blair said simply, "Aside from Martha, there's no one I'd rather work for."

The others crowded around to congratulate him as well. "I'm not really on office man," Les said. "I'll need the help of every one of you in that area."

"What about Mike?" Bill asked.

"My last job as interim CEO will be to tell him he violated his contract," Harriet said, "and that he is dismissed. Les starts out fresh. David, please take this group to Martha's office and show them the bar. I will join you in about fifteen minutes."

As the men began to move toward Martha's office, Harriet turned to her secretary.

"Violet, call security. Have them meet me in Mike Carlson's office."

"I should go with you," Les said.

"Thank you, I'd like that."

The two entered Mike's office and found him at his desk.

"Busy?" Harriet asked.

"As a matter of fact, I am," Mike responded.

"Well, that is about to cease," Harriet stated coldly. "You missed a mandatory meeting and thus violated your contract."

"You can't call any old meeting mandatory," Mike spat out irritably.

"You didn't believe announcing Mrs. Cook's retirement was important?" Harriet asked.

"I agree I made a mistake there," Mike admitted.

"That didn't give you a clue that this meeting might also be important?"

"Some people think everything they say is important," Carlson sneered.

He wasn't going to kowtow to this woman.

"Well, at this meeting, with Martha's approval, I named her successor," Harriet said. "I'd say that was important."

Mike's expression went from utter disbelief to outrage. "On what basis? You don't know anything about us or this company. Half the department heads want me."

"Well, they did a good job of trying to excuse your absence," Harriet informed him. "But when I told you I had the authority I meant it. And you had a contract. One thing you should know about bankers. We believe in rules."

"Rules? What rules?" Mike asked, apprehension seeping into his voice.

"You know which one," Harriet said. "You're fired."

"I'll appeal."

"Go ahead," Harriet said. "But in the meantime, you have fifteen minutes to pack your personal belongings, and leave. Security is here to watch you."

"You don't trust me?" Mike asked aghast.

"Not for a second," Harriet said. "You've shown me nothing but contempt. I am Martha's chosen representative and, as such, contempt is not something I should have received. I have not misused my power and I have accomplished my assigned task with a minimum of disruption to this company."

"I'll fight this," Mike said. "You won't get away with it.

"Actually, she will," Les said. "She told you she had the authority. I believed her. So did the rest of the department heads. You didn't. It was a big mistake."

"Les, you need me. You'll be no good in board meetings."

"I have David. He can handle those."

"You know nothing about office management. Stats. Projections. Costs."

"I have Matt. He knows just about everything."

"You're a field man."

"You are so right," Les said. "If you had treated me with the contempt you showed Mrs. Locke, you'd have been off my crew so fast you'd be lucky if you held onto your pants. So get cracking. We have a party to go to and we're late."

He turned to the security guards.

"Okay, men. He's all yours. He has fifteen minutes. No files. No paperwork. Pens, pictures and book ends."

"Yes. Mr. Swekla."

Violet had obviously filled them in.

Chapter 13

Harriet breezed into Martha's hospital room and said, "I have your new CEO outside in the hallway waiting to see you. Please, please say it was your idea."

Aleta caught the panic in Harriet's voice, "Grams, what's wrong?"

"I'll explain fully later, but I had a vision and I couldn't figure out how to save his life except to tell him you wanted to meet the person I selected."

"In my condition?" Martha mumbled.

"I told him we're waiting for Wayne to join us," Harriet said, her voice shaky. "I've never been anything but straightforward. But my God! What have I done?"

Aleta laughed.

"Well, you came to the right place. We do understand."

Martha mumbled. "I do want to see my successor."

"I actually understood that!" Harriet exclaimed. Harriet heard Wayne greeting Les.

"Les?" Martha asked.

"The men love and respect him just as they did your husband. He's a man of integrity. You said so yourself. I'm not sure he'll make a lot of money but the company will remain one to be proud of."

"Are you giving away the surprise?" Wayne asked, entering the room. "Come on in Les. Grams has only recovered part of her speech, but her brain is still firing on all cylinders."

Les came in and pulled up a chair and sat beside Martha. "You don't have to be locked into this retirement or to my taking over. You can get well and then look around. I'm sure that this move was to prevent anyone from fighting you for control. And it was a good move."

"Aleta, translate," Martha said and then she began to speak rapidly and Aleta translated as she spoke. She told Les about her husband and her desire to keep his goal of building houses that he would be proud of. She told him about his feel for wood and the working of it. She explained how much she had worried when the company grew so large. She worried that it would need a professional corporate manager and it would go downhill from there. By downhill, she wasn't talking about profit, but loss of standards.

"Just keep the men employed," she finished. "And don't try to cut costs by reducing the workforce. Think of the men first."

"I can do that."

"Don't be afraid to fire someone who lies or cheats. No kickbacks, no under the table deals. Our reputation is our stock in trade."

"You are talking to me as if I'm your new CEO," Les said. "Are you certain you don't want more time?"

"Les," Martha said slowly, "You are my choice. I wanted you to hear me say that."

"Thank you," Les responded. "Remember, in my eyes you are still the boss. I know what being a major stockholder means, but I'm not referring to that. You have been the head of Cook Construction since I started. And I would miss dreadfully if you stopped calling me and telling me you have a special little job that my men must do immediately. The men love those interruptions too."

He turned to Aleta and thanked her for acting as Mrs. Cook's interpreter and then asked her name.

Aleta replied, "Aleta Praetzel, attorney from California, wife of Stanley Praetzel. We are the attorneys for the Tontine whose members have hired you to build the new physical therapy wing, the homeless compound, the dog and cat shelter and the homes around the lake outside Arborville."

"And your own house expansion," Les said. "I remember you wouldn't marry your husband until we finished the kitchen and then you agreed to let our oldest carpenter do your cabinets--the one man no one could ever hurry."

"That's me," Aleta said cheerfully. "Your man did a fantastic job."

"We replaced all your windows with bulletproof ones too, if I remember correctly."

"I keep getting shot at," Aleta said. "You bulletproofed the window in this room too."

"Well, that's nice to know," Les responded. "But I thought that was to protect Wayne."

"It was. He's my doctor. Martha didn't want him shot while he was taking my pulse."

"You're not one of the targets these psychics keep naming, are you?"

Aleta laughed, "We're the psychics."

"Who are?"

"Martha, Harriet and me."

"But you're professional women."

"That part's hard for us too," Aleta said. "It's the reason you're here. Grams saw you die in a car crash on the way home from work. She couldn't bring herself to tell you and so she brought you here."

"Well, that makes sense," Les said. "You ladies have a great track record."

"Get your car checked before you drive it again," Harriet said. "I think the brakes failed."

"It's a new truck," Les pointed out.

"You came to an intersection and the light was red. You couldn't stop and you were broadsided by a truck."

"Wow!" Les said.

"My friend's only prophecy murder," Martha said. "We call ourselves prophets because we are pretty much limited to that."

"Murder?" Les gasped. "But who?"

"All we ever see," Aleta explained, "is the murder itself."

"Well, call me anytime you see me murdered again."

"While I have you here," Aleta said, "I have an urgent request."

Stanley entered the room in time to hear the last sentence.

He protested at once. "Aleta, I told you, Hubbs is comfortable."

"Is this your husband, the lawyer?" Les asked. "Why is he half dressed like a cop?"

"I'm a substitute cop," Stanley replied tersely.

"How'd you get that job?" Les asked with open curiosity.

"I'm a crack shot."

"Your wife gets shot a lot," Les said, smothering a grin.

"One has nothing to do with the other," Stanley said seriously. "And who are you?"

"Les Swekla, Cook Construction Company's new CEO."

Stanley's demeanor softened. He extended his hand.

"Congratulations," he said warmly. "That was fast."

"So your wife is about to hire me to do a rush job."

Aleta butted in.

"My horse was shot."

"Him too?" Les exclaimed. "We get hazard pay then."

Stanley scowled, "Aleta, what have you been telling him?"

"He remembers replacing our windows."

"So you want me to bulletproof your horse's stall?"

"Heavens no!" Aleta exclaimed. "Hubbs, our horseman, insists on sleeping in the barn. There's a space in back that would make an excellent room, but it needs everything--walls, floor, heat, light, water, insulation."

"How much do you want to pay?"

"Put in whatever Hubbs needs. You can put in windows too."

"If you want an estimate, I need some parameters."

"I don't need an estimate. Just make the space livable and Stanley'll pay for it."

"Me?" Stanley said. "It's your idea."

"He's part of my Christmas present. Hubbs can't live in a stocking."

"It's a sleeping bag, Aleta. And he likes to feel the wind on his face and have the sun wake him. He likes the smell of hay and horse liniment and leather."

"You talk to him, Les. Be aware he may be afraid to ask for much. He's old. And he has a horse. It was hard for him to find a place. But he's perfect for us. And he deserves the best."

"I'll go out there tomorrow and talk with him. Then I'll give you a rough estimate. It prevents future shock."

"Give it to Stanley. He won't give you trouble, I promise."

"I'll be hard to get hold of tomorrow," Stanley said. "Just start the work. Twenty thousand is my limit."

"I can do it for under that."

Stanley took his wife's head in his hands, kissed her, then said, "Next year, Aleta, I'm giving you diamond earrings. This horse is costing a fortune."

"But it was the gift of a lifetime. You don't ever have to match it. I'll remember it forever," Aleta said with an honest gratitude that pleased every ear that heard it. "Next year give me another baby."

Stanley gasped,

"You haven't even had this one yet!"

Laughter erupted among the onlookers.

"Les, let me take you home," Harriet said. "I don't like to be on the road too late at night."

"Grams, no!" Aleta said suddenly. "Your car's been tampered with too. Brakes."

"It got here just fine," Harriet protested.

"Grams! Not you!" Aleta cried.

Tears burst forth.

Harriet rushed over. "Oh, Aleta, I'm so sorry. Of course I won't drive Mr. Swekla I'll call him a cab."

Stanley called Lyle on his radio. He spoke briefly, then turned and said to Harriet, "The police are going to impound your jeep. Hawk will go over it immediately."

"What do I do about my truck?" Les asked.

"We'll call you as soon as we have a report," Stanley said. "And then you call the Des Plaines police."

"Use a company car," Martha added.

"I'll be at your place in the morning, Mr. Praetzel," Les said. "I'll see Hubbs has a warm place to sleep quickly."

As soon as he left, Aleta began to cry. Stanley sat on the edge of the bed and hugged her gently. The sobbing worsened.

Dr. Cook came over. While Stanley held her, Dr. Cook took her pulse.

"Normal misery," he assessed. "Nothing to be alarmed over.

Martha began speaking rapidly and Aleta's sobs lessened. She rubbed her wet face on Stanley's vest and then drew back.

"We have got to get you a job where your shoulder is softer.

Stanley wiped her face with his fingers. "What did Martha say?"

"That this time it was an ordinary murder attempt by an angry person who'd just been fired. And God protected her, so I should stop worrying."

"Oh, Aleta," Stanley cried softly. "When will you let go?"

"It's Dr. Cook's fault."

Wayne Cook's face registered his surprise."

"Mine?"

You ordered me to stop worrying about Stanley, but you forget to include Grams."

Dr. Cook laughed. "Leave it to a lawyer!"

"You just saved a life," Stanley said.

"We lost one too."

"You didn't lose her," Stanley argued. "She decided to ignore the warning. That was her choice, not yours. Haven't we been over this? Did you forget?"

Dr. Cook came over and pulled the curtain.

"Stanley, put Aleta to bed and see that Harriet's visit is short. These two need their rest. I can't believe how busy these two are lying flat on their backs in hospital beds. If this keeps up, I'll have to keep them here two weeks."

"Oh, no!" Aleta exclaimed. "We'll rest. I promise."

Stanley lowered the bed and Aleta asked him to take off his vest and gun.

"Why?" he asked.

"Because I'm asking," she replied.

He removed them and put them on the chair in the corner. "Don't let me forget them."

As Harriet and Martha conversed on the other side of the curtain, Stanley carefully removed Aleta's gown. She reached up and stroked his cheek and he tucked her hand back under her covers. Once his hand was under the covers with hers she put it on her tummy and held it there with her hand.

"The baby is moving. I can feel it," she whispered,

In a few moments, he felt it too. It was a precious moment.

"Isn't it early?" he whispered.

"You're asking me? How much experience do you think I've had?"

"Don't you women know these things?"

"You mean, is it wired into our DNA?"

"Something like that."

"I hate to burst your bubble, but I'm no expert."

"So, he survived the operation."

"He did indeed." Aleta smiled slyly. "That's because he's a she."

He left shortly afterward. Neither remembered the gun on the chair.

After their visitors had left, Aleta and Martha lay quietly for a few minutes, each staring at the white ceiling.

"You sleepy?" Aleta asked.

"No. Are you?"

"Tell me about Harriet's visit to your company."

And Martha did.

"It's exciting, isn't it?" Aleta asked, "To be entering a new phase of one's life."

"I thought I'd die working," Martha said.

"I thought I'd probably never marry."

"You had a boyfriend."

"Before Stanley there was really no one. Stanley turned my life around."

"I think you've reciprocated."

"We felt the baby move this evening."

"Exciting?"

"Very."

"Good evening, Ladies," said a familiar voice. "Why are you all alone and tucked for the night?"

Chief Lyle West entered their room.

"We were put to bed," Aleta giggled, "and told to go to sleep."

"But you're talking."

"We aren't sleepy."

"Good. I have news."

"We heard that Harold Moshansky cancelled his racquetball date," Aleta told him.

"We've narrowed the field of suspects to five families, but we have one that seems the most likely. We have men watching all five houses now," Chief West said.

"That's great."

"We haven't a shred of evidence, just theory, but that's a whole lot better than being nowhere," West went on. "But that's not why I'm here. It seems our perps have taken a new tactic. They've drained Jackman's bank account. They've also drained Harold Moshansky's. I believe they'll go for yours next, Martha."

"Who's your best suspect?"

"The Hepner brothers. There are three. Their father was dismissed while their mother was undergoing expensive experimental treatment not covered by insurance. He couldn't focus enough to find another position. All three sons had to leave college. The mother died, but the family finances had been completely drained. The father couldn't find work. The sons eventually gave up hope of returning to school and took jobs of various sorts--all low level positions. The father's ended his own life and the boys buried him last year. Christmas Eve was the father's birthday."

"Multiple losses followed by multiple deaths," Aleta said. "I think you've identified the assassins."

"You think they'll go for my money?" Martha asked.

"We can't prove it's them. The money gets transferred into a bank account in Switzerland and is transferred to another elsewhere. All we do know is that large sums of money have appeared in the five bank accounts of those we have under surveillance. A couple asked their bank managers to investigate which is why we know about it. Others used the money to pay creditors."

"So they're playing Robin Hood," Aleta concluded.

"Eventually, we'll get them," Lyle said. "I have Ed working on it. They've given our police computer a virus. We're down for a day at least."

"I have an idea," Martha said. Her next words came so fast Lyle missed most of them. Aleta summarized her suggestion.

"Martha wants Ed to transfer all the money in her checking account to the Hepner brothers' local bank account."

"Why?"

"Two can play that game," Martha said coyly, speaking slowly. "When they access my account, I want them to find it empty. They will look for the money. They will assume that I opened a new account."

"That was going to be my suggestion," Lyle said.

"Won't do any good," Martha declared. "But what will they do when they find the money has been blatantly transferred to their own account?"

"How much money are we talking about?" Aleta asked.

"Quarter of a million."

"Do you know what people in California do when an earthquake hits?" Aleta asked.

"No."

"First, they're surprised. Then slightly awed. Then scared. And if they aren't dead when the shaking stops, relieved and slightly giddy. Then come the aftershocks and hours of apprehension."

"What's that to do with this?" Martha asked.

"You will have rocked their world," Aleta said.

"You can't report the money stolen," Chief West cautioned.

"You don't think my bank manager will notice that a quarter of a million has been sucked from my account overnight?

"He'll call you."

"He can't. I'm in the hospital," Martha shot back. "Under protective custody, which means no visitors."

"He'll insist on an investigation."

"So you tell him the truth," Martha said.

"Which is?"

"I ordered the money transferred since I believed they were going to take it anyway."

"Wow!" Aleta said. "Martha, it's beautiful! No lies. No direct accusation. But you point a finger. And no more."

"You realize if they accept it, it can't be considered stolen," Chief West told her.

"I want to shake them up."

"Why not just transfer a part of it?"

"They'd gleefully take the rest," Martha stated knowingly. "These are men whose success has made them feel invincible. Let's change that."

Shortly after Chief West left, Aleta spotted the gun and vest lying on the chair and told herself that she'd return them in the morning. She had no idea how early she would do that.

Chapter 14

In the Hepner house near the outskirts of Arborville, the youngest of the three brothers yelled at his brothers to come to the rear bedroom at the same time the eldest shouted for his brothers to come into the living room. Toby answered Sam's call first.

At Sam's direction, Toby slid behind the half-closed drape and peered out into the darkness. The streetlight just barely caught the bar on the car parked in the shadows down the street far enough away not to be easily spotted.

"It's that damned paper," Toby lisped. "The first stories were good for us, but today he went over the line."

"He didn't name names," Sam reminded his brother. "He just told the stories of the families whose breadwinner was arbitrarily downsized by Jackman."

"He picked our five families," Toby complained. "All of us with deaths within this last year."

"Deaths drive the point home quicker than anything else," Sam said, his sudden good humor a contrast to his brother's blatant irritability.

"I didn't like the unspoken implication," Toby grumbled. "I think that's why the cops are out there."

Fred appeared, his angry scowl followed by sharp words. "I called you guys. I got something important to show you."

"Cops are watching the house," Sour Sam announced. "Toby thinks that reporter pointed at us."

"Sam thinks the cops don't read the papers," Toby growled.

It was his turn to be the angry brother.

"You're both wrong," Fred snapped. "That's what I wanted to show you."

"Show us? To impress us by pushing buttons on the computer screen until you get to something you could just have told us straight out," Sour Sam snapped, his anger rising to match Toby's. Fred was always showing off his prowess on the computer and it was wearing as thin as his penchant for wearing his hair over his eyes.

"This you gotta see!" Fred declared, adamantly.

His tone told his brothers to pay attention. They followed him back to his computer set-up where they found themselves staring at Martha Cook's bank account.

Sour Sam reacted first. "So you transferred the quarter million. We knew it was there."

Fred pushed a couple keys. "Here's the account it went to."

"That's our personal account!" Sam exploded. "That was a stupid mistake!"

Toby eyed his younger brother inquisitively. There was no apology in his manner. He hadn't made a mistake.

"Who did this, Fred?" Toby asked.

"Martha Cook is behind it. She knows it's us and this way she can force the cops to move in," Fred announced.

"Put it back!" Sour Sam shouted.

"Can't," Fred shot back, his exasperation bursting forth. "That'd be like admitting we can play around with bank accounts."

"Then let's take the money out," Sam said heatedly.

"You think the bank manager is going to hand us a quarter of a million in cash and not ask questions?" Toby lashed out.

"We can't leave it there," Sam declared.

"Our only choice is to move it to our Swiss account," Fred said.

"Wait!" Toby shouted, reason taking over. "We can't do that. We'd be leaving a trail that will connect us to the money that went through that account."

"You mean leave it?" Fred gasped.

"Why not?" Toby lisped. "We didn't steal it. Legally it's ours."

"There will be questions as soon as the bank opens," Fred remarked, shoving his hair out of his eyes so his brothers would know he knew what he was talking about.

"We move it!" Sour Sam declared, grabbing hold of the leadership role again. "And then we move."

"You mean we start running?" Toby pressed, perturbed.

"That's a mistake!" Fred declared.

"We've been given the money," Sam argued. "We didn't ask for it. So we do what anyone would do with such a windfall, we take it and split."

"What about the car?" Toby threw in, not able to think past the one thing that was his.

"Yeah," Fred reiterated. "What do we do with his car?"

Back in control, Sam relaxed into issuing orders. "Fred, pack up your computer and take it to my truck."

"What about my car?" Toby pressed.

"It's parked in front. We can't take it," Sam decided.

"We just leave it?" Toby grimaced.

"We'll buy you a new one," Sour Sam snapped.

"And my car?" Fred said, referring to the brown car which was currently hidden in the garage.

"Toby and I are going to torch the car," Sam announced matter-of-factly.

Fred's eyes widened, and his jaw dropped.

"While it's in the garage?" he gasped. "The house will go up too."

"We can't come back ever," Sam said stoically. "We've got to disappear, but before we do we've got to take care of those two psychics in the hospital. We can't hide from them."

"My gun," Fred said. "It's in my car."

"Get it," Sour Sam ordered. "Take it and the computer to the truck. Go out the back. The cops are only watching the front.""

He turned to his middle brother. "Toby, can you set up a device to switch lights on and off in progression?"

"Sure, but why?"

"We aren't going to be here when the garage goes up, but I want the cops to think we are," Sam responded, his plan taking shape quickly.

"When do we take out the psychics?" Fred asked.

"Tonight," Sam replied with steely determination.

At two in the morning Aleta buzzed for the nurse. The nurse noticed the gun and the vest.

"Do you want me to remove those things?" she asked.

"Do you know anything about guns?"

"No," the nurse replied.

"Then just leave it."

"I could call one of the guards in."

"With me naked, please don't."

The nurse shrugged. "I guess those things aren't going anywhere."

Aleta lay awake for a long time after she lay back down. Martha put a quarter of a million dollars on the line just to rattle a group of assassins. Just suppose they didn't react as expected.

Just how did she expect them to react? How do people react when they're shaken? Her mind drew a blank. Usually so full of ideas and thoughts, she was suddenly without any.

She put her hand on her tummy. Even her baby was asleep. She stared at the ceiling, a soft gray under the low light from the nightlight.

Her eyes closed but her mind stayed awake noting every sound. Most of those she heard were muted and barely distinguishable. Sometimes the only sound was the soft blowing of the hot air through the ventilator. Martha rolled onto her back and began to snore softly. The sound soothed her.

Somewhere on a floor far below, the service elevator started its climb. Its machinery didn't stop and Aleta realized it was going to stop at one of the top floors. There were no patients on the fifth floor.

She wondered briefly if the guards on the door were awake. For some reason she glanced over at the gun. She could maybe walk to the chair. She hadn't been out of bed since the operation. Her shoulders had not supported the weight of her arms for more than a few seconds let alone a heavy revolver.

I'm panicking, she told herself, over nothing. I've been asleep most nights at this time. I have no idea if the cleaning crew comes up in the elevator every night at this time or if the guards change shifts at this time, or nurses on break return in the service elevator.

She heard the elevator stop. The stairway door opened. She heard male voices.

She felt a chill. She sensed danger. Pushing her sheet aside, she sat up. She wavered slightly but ignored the momentary dizziness and slid her legs down over the edge of the bed. The icy floor was a shock to her bare feet.

One of the voices outside demanded compliance. She could barely discern the words.

"There are three guns on you and we are all expert marksmen."

Aleta straightened up and moved toward the chair. She snatched up the vest and drew the gun from its holster, surprised that Stanley left the holster unsnapped.

She hurried over to Martha and whispered in her ear. "I'm putting a vest over your face and chest. Don't move. Don't look. No matter what happens, play dead."

She laid the bulletproof vest lengthwise from the tip of Martha's head to her waist. Then she drew the sheet over the vest covering it completely.

Looks like someone just died, she thought.

Then she opened the gun and looked inside. It was fully loaded. She snapped it shut and stepped away from Martha.

She backed up toward the window. There had been scuffling in the hall the whole time she was at Martha's side. She wasn't aware of it until it ceased. Her back hit the cold windowpane and she stopped dead. She shivered. For a second her hand trembled.

She was a perfect target outlined against the window, her head wrapped in white gauze, her body completely nude.

She briefly thought about grabbing her sheet, but brushed aside her modesty and with both hands, raised the gun. The trembling stopped. Pain took its place. The first man through the door spotted her and stopped short.

His rifle, which was lowered as he entered, was raised immediately. Aleta said not a word. Her trigger finger moved and a round hit the lead man in the shoulder. That hand fell away, but the man didn't falter.

He grabbed hold of his rifle with his left hand. The next round took out that shoulder. The rifle dropped to the floor as the second man pushed past his brother with his rifle aimed straight at the place he assumed the shooter was. He took a second to check on Aleta's exact location and found himself staring at a totally naked woman of remarkable beauty who was holding a gun. His hesitation measured only fractions of a second. Aleta's reaction was faster.

Her first shot hit the side of his face. It wasn't a fatal shot, but it shook him. Before he could respond, her second bullet bore into his upper arm. His gun fell to the ground.

He grabbed his brother with his good arm and pulled him back through the door.

"Fred, get us out of here," Toby yelled.

Aleta heard scuffling in the hallway, but she didn't move. She kept her gun raised, pointed at the door. Her shoulders both ached, but she didn't lower the gun.

"Let me waste her!" she heard the third man say.

"She'll kill you, you fool!"

She heard the distinctive lisp of the man she'd shot in the face.

Had she hit his mouth she wondered.

"No, she won't," came the protest of the unseen third man.

"Get the hell in the elevator and get us out of here. Right now!"

Despite the lisp, the words were delivered with authority.

Aleta's arms began to weaken; but she didn't dare let them drop. That third man was angry. He might disobey.

She heard the elevator descend. Still she didn't move. He might still be there.

Then one of the guards shouted, "It's clear. Release us."

Aleta hurried toward the bed and took the vest off Martha's face.

"Are you okay?"

"I didn't get shot?" Martha mumbled. "Did you?"

"No," Aleta replied. "I shot them."

"All four shots were yours?"

"Yes.

The shout from the hallway was directed at the occupants of the room. "Will one of you please unlock these handcuffs."

"Are you going to do it?" Martha croaked.

"One of the nurses can do it," Aleta said. "They have clothes on."

"Hurry," Martha said, "before someone sees you."

Aleta rushed back, dropped the gun and vest on the chair and climbed into her bed. She reached for the sheet and wished she hadn't. Still her fingers had hold of the hem and so she tucked her hands under her chin and fell back into her bed covered.

"On, my poor baby," she murmured, her hand on her tummy. "At this rate I'll never be able to hold you."

She stared at the ceiling. Silently, she wept.

Chapter 15

Dr. Cook was the first to enter the room. He stepped over the blood and the two rifles and glanced over toward Aleta. There was no blood on her sheet. His attention went back to the woman nearest him. He calmly picked up her wrist and read her pulse. It was strong and even.

Martha opened her eyes and smiled.

"She shot them four times and hit them every time."

"Were either of you hit?"

"No," Martha said. "She shot first. She covered me with the vest. They didn't see me even though I could smell them they were so close."

"Any dizziness or headache or chest pain?"

"No. Check Aleta. I think she's hurt."

Dr. Cook immediately left his grandmother and went over to Aleta who hadn't even turned her head since he came in.

"Where do you hurt?" he asked as he took her wrist. Tears continued to flow down her face but she didn't answer.

Dr. Cook tried to reassure her on several levels. "The men aren't here. You didn't kill them."

Still no response. He took out his stethoscope and listened to her heart.

They both heard Chief Lyle West's voice in the hall.

"What do you mean Dr. Cook is in there? How did he get here before me?"

There was a mumbled response.

"Keep anyone else from disturbing the crime scene," he ordered and then entered the room.

"Martha, you okay?" he asked, his voice softer.

She nodded then spoke. "Don't blame her for anything. She saved us."

Lyle patted the old woman's hand. "I know."

He walked over to the other bed and Aleta pulled her sheet up under her chin.

"Did you call Stanley?" Dr. Cook asked.

"First thing," he replied.

"Aleta where is the gun you used?" he asked turning away from the bed.

She pointed at the chair. Chief West went over and picked up the vest.

"Why is it under the vest?" he asked, hoping to break Aleta's silence.

"The vest covered me," Martha said.

Lyle saw the hospital gown at the bottom of the pile. "She shot it out with two armed men with no…"

Martha interposed, "Yes, she did. My face was covered, but I think she surprised them."

"I imagine she did," West responded.

Dr. Cook put his hand on Aleta's. "Thank you."

Aleta's tears began to flow faster. "I ruined my shoulders. I'll never be able to hold my baby."

"You saved its life," Dr. Cook said. "Let's put aside future fears and rejoice in the present. You're alive, and so's your baby. Your shoulders will heal. In fact, Aleta, I promise you that you will be able to hold your baby."

"You can't promise that!" Aleta charged, coming to life again. "And pull the curtain all the way. Lyle is not getting a show."

Lyle's voice was heard on the other side of the curtain. "You mean only the bad guys get to see you naked?"

"I shoot people who see me naked!" Aleta quipped.

"I'll stay out here," Lyle responded, happy to hear the lilt in her voice.

"Whose blood is this?" Stanley asked noting the closed curtain as he entered.

"Not Aleta's," Lyle said. "And be careful where you step. It's a crime scene."

Dr. Cook looked up. "Glad you're here, Stanley. Tell your wife I keep my promises.

"He keeps his promises," Stanley said. "What promise are we talking about?"

He sat down on the bed and took Aleta's hand.

"That she'll be able to hold her baby five months from now. I'll admit I am having trouble getting these shoulders to heal twice as fast as normal, but I can manage to do the job in five months."

"I wouldn't promise the reasonable with Aleta," Stanley said gently rubbing her hand. "I gather she didn't just lie in bed during the assault."

Lyle responded from the other side of the curtain.

"My men were on their stomachs, their hands handcuffed behind them. She took the two gunmen on, armed with the gun you left here and a surprise."

"What surprise?" Stanley asked, looking at Aleta.

She blushed and he knew. Lyle's words confirmed his suspicion.

"She needs to get dressed so I can show her some photos."

Stanley raised a brow in silent query.

"It worked," Aleta said defensively. "I got two shots off before he... Oh, Stanley... I didn't do it on purpose... There was no time."

Martha called from the other side of the curtain.

"That's because she chose to save me over saving her modesty.

Aleta continued to explain.

"I put the vest over her head."

"And you think I'd disapprove of your actions?"

"Don't you?" Aleta charged. "You don't like me sleeping nude."

"That's not true," Stanley protested.

She glared at him.

"Okay, so I want you to stay clothed in the hospital," he conceded. "But in this case, your penchant for nudity saved three lives. Besides, the guys who saw you, you shot, right?"

"Yeah."

"Let's get you dressed, so we don't have to shoot anyone else."

Dr. Cook went to the closet and took out a clean gown and handed it to Stanley. Then he went to sit by his grandmother.

"Who'd you hit?" Lyle asked Aleta still on the other side of the curtain.

"Not Fred. One of them told him, he needed to drive. He was ready to come in here. Oh Stanley, it was so close. He would have come in shooting."

"So it is the Hepner brothers we're after," Lyle commented matter-of-factly. "Did you get a good look at the men who came in?"

"Yes," Aleta replied.

Lyle was on his radio. "French, put out an APB for Sam, Toby and Fred Hepner. Armed and dangerous. Check the DMV and see what cars they own besides that old brown

Chrysler. And fax me over some photos so Aleta can make a positive ID.

There was a momentary pause before he spoke again.

"Yeah, wake up Milani and Peets. We need everyone if we're going to catch these guys."

Aleta gripped Stanley's hand. He could feel her trembling.

"Dr. Cook, she's cold."

"Nurse," Cook shouted out the door. "Warm blankets!"

He pushed back the curtain and told Stanley to climb in bed with her and hold her. He pulled a blanket from the closet and wrapped it around Aleta's bare legs.

"Her shoulders," Stanley ventured.

"We'll deal with those later. Right now we need to warm her."

"She seemed fine a few minutes ago," Stanley pointed out.

"Ask her if she had another vision," Dr. Cook suggested, going to the door to receive two warm blankets and ask for two more.

"Did you?" Stanley asked.

"I don't want it. If I don't do anything, God will give it to someone else, won't He?"

"I have no idea. But you always have a choice."

"Disobey God?" she ventured with obvious trepidation.

"He'll understand," Stanley said. "He gave us free will. That's what free will means."

"I don't want any more visions of death."

"If you want this to stop, you have the power."

"But someone might die," she said, her voice breaking.

"All choices have consequences," Stanley stated calmly. "Whatever you decide I'll support you."

Dr. Cook came over with the warmed blankets. Stanley asked if he should move, but Dr. Cook told him to stay where he was. "She needs you. I can work around you."

"You heard?" Stanley asked.

"Yes," Dr. Cook said, but didn't elaborate.

"No input?" Stanley asked.

"You're asking the wrong Cook."

"Martha, any help would be appreciated," Stanley said.

"Aleta, this one is yours because there's a complication I can't handle," Martha said.

"You had the same vision?"

"No, just that bit of advice," Martha said. "It's Aleta or nobody."

"That's no help!" Stanley exclaimed.

"Sure it is," Martha said. "The decision is not between her and someone else. It's between her and no one."

"It's a fire," Aleta whispered. "I only saw the body carried out."

"Out of where?"

"I don't know," Aleta said. "I don't want to see anymore. Fires scare me. I'll have nightmares for years."

"You're shutting off your vision?" Stanley asked awed. "You can do that?"

"This time I can," Aleta responded.

"Don't look at the death," Stanley said. "See if you can see who's around the body when it's carried out."

"I already know. Chief Milani."

"His family?"

"No. He's not even in Willow Glen."

"Where's Milani?" Stanley asked Lyle.

Lyle spoke into his mike briefly.

"He's at the Hepner house in Arborville. I asked him to check out the Hepner house. I'm spread too thin. He loaned me a couple of men. They must have called him. His men have just gone in to search for clues as to where the Hepner brothers have gone."

"No!" Aleta cried. "Tell him to get them out of there."

Lyle told Tom the house was going to go up. "Get the men clear now!"

He heard Tom shouting at his men to leave the house.

"All out," he reported a few minutes later. "Nothing's happening."

"Aleta says it's going to go up," Lyle reported.

"Oh God! No!" Aleta screamed. "One man's inside. Oh my God! Oh, please, God, take it away. Please! Please!"

"There's one man still inside," Lyle told Tom. "He's out of time."

Tom grabbed his bullhorn. "Whatever fool is still in the house, get your butt out here now!"

He turned to his men. "Who's not here? Give me a name."

"Tell him to shoot," Aleta said.

"Shoot!" Lyle cried over the radio.

Tom took out his gun and began firing into the bushes.

A young officer appeared at the door, gun in hand. He looked around.

"Hey I found something!" he cried, turning to go back inside.

Tom shot him in the leg.

The man fell in the doorway as the house exploded into flame.

"Get him!" Torn shouted.

Two men ran forward and dragged the man out and rolled him in the dirt and dried weeds that comprised the front lawn. A third cop tore off his coat and threw it on the burning jacket.

The fire truck screeched to a halt seconds later. Chief Milani had alerted them when he was ordering his men to leave the house.

Lyle heard Tom Milani shouting at the man who was saying he didn't know there was any danger.

"When I give an order, you obey it! I don't care whether it seems reasonable to you or not," Tom yelled. "I'm the goddamn Chief of Police. That means you do what I say."

"Thanks for shooting me," the young cop said.

"That better not be sarcastic!" Tom bellowed. "You're lucky to be alive!"

"Like I said. Thanks!"

Tom spoke to Lyle. "Thank Aleta. She saved this dumb kid's life. He may be confined to the file room for a decade."

Lyle turned and said simply, "Tom says thanks."

"You did it, Aleta," Stanley said. "You saved a young man's life."

"I saw him die," Aleta murmured. "I know he didn't die, but I saw him burn to death."

"But he didn't."

"I didn't get an image of him being saved, just of the flames engulfing him. I can still hear his screaming. That's what's burned into my memory. Why did I allow God to show me that? How could I have been so dumb! "

Lyle came over.

"Aleta, if you're going to survive this psychic business, you have to learn how to forget."

"How can I?" Aleta challenged. "The images are too real to be able to dismiss lightly."

"I'm going to give you an image to replace the vision of what might have been but wasn't."

"It won't work!" Aleta declared.

"Aleta, be reasonable. It will work. You see things that might happen. I see things all the time that have happened."

"I have those too," Aleta said.

"But at this moment we are only dealing with what happened a few minutes ago," Lyle said. "Now relax while I paint a new picture."

He began to speak.

"The house hasn't burned down yet. The men are inside looking for clues as to where the fugitives could have gone. One is in the kitchen opening drawers; one is at the desk, rifling through papers; one is in the back bedroom where the computer geek lived. He notices that the computer is gone. He looks around far back-up disks. He finds a stash of them. He's sorting through them when he hears his chief yelling at everyone to get out of the house. He hears the guy in the next room complain about the smell of gasoline and he decides he can stand it for a few more minutes. In fact, he opens the window, so he doesn't have to leave so soon. He figures Milani is calling everyone to come out and put on masks. He puts down the first bunch of disks and picks up a second.

Then he hears the bullhorn. What's with Milani, he wonders. He's got air. Gun shots rip through the quiet inside the house. He drops the disks, draws his gun and dashes to the front of the house. He opens the door and sees a row of cops standing at the edge of the property. He remembers the anger in Milani's voice and decides to go back far the disks to show Milani he had a reason for not obeying. He turns. Milani fires a shot. He feels the sharp sting of the bullet in his calf. His leg collapses and all he can think is that his chief shot him. He lands face down on the floor, hurt and angry and frustrated. Suddenly, the house bursts into flame and because he's lying on a gasoline soaked rug his jacket catches fire. He feels hands grabbing his feet and dragging him through the open doorway. He yells at them that he's on fire and he's been shot. He realizes that the men know this.

They roll him around on the dirt and a coat is thrown over his burning jacket and hands beat on his chest and he wants to tell them to stop knocking the air out of him, but the men continue to beat on him ignoring what he now realizes are his howls of pain.

The chief begins to shout at him. He offers a lame excuse. It doesn't mitigate Milani's anger. He tries a new tact. He thanks Tom for shooting him. Torn thinks he's being sarcastic and bellows even louder. He realizes that had he walked back into the house, no one could have saved him. He thanks Tom again. This time it takes. He hears Tom on the phone with me. He's not going to be fired, but he's going to be in the dog house for a long time. Then he realizes he's sort of a celebrity. His chief shot him. The firemen tell him his burns aren't too bad. They've seen worse. He's bundled off to the hospital, alive, with only minor injuries and a tale to tell."

Aleta listened with rapt attention as Lyle spun his tale-- half imaginary, half real--and she found herself smiling.

"Milani's never going to live that one down is he?" Aleta murmured.

He'll probably use it for years to come when he lectures his men an obeying his orders in the field," Lyle concluded. "Obey me or I'll shoot you!"

"This was a happy ending, wasn't it?" Aleta asked. It was a rhetorical question.

Stanley held Aleta in his arms long after Dr. Cook and Chief West departed, long after the forensic team finished and the cleaning crew took over. He held her through the darkest part of the night and into the graying of the pre-dawn hours. He held her after she had fallen asleep and he kept the covers wrapped around her arms holding them still. He thought about what she had done and marveled that she not only hadn't been killed, but had come through physically unscathed.

He held her tenderly and when she moaned in her sleep he rocked her gently back and forth until the moaning stopped.

He was still holding her when the hospital began preparing for the day. A nurse entered to dress and bathe Aleta and he sent her away. The nurse had heard the tale of the shootout and guessed why Stanley was in the room cradling his wife.

Aleta woke at nine in the arms of her husband.

"It's light out," she observed. "I missed breakfast, didn't I?"

"By the time you have your bath it'll be time for lunch."

"You expect my bath to take a long time?"

"It will today. I'm your bather."

"You can't do that!" Aleta exclaimed.

"Sure I can. I've done it lots. I'm practiced."

"This is a hospital," Aleta explained in parental tones. "It's not appropriate."

"I didn't say I was going to make love to you. I said I was going to bathe and dress you."

"The doctors make their rounds between now and lunchtime," Aleta said. "They'll catch us."

Stanley got up. "You wait right there. I have some arrangements to make."

"Stanley, it's not going to happen," Aleta declared.

"Tell her Martha," he said as he disappeared through the door.

"Tell me what?"

"Stanley and I have a deal," Martha said. "You and I can't watch the news. Wayne is afraid it'll upset us. So Stanley is going to rescue us an hour. I get to watch TV and he gets to give you a bath and a massage."

"He may go past that," Aleta said sheepishly.

"I would hope so!" Martha said. "But it's up to you. My attention is going to be on the news."

"This is practically a public place."

"But not quite," Martha said. "He held you all night long. He was more traumatized by your escapade than you realize. Give him a chance to work his way back to normalcy."

"It's all set," Stanley said. "The guards will keep everyone out, especially Wayne and Lyle. Here's the remote, Martha. And for you Aleta, I have lots of good stuff planned.

"A massage?"

"Lauren taught me how to do shoulders," Stanley said. "Dr. Cook has already okayed it. It was supposed to be a present at the end of the day. I figured the riding might have stressed your shoulders."

He drew the curtain and the two heard the television click on. Stanley pulled back the sheet and began unwrapping Aleta from her cocoon of blankets. She decided to relax and enjoy her hour. It passed by swiftly. Too swiftly.

"Five minutes!" Martha called.

"No," Aleta said softly. "Must you stop?"

"Yes, I must. But if you want another massage tomorrow, I can arrange it. How do your shoulders feel?"

"So much better. So does the rest of me. You are one helluva bather!"

"Ready for the world?" Stanley said carefully turning her over and helping her into her hospital gown. The slings came next. Then he adjusted the bed so she was in a sitting position and he covered her legs with a fresh sheet. The pile of used linens lay in a heap on the floor. He drew back the curtain, took the remote form Martha, waited for the commercial break, then turned off the TV and returned the remote to the top of the TV.

"See you two ladies later," he said and then opened the door.

"The ladies are ready to receive callers now," he announced with a wry smile.

"You can't do this," Dr. Wayne Cook said.

"You can't do this," Chief Lyle West repeated.

"Exactly what did you do?" Dr. Chesney asked thoroughly enjoying the scene.

"I can and I did. And tomorrow there will be a repeat, Gentlemen. Live with it."

"It won't happen again," Lyle said firmly.

"Check with your boss, Lyle. It will."

"I need access," Wayne said annoyed. "This won't happen again."

"Check with your patients, Wayne. It will."

Dr. Chesney grinned. This was delicious. He wasn't going to miss the rest of this play. He followed the two into the room and went straight to the nightstand drawer and took out the box of chocolates.

"Care for dessert?" he asked the smiling women.

He let Martha select her truffle and fed Aleta hers, saying, "I understand you gave those arms quite a workout last night."

"They hurt."

"You held the gun out in front of you?"

"Yes.

"And held it there?"

"I didn't dare put it down until I knew they were gone."

"Even my muscles would be sore doing that," he said.

"I think I hurt my shoulders all over again."

"Do they feel better now?"

"Yes."

"Then it wasn't serious."

Wayne Cook was checking out his grandmother as Dr. Chesney was talking with Aleta. Martha stroked his cheek with her hand.

"Do be a good boy and let us have our hour with Stanley tomorrow."

"I heard the TV going."

"If that's all you heard, then our plan worked."

"What were you doing?"

"Having a bit of fun. We deserve it don't you think? We've both been model patients."

Lyle spoke up. "He can't order my men to keep me out."

Martha grinned. "I can't believe he managed that."

"He threatened to sue me!" Lyle exploded.

"He wouldn't do that."

"He talked my men into believing him."

"He is a superb lawyer," Martha stated calmly. "Only you know how much he respects you. He counted on the loyalty of your men to put your wellbeing over their own. I must admit that that impressed me."

"It can't happen again."

"You are absolutely right," Martha said.

Lyle smiled. He'd won.

"Tomorrow you will instruct them to give Stanley an undisturbed hour with us."

"Grams!" Wayne exclaimed. "No."

"And you, dear boy, will be busy elsewhere," she finished.

Dr. Chesney added his two cents.

"Well, whatever he did during his hour, the results are good. We might consider hiring him as an adjutant to our nursing staff."

"You won't succeed," Aleta predicted. "He's told me a thousand times he's a child advocate and that's all he wants to be."

"Well, ladies, you win this one," Dr. Cook acquiesced. "Whatever you three did, it seemed to have bolstered your spirits. And that's a plus."

Aleta directed attention toward Lyle.

"Is it over? Are we safe?"

"We didn't catch them," Lyle said. "They invaded an all-night urgent care facility and the doctor dug out the bullets. He reported it this morning when the day crew came on and untied everyone.

"So no one died."

"The older one, Sam, won't be holding a gun or anything else for a while. Toby won't be able to shoot for a while either. They managed to withdraw twenty thousand of Martha's quarter million from their personal account. We found their truck halfway between here and Canada. They traded it in for a van. We assumed they crossed into Canada. The Canadian police are helping us."

"They'll hide for a while," Aleta said.

"Is that a prophesy or a guess?"

"Wishful thinking," Aleta returned.

"We arrested Mike Carlson for tampering with Harriet's brakes. Harriet insists on pressing charges. Les is hesitating.

"Harriet is correct," Martha said. "I'll speak with Les."

"We have Carlson's fingerprints on the underside of both cars," Lyle went on. "His lawyer says he'll plead guilty to a misdemeanor. Harriet says no. She wants him to serve time for a felony."

"Grams doesn't like people who try to kill her," Aleta said.

Martha chuckled. "Aleta shoots such people."

After everyone left, Aleta stretched her legs out and said happily, "Isn't it great to be done with this mess?"

"The three are still out there," Martha countered.

"But coming after me now isn't reasonable."

"Hatred pushes aside reason."

"Not one of us got any hint about that attack," Aleta worried.

"God expects you to use the reasoning power he gave you. And you did."

"Was anything on the news?"

"Everything was on the news except for your state of undress."

"I would have thought that would have been the headline."

"Only the shooters saw you."

"Stanley really stayed up all night?"

"Yes he did."

"I'd feel guilty if I didn't know he'd head straight home to catch up on his sleep."

"How can you be so sure?"

"He was wearing jeans."

But Aleta was wrong. Stanley breezed into his office. "Am I late?"

"Robert called. The judge is running fifteen minutes late," Alice said. "Your clothes are in the bathroom as well as your shaving stuff."

Stanley headed for the bathroom and called out as he began shaving. "I'm going to be busy an hour tomorrow morning too. How's my court schedule look."

"Chock-full," Alice responded. "If you tell Aleta, I'm sure she'd understand."

"Not a word to her. As long as she thinks I'm home sleeping she relaxes."

When he walked into the courthouse, Stanley was immediately surrounded by people. The first man shoved an old teddy bear at him and asked him to give it to his wife and see if she could see where his baby was. A second woman waved a tee shirt saying it was her son's favorite. Stanley saw the image of Pooh Bear on the front of the tiny shirt.

How could one so small have a favorite shirt, he wondered as he pushed through the group. A man held out the financial section of the newspaper and begged for a stock tip. Half the people appealed to him directly as if being married to Aleta gave him psychic powers.

Exasperated with the demands, he finally addressed those pressing in on him, "My wife is not a psychic. She's a prophet. But she only prophesies murders and then only some of those. Her predictions are not of her own making. They are a gift. And she shares them with the people involved. As for me, I can foresee nothing. If I could, I would never have come in the front way this morning."

With that he pushed open the court room door and the bailiff told those that tried to crowd in with him that this was a private hearing.

He walked over to Robert Locke. "Did you know about them?"

"I saw the mob, but I didn't know they were waiting for you.

"Aleta's going to have no peace at all," Stanley fretted.

"You have about five minutes to get your head wrapped around this case," Robert Locke leaned over and whispered.

Stanley reached into his briefcase and pulled out a file.

"We'll deal with Aleta's problem later," he decided.

"The judge is ready," Robert said, and the conversation ended.

When Stanley emerged from the courtroom after his last case, Chief Milani was waiting with two police officers. The corridors were empty.

"Where were you this morning when I was mobbed?"

"If you think this morning was bad, take a gander through the window at your waiting public."

Stanley walked over to the window and stared at the group of people being kept out of the courtroom by police in riot gear guarding the door.

"Who called you?"

"Several judges who attempted to go to lunch."

"Robert and I worked straight through."

"You were fortunate to have your first few cases in the same courtroom."

"Now what?" Stanley said. "I don't want those people all over my property. What's wrong with them anyway?"

"Justin wants to interview you for the six o'clock news."

"What good will that do?"

"He got some of what you said on tape this morning. His TV contact will give you some time to answer questions."

"What do I know? I'm not a prophet."

"You're the closest thing we've got. West picked up Harriet early and she's spent the day with Martha and Aleta. She said she'd do the interview, but West said no."

"Glad he took her off the hook."

"So you'll do it?"

"Do I have a choice?"

"I have a car waiting to take you to the studio."

Stanley shrugged his acquiescence.

"Let's go."

When Stanley arrived at the studio, he asked Justin if he was certain he wanted to attempt this interview. Justin smiled broadly.

"Just follow my lead," he said, "and we'll be fine."

"I'm apprehensive," Stanley said, "but I'm not nervous."

"Apprehensive, nervous--what's the difference?"

"If you don't know," Stanley quipped, "we're in trouble."

"Are we going to quibble over words?" Justin asked, his smile fading.

"You'd better refrain from that term during the interview. I have no intention of quibbling."

"Good," Justin said a bit too heartily.

"Keep it simple," Stanley suggested as the countdown began.

"Good evening. I'm Justin Conway and I have with me in the studio Mr. Stanley Praetzel, husband of the new psychic…"

Stanley interrupted Justin at that moment.

"Wrong word," he said.

Justin's surprise was evident and replayed on every news station that picked up pieces of the interview.

"Aleta is not a psychic. Aleta is a prophet. She can predict with accuracy certain murders."

"I don't mean to quibble," Justin said scrambling to save face, "but isn't that what a psychic does."

"Aleta's powers are more limited than a psychic's."

"Limited," Justin shot back. "I'd say they were far-reaching. She didn't even know some of the people."

"I hate to burst your bubble, Justin, but Aleta predicted relatively few of the murders that took place in this country."

"How do you account for those she did predict?"

"I don't."

"No connection, say, to some evil God wants to stop."

"Well, murder is evil. Obviously, He wants certain murders not to take place. That's all I know."

"Your wife recently predicted the deaths of a number of homeless men, yet she missed predicting those who would be hurt."

"She only predicts murder. She doesn't predict attempted murder. That's the reason I said her foresight is limited."

"Perhaps she can see other things, but just doesn't think they're worth her while."

Stanley's face reddened and Justin knew he'd struck a nerve. "That's what some of the people who accosted me this morning said. And they're wrong."

"Wrong? How can you be so sure?"

"You know my wife's in the hospital, correct?"

Justin acknowledged the query with an affirmative nod.

"And you know she's there because someone shot the horse she was riding, Stanley went on. "What you may not know is that she loves that horse. If Aleta had known that those bullets were coming, she'd have thrown herself in front of them. She didn't know."

"What about the attack on her at the hospital last night. Are you going to try to convince me she didn't foresee that one?"

"I can't convince you of anything," Stanley said. "All I can do is tell you the truth. People don't always let the truth prevail. Half the people who see this interview won't believe what I say because they their beliefs are firmly entrenched in their minds."

Justin wanted him back on the events of the night before. Reports had been scarce. Police were never good at filling in details.

"I'm ready to listen," he said coaxingly. "Tell me about last night."

"Aleta didn't know."

"She got the drop on two gunmen."

"She heard voices in the hall."

"So what?" Justin probed.

"They were men's voices. The nurses on the floor were women."

"So, why not a doctor?"

"He would have spoken softly."

"Where'd the gun come from?"

"I left it there."

"Wasn't that foolish?"

"As it turns out it wasn't; however, I didn't leave a loaded gun in a room with a child. I left a gun in a room with a woman who knows how to shoot."

"She missed," Justin observed. "Four shots and still the men walked away."

"She didn't shoot to kill. She hit what she aimed at. Both men dropped their rifles."

"So she came out unscathed, and you still want me to believe she didn't have a hint."

"If she had, she…," Stanley began and stopped.

He was about to say she would have put on a robe. His mind raced.

"She would have what?" Justin prompted.

"Warned the guards in the hall," Stanley said. "The confrontation left her in a state of shock."

"Not too much shock for her not to save the life of a policeman almost caught in a house fire."

"That added to it," Stanley said. "The point is she doesn't want to see these murders. The vision is so real she's haunted by it. And it doesn't make any difference whether it happens or not, she still is left with the memory of it. She would like to shut these visions off, but…"

"She's not eating up the publicity?" Justin asked.

"She doesn't know about it. She's been without TV, radio or a paper for days."

"How much longer will she be in the hospital?"

"Until she's well enough to come home."

"Come on. She didn't even fall off the horse," Justin charged. "Is she hiding?"

"No, she's not. She had brain surgery," Stanley said.

After the interview, Stanley complained that he now had no time to change and Tom told him hiding the situation from Aleta wasn't a good idea.

"Wives hate that," Tom finished.

"But it's for her own good." Stanley argued.

"Wives hate that reasoning even more."

"So what do I do? I don't want to upset her."

"Counselor, since when did you need lessons in handling Aleta? You're a master at it."

"This is new territory."

"It's always new territory."

"Is married life always so... so unsettling?"

"Only when you're actually dealing with your wife. Otherwise it's fine."

"I feel like I'm always dealing with Aleta."

Tom clapped Stanley on the shoulder. "So, my man, do I."

Shortly after that conversation, when Stanley entered Aleta's hospital, he could tell immediately that she was upset.

"You're late," Aleta said perturbed.

"You noticed," Stanley said evenly. He walked over to the television set and picked up the remote and turned it on.

"Has Wayne Okayed this?" Martha asked.

"I have to bring Aleta up to date," Stanley said.

He continued picking up segments of news broadcasts until the three women had a good understanding of what was happening outside the hospital walls.

At one point Aleta exclaimed, "That's you!"

They watched his brief statement several times before one channel announced the interview.

"You were interviewed?" Aleta exclaimed.

"That's what delayed me."

They watched the interview several times.

They weren't the only ones who watched it more than once. Toby spotted it first and drew his brother's attention away from the computer in ample time for them to watch it several times.

"Do you know what this means?" Toby asked.

"That she's going to be even more protected," Fred guessed.

"No!" Toby shouted. "They can't see anything but murder!"

"So if we don't kill Jackman, we can do whatever we want to him," Sour Sam postulated. His tone wasn't happy.

Fred screwed up his face. "But the idea has always been to kill him."

"What's wrong with you two? I'm not scrapping our plan to kill Jackman. I'm saying the psychics can't see nothing but murder," Toby lisped.

"We heard you!" Fred retorted brushing his hair from his eyes.

"Tell us what the hell we're missing." Sour Sam insisted.

"Didn't you listen at all?"

"Cut the crap!" Fred burst out impatiently. "Tell us what you're thinking."

"Aleta Praetzel would have taken a bullet for her horse. I wonder what else she'd do for him?"

"We don't want her to do anything!" Fred said.

"Now you're getting it," Toby returned.

"Getting what?" came the bewildered response.

"We don't want her to do anything. We don't want her to predict Jackman's death. We want her to keep silent."

"So we kill her," Fred said, still slightly confused. "That was always the plan."

"You only got one track in that brain of yours?" Toby growled, exasperated. He rarely attacked Fred.

It was Sour Sam who finally realized what Toby was suggesting.

"You mean we threaten to shoot her horse unless she agrees not to predict anymore Jackman murders?"

"That's it!" Toby exclaimed.

"Now it's you that didn't listen to the news," Fred sneered. "She's being held incommunicado. It'll be as hard to threaten her as to kill her. I say we stick with the first idea."

"I vote for Toby's plan," Sour Sam said unexpectedly. "We'll figure out something.

"Which of us do the people know about?" Martha asked.

"I'm not sure," Stanley said. "The majority appear to only know about Aleta."

"You did a good job in the interview," Aleta commented. "You were very clear."

"That's not always enough," Harriet observed, her rough voice somber. "It's only a matter of time before we'll all be besieged everywhere we go."

"Oh, Stanley, what do we do?"

The anxiety in Aleta's voice was reflected in the faces of the two older women.

"We take it one day at a time," Stanley said. "First, we see if my little talk did any good at all. And we use this time to think about how we want to handle this if it doesn't go away. There's not one of us who wants to move, so we scratch that off the list right off."

"I'm glad that's not an option," Martha rejoined.

"I think we need guidance," Harriet said. "Are we all agreed to ask God for that?"

Stanley saw Martha nod and then his wife. The three looked at him.

"What?"

"Are you with us?" Harriet asked.

"You mean we're evoking this 'Wherever two are gathered in my name…' bit of scripture?"

Aleta smiled when she saw the surprised look on the faces of the two elderly women.

"He's quite versed in the scriptures," she said, "and he believes too."

"So do you agree we ask for guidance and go from there?" Martha pressed.

"Not if we're told to move!" Stanley declared staunchly.

"We can't put a caveat on our request," Aleta said. "However, we're only asking for guidance. We can choose not to follow it."

"Well, as long as everyone knows which plan I won't follow," Stanley said.

"I'm sure you've made your point with God as well," Aleta said.

"I'm not trying to make a point with Him. He already knows how I feel. What I want to be sure is that you three ladies don't think that when I agree to ask for guidance that I promise to follow it."

"But would you be open to listening to His suggestion?" Martha asked.

"I hate to say that to three prophets," Stanley said. "I will believe what you say. And that's all I'll promise."

"Good enough!" Martha said.

The three women bowed their heads.

"Okay, God, we're ready," Martha said.

"Thy will be done," Aleta chimed in.

"Amen" Harriet finished.

"That's it?" Stanley asked.

"He heard our discussion," Martha said. "We don't have to repeat ourselves."

"Let's treat ourselves to a chocolate," Harriet suggested. "I've been dying for one all day."

Stanley looked at the three faces. All were relaxed.

Chief Lyle West popped in. "Ready to go Harriet?"

"See you tomorrow, Grams," Aleta said.

"No you won't. I'm going duck hunting."

"Season was over December 14," Aleta stated.

"Only in Northern Illinois. Seems Hubert Praetzel has friends who are members of Hunt Clubs in Southern Illinois and Lauren and Lydia concocted this joint Christmas gift--a two-day duck hunting trip. It'll be Hubert's first venture into hunting. When Lydia called Hubert's friends, they asked if Hubert could bring down a second dog, so Stoney was invited and me with him. We're flying down tonight."

"You've been here all day. When did you pack?"

"I've known about this since before Christmas. I'm packed. And Stoney is always ready."

"Won't Mr. Praetzel need a copilot?" Aleta asked.

"That was part of Lydia's package," Harriet said.

"That's why they needed another dog. One of Hubert's flying buddies is coming too."

"And to ease the pain of my departure," Lyle said, "I invited Tom Milani to come over with some peace offerings from Rachael--her famous lasagna for our starving Stanley and chocolate cake for you two chocoholics."

"That would do it," Aleta said. "Have fun!"

At eight o'clock just as Stanley was finishing his second piece of chocolate cake, Chief Milani got a call on his radio. The stout police chief swallowed his mouthful of cake and asked, "You guys allowed TV yet?"

"What's up?" Stanley asked.

"Jackman's on TV," Tom said. "Evidently he dropped a bomb."

"Let's turn it on," Stanley said, looking at his watch. "Dad'll be halfway there by now. He won't turn back."

"I told Lyle he better not come back without ducks for us," Tom put in. "Rachael can sure cook a duck!"

"He might in an emergency," Stanley ventured.

Tom shook his head. "He reminded me that you're still deputized and to give you a gun and vest and set you to guarding your wife."

"I've got a full day of court tomorrow," Stanley reminded him.

"Don't worry. I'll only use you from eight at night to eight in the morning. The day is yours."

"Gee, thanks!" Stanley quipped.

The commercial finished and Jackman's face appeared on the screen.

"No, I don't believe in this psychic nonsense."

"They saved your life," the reporter commented.

"My actions saved my life," Jackman corrected. "They warned me, it's true; but since the perpetrators live in their town, it's possible they got their information from them somehow. Maybe they may even have made a deal. The men who are after me wanted to make a statement. What better way to do it than to have a psychic predict their actions? They'd get the news coverage they wanted."

"So you aren't counting on them to save your life in the future?"

"I told my house staff not even to take their calls."

"I understand these perpetrators have been siphoning money from your bank account. Do you think they've chosen a new revenge tactic?"

"No, I think the money was the goal of the brothers the whole time," Jackman stated unequivocally. "And those women are in on it. They distract us with prophesies of our murders, and we look away and their associates invade our bank accounts."

"Two CEO's were killed," the reporter painted out.

"To make those psychics seem all-powerful," Jackman concluded. "It's a scam, Gentlemen, and it's not over. People are lining up willing to throw money at these women hoping they can get a glimpse of their own future."

"The three women have money."

"No one ever has enough!" Jackman scoffed. "Especially, the rich."

On that note the interview ended.

Martha was the first to give voice to everyone's thoughts.

"What a stupid, ungrateful man!"

"Well, I guess that leaves you women off the hook as far as he's concerned."

"Not really," Aleta said. "We still have to tell someone. And if Jackman's refusing our call... well... Guess who's our number one receiver for the next two days?"

"Lucky me," Tom grumbled good-naturedly. "Lyle better bag the limit both days. And he better get at least two wood ducks."

"Well, I can tell Jackman right now that the men targeting him still have him in their sights," Stanley responded. "In fact, after that interview I'd say they're going to be more determined than ever."

"Maybe God will leave him to his fate," Aleta said. "I don't understand why God would want to save him."

The group heard voices in the hall. Aleta tensed. Stanley held her closer.

"It's nothing bad," he whispered. "The men are laughing."

When Lieutenant Peter French, Lyle's first in command appeared, his presence surprised Torn as well as the others.

"We're allowed television now?" he commented, knowing full well that it was still forbidden. "I liked your interview, by the way."

Stanley turned off the set.

"I know you didn't come over here just to chat," Stanley said. "What's up?"

"We heard from the Hepner brothers."

Shocked, Stanley could only ask, "They contacted you?"

"Not me. Justin Conway, the reporter who's made this his story."

"How?" Stanley asked.

Before French could reply, Aleta spit out her question. "What did they want?"

"By computer," French replied, choosing to answer Stanley's query first.

"Are you sure it was them?" Stanley asked.

"The message described details about the shooting of Aleta's horse that not many know."

"They threatened me, didn't they?" Aleta surmised. "They want me not to tell Jackman when they plan to hit him again."

"What was the threat?" Stanley asked.

"They got very broad in their scope," French went on. "If any of the three prophets utters another prophecy, they will shoot Aleta's horse."

Appalled, Aleta could barely utter her horse's name. It came out as a hoarse whisper. "Shadow?"

"And unless they have an answer on tonight's ten o'clock news, they'll take out one of those dogs running around your house to show you they mean business."

"Scooby?" Aleta cried softly. "He's just a pup."

"They didn't give us much time, did they?" Stanley cut in, hoping to divert Aleta's attention.

"None at all," French said.

Stanley turned to the women. "What's your call?"

"It's an answer to our prayer," Martha said.

"I agree," Aleta said. "Do you understand, Stanley?"

Stanley rose, "Let's go."

Flabbergasted, French shot out, "Do you know what they want to do?"

"You came in the middle of the play. Some plays you have to see from the beginning," Stanley said. He handed the remote to Martha. "Not until the ten o'clock news."

Aleta's eye was on her husband's departure.

"You aren't coming back?" Aleta asked dismayed.

"I need to check on Hubbs," he said.

Chief Milani and Acting Chief French rushed out after him. When Peter French caught up to Stanley, he asked, "Do you know where you're going?"

"You're going to tell me."

"Lobby, downstairs," Peter said. Tom stepped into the elevator with them.

Justin approached them when the elevator doors opened.

Stanley shook Justin's hand and said, "You read the threat you received, let me answer and then ask whatever questions you want."

"Your plan works for me," Justin responded, ushering Stanley into his spot. This time they'd do it exactly as Stanley wanted.

Justin's introduction was succinct. He read the email note with a sonorous tone that gave added weight to its words. When he finished Stanley took over. His voice, also a rich baritone, carried the weight of the moment well.

"The three prophets have agreed that they will not prophesy as long as the three Hepner brothers are free to carry out their threat."

The brevity of the statement almost caught Justin unawares; however, the first question jumped out at him. "They will stop saving men's lives to save the life of a horse?"

Stanley read Justin's shock as the typical reaction to his bold declaration that there would be no more prophecies forthcoming.

"These people, who would maim a horse, wouldn't stop there. Before they escalate their demands to include people, the three prophets have agreed to cease sharing their prophecies."

"They might not..."Justin began.

Stanley interrupted him. "These men have killed what they consider extraneous human beings to cover up their real targets. You better believe they would move on to people if Aleta's love for animals wasn't as strong as they believed."

"Why did the other prophets agree?" Justin protested. "Don't they feel obligated to the people whose deaths they can prevent?"

"These women don't believe God would ever ask them to exchange one life for another."

"This is a horse," Justin objected again.

"God likes horses. One of the first things He told us to do was to take care of animals. And we need to remember these women are God's prophets."

"So you believe they are true prophets."

"Yes, I do."

"But you're a lawyer, a man of reason," Justin prodded.

"Yes, I am."

Justin recognized at once that he wasn't going to be successful baiting this man so he summed up Stanley's responses and ended the interview.

The TV crew leader objected to the brevity. Justin spotted Chief Tom Milani and Lieutenant Peter French standing nearby. And while he expected a no comment from either man, he tried for one anyway. After Chief Milani gave the expected reply, Justin took a different tack with Peter French.

"Sergeant Peter French, are you in charge in Chief Lyle West's absence?" Justin asked casually.

"Lieutenant Peter French," Peter corrected him.

"This promotion is new?"

"Yes, it is."

"Well, congratulations!" Justin said warmly. "Do you expect any more trouble this week?"

"No, I don't."

"What do you base that prediction on?"

"Chief West left town."

"I would guess his actions tell us what he thinks," Justin said finishing that segment.

As the camera crew was packing up, Stanley asked Justin if he'd like to add some live footage of the horse.

At the barn Hubbs, not knowing the camera was on, pointed out to Justin where the bullets had grazed Shadow. The cameraman stepped up on a bale of hay and zoomed in on the horse's back. Justin asked Hubbs what angle would be a good one to photograph the horse from.

"He ain't no prissy actor," Hubbs said. "He's a horse. Besides he ain't got a bad side. Here, let me show you."

He brought Shadow out of his stall and walked him in a circle.

"See, he's beautiful all over," Hubbs said. "And a gentler, nicer horse don't exist nowhere. He ain't a horse should be shot at. He don't deserve that!"

The ire in his voice added a nice note, Justin realized. He stood next to the horse and reiterated the declaration of the three prophets that they had promised not to disclose any more prophecies as long as the Hepner brothers were at large.

When the segment aired on the ten o'clock news, Aleta squealed with delight when she saw Shadow on the screen.

"He is beautiful, isn't he?"

"Who?" Martha joshed. "The horse or Stanley?"

"I've got two handsome males in my life, don't I?" Aleta giggled. "This time I was talking about the horse."

Martha grinned.

"You definitely are in the right profession."

"It's nice to be free of this mess," Aleta observed, settling down in bed. She was ready to sleep now.

Chapter 16

At seven the following morning Aleta was awakened with a kiss.

"Stanley," she exclaimed, "what are you doing here?"

"Giving you last night kiss for starters."

"You noticed?"

Stanley raised an eyebrow. She realized the query offended him. Never one to go on the defense, she changed direction.

"You're early."

"I have a full day in court."

Aleta noticed the towels.

"If you're going to rush my bath, the nurse can do that."

She hadn't forgotten how deserted she felt when he'd left without kissing her.

"Don't get your tail fathers ruffled. You're getting the full treatment," he said calmly. "But before we start, what's really bothering you?"

"You haven't time," Aleta snapped.

He sat down on the bed and took her hand in his. "For you, I always have time."

"You're on the clock," she accused.

"If I don't show, Robert will tell the judge you had a relapse and I was needed here."

"I'm not having a relapse!" Aleta protested. "We can't lie to a judge every time I get upset about something."

"Considering the fact that you're less than a week from brain surgery and you're four months pregnant and you've had a serious threat leveled against you, I believe I can safely call this altercation we're having a relapse."

"Relapse means a return to a former state," Aleta argued.

"And isn't that what's happening?"

"What former state?"

"The one where you're sure my love is waning."

Embarrassed, Aleta scowled.

"You always kiss me goodnight.

"Guess it's time to change that 'always' to 'usually'."

"When have you ever missed?"

"The night I was operated on, for one."

"Well, that was different," Aleta started, and then remembering a promise she made to herself, backed off.

"I'll settle for 'usually', only I want make-up kisses."

"Can I do them while I bathe you?"

"Those won't count. You always kiss me when you bathe me."

"There is no such thing as a make-up kiss, is there?"

"Now, you're catching on," she snickered. "Hurry up or you'll be late for court and Dad will have to use that awful excuse and I'll have to live it down."

"I love the way your mind works," Stanley said rising to pull the curtain.

He winked at Martha as he did so.

At ten o'clock Dr. Cook entered.

"Today is the day!" he announced.

"I get to go home?" Aleta asked, eyes alight.

"You get to ride around the corridors in a wheelchair."

"That's it?" Aleta queried. "What's there to see?"

"If you're very good, I'll let you go to therapy with Grams. And we can do some preliminary therapy on your arms and shoulders while you're there."

"Okay!" Aleta exclaimed happily.

"Grams, I understand you wolfed down same lasagna last night," Wayne poised. "Any trouble swallowing?"

"Why?"

"So, I'll know whether to schedule speech therapy."

"My speech is coming back by itself."

"But your swallowing could have been affected. It's important for me to know if it is."

"Why?"

"If you aspirate a bit of food, in other words, if a bit goes down the wrong way when you're talking or sleeping, it could lead directly to pneumonia."

"Oh."

"So I've scheduled a swallowing test this morning."

"Is that why I've been eating goop?"

"Soft food diet," Wayne corrected. "If you want good stuff, you've got to let me do my tests."

"I have other resources, you know," Martha countered.

"He just left for several days of duck hunting."

"Two days," Aleta said.

Dr. Cook smiled. "I told your father-in-law to keep him one more day. The man's been under a lot of pressure. He needs to unwind."

"So have the other chiefs," Aleta commented.

"Lyle's been here more than usual because you and Stanley are close friends. I think he's clocked in more hours than I have and running an investigation on multiple levels."

"I'm surprised he went," Aleta said.

"He wouldn't have if it hadn't been Lauren's gift to him. He loves her too much to dishonor her gift," Dr. Cook explained. "Even so, it took a lot of pushing from me and Tom to get him to go."

"He took Grams," Aleta pointed out. "I bet he told himself he's guarding her."

"That fantasy does no harm," Dr. Cook said.

"And it is a fantasy," Aleta agreed. "There's no way the Hepners know where they are."

But Lieutenant Peter French's comment about his chief being out of town stirred the Hepner brothers into wondering.

"Why would he leave town in the middle of an investigation?" Sam asked.

"Does he know where we are?" Fred queried. "Is he coming for us?"

"Alone?" Sour Sam asked. "No, something else is going on. Fred, get on your computer and see if you can find out where he went."

"He must have gone for more than a day," Toby put in thoughtfully. "Or that French guy would have acted different."

"I'm going to need a lot of luck," Fred commented. "The chances of me finding anything on West's home computer are remote. He doesn't use email. And we don't have any way to recreate phone conversations."

"What about the police computers?" Sour Sam asked.

"We gave them a virus, remember?"

Sam turned to Toby. "How's that arm?"

"Sore, but I can shoot with my other hand. How about you?"

"Not yet. The damn broad hit me in both shoulders. Every time I even try to lift a gun my arms never let me get it past my waist."

"So, I'm the shooter, huh?" Toby asked.

"You're better than Fred."

"Hey guys, stop discussing what I can't do and look at what I can," Fred called from over his shoulder. "Mrs. West got an email. I know where Chief West went. And guess who went with him?"

When Hubert Praetzel came down the stairs of Professor Claude Luther's spacious Carbondale home, he spotted Harriet, fully dressed for the day's hunting sitting on the couch deeply immersed in the financial pages.

"You beat us all," he observed.

"Our host is in the kitchen," Harriet offered. "The cook is packing breakfast."

She looked up from her reading. "So who won the toss?"

Hubert chuckled. That's what Lydia would have asked.

"I did."

"So Mr. DuMont is stuck with me?"

"On the contrary," Hubert said. "I used a two-headed coin I save for such occasions."

"Lyle will be a great teacher," Harriet said graciously. "You'll enjoy hunting with him."

"Maybe tomorrow we'll switch," Hubert said. "But today you're my partner."

Harriet wasn't certain she heard right. She decided to hedge, "It's your gift. You can decide. I'm just grateful to be here."

Hubert smiled. "I'm more fun than Avery."

Then Professor Luther came in from the kitchen. "Lyle told me last night that your dog can get in and out of a boat."

"So can his."

"Two pairs of hunters will be in boats. One will be in a pit.

"I don't even like the sound of that," Harriet commented.

"It could be dryer than a boat with a wet dog getting in and out," Professor Luther commented. He was a tall, hefty man and Harriet considered it a gracious act to offer the smaller lighter man, the land spot.

"Avery voted for the pit, so Morgan will run off the land," Lyle interjected. "Sorry, Hubert, I didn't give you a choice."

"I have no opinions on where I'd rather be," Hubert said. "Besides I'd like to give this outfit a good baptism."

Stoney sat still in the boat as Hubert rowed. The professor's guide led them to their spot and then rowed further on.

"Get the boat well back into the reeds," Harriet suggested. "We want to be stationary and hidden."

"Once Stoney gets wet, won't he get cold?" Hubert asked.

"Chessies have a coat designed for swimming in water with ice," Harriet explained, stopping Hubert and having him lay the oars on the bottom of the boat. She then fastened the dog perch to the side of the boat. Stoney, however, stayed in the boat.

"Now what?"

"We wait for dawn to break," Harriet said, her voice lowered to a whisper. "One rule. We don't shoot the dog."

The two sat in silence, waiting. Harriet liked the early morning hours before dawn. She felt safe in the pre-dawn darkness. The promise of light piqued the gray dullness into a yawning of color.

Just before the gold-orange glow was birthed, a loud honking accompanied by splashing told the two hidden in the reeds that a flock was taking flight. In the early still uncolored light of dawn, the two hunters raised their rifles and shot.

Two ducks. On lay still on the slightly choppy water, the other, however, was moving.

"It's a cripple," Harriet assessed aloud. "Hang on, Hubert."

She pointed toward the fluttering bird, then said Stanley's name. He leaped into the water. The boat rocked from the thrust of his back feet.

"I can't see my duck," Hubert said dismayed.

"Dogs have better vision in dim light than we do," Harriet said. "And Stoney has a good sense of direction."

"Where'd my duck go?"

"Into the reeds."

"I can't see your duck either."

"It'll float into the reeds, but it's dead so it won't go in deep."

They heard multiple shots at a distance.

"They're getting a lot," Hubert said piqued.

"Or missing a lot," Harriet commented. "How good a shot is Avery?"

"Not as good as me."

"Then I'll wager Morgan will have to run down a cripple too," Harriet commented.

As the sky lightened, Hubert shouted, "There's your dog!"

Harriet said not a word, but took the duck from the big dog's mouth and pointed to where her duck lay. She could only guess, but Stoney took off as if she knew exactly where it had fallen.

"It's still alive," Hubert commented, staring at his duck's wing flapping. "The dog didn't kill it."

With one swift twirl of her hand, Harriet dispatched the duck.

"He had a broken wing," she said simply.

Stoney returned with Harriet's bird and she took it from him and laid it beside Hubert's in the bottom of the boat. Stoney climbed on his perch just above the water and, after a quick shake which showered both gunners with cold water he sat down.

Hubert laughed at the cold shower and Harriet relaxed.

When the next flight came by, the two shot four times and four ducks fell. At Harriet's command, Stoney took off.

"You are one hellava marksman," Hubert commented. "Will he remember all four?"

"He marked them," she commented. "He'll pick up the outside ones first."

"How do you know?"

"That's his pattern."

At noon, Hubert rowed them out of the reeds and headed for the dock. In the bottom of the boat were six mallards, two wood ducks, and two Canadian geese.

"We did well," Harriet said.

"I really did want to beat Avery," Hubert confessed. "There were so many shots from their direction."

"I would guess Lyle got the limit," Harriet predicted lightly.

Professor Luther and his guide-joined them and as the birds were being cleaned, stories were exchanged.

"What will you remember the most?" Lyle asked Avery who'd only bagged two birds.

"Morgan looking at me with disgust when I missed."

Lyle laughed. "He doesn't like being disappointed."

"Well, you gave him plenty to retrieve," Avery commented dourly.

Lyle turned to Hubert. "What will you remember the most? "

"When Stoney brought back my first bird, it was still alive," Hubert started.

"He has a soft mouth," Lyle interjected.

"What I'll never forget is how deftly Harriet finished him off. I never thought I'd ever see a woman do that."

Harriet laughed. "In times past, who do you think used to catch and kill the chickens for Sunday dinner?"

"I suggest we switch partners tomorrow," Avery said. "I can't spend another day with Morgan looking at me like that whenever I miss."

"Shoot better," Hubert snickered. "You're not getting Harriet."

"You know, Hubert," Harriet said, "It was, after all, your wife and Lyle's that cooked this vacation up. You two have a lot in common. Go on and hunt together."

"You don't mind?" Hubert asked.

"Avery and I will…," Harriet started when Professor Luther butted in.

"Avery can have my guide. His dog is used to people missing shots. He actually expects it."

"You want to hunt with me?" Harriet asked surprised.

"It would be an honor. You are a legend in the world of finance, you know."

"Retired," Harriet said tersely.

"I understand," Professor Luther acquiesced. "No shop talk. But I still would like to shoot with you. I can offer you blinds on the shore tomorrow. Your dog gets to swim, but not us."

"That's for me," Harriet said.

Just before dinner that evening, Professor Luther found himself temporarily alone with Harriet.

"I owe you an apology," he said.

"Whatever for? Your hospitality has been everything one could wish for."

"I'm a recent widower and, frankly, I thought when I was told there was a single, older woman in the party that Hubert was trying to set me up."

Harriet laughed. "He wouldn't dare!"

"I soon discovered that wasn't the case," Claude Luther said. "My first inkling came when you showed up with a Chessie; my second, when you rose just after me and immediately buried your nose in the financial pages.

"I'm sorry if I was rude," Harriet began.

"No apology necessary," Claude Luther said smiling. "The clincher was when you bagged almost as many as Lyle."

"Stoney and I haven't gotten out much this year. We are having a whale of a good time," she responded slightly abashed by her read in this conversation.

"I know that Hubert and Lyle have wives and jobs waiting for them, but I would like to invite you to stay a bit longer. I love to hunt and it would give me pleasure to show you some of my favorite places."

"Well...," Harriet hesitated.

The offer was unexpected.

"Stoney would love them all, believe me," the professor urged. "And when Morgan's gone, he can have the run of the house.

"Just a couple of days. I want to be home when my granddaughter is released from the hospital."

"I'll fly you back myself."

"You fly?"

"Didn't you know?" Claude Luther asked, and then before she could respond, added, "Hubert truly didn't plan this."

To his further surprise, when Claude mentioned that he'd invited Harriet to remain tor a few extra days of hunting, both Hubert and Lyle objected. Claude jumped to the wrong conclusion.

"I can invite another guest to chaperone."

Harriet giggled.

"Lyle, Hubert, this isn't a romance that's blooming. Claude's going to be alone over New Years. So am I. And we both like to hunt; so why not?"

"I can't leave you here!" Lyle said. "You'd be so far away. "

Claude raised his eyebrows. "This is getting interesting."

"Mike Carlson isn't going to come down here," Harriet said.

"He's not the one I'm worried about."

"Who's Mike Carlson?" Claude asked and, thus, he learned the story of Harriet's stint as CEO of Cook Construction minus the prophetic visions Harriet and Aleta had had.

"Who are the other guys?"

"The Hepner brothers," Lyle said.

Suddenly Claude's frown disappeared and his eyes brightened.

"You're one of the psychics, aren't you?" he exclaimed.

"Yes, I am."

"Talk about an interesting woman!" Claude exclaimed. "Hubert, why is it exactly you didn't tell her what a great catch I was?"

"Now I know she's not staying without a proper chaperone," Hubert exclaimed.

"Or police protection," Lyle said firmly.

"Oh, for Heaven's sake!" Harriet exclaimed. "Claude's hoping to pick my brain, not... well... whatever you were thinking."

"I know him!" Hubert said. "We went to college together. He likes older women."

"In college older women were tempting to every one of you," Harriet countered. "Tastes change with age."

Avery DuMont finally piped up. "Whatever's going on, I need to be home for my wife's New Year's Eve party. And that's not negotiable."

Hubert looked at Lyle, "We could squeeze in a hunt Saturday morning and fly home in the afternoon."

"Sure," Lyle said. "Whatever brain picking Claude wants to do, he'll have to do in the next two days."

Harriet winked at Claude and he agreed heartily.

Meanwhile at the airfield, Sam Hepner approached an employee in the hanger and waved a piece of paper telling the man he had a work order. He was passed along to the man's supervisor who looked at the order and then told him where the plane was parked. With nineteen small planes on the ground, directions were important as well as having the supervisor believe the three had a legitimate reason for being there.

Toby had spent the night before studying the engine of the small jet Hubert Praetzel flew. He'd devised a system that would kick in at a certain altitude and disrupt the electronic mechanism, thereby stalling the engine and preventing the influx of fuel which was essential to recovery from the downward spiral generated by the stall. The plane would crash for no apparent reason.

It was a clever design and Toby was proud of it.

Even if Harriet predicted the crash and the group called for an inspection of the plane, Toby assured them his work would pass any casual inspection. An expert airplane mechanic would question the addition of an altimeter, but a bomb expert, while he would notice it, would note there was no explosive device and slough off its presence. At least that was the theory under which the Hepner brothers were working.

It took Toby almost an hour to complete the job. No one came by to question them. The three left as unobtrusively as they had arrived and headed north.

Home was now a small two-room apartment on the first floor of a beat-up old farmhouse on the outskirts of Indianapolis. They had fled toward Canada and then decided that they needed to stay in familiar territory, so they had sold the truck, bought a van and switched direction. Indiana was familiar territory, especially Indianapolis. Their father, a racing fan, had taken his sons to see the Indianapolis 500 twice.

For rent signs abounded in the city, but the brothers wanted to be somewhere less crowded. The more people, the more apt recognition would happen. So they picked a spot on the outskirts of Indianapolis and settled down.

That evening Stanley arrived at the hospital late and in an agitated state.

"We saw Jackman on the news," Aleta said. "He can't actually sue us, can he?"

"I can't believe he found a law firm willing to take on so spurious a legal action," Stanley raged. "I can't believe a judge won't throw it out as trivial, groundless and totally without merit."

"It's a nefarious attempt by Jackman to recoup his monetary losses," Martha commented, her speech suddenly, inexplicably understandable. "And a way of getting back at us from his grave if we failed to save his life which he is certain we can't do, but just in case, we could have, he wants us to regret our promise not to."

"You mean this is about money?" Aleta asked.

"The man is suing the three richest women in the state and you don't think he's seeing dollar signs?" Stanley queried.

"As are his lawyers," Martha added.

"But we're not...   Aleta began.

Martha shook her head.

"How am I wrong?" Aleta protested.

"You married into wealth, my dear," Martha responded.

"We have some money, sure," Aleta said. "But we aren't rich enough to..."

Martha shot a questioning glance at Stanley who cleared his throat.

"Martha is right, Aleta," Stanley said calmly. "We are wealthy. And Jackman's lawyers know it."

"They want a settlement," Martha concluded.

"They know we don't want to go to court," Stanley agreed.

"Why not?" Aleta pushed. "You can't sue a prophet. That's like suing God Himself. He is the one who provides the visions after all."

Martha looked dejected. "We really have to settle. I see no other reasonable way out."

"No, we fight!" Aleta insisted. "We counter sue and refuse to negotiate and we go to court."

"On what grounds?" Stanley charged. "That the Hepners are endangering the life of a horse? Much as a lot of people will sympathize with that, I think the court will find that the life of a man is eminently more valuable."

"We don't stoop lower," Aleta said excitedly. "We move to higher ground."

Stanley sat down. "Go on. I'm listening."

"We sue Jackman for interfering with our practicing our religion. We are God's prophets doing God's bidding. We are following His direction in this matter. It surprised us that He chose the life of a horse, which has harmed no one, over an unrepentant unbelieving man, who has harmed many; however, we did not question God's decision. We are violating no laws of God or man. Furthermore, each prophecy is a gift. We are not the givers. We are the receivers. To demand that we produce what we cannot is ludicrous."

Stanley considered her argument. No one spoke as he sat unmoving considering her argument. Minutes passed. Aleta knew it would be unwise to interrupt him. Martha followed her lead.

Twenty minutes later, Stanley said, "Jackman is suing to force you to reveal a prophecy if you receive one."

"The problem is," Aleta countered heatedly, "that he thinks we are liars. His lawyers won't believe we didn't get one. We have to go with this. God chose the horse over him."

"I like it," Martha said, her spirits rising.

"No one will take such a case," Stanley said.

"You will," Aleta said. "I'll do the work."

"Aleta...," Stanley moaned. "Do we want to spend time on this?"

"Do we want our lives back?" Aleta questioned. "We asked for a way out. We didn't ask for an easy way out."

"You win if Martha agrees," Stanley acquiesced with a tinge of regret. This was going to take him away from his practice again.

Martha Cook smiled. "Wholeheartedly! I only wish Shadow was a jackass. That would have made a statement I could have had same fun with."

"I assume you two ladies will guarantee Harriet's acceptance of this plan?" he asked.

"We're just taking the next step," Aleta said. "Grams has never backed away from a fight."

"I could call," Stanley said.

"Don't disturb her," Aleta decided. "She was really looking forward to this trip."

"They get the news down there," Stanley said.

"So she'll get our answer," Aleta said. "She'll call us if she disagrees. But my guess is that she'll go on enjoying herself knowing we're taking care of things.

"I agree," Martha mumbled.

Thus the eight o'clock news carried a statement by the lawyer representing the prophets in response to Jackman's alleged suit.

Stanley announced that he was puzzled by the suit as Mr. Simon Jackman had gone on record stating that he giving no credence to the validity of the prophecies. He then told the media that the prophets planned to file a countersuit on constitutional grounds. He stopped there and said he'd answer any questions not legal in nature. The first five questions were brushed off as legal.

"What's your personal take on this?" Justin Conway asked.

"That's a broad question," Stanley responded. "Would you care to narrow it a bit?"

"Isn't this a matter of a horse being more important than a man?"

"It might appear so on the surface," Stanley Praetzel replied. "And the threat to Aleta's horse was the so-called straw that broke the camel's back. The women are tired of living under the sentence of death by whatever criminal is thwarted by their prophecies."

"But they save lives. Isn't that worth the risk?"

"Perhaps it would be if it weren't for the bitter acrimony poured on them by the likes of Dr. Dunlap and Mr. Jackman, as well as those whose lives they tried to save. These are women of principle, Gentlemen, and to have their integrity questioned is hurtful."

"All people in public eye are viewed as either heroes or villains," Justin shot back. "These women seem a bit sensitive."

"It is their sensitivity that allows them to prophesy in the first place."

"People have a right to question a so-called prophecy," another reported shouted out. "Do you disagree?"

"Absolutely not," Stanley said. "And a person can die for his disregard if he likes. It's his choice."

"Shouldn't we have the right to see whatever these woman see?" asked another harsh voice.

"Be careful what you ask for," Stanley said knowingly. "God may just grant your wish."

"I can handle it," the young reporter said boastfully.

"Really?" Stanley asked. "Have you ever seen a man burned alive? Not in a movie, but in real life."

"No, but…"

"Anyone who's seen a man burn to death, raise your hand."

No hands went up.

"I was rather hoping one of you had," Stanley said.

"Whatever for?" asked the brash young reporter.

"So I could ask how long before the image faded from his memory or if it ever has."

By now everyone knew to which vision he was referring.

"But the man was saved!" the young man pointed out.

"But she wasn't there to see it. The image she is left with is him dying in agony. It's as real to her as if it happened in her presence. Would you want to live with that horror for the rest of your life?"

"But it didn't happen," another reporter pushed in. "We see stuff like that an newscasts all the time."

"Actually, we don't. The news is edited," Stanley contended. "But to take your argument further, these images aren't like a movie an a screen in a theater where your brain tags them as fantasy. These images appear inside the brain. You can't close them out by shutting your eyes. You can't shut off the sound by putting your hands over your ears. Your brain registers them as real. And that's how your memory stores them. Frankly, I hope she never has another vision like that the rest of her life."

At Professor Luther's house, the group of hunters watched the entire interview without comment.

"He's a sharp young man," Claude remarked at the end. "He's got my vote."

"Very insightful," Harriet commented.

"Well, those ladies have themselves one smooth lawyer, but Jackman's hired a pretty sharp law firm," Avery said. "Your son'll need better arguments in court."

"Believe me he knows the difference between the pressroom and the courtroom," Hubert responded matter-of-factly.

"I notice he didn't touch on any legal issues," Lyle said. "He stuck to his personal opinion and painted a rather vivid picture of the toll exacted on his wife."

"You don't buy into this prophesy nonsense?" Avery quipped. "You're a cop."

"As a matter of fact, I do."

"Go ahead, convince me," Avery challenged.

"Sorry, but I can't talk about an ongoing investigation," Lyle said coolly.

Harriet rose and excused herself. The group broke up shortly afterward.

Lyle knocked on her bedroom door and when she opened it, he asked if she was okay.

"I was proud of Stanley," she commented. "The case is in good hands."

"I'm glad you aren't going out with Avery tomorrow."

"Me too," Harriet smiled. As she closed the door, she winked at him.

Chapter 17

By seven the next morning, Harriet and Claude had two wood ducks and one mallard drake each. Stoney had showered them each several times and now sat, a thoroughly satisfied dog, next to the blind waiting for the next falls.

At that very hour Stanley entered Aleta's hospital room. He was dressed casually.

"No court today?"

"Not until ten," Stanley said, preparing to give Aleta her bath. "Mother heard from Dad. They are staying an extra day. It seems Harriet has a beau."

"A what?"

"You heard me," Stanley snickered. "Their host has taken a fancy to your grandmother."

"You're joshing."

"Harriet says the professor just wants to pick her brain. He teaches economics at Southern Illinois University."

Aleta relaxed. "That makes sense."

"She wants to stay the weekend. He says he'll fly her home to be here when you're released."

"She's going to stay there with him alone?"

"That's her plan."

"She can't!"

"Why not?"

"Just because."

"What's wrong with your grandmother wanting a little sex," Stanley said with a straight face. He watched Aleta redden and added, "You like it. Why wouldn't she?"

"Stanley!" Aleta cried, completely unsettled.

Stanley realized he may have gone too far.

Quickly he added, "Lyle said there was no way she was staying."

"You'll pay for this!" Aleta growled.

Stanley lost his newfound sympathy for his bedridden wife.

"Lyle did add that when he bid Harriet goodnight, she winked at him."

Aleta did an about turn. "Stanley, you've got to call her and talk sense into her."

"Me? "

"Who else? Your dad and Lyle West are with her."

"Exactly!" Stanley returned. "Two men who would have far more influence on her than me. And there are two of them. And they're there."

"You've got to do something!"

"Aleta, she's a grown woman. Not only that. She's just like you except that she's not in love with me."

Aleta grew thoughtful. "I guess she's old enough to be trusted. But if anything happens to her, I'm holding you personally responsible."

"You mean if she falls in love I'm responsible?"

"You know what I mean."

"You were vague, Counselor," Stanley said.

After a few minutes of silence, Aleta said, "You know this man, don't you?"

"He's a friend of my father's."

"But you know him. That's why you could tease me."

"You're right. I'm not worried."

"So, he's safe."

"He's a man."

Aleta frowned. "Stanley, tell me he's safe."

"Your grandmother's a good looking woman."

"I'm not speaking to you anymore until after my back rub."

"That's how I like my women--sexy, silent and stripped naked," Stanley quipped.

"You just better hope no one's within earshot."

"It's before eight. Just how early do you think physical therapy begins?"

"The television isn't turned up very loud," Aleta noted, knowing that Martha relished her undisturbed television time.

"I spoke softly, but your exclamations…" he paused and let the corners of his mouth twitch just enough to rile Aleta. "…could be interpreted in more ways than one."

"Stanley!" she exclaimed.

"You fall into my traps so neatly each time," he grinned.

Suddenly, she broke into a smile. "I do, don't I?"

"So, now you have something new to worry about."

"I don't need things to worry about," Aleta protested.

"Sure you do," Stanley said with certainty. "But I love you anyway."

Aleta flared up. "It's not a fault!"

"I said I loved you," Stanley said calmly.

"You added 'anyway' and I know what that means."

"Good!" Stanley said firmly. "Just remember it!"

"I give up! Rub!"

"Finally!" Stanley quipped.

"You're impossible!"

"I thought you gave up."

"That's me giving up."

The time between the flights of migrating birds, Harriet and Claude talked softly. The lake was less choppy than the day before because the wind wasn't so strong. The air was cold however. Sitting still, even warmly dressed, let the icy air slip its cold fingers into every opening in the outer garments. Talking seemed to help ward off the cold. Anticipation had the same effect.

When a flock of Canadian geese flew over, Harriet brought one down. Claude missed his shot. They heard multiple shots down the way and saw a second one fall.

"Lyle," Harriet said.

"That'd be my guess to," Claude agreed. Harriet sent Stoney for her bird.

"You seem more relaxed today, Claude remarked.

"I am," Harriet said. "Hunting is like stepping into another world for a bit. It's a real vacation for me."

"It's more than that," Claude observed. "I love to hunt. But you enjoy it more. Why is that?"

"Stoney is the added pleasure," Harriet said. "I can't explain the thrill I feel when he is returning with the fall. His excitement and pleasure infect me. He's the difference."

"A dog? That's the difference?"

"Not just any dog. A dog that I'm connected with. A dog I've trained myself. That's the difference."

"I think I'd like that experience."

Meanwhile in the far northern part of the state, in a house opposite Jackman's, with its owners tied, gagged, blindfolded, and stashed in an upstairs bedroom near the one they occupied, the Hepners were still waiting for Jackman to exit his house.

"I thought you said he had an appointment," Sam complained, irritable because it was Fred with the gun at the window and not him. He was relegated to watching their hostages.

"He has several," Fred responded. "He may have canceled one or he's running late. Was there anything on the news?"

"No," Sam said. "But that doesn't mean, one of the women didn't tell someone."

"There is one cop on the door," Fred said. "And that's it. We been here for hours and ain't seen a hint of anymore."

"You really think the women meant it when they promised not to tell?" Sam asked. "Because I don't. I think it's something else."

"Like what?"

"I dunno. Maybe they didn't get a vision at all because I can't see them not telling if they did no matter what they said."

"I can," Toby lisped. "That lawyer of theirs made some good points. I think they're going to fight for their right not to tell. I think they've got a new goal now."

"Hey, guys. Shut up," Fred hissed. "I think the door's opening."

"I don't see nothing," Toby whispered back.

"The guard outside turned," Fred said. "He heard something."

Toby lifted his rifle. His arm didn't like the weight. His cheek didn't like any movement which included Toby cocking his head slightly to gaze down the barrel of the gun, through the sight.

The door opened.

Sam noted Fred's eagerness and cautioned him to wait for Toby's signal.

A cop in full protective gear stepped out.

Fred let out a huge breath. It was a release of tension as well as a sigh of relief that he hadn't squeezed the trigger.

Sam watched through the window above his head. "Could be a second cop," he warned.

He was right. A second cop in protective gear emerged.

"Damn!" Fred growled.

"Relax," Sam said. "He'll come out next."

Jackman stepped out. The two policemen blocked any shot all the way to the car. Toby and Fred kept what little they could see of Jackman's head in their sights.

The car door opened. The men parted slightly as Jackman began to fold himself into the driver's seat.

Toby didn't say a word as he squeezed his trigger. Fred heard the shot and instantly reacted. His round followed his brother's within seconds.

Toby's bullet hit Jackman in the head. Fred's hit the headgear of the cop who was at that moment bending over to cover Jackman. Both men went down.

The rifles were withdrawn immediately. Sam saw the cops aiming guns in their direction. No shots were fired, however.

The three ran down the stairs and into a television van parked in the driveway.

Fred backed out of the driveway slowly and proceeded down the street. He heard sirens approaching and pulled off to the side to let the police pass.

The three were unseen when they left the van and climbed into their car and drove south.

The news hit the airwaves as they were driving. Simon Jackman was shot while under police protection. One policeman was wounded as well. Jackman was in critical condition at Cook County Hospital.

The newscaster went on to elaborate that the police received no warning of any kind about this attack.

Later, speculation was aired as to what this silence on the part of the prophets meant.

Talk radio took over the speculation and the opinions ranged from outrage that the women would withhold a warning for the sake of a horse's life to people who felt that a horse was an animal worthy of consideration and Jackman got what he deserved.

Soon public opinion began to rage against the greedy men who masked as leaders in the business world when what they were good at was fleecing corporations.

One caller offered his opinion that the trustees who did the hiring of the top men in hopes of quickly raising the price of their stock never learned that greedy people made poor bedfellows. They demanded all the blankets.

The brothers liked that offering so listened eagerly to see if there were more who understood their position. To their dismay, emotion began to take over as if emotions were to be valued above reason. The few intelligent and thoughtful comments offered were lost in the barrage of stupidity that raged on like a rushing river at flood level. The small boats of reason were soon overturned by the swirling waters of emotion leaving rational men disgusted and irrational men inflamed.

The Hepner brothers listened hopefully to the blather on the long drive through Chicago but eventually, they too tired of the opinions of people who were speaking despite having nothing to say.

"It seems the ladies kept their word," Toby concluded.

"Only if they knew," Sam countered. "He's still alive."

"Why's that important?" Fred asked.

Toby answered him to show Sam that he understood his comment.

"The women only predict murders, not attempts."

"You shot him in the head!" Fred exclaimed. "It's only a matter of time."

Harriet found out about Jackman shortly after the group arrived back at the house after the shoot.

The shock on Harriet's face told Lyle she had had no warning. The reaction of the two hospital patients told Stanley they hadn't either.

"He's still alive," Aleta said. "That's probably why."

Her words were spoken in response to Stanley's unspoken query.

"You mean he's going to live?" Stanley asked.

"Well, he isn't going to die," Martha said.

Her words hung as an enigma in Stanley's mind. Inexplicably, he was certain those words were carefully chosen. How could one not live and not die?

He tucked the saying in his memory and told the two women that Bertha had made supper for them.

"She is upset at having so little to do," Stanley reported. "She brightened right up when I told her you might be coming home Sunday.

"So I'm really going home on Sunday?"

"Bertha's planning a nice dinner for the family to celebrate."

"Is it safe?"

"Milani thinks the danger is over. The guards are mostly to keep reporters out of here."

"You said you had a short court calendar today," Aleta said. "Why weren't you here earlier?"

"I was working on your case against Jackman."

"I told you I'd do the research," Aleta said. "This attack on Jackman may force Jackman's lawyers into pushing for an early hearing. Tomorrow is New Year's Eve. I'll be home Sunday. I can start then."

"It would not be unprecedented for them to wrangle a preliminary hearing tomorrow," Stanley said.

"What's our position?" Aleta asked.

"It all hinges on the belief you three have that God is directing you. This is a religious belief. No one can force you to do something against your belief unless your action or, in this case, inaction causes greater harm."

"But isn't that a moot point now?" Aleta asked.

"I need time to pull together my argument," Stanley said. "I haven't found any pertinent case law so far. There may, in fact, not be any."

"So you want to go, don't you?"

"I don't want to. I need to."

"Martha and I are big girls," Aleta said. "You can go, but you need to eat first."

"I really can't take the time…," Stanley began but a scowl from both women stopped him. "You're right. I'll last longer with a full stomach besides who's going to feed Aleta if I don't."

"Glad you finally got your priorities straight," Aleta said.

"Not really," Stanley returned. "It's just that when two of my clients scowl at me, I pay attention."

"Ask Dad to help," Aleta said. "It's his daughter and mother who are being sued. He's got a personal interest in the case."

"I tend not to ask anyone to…"

"I know," Aleta interposed, "but this time he'd actually appreciate it."

"You're in a time crunch," Martha put in. "I've discovered my men like to work under real pressure and at odd hours on occasion. Gives them a sense that they matter."

"You win. It's a good idea."

Saturday morning the early news broadcasts reported that Simon Jackman had undergone surgery and his condition was stable. He was expected to recover.

Harriet and the hunting group had departed for their last day of hunting without checking the news. Whatever was happening in the world was put on hold as their minds focused on that morning's hunt.

The Hepner brothers, however, had slept fitfully, not knowing whether they had succeeded or not. They drank in the news with their morning coffee.

"Now what?" Fred said.

"We still don't know about the prophets," Sour Sam declared.

"Well, soon we'll only have two to worry about," Toby reminded his brothers.

"They're still in the hospital--the other two," Fred said. "We could try again. No one would expect that."

"Little brother has a point," Toby lisped. "And up close neither of us will miss."

"I can't hold a gun," Sour Sam protested;

"We can rig a harness. All you'll need to do is pull the trigger," Toby suggested. "But we should do a couple of things differently this time."

"What do you have in mind?" Sam asked, for the first time willing to listen to Toby's ideas.

When Dr. Cook arrived that morning, he found both Martha and Aleta sitting in wheelchairs in front of the window watching the snow fall. He affirmed that Aleta was being released the next day.

Martha looked at her grandson hopefully.

He shook his head. "You won't tolerate the help you need at home; however, if your therapy keeps going as it has, it'll only be a few more days. We did reverse the permanent damage."

"I'll do whatever you ask," Martha said, "if you'll let me start the New Year in my own home."

"You'll accept a full-time nurse and sleep downstairs for a week? And you won't drive? And you'll come to therapy every day?"

"Yes," Martha promised. "I'll do everything you ask."

"I'll take you home myself around five," Dr. Cook said.

"So late?" Martha asked upset.

"Why not let her come home with me?" Aleta said. "Bertha is cooking a welcome home dinner for me. It'll just be family. And you can pick her up when you're free. We know how it is with doctors."

"How is it?" Dr. Chesney asked entering. "Good to see you two up. I came to say goodbye."

"Why don't you come to my welcome home dinner?" Aleta said. "It's a small one--just family--and I hope Martha."

"You're leaving us too?" Dr. Chesney asked the older woman.

"Wayne said I could go. I had to promise him the earth in exchange," Martha quipped.

Dr. Chesney turned toward his fellow doctor.

"I thought you were on tomorrow."

"I'll take her home when I get off."

"I'll take Martha to Aleta's party," Dr. Chesney offered. "If she tires, I'll take her home."

The eager hope on the face of his grandmother washed away Wayne's residual reticence.

"Can't ask for better hands to put you in, Grams. Okay."

"Did we miss Stanley?" Dr. Chesney asked.

"He didn't come," Aleta replied. "He and Dad spent all night trying to find cases to bolster our arguments in case Jackman's lawyers get an early court date... But if Jackman died..."

"He didn't. Taekman did him," Dr. Cook said.

"Tell Taekman I owe him," Aleta said. "Now, since you two aren't busy, how about wheeling us up to physical therapy."

"The techs will come...," Dr. Cook started but Dr. Chesney took hold of Martha's chair and turned her toward the door.

"Come on, Wayne, let's do it. Stanley just might pop in and he'd find empty beds. It'd be good payback for the last few days he made us wait outside the door.

Wayne smiled. "Yes, it would."

When they arrived there was no one in the therapy room.

"It's early," Aleta said. "Just leave us. We'll be fine."

"We'll talk," Martha added.

The doctors agreed that they'd be okay. The guards were on the door.

When they left, Martha asked Aleta, "Why would it be so terrible if Harriet fell in love?"

"He lives so far away."

"He could move here."

"Men don't do that."

"Men do a lot of unexpected things when they're in love."

"All we have is a little fanciful flirting," Aleta contended optimistically, "Nothing more. Grams is a sensible woman."

"We are all sensible women and sensitive women as well. And we are women capable of love. The question is can you love her enough to let her go?"

"What do you know that I don't?"

"Harriet never flirts."

"You flirt."

"I've also fallen in love since my husband died."

"But you never remarried."

"I was too engrossed in the company to give the relationship what it deserved. It was not my best decision."

"I want Grams to be happy, but why not with someone close by like Dr. Chesney."

"You'll never be a good matchmaker. Your criteria are all wrong," Martha stated flatly.

"What's wrong with Dr. Chesney?"

"Nothing. But your grandmother and he have nothing in common."

"Well, neither did Stanley and I, and Grams paired us."

"You had the one quality Stanley was looking for and vice versa."

"And what quality was that?"

"What quality does he have that you value the most?"

"In him I've met my match."

"Exactly."

"But that's so elusive."

"Which is why matchmaking is so hard. Think about your dad. Would you have picked Bertha?"

"Never even gave her a thought."

"Still you think they're well-matched."

"Strangely enough, yes."

"Well, when Harriet brings this professor home…"

"She won't!" Aleta exclaimed. "That would broadcast that she was serious. She's only known him two days."

"Stranger things have happened."

"But it's too fast," Aleta cried. "Only a con man works that fast. He's after her money."

"He flies his own plane. He's a professor at a university. I'd say he was both wealthy and established."

"But he lives so far away."

"He flies a plane."

"Okay. Okay, I give in. I'm being petty."

"Your grandmother has her family here and a large number of close friends. She's about to become a great-grandmother. She isn't going to toss all that aside casually."

"Can I pray about this?"

"Only if you limit your prayer to the four words Jesus taught his disciples."

"Thy will be done?" Aleta grumbled.

"Those are the ones," Martha said. "Now, are we out of danger yet?"

"You knew?"

"Only that we were really early for therapy."

"While we wait, why don't you tell me about your pregnancy with Wayne's father."

"No one's asked me about that in a long time," Martha said.

Aleta hung on every word that followed.

In one of the duck blinds on a lake in the Crab Orchard Region, Harriet suggested that perhaps they were going to have to stop soon. She said so regretfully.

"I wish you would stay," Claude said. "I had gotten pretty excited over the idea of spending the New Year's holiday in your company."

"Would you like to spend it with my family? They're a pretty interesting bunch. I'm sure Hubert would love to return your hospitality. We're spending New Year's Day celebrating Aleta's homecoming; but New Year's Eve you and I could do anything you'd like. I've been invited to a party at Kurtz West's house. That's Lyle's father. I'm sure he and his wife will be there, so you'll know at least one person besides me."

"I won't be imposing?"

"On whom? The Wests want me to come and bring a friend. As for Aleta's party, she always expands them. My guess is Bertha has already been told to set a couple extra places. Bertha's very flexible. She knows Aleta. My son will be delighted that he doesn't have to squire me around and can concentrate on Bertha."

"Bertha? Your granddaughter's cook?"

"And Robert's fiancé. He loves her cooking as well as her other attributes. She is a gem. He's a fortunate man."

"I'd love to come."

"I need to warn you about one thing," Harriet said pensively. "Aleta hates change she hasn't generated, so be prepared."

"I gather she will think that your bringing me back with you has a special significance."

"She would be correct."

"Good! As long as you and I are on the same page, I'll be fine."

"There are probably two things you should know before we go any further."

"You've already told me you're one of the psychics?"

"We prefer the term prophet," Harriet explained. "We can only see future events and only people being murdered. The police wish we could identify the murderer but we can't. There are three of us: Martha Cook, Aleta and me."

"And the second thing?"

"I'm part Negro."

"And what? That's it?"

"Yes."

"The prophet thing was bigger," Claude said. "How many people know you're passing?"

"Most of my friends, but not all."

"I can be discreet," Claude said. "I'm curious as to why you told me."

"My son's wife divorced him when he told her. His middle daughter lives with her mother and accepted her mother's lie that she had an affair and that she has a white father. His other two daughters are with us. They accept the truth. Jocelyn lives with me as does her father. There are no secrets in our house."

"And you're telling me this because Avery doesn't know any of it and so you can't speak of it in his presence."

"It's now or never," Harriet said. "I don't want you to wind up in an awkward situation. We can cancel our plans now if you wish. We can part amicably."

Claude took her hand as he stood up. "You have no idea how long I've wanted to do this."

He drew her to her feet, embraced her and gently kissed her. Harriet closed her eyes and let herself enjoy her first such kiss in many years.

Back at the Tri City Hospital in Arborville, the Hepner brothers found the room on the fourth floor empty. They cornered the nursing staff.

"Where are they?" Sam growled.

The nurses knew exactly who the 'they' were.

"Physical therapy," one nurse replied, looking at the barrel of a rifle pointed at her midsection. "That's one floor up."

"No," a second one interjected. "Dr. Chesney and Dr. Cook took them. They didn't say where."

The rifle poked the first nurse in the stomach.

She explained quickly, "Dr. Chesney might have taken Mrs. Praetzel to OB. She's pregnant."

"Mrs. Cook isn't," Sam snapped, his rifle barrel prodding the frightened nurse.

"Maybe Dr. Cook wanted her to have another CAT scan," the first nurse suggested. "It's his grandmother. He does a lot of tests on her."

The second nurse was mute. She'd seen which doctor had which patient.

It was Fred who spotted the arrival of police cars through the window of the nurse station. He warned his brothers they were being surrounded.

Sam prodded the first nurse. "Move."

She stepped back.

Toby told the second nurse to move.

When she stepped back, he spotted the alarm button on the floor.

Sam signaled Fred and he hit her on the back of the head. She fell at Toby's feet.

The other nurse screamed. The sound was cut off by Fred's second swing. She fell on top of her fellow nurse.

The men ran to the service elevator, picked up the block of wood, keeping the door open and descended to the basement level. They ran through the tunnel and burst through the far door just as Peter French's men entered the front door of the new Physical Therapy Wing.

Toby led his brothers up the stairway to the second floor. The brothers hid there while the police pushed through the main floor to the tunnel.

On the fifth floor, Aleta smiled at her elderly companion. "We're safe now."

"Yes, we are," Martha agreed.

Chief Tom Milani entered a short time later. Lieutenant Peter French was with him.

"You knew, didn't you?" he questioned, not expecting a reply.

"We should warn Harriet," Aleta remarked.

"There's no way the brothers know where she is," French replied. He looked at his watch. "Besides they're boarding the plane practically at this very moment to come home. There's no way the Hepners could make it down there even if they sprouted wings and flew."

Tom pondered the suggestion, then said, "I'll have someone meet their flight."

Chapter 18

The dog crates were transferred from Claude's vehicle to Hubert's plane while Harriet and Lyle held onto their dogs. Harriet approached the plane with Stoney first.

The big Chessie balked at the bottom stair. Harriet urged him forward. As she did so she put a hand on the stairway railing. While touching an object before had not resulted in a vision, this time it did.

Lyle brought up Morgan.

"Maybe Stoney just doesn't want to be first," he said.

"We can't fly home in this plane," Harriet said. "It's going to crash."

"Explode?" Lyle queried softly. "A bomb?"

"No explosion. It's just going to go down."

Hubert poked his head out the door just as Morgan pulled away from the stairway and Lyle turned around and looked at his black Lab.

"What's wrong?" Hubert asked.

"Stoney doesn't want to board the plane," Harriet said simply. "And neither, evidently, does Morgan."

By now Avery and Claude had moved close enough to hear the exchange.

"For God's sake!" Avery snarled. "Drag them in!"

Harriet eyed Avery with contempt. "One does not drag a Chessie anywhere!"

"And I listen to my dog," Lyle announced. "I guess we get the plane checked out."

"That's crazy!" Avery exploded. "The dogs just want another day of hunting."

Claude interjected a consideration that seeing as how it was New Year's Eve, they'd have trouble finding a good mechanic.

"Still," he finished, "if there's any question, I'd rather be safe than sorry."

"Screw you!" Avery said, his ill-temper rising. "Screw the dogs. Come on Hubert, use your head! Not a speck of trouble on the way down!"

Hubert turned to Harriet.

"Do you advise against it?" he asked openly.

"Yes, I do."

"Then this plane stays on the ground until it's checked out," Hubert decided.

"All because of some dogs?" Avery said contemptuously.

"These dogs have warned us before," Lyle said. "My guess is Stoney picked up a smell he didn't like."

"I'll believe that the day dogs fly," Avery quipped. "You people are stupid--listening to dogs and believing in psychics! Hubert, I'm never flying with you again."

Claude eyed Avery DuMont with disgust.

"Don't get your panties in a tangle," he mocked. "It's you who are stupid. But I do have a solution. I'll fly us all north."

"Will your plane hold all of us?" Avery asked skeptically.

"Oh, I think I can manage to squeeze a everyone in," Claude said. "Avery may have to hold his goose in his lap."

Lyle put his hand an Avery's shoulder. "He's joshing with you. I'm sure we can find a place for your goose."

Avery scowled, but didn't respond.

"I'll be a few minutes," Claude said. "I have to fuel the plane. Harriet, walk with me."

"I'll park my plane," Hubert said returning to the pilot's seat. He looked at Harriet when he announced his intentions and she didn't object. Whatever she foresaw wasn't going to happen on the ground. He relaxed as he taxied his plane back to its spot.

"How far is your plane?" Harriet asked as she strode beside the tall, hefty man whom she found so attractive.

"It's a bit of a hike," Claude said. "We could have driven, but I wanted a bit more time alone with you."

"Thank you for offering your plane."

Claude came straight to the point. "You had a vision, didn't you?"

"Yes," Harriet replied.

"And you told Lyle. And he believed you."

"Yes," Harriet said again.

"And Hubert suspected which is why he asked your advice."

"Correct again. Now I have a question for you," Harriet said. "Before when I told you about my heritage, you seemed to feel there was something else I was concerned about. What was it?"

"The disparity in our ages."

"You had an argument ready, didn't you?"

"Of course. It seemed the most obvious question to be resolved."

"So what's your argument?"

"Since you appear not to have a problem with the age difference, my arguments are moot now," Claude responded. "But I'm curious as to why the age factor never came up."

"I figured you were good with numbers," Harriet remarked. "And you probably have the actuarial tables memorized."

"We are serious, aren't we?" Claude asked.

"It would seem so."

"Because if we're not, I'd like to know."

"We've only known each other two days," Harriet remarked.

"I never thought I'd be as attracted to a woman again, as I am to you."

"Do I remind you of your wife?"

"Strangely, not at all."

"Good. Because you're not like my late husband either."

"Good. Then I don't have to measure up to a memory."

"Exactly!" Harriet responded. "What are you looking for?"

"Companionship, mostly."

"Really?" Harriet said with a sly smile. "I was rather looking forward to great sex."

Claude stopped dead. "Sex?"

"You were afraid to hope, weren't you?"

"As a matter of fact, I was willing to forego it to have you as part of my life."

"With me, you're better off being honest," Harriet stated.

"I can see that. But give me a chance to get used to being that way."

"What won't your children like about me?"

"Nothing."

"Honesty is required here," Harriet said firmly.

"They'll think you're after my money," Claude confessed.

"You have money?"

"I have a large house, servants and a plane," Claude said. "Isn't that obvious."

"I know you're wealthy, but do you have money?"

"Yes."

"Well, as you probably know, so do I. And my granddaughter Aleta might think the same thing, but not because she wants anything, but simply because she wants to protect me."

"Not your sons?"

"They won't care. They didn't find out I had any real wealth until a few months ago. They haven't grasped the concept yet," Harriet explained. "However, a pre-nup should take care of your children's worries, so I'll happily sign one."

"As will I," Claude said as they reached the plane.

It was bigger than Hubert's. Harriet took a deep breath.

"My you do indeed have a plane!"

"We're alone," he announced abruptly.

"Stoney's here."

"What's his view on sex?"

"Positive."

"Good," he responded drawing her to him. "I know I have to be discreet for the next few days, so let me get a kiss under my belt now."

"Literally?" Harriet asked.

"You are a surprising woman!" Claude chuckled.

Gently, he embraced her. Their kiss was long and passionate. When Stoney whined, they paused and looked around.

"Let's go inside," Harriet said.

"Do we dare proceed so fast?"

"I have an idea," Harriet said. "I'll tell you in the plane."

Stoney scrambled up the stairs without hesitation and began investigating every nook in the luxuriously appointed plane that could accommodate eight besides the pilot and co-pilot.

Once inside, with the door closed, Harriet said, "We need to be married."

"I'm ready."

"Hold my hands," she said, "and make your vows before God and me."

Claude said simply, "I love this woman, God, and I promise to cherish and honor her as long as we both shall live."

"God," Harriet said softly, "I promise to be faithful and true to this man, to love and honor him until death do us part. Bless us this day and thank you."

Claude drew her to him and kissed her tenderly.

"This is for real," he said.

"For us, this is it," she responded. "Later we'll do it for others."

"Anytime you say," he murmured as he kissed her again.

As she responded, Harriet felt the quickening of her heart and the arousal of her long-buried sexual energy. She could scarcely believe how alive she suddenly felt in the arms of this man.

She had thought such feelings had long ago died. Part of the wonder as they progressed slowly toward their final coupling was that God had blessed her when she least expected it and in a way she never dreamed possible.

Afterward, they lay on the carpeted floor of the plane, neither wanting the moment to end.

Stoney's whine woke them to the fact that people were waiting.

Harriet looked at her watch. "How long have we been?"

Claude looked at her and traced the outline of her naked body with his finger. "You expect me to be logical after this?

"Well, you better be because I can't even focus on the time."

"Let's just say it's time to get dressed and fuel the plane."

"And if we're asked?" Harriet said.

"I'll leave the answer to you," Claude said. "Whatever I say will be wrong."

"I love a man who's been well-trained for marriage," Harriet said.

She leaned over and kissed him.

"Don't start me up again," he warned her, "or we'll never get off the ground."

"Do you feel married?" she asked.

"Completely," he said softly.

"Me too," she whispered.

Neither moved at all. They lay, their bodies touching, savoring the feel of a loved one's warmth once again.

Stoney, however, not too sure what was happening, decided to check on these two lying on the floor unmoving. He walked alongside Harriet and licked her face. Stoney's ministrations were successful.

Shortly afterward, Claude taxied the plane to where the group was waiting. Lyle and Hubert were chatting amicably in Claude's vehicle while Avery paced outside.

When the staircase was lowered, Avery barely let the two descend before he tersely inquired as to the delay.

"We... er...," Harriet began.

"...got married," Claude finished.

Harriet smiled and nodded.

All three men looked at them quizzically.

"We'll do the legal stuff later," Harriet added.

Hubert and Lyle both rushed forward, congratulations bursting forth. They hugged Harriet and wished her happiness and shook Claude's hand.

Avery scowled in disbelief. "You didn't get married. You couldn't have gotten...."

Hubert cut him off. "I've never known either Claude or Harriet to lie. Have a little faith, man."

"He just wanted a...," Avery began.

This time it was Lyle who cut him off. "Don't say it!"

"I call a spade a spade. You can put all the pretty words to it you want; but the fact of the matter is they kept us waiting in the cold while they went at it hot and heavy."

"I certainly hope they did," Hubert said.

"It completes the vows taken," Lyle added.

"No vows were taken!" Avery said. "Maybe he fed her a line promising marriage in order to... well, you know what, but that's all it was."

"Oh there were vows," Harriet said. "God heard them."

"You weren't in a church. There was no minister. There was no wedding," Avery spouted. "You remind me of the hippies in the sixties. They were full of garbage too."

"Sometimes, Avery, you shock me," Hubert said. "You're so... so provincial."

"This is why women don't belong on hunting trips," Avery blurted out. "They mess things up."

"Ignore him!" Hubert said. "He's still peeved because Harriet managed to shoot more birds than he did."

"I got a goose today," Avery shot back. "She didn't!"

"Cool it, Avery," Hubert said.

"So when are you telling Aleta?" Lyle asked, grinning.

"Why Aleta?" Claude asked.

"Because Aleta will have a reaction. And I want to be there."

"Me too," Hubert said.

"You expect fireworks?" Claude asked.

Aleta is unpredictable," Lyle said. "You're going to love her. We all do."

"Should we not tell her right away?" Claude asked.

"She doesn't handle deception well," Harriet said.

"You said she was married," Claude asked cautiously.

"To my son," Hubert chimed in. "She's added excitement to his life as well as great joy."

"She must be like her grandmother," Claude remarked squeezing Harriet's hand.

"She is," Hubert said.

"Then I'm going to love her."

Harriet squeezed his hand.

Chief Milani was waiting at the airport personally when Claude landed his jet. He had two officers standing by, two more in squad cars.

Lyle spotted him from the side window.

"Something's up," he said.

"Wouldn't they have called you if something happened?" Harriet asked.

"No," Lyle replied. "I couldn't do anything, but their presence tells me that you're in danger.

"I need to see Aleta."

"I'll see to it."

"I need Claude with me."

"I'll take you there myself," Lyle said.

He lowered his voice. "Does Claude know you're one of the prophets? "

"Yes," Harriet responded. "He knows about that and a whole lot more."

"Good, because he's about to be dipped into some really deep… er… stuff."

"Thanks for not doubting my choice," Harriet said softly.

"You're welcome. Let me talk with Tom."

After Avery left, Lyle told the rest what Tom had told him all about the brothers' thwarted attempt at the hospital.

"It appears that your plane might have been tampered with, Hubert," Lyle finished. "Chief Milani wants Harriet under constant surveillance."

"We need to take care of certain matters that I can't do alone," Claude protested.

"Those will have to wait," Chief West said. "I'm sorry. But Chief Milani wants Harriet confined to her house."

Claude saw Harriet's face crumble and, taking her by the arm, escorted her back into the plane.

"I want to marry you," he said. "That hasn't changed."

Harriet swallowed back her tears. "I had this lovely plan in my head. It all seemed so right because it was... well... sort of a package."

"I know I can't live with you," Claude said. "I'm sure Hubert's house is equipped with cold showers."

"I don't want you taking cold showers," Harriet declared.

Claude put his arms around her and hugged her. "Me neither."

"But you're right. Jocelyn wouldn't understand."

As Claude held her, he looked around.

"We're in a plane," he said.

The comment was inane except as a preface to a new idea.

"You aren't suggesting we stay here?"

"Only as long as it takes to get to Las Vegas. You can get married in a day there."

"It's New Year's Eve."

"Las Vegas should be in full swing. Nothing will be closed, but we don't come back until we're married. Are you game?"

"I'm in all the way," Harriet decided instantly.

"That's what I love about you," Claude said, "well, one of the things."

"What? That I'm ready to follow you anywhere?"

Claude closed his arms around her. "That's a bonus."

He kissed her with a passion that made her heart beat rapidly. Reluctantly, she pushed away.

"You keep this up and I'm going to need a cold shower."

Back outside the plane, they found Lyle and Hubert involved in an earnest conversation.

"We think the Hepner brothers have locked into one of our computers somehow," Chief West said.

"Harriet and I want to fly to Vegas and get married," Claude announced. "Hubert, would you and Lydia be our guests on the junket? We need you both."

Harriet jumped in. "I'm not leaving the plane. Tom can guard me here until we leave."

Lyle waved Tom over and the group ironed out the details for the trip. Hubert would call his wife, have her pack for an overnight trip, but not tell her the destination."

Tom insisted on that level of secrecy. "The leaks are coming from here."

"Lauren and I will personally take care of housing Stoney," Lyle said. "We'll get your ducks in the freezer and tell your family not to worry."

"What will you tell them?" Harriet asked.

"That you had a legal matter that required you to fly somewhere. When I tell them that Hubert is going with you, they won't ask me what legal matter."

"Stanley and Aleta are the Tontine lawyers," Harriet said.

Tom spoke up. "Stanley's tied up in court on the Jackman case."

"Are you coming back for Aleta's coming home party tomorrow," Lyle asked.

"We plan to," Claude said.

"I need to make some phone calls," Harriet said. "I'll use the public phone in the terminal."

"Who are you calling?"

"A jeweler and a clothing store," she said, trotting off. Tom told one of his officers to go with her.

She returned a short time later and climbed into the plane. Hubert and Lyle were transporting the birds to Lyle's van. Stoney was already in a crate in the West's van alongside Morgan. Harriet was told Claude was filing a flight plan.

"Hubert, we're going to need pre-nups," Harriet said.

"From me?"

"You're a lawyer, aren't you?"

"I don't handle domestic issues."

"It's easy," Harriet said. "Everything he owns before, including today, is his. Same for me."

"Lydia deals with that all the time. Have her write it."

"You write it. She can review it."

"I need my briefcase," Hubert said, flicking open his cell. He was brief and refused to answer any of his wife's questions until he saw her.

The jeweler was the first to arrive. He was ushered into the plane by an officer. He looked frightened when he entered, but Harriet assured him that he was in no danger. Hubert was sent to fetch Claude.

Harriet looked at the ruby necklace she'd spotted once in the store window. It was as beautiful this time as last. She bought it and the jeweler happily wrote up the sales slip for the four thousand dollar purchase. A ruby tie clasp and cuff links were purchased as quickly. She was glad she'd insisted the jeweler bring boxes. The Rolex she selected was gold with few features. Claude wouldn't like a gimmicky watch, she knew instinctively.

She was writing the jeweler a check when Claude entered.

"You're done?"

"Just some gifts for our best man and matron of honor," she said. "I haven't looked at the rings yet."

The jeweler opened a case with a number of ring sets.

"I can size any ring you like," he said.

"We need them to fit today," Harriet said, selecting an intricately woven gold and platinum double band. She slipped it on her finger.

Claude picked up the larger one in the set and slipped it on his finger.

"Fits!" he said. "I like it."

"The rings can stand for anything you like," the jeweler said. "Some people think of one band as standing for friendship, the other for love."

"We'll take them," Claude said decisively. "May I pay with a credit card? Mine would be an out of town check."

"Either will be fine," the jeweler said.

As the purchase of jewelry was completed, the manager of the small apparel shop in Willow Glean entered with a number of boxes and two garment bags. Harriet asked a few questions and wrote a check for everything.

Claude stared at her aghast. This wasn't how women shopped.

"He knows my size and taste," she said. "I don't like to shop. Now I'm ready to get married."

"What've you got in those boxes?"

"A flannel nightgown, waders… you know, the usual stuff to turn a man on."

"The nightgown better be satin," Claude quipped, "or better yet, invisible."

"Where's Hubert?"

"Making hotel reservations," Claude said. "We're alone."

"We are not…," Harriet started.

His kiss cut her off. She put her arms around his neck and returned his passion with hers. Before they went any further, she put her hand on his which had slipped to her waist and had begun to push her slacks down.

"The door locked," he whispered.

"Our friends are standing outside in the cold," she returned. "We can't do this now."

"You drive me wild," Claude responded. "For God's sake, I'm a university professor. An economics professor. We're a stuffy lot."

"As are retired bankers," Harriet added. "I guess we're burying those myths."

"Doesn't it scare you a little?"

"Terrifies me," Harriet said. "But I've never felt so alive, so happy."

"Me neither," Claude said. "We may need a longer honeymoon than one night. We're not fit company for decent people right now."

"You are so right," Harriet agreed. "But maybe we should let our friends back inside. It's cold out there."

"I hope you got them nice gifts, really nice gifts," Claude mused aloud.

Later, as Claude and Hubert guided the plane down the runway and into the air, Lydia told Harriet that Stanley had exhausted all his arguments for postponing the Jackman case; he was going to have to be ready by two.

"The judge told him this appeared to be an emergency situation so she was hearing the case this afternoon."

"He's all alone," Harriet said.

"Robert's with him and while he can't argue in court, Stanley says he's contributed a lot and he's counting on him to see holes he might miss. He says they're a good team."

As Lydia was telling Harriet about Stanley needing to appear in court that afternoon, Jackman's lawyer rose to present his case. He was just finishing when Lyle West entered the courtroom in full uniform and stood beside the door. Stanley asked for a short recess which was granted.

"Your Honor," Stanley said, "I would like a continuance."

"On what basis?" Judge Ellen Cohen asked.

"We just learned of an attempt on Harriet Locke's life. Mrs. Locke was vacationing in Carbondale. Very few knew of her departure, but we know that Mr. Jackman has had men tracking her movements. He is a suspect."

Jackman's lawyer sprang to his feet. "That's ridiculous, Your Honor. Mr. Jackman's life is at stake here."

Stanley broke in. "Excuse me, Your Honor, Mr. Jackman is recovering nicely. He is under police protection."

"Mr. Jackman was attacked and not one of the three women warned him," Jackman's lawyer charged vociferously."

"Your Honor, all three prophets say they were following God's direction. Their religious belief does not allow them to violate a directive from God."

"I thought this was about a horse's life being more important than a man's," the judge said.

"Mr. Jackman's lawyers want that to be considered the heart of the case. But this is a case about Mr. Jackman, who is a nonbeliever, trying to force his beliefs onto these three women. To force them to deny their God is to violate their religious freedom."

"Are you telling me that God wants this man to die?"

"No, Your Honor. What I'm saying is that God has told them to announce that they were no longer going to be the prophets chosen to give Mr. Jackman a warning about the future. They did not decide not to prophesy. They prayed and asked for guidance which they agree they received."

"Mr. Jackman received no warning from anyone about this attack," the judge remarked.

"That could be because no one received a vision," Stanley suggested. "The prophecies are not self-generated which means none of the women has any control over receiving one."

"I'm going to order Mr. Jackman to remain under protective custody and ask that you present a brief on how his request violates the religious freedom of the three women. Tuesday morning."

After court was adjourned, Robert leaned over. "She gave you an extra two days."

"Yes, she did," Stanley said. "And we're going to need every second."

Chapter 19

"Give us an hour to shower and change," Harriet said as they reached their room on the eleventh floor.

"Or we could just wait until you knock on our door," Hubert offered smiling.

"We'll be ready," Harriet said firmly.

When she entered the room, Harriet took a deep breath. Across the beige carpeted floor, spanning the entire width of the spacious room, the window overlooked the bright lights of the main street of a town already preparing to ward off the coming darkness. The setting sun had painted the sky bright orange with wide irregular bands of yellow.

Harriet didn't take her eyes off the sunset as she laid her boxes on the brocade bedspread and kicked off her shoes.

The carpet felt like soft grass beneath her feet. Claude came up behind her and put his hands around her waist and hugged her.

"A penny for your thoughts," he whispered.

"Are you sure?" she asked.

He knew what she was asking.

"Yes. Are you?"

"You talked with Hubert about me all the way here, she stated as a fact with only a hint of an inquiry buried in it.

"I didn't want to do anything that would dissuade you from marrying me," he replied evenly.

She turned, surprised.

"That was it?"

"What did you think?"

"It…it doesn't matter."

"Maybe you thought that this was moving so fast I couldn't think straight?"

"Yes," she replied.

"It is," he replied staunchly. "I'm trying my darndest to sweep you off your feet before you discover I'm an ordinary man without any special qualities."

"You do know how to turn a phrase," Harriet said kissing him lightly and pulling away. "I'm going to take my shower now."

He let her go. When she left the bathroom door ajar and he heard the shower running, he quickly undressed and entered. The bathroom, like the bedroom, was huge. The shower stall was in a corner with glass on two sides. He watched for a few moments and marveled at lithe body that seemed ageless. He opened the door and taking the soap from her hands he began to wash her.

His touch was gentle and light and again she felt stirrings inside her that she believed belonged to a younger woman. He sensed her rising excitement and wordlessly he took her as the warm water cascaded down upon their union baptizing it with an exquisite joy.

She wanted to protest that she was too old to arouse such passion in a man, but she couldn't reason away the fact that she had. Could he possibly be enjoying this as she was?

Just before he turned off the water, he said in a subdued voice, "You arouse a passion in me that I didn't even know I had."

"I don't understand myself anymore either," she replied.

"Let's dry off and go get married."

"Let's. According to Lydia, you're quite a catch." Claude smiled as he grabbed the towels.

"According to Hubert, you are too," Harriet said. "I'm older, you know."

"I know."

"I may fade fast."

"Well, just try to hang on until we're married and then fade all you want."

"Who would want a rose almost bloomed out when there are so many just opening up?"

"Some roses last a long time in full flower. Some buds never fulfill their promise."

Claude threw down the towels and embraced her one more time. "You are exactly the person I want to spend the rest of my life with."

"Well, since you've erased my last remaining doubt," Harriet said, "let's go. If we're not ready when Hubert gets here, he'll never let us live it down. And we have a lot of years ahead of us."

Claude laughed.

Back in Arborville, Lyle West was telling Aleta that she and Martha were going to be visitorless that night.

"Stanley and your dad are working through the night and probably the whole weekend on the case. They have to file a brief Tuesday morning."

"There's always Grams," Aleta ventured, suspecting that she was unavailable. She assumed that Chief Milani had put her under police protection and confined her to her house.

"Afraid not," Lyle said. "Harriet flew out of town this afternoon to take care of a legal matter. Hubert and Lydia went with her."

"Stanley and I are the Tontine lawyers," Aleta pointed out.

"It was a personal legal matter."

"What personal legal matter?"

"She'll tell you about it when she returns."

"Where'd she go?"

"I can't tell you. Her safety depends on no one knowing."

"Are you telling me that Stanley's parents left town and didn't tell him where they were going?"

"That's correct," Lyle said. "That's the bad news. The good news is that Bertha is fixing a special supper. And Aleta, Wayne said that you can use your hands to feed yourself starting tonight. Lauren and I will bring the food to the hospital tonight. She wants you to see the new outfit she bought for the party at my parent's house as well as her Christmas present from me. I wasn't as creative as she was but..."

"You bought her jewelry," Aleta guessed immediately. "And you're taking her out to show it off. That's creative enough for any woman!"

"Don't worry about us," Martha said. "We'll be fine. It's not as if we're alone."

"We've beefed up the security here and put some at your place to protect Hubbs and Bertha. She's spending the night to care for the pup and get things ready for your party tomorrow."

"Wayne?" Martha asked.

"He's taking Yancey to the same party. Tom and Rachel are going too, so try not to get into any trouble tonight."

"Us?" Aleta said. "I'm worried about Grams. She isn't planning to come back tonight, is she?"

"Not a chance!" Lyle said. "No one has to worry about her tonight."

Martha smiled, but said nothing.

On the eleventh floor of the famous Golden Nugget, Hubert knocked on the door to Claude and Harriet's room. To his surprise it was opened right away.

"You cost me five bucks, you know," Hubert grumbled.

"That'll teach you to try to predict our actions," Harriet grinned.

"Everything's set. First we get your license. I hope one of you has fifty-five bucks because they only take cash."

Lydia chuckled as Claude checked his wallet and Harriet went for her purse.

"I have it," Harriet said.

"I booked a small chapel--and I mean small. It only holds six. For seven thirty," Hubert said. "Photographer will be there and you get twelve photos."

"I have the rings," Lydia added. "And we ordered a bridal bouquet for you and another for me."

"At eight we have dinner reservations and, after that, we can each choose what to do with the rest of our evening," Hubert finished.

"What he means," Lydia explained, "is that we can separate if you'd like. We plan to go dancing."

"No dancing for us," Claude said. "Not tonight."

"Too provocative," Harriet explained. "We aren't in control yet."

Lydia laughed. "Those were Stanley's exact words when he called us during his honeymoon."

"Well, I know why Aleta got pregnant so quickly," Harriet quipped. "She sure rubbed off on me."

Hubert joined in. "She's to blame?"

"Who else?"

"We'll have to drink a toast to Aleta tonight," Hubert said. "She certainly has influenced us all immeasurably."

Before they left the room, Hubert presented the pre-nups and each signed one.

"It's to make my children happy," Claude said as Harriet signed.

"And to put Aleta's mind to rest," Harriet said as Claude signed.

Harriet noticed Claude signed an additional piece of paper which he folded and put into his pocket. She didn't inquire about it. If he wanted her to know, he'd tell her.

The gifts were presented to the Praetzels. Lydia was delighted and immediately replaced the diamond necklace she was wearing with her new ruby necklace. The look of pleasure when she looked in the mirror told the two givers it was a good choice. Then Lydia fastened her necklace around Harriet's neck.

"Something borrowed," she said.

Hubert handed Claude a blue garter. "They sell these by the truckload here for the traditionalists."

As Harriet slipped on the garter, Hubert donned his new jewelry.

"We're all looking grand tonight!"

"Something old," Lydia mumbled.

"Last time I was home, my sister gave me a lace handkerchief that belonged to my mother," Harriet said. "It's in my purse."

"Now we're ready," Lydia said.

The license bureau was near the Golden Nugget and the line was relatively short. The chapel was tiny with a small raised platform with flowers hanging from baskets on each side. The two stood before the minister and repeated simple vows. Rings were exchanged and the wedding kiss was as momentous as their first one.

The two beamed for the photographs and Hubert and Lydia were drawn into most of the shots by the happy couple. The photographer shot several extra shots, hoping to capture the joy he felt in the presence of this older couple. There was something special about them. He wished he could hear their story, but his schedule didn't allow time for that. It was a busy night. He was surprised they were squeezed into the time between two weddings that was so tight it was rarely used.

When he saw the best man pay the minister with a single bill, he realized that it was a large denomination bill as the service generally cost several hundred. He wondered what made these people so anxious to marry on the spur of the moment.

Hubert asked him to deliver the photos before ten to his room. He didn't explain except to say that the newlyweds needed privacy. That the photographer understood.

The newlyweds went back to their room after dinner with the Praetzel's blessing.

"We have plans for our evening," Hubert said. "We'll call you around ten tomorrow morning."

Harriet blushed slightly. It was one thing to be caught up in the unexpected onslaught of passion. It was another to plan to have sexual relations. She was nervous. Suppose they'd ruined things by getting married.

"Don't be surprised to see us wandering around on the strip," Claude said. Harriet was grateful for the out.

They weren't locked in.

"Nothing you two do would surprise me," Hubert said. "Just relax and enjoy yourselves."

Once back in their room, Claude asked. "What would you like to do this evening?"

"Not concentrate on sex," Harriet blurted out, then hurried to explain. "I mean not to plan to have it."

"That works for me," Claude said. "Want to put your flowers in some water?"

"Yes, I do," Harriet said, taken up with the mundane task. She took the water pitcher to the bathroom and filled it with water.

Claude was on the phone ordering room service.

"We just ate," Harriet said, coming into the room.

"I felt like some ice cream," Claude said.

"Hope you ordered some for me."

"Of course."

"What kind?"

"Chocolate, vanilla, strawberry and butter pecan."

"That's a lot of ice cream."

"I was hedging my bet as to what you liked."

"Well, you hit one hundred percent!" she laughed. "I like any ice cream not marred by candy bits. But I can't eat ice cream in this dress."

"Take it off then," Claude said. "There's a robe in the bathroom."

When she returned to the room, she was gratified to see that Claude had only removed his coat and tie. Somehow this comforted her. Still, it looked as if they were going to wait for room service in uncomfortable silence until Harriet remembered she hadn't given Claude the gift she'd bought for him.

She made him close his eyes and hold out his hands. He opened them when she put the box in them.

He looked startled when he saw it was a Rolex.

"I don't treat watches well," he said.

"What do you do to them?"

"I keep taking showers without removing them."

"It's waterproof," Harriet remarked, "and if the Rolex Company says its waterproof, you can dive into a swimming pool or go snorkeling and not damage it."

"What's this?" he said, unrolling a slip of paper.

"That's what the jeweler is going to engrave on the back whenever you can part with it for half a day."

He put on the watch and stared at it. "I've always wanted one, but could never bring myself to buy one."

He rose and drew her towards him.

"Just a thank you kiss. That's all."

As their lips met, she took his hand and slipped it under her robe. She was naked underneath. His hand let her hand guide it. He felt her body quiver at his touch and knew her shyness was a temporary affliction.

Still, he held back. To rush now might bring that reticence back.

"We need to be on equal footing," she said, releasing his hand and drawing away. "There's another robe in the bathroom. Hurry or I'll eat all the ice cream."

"I have a gift for you," he said as he headed for the bathroom. "It's in my coat pocket."

"The paper you signed?" she asked.

"Read it," he said as he disappeared into the bathroom.

Harriet unfolded the single sheet. It was a simple will leaving her half of his entire estate. The remainder he left to his three children.

Harriet could see Hubert's hand in this. Hubert had said repeatedly that simple wills were difficult to break.

"You know I don't need your money," Harriet said when he emerged from the bathroom.

"I know. And I don't need a Rolex either, but I wanted to let you know how important you are to me."

"Well, you certainly did that," Harriet admitted. "You surprised me."

"For once," Claude remarked. "I feel like I'm the only one being constantly surprised."

"Everything about this relationship surprises me," Harriet returned. "I thought this part of my life was over."

"Actually, so did I."

"You've been a widower for almost a year. Surely women have been lining up to get your attention."

"They have. And some quite beautiful and fairly young," he replied. "But no one stirred me the way you did. I thought my ability to love had died along with my wife."

"Well, if today's been any type of measure, I'd say it had merely lapsed into a coma."

"Well, we are both certainly awake again."

Harriet moved toward him and taking his hands guided them both under her robe.

"I don't want to rush you," Claude said. "I can wait until you're ready. And I want you to know that if we never have that kind of sex again, I still want to spend the rest of my life with you."

"Hey, I'm in this tor the sex," Harriet quipped.

"Are you really?"

"Oh, for heaven's sake, Claude," she said pulling his hands around behind her back. "I love you so much I can scarcely think. I joke about the sex because it seems to break down whatever barriers my reason has imposed that this is too fast, too exciting, too wonderful to be real. Every time we join, those doubts disappear. I can't explain it. But whatever the future holds, I'm game. You are an exciting man and I'm ready to enjoy every moment we are given."

The knock on the door startled them both into dropping away from each other.

"We're married," Harriet laughed. "We can be in our room in our bathrobes."

"Where's my money?"

"Just sign the bill and add the tip," Harriet said.

"You aren't the only one addled by this relationship," Claude remarked, heading for the door.

The steward wheeled the cart in and Claude signed the bill. Harriet smirked at her new husband's attempt to be cool, but refrained from voicing her slight embarrassment with a smart joke that would only wound Claude.

She looked at the tray as the steward closed the door. "You ordered cake," she said.

"At weddings they serve cake. It's traditional."

"The cake can wait, but the ice cream can't. Neither can I."

"I can order more ice cream," he said.

"I have a better idea," Harriet said. "We eat the ice cream. You're going to need your strength for the night ahead."

"Is that a threat or a promise?"

"Neither. It's all going to be up to you. After we eat, we'll go to bed and let whatever happens, happen."

"Suppose I fall asleep."

"You won't."

"But what if I did?"

"Eat your ice cream."

"I want an answer."

"You won't. Neither will I. Not until after."

"Hey, don't eat all the butter pecan."

"Hurry up and dig in."

Thirty minutes later as they lay side by side, Claude worried aloud about being able to fill Harriet's desire.

"Relax," she said. "I'm going to sleep. You can wake me anytime you want."

"It won't be until morning," Claude said sleepily.

When he woke her with a kiss several hours later, she asked, "Is it morning?"

"It's the New Year," he whispered.

"How many minutes into the morning," she asked sleepily.

"About three minutes."

"How long have you been waiting for it to be morning," she joshed.

"About twenty," he confessed. "I told you drive me wild."

She rolled over and faced him. "Delicious, isn't it? Let's just enjoy it."

At four he woke her again. That time they ate the cake.

She woke him at six to make a suggestion about telling their children and he kissed her and the children were forgotten.

At eight Hubert called, apologized for waking him and said. "I forgot about the time change. We need to be in the air by nine."

"Honeymoon's should be longer," Claude said. "A man needs some sleep."

"Sorry, old man. That's not going to happen. You can't miss Aleta's party."

"Who's that?" came Harriet's sleepy voice.

"Hubert. He says we need to be airborne in an hour."

"Tell him we'll be ready to go in an hour," Harriet said rising and stretching.

Claude choked out the words as he watched her move gracefully toward the bathroom.

"Order breakfast: toast, eggs, bacon and lots of coffee," she said. "I'll meet you in the shower."

Harriet had barely rinsed her hair when he joined her. "Do we have time?" he asked, knowing if she said no he'd have to linger under cold water after she was done.

"That we have time for," she replied cheerfully. "Shave while I pack, but don't take too long."

He watched her leave and reached for his razor. If he weren't going to meet her family, he wouldn't have taken the extra time to do it well.

When he entered the bedroom, his clothes were neatly laid out on a chair and she was taking the tags off one of her new outfits.

"You have on your nightgown," he observed, surprise coloring his tone. "Did I miss a day somehow?"

"You said you liked the feel of satin," she replied. "I thought you should have the pleasure of removing it at least once."

"You keep surprising me," he said. "I'm certainly glad you're as old as you are. I would never have survived being married to a younger you."

Their lovemaking was not one whit less satisfying than previously. That surprised them both.

"What a wedding night we've had!" Harriet exclaimed as they lay on the bed, spent and fulfilled.

"I would never have believed I could do it that many times."

"Do you think we can last the day?" Harriet asked wryly.

"Only if you keep your clothes on."

The knock on the door electrified them both into action. Claude threw on his robe and let in room service. Harriet noticed that this time, he didn't act cool, he was cool.

At exactly nine, they opened the door and found Hubert raising his hand to knock. He handed them a packet.

"Your photos," he said.

"If ever I marry Harriet again, I'll be sure you're my best man."

"You both look great," Hubert commented. "So you got a good long night's rest after all."

"You've got to be kidding!" Claude exclaimed. "People don't sleep on honeymoons."

"Are you up to flying home? We didn't get in until late and I'm barely awake."

"Stow it!" Claude ordered. "I know you got more sleep than I did."

"If I could fly that monster of yours by myself, I'd tell you to stay here a couple more days. You need a smaller plane."

"I'll buy us one," Harriet said. "We'll need it if you're going to fly back and forth on weekends."

"I'm not flying back and forth on weekends," Claude said. "I'm living with you."

"At my house?" she asked, her surprise coated with hope.

"Where else?"

"What about your job?"

"The quarter's over. I'm resigning."

"When did you decide this?"

"This morning. The satin nightgown did it."

"Did what?"

"Made me resort my priorities. I want to wake up every day beside you, not one morning or two a week."

To his utter amazement, Harriet burst into tears. He embraced her, bewildered.

Hubert smiled at Claude's confusion.

"I'd say you just made her the happiest woman in the world."

"But she's crying."

"Aleta does that too," Hubert commented knowingly. "It always takes Stanley aback. I think it's a family trait."

Chapter 20

Four hours earlier, a bomb exploded in the bedroom of Harriet's new house. Ed and Beatrice, startled awake by the loud noise, called the fire department and rescued the dogs.

The response was quick enough so that only the master bedroom and the two rooms below it were severely damaged. The house, however, was rendered instantly unlivable.

The news hit the airways at six and Les Swekla was at the house an hour later. The police and fire departments had the whole front end cordoned off, but Les told Chief Milani that he was the new CEO at Cook Construction and had originally built the house and Chief Milani told Les he'd be allowed to check the house as soon as the forensic work was finished.

Ed Ornstein invited Les over tor coffee and homemade cinnamon buns and they chatted amiably for an hour. Milani joined them and told them Harriet was returning later that morning.

"The Hepners didn't cross the border into Canada after all," Ed said. "Too many strikes near us. Canada's too far away and the area north of us has had frequent storms."

Milani hesitated telling Ed more but as he sipped his coffee and looked at the blackened remains of the front half of Harriet's house, he decided now was no time to play it close to the chest. West had solicited Ed's help and narrowed the search area before. And West was always careful not to jeopardize the future court case.

"They did something to Hubert Praetzel's plane, the one Harriet flew to Carbondale in," Chief Milani revealed.

"Do you know what?" Ed asked.

"Not yet, but Harriet had a…," Milani hesitated.

"Premonition?" Ed asked not knowing if Les knew she was a prophet.

"Yes, that… So they took another plane home."

"How long was that plane parked?"

"Several days."

"What did West find out?" Ed asked.

"A mechanic worked on the plane."

"Yeah. That figures," Ed remarked. "They gotta be holed up between here and there."

Milani expression asked his question. Ed read him correctly.

"Because they didn't think the trip was too far to make by car," Ed explained. "But they got no relatives down there. None in Indiana or Iowa, neither. Did the cop who was burned give you a clue?"

"I can practically recite his report," Milani said. "It kept coming out of him the same way over and over. He went into the bedroom in the back, the kid's bedroom. He was surprised it still looked like a ten-year-old's bedroom. The kid was in his twenties. He said he would've thought there'd be pictures of girls on his walls, but the walls were plastered with posters of race cars. Old ones, he said. Maybe ten years old. He found the computer disks but he left them so we don't know what they might have told us. We've got nothing."

"The race car posters," Ed probed. "How'd your man know they were ten years old?"

"He's a race car fan."

"The Hepner brothers are in Indianapolis," Ed announced.

"That's a big city and way too far away for us to deal with." Chief Milani remarked.

The men drank their coffee silently, each one thinking his own thoughts.

"Could you find those guys?" Chief Milani asked Ed finally.

"If they're in Indianapolis, I could," Ed stated flatly.

"I'll get back to you," Milani said, rising. "Thanks for breakfast."

After an hour in the air, Hubert said he needed a coffee break.

"You can take one after me," Hubert told Claude as he got up.

"Don't even suggest it! You just bring me back some coffee."

Hubert settled back in his seat, his curiosity aroused. Claude had been reticent about talking about his wedding night.

"Demanding, huh?"

"Her? Not really. Compliant is a better word."

"They why don't you want…"

"To be near her?" Claude asked, looking over his shoulder. He saw Lydia and Harriet engaged in a lively conversation and continued. "She excites me beyond reason."

"Really?"

"I kept waking her up," Claude confessed. "She not only never said no, she… it was the most exciting night of my life and I'm exhausted. My own desires are out of control. I didn't know I even possessed such an ability."

"Compliant huh," Hubert mused. "That's not a term I would ever have applied to Harriet."

"I need more of a honeymoon than just one night."

"Take it then."

"She needs to be with her family, especially Aleta."

"Her family will understand."

"I won't ask her to leave them now."

"I'll get us both some coffee," Hubert said, rising. "At least put on the automatic pilot so I don't feel so guilty."

Claude pressed a button and stretched in his seat.

A few minutes later, a hand presented a cup of coffee on the tray. A second hand, one with a ring matching his own rested on his shoulder. A head came around and he found himself being kissed. It was a short kiss.

"Now, what's this nonsense about you being afraid of me," Harriet purred.

"I'm not afraid of you!"

"Hubert said you were afraid to take a break."

"That is sort of what I said," Claude admitted. "You are the most unsettling woman I've ever met."

Harriet plunked herself down in the copilot's seat. "Why didn't you tell me you wanted a longer honeymoon?"

"Hubert has a big mouth," Claude grumbled.

"Hubert wants us to be happy."

"You have a family that needs you. I don't want to deprive them of your presence. I want them to like me."

"Let's go to the gathering to celebrate Aleta's recovery and take it from there. But I still think a smaller plane isn't a bad idea."

"I like my plane."

"We're rich enough to own two," Harriet said simply. "And we have family scattered all over."

"You have a point."

"Think of it as an investment."

"But not a very good one."

"It depends on whether you're locked into a monetary return only or you realize that there are other values as real as money that owning a second plane will provide."

"You're saying it's an investment in our well-being."

"Nicely put," Harriet said. "Now, tell me what are you planning to do next."

"Besides being married to you which, so far, has proven to be a full-time job."

"You can think about it the rest of the trip," she said rising. "Robert retired. He lasted less than a week before he was back in the game, but at a different pace."

"What about you? You're retired."

"I changed jobs, cut back to just responsibilities for the Tontine Trust."

"Until I met you, I thought I would drop dead teaching."

"Well, you've met me. So deal with it. When our honeymoon's over, you go back to work."

"Is our honeymoon over when this plane lands?"

"Only if you want it to be."

"You know what I want."

"Then go for it!"

Having said that, she left and Hubert took her place in the copilot's chair.

"If you were asked to choose between extending your honeymoon and going to work, what would you choose?" Claude asked.

"I thought you retired."

"So did I."

Chief Milani personally met the plane when it landed at the small private airstrip north of Willow Glen. He climbed on board, and in the privacy of the plane's plush interior, he began to tell them all what had happened that morning.

"My dogs?" the words sprang from Harriet's mouth before he'd finished.

"They're fine. When Aleta heard what had happened she had Beatrice and Ed bring the dogs and their crates to her house. Robert and Stanley set them up in the family room."

Lydia was the first to surmise that Harriet was now without any wardrobe except for the few items she had with her.

"Well, I have my hunting gear and gun," she said calmly. "And a new coat and dress, so I'm okay. How about Jocelyn's stuff? She doesn't have much, but what she has is precious to her."

"Her bedroom is the farthest from yours. Swekla is sending his engineers in tomorrow to check out the stability of the house. It looks as if her belongings will be okay except, of course, for heat and smoke damage. The furnace came on before the fireman arrived and circulated the smoke into every room in the house. Water from the hoses did a lot of damage to the downstairs rooms. The guest bedroom acted as a buffer upstairs."

"Les came so soon?"

"We had breakfast together at Ed's house," Milani said.

"Then he came without being called?"

"He heard it on the news," Milani explained. "He plans to start the restoration as soon as the insurance adjuster finishes his inspection."

"Outstanding!" Harriet exclaimed.

"West and I need to talk with you about hiring Ed to find the Hepner brothers. He figured out they are probably holed up in Indianapolis."

"I'll gladly hire him," Harriet said.

"We don't mean as an individual. Robert said the Tontine should do it."

"That works. The members voted once before to protect our lawyers, who are still Stanley and Aleta, so I have precedent for doing it again."

"Chief West is at Stanley's house," Chief Milani said. "He and I set up some rules which so far no one likes. Lyle suggested the group work it out for us, remembering that we have limited man power what with the rounding up of the homeless and the other investigations going on."

"That'll make interesting dinner table conversation," Hubert commented.

"We'll see if we can't inject a bit of joy into the day," Harriet said.

The drive was relatively short. Harriet could feel Claude's nervousness. She tried to calm him. "You already have Lyle West's approval and Hubert's and Lydia's. You aren't going in as a complete stranger."

He didn't answer. Her assurances did little to quell the rising nausea.

When they arrived at the house, Harriet said, "Let me introduce you, relax and go with my surprise."

"Oh, Harriet," he groaned. "Don't surprise me in front of strangers."

"They're family," Harriet assured him. "And I won't embarrass you."

"Promise?

"Go with the flow."

She took his hand and they followed the Praetzels through the front door. The living room was filled with people.

"There are more than family here," Claude whispered in Harriet's ear. His dismay was obvious.

Harriet stepped up. "Hi, everyone. This is Claude Luther, my husband."

The response was one of shocked silence. No one had expected that.

"We were married yesterday in a little chapel in Las Vegas. Hubert and Lydia stood up for us. I know some of you might be upset because you missed the ceremony, but we brought a piece of it home to share. After we exchanged rings, the minister said 'I now pronounce you man and wife. You may kiss the bride.' That's the part we brought back to share."

She turned to Claude and gazed into his eyes. He looked at her. He felt the same thrill he had that night. So he embraced her and kissed her as fervently as he had at the end of the wedding ceremony in the little chapel in Las Vegas.

When they parted, Lyle West was the first to step up and congratulate them. Robert kissed his mother and hugged her.

"Such wonderful news, Mother! I'm so happy for you!"

Stanley shook Claude's hand and, with genuine warmth, said, "Welcome to the family. I couldn't be happier for both of you."

People made way for Martha Cook who extended her arms. Harriet embraced the older woman as Dr. Chesney shook Claude's hand and congratulated him.

"Are you her grandson?"

Dr. Chesney smiled as he shook his head. "Wayne is tied up at the hospital. I'm Martha's... Martha, what am I?"

"You're the doctor I'm madly in love with."

Laughter dissipated what little tension had lingered. Martha took Harriet's hand and looked at the ring.

"Lovely," she said.

She shook Claude's hand. "Congratulations! I've never seen Harriet so happy."

She looked around. "Aleta, get over here and meet your new grandfather."

The group parted as Bertha pushed Aleta's wheelchair forward. Harriet stepped forward and embraced Bertha. "This is my soon-to-be-daughter-in-law. Bertha. And in the chair is my eldest granddaughter, Aleta Praetzel."

Claude looked down at the bandaged head of the young woman with a face so like her grandmother's it was uncanny.

Both arms were in slings. Noting the recent scars on her head, he realized more completely how much trauma this young woman had been through. No wonder Harriet had been so driven to return.

"You are as beautiful as your grandmother," he said.

Startled by the unexpected compliment, Aleta blurted out, "Hairless."

"Real beauty doesn't need hair. It's etched in the face," Claude returned. "I'd get rid of that bandage as soon as you can though. You have a terrific collection of scars."

Aleta tittered. "I've decided to collect other things. Scars are too expensive."

"Expensive?"

"Doctors charge a fortune for putting them there."

"Dr. Chesney put any there?"

"He's my obstetrician," Aleta said gaily. "You joined the family just in time to be a great-grandfather."

"He'll be my first."

"You said 'he'. Why do you think it's a boy?"

"Isn't it?"

"We don't know yet."

"I do.   It is."

"And if you're wrong?"

"Then I'll eat crow, I guess," Claude said good-naturedly. "Or anything else you choose."

The howls of laughter that greeted that put everyone in a mood for dinner. Harriet was delighted that the entree was duck, the very ones she shot on her wedding day.

Lauren, as usual took charge of the seating.

"No more than three men to a table and no pairs together," she ordered.

It took a while for everyone to sort themselves out because Lauren wouldn't let anyone sit down until every table was mixed properly.

"Is she going to tell us what to talk about too?" Claude asked the short plump man that wound up next to him.

"Ask West. She's his wife," Ed replied.

Lyle smiled. "No comment."

Claude turned back to Ed. "Do you like your work?"

"Sometimes."

"Do you do mostly cheating husband stuff?"

"Nope. I do other investigative work," Ed said. "Sometimes I help the police."

"And he's good at it," Lyle said.

"He helped us get back my stolen books," Bessie put in. "The thief tried to sell them on the internet."

"You collect rare books?" Claude asked.

"Just a few."

"I'd like to see your collection sometime," Claude said.

"Bessie paints," Lyle said. "The painting over the fireplace is hers."

"That fantastic one with the rain sheeting down the window?"

Bessie nodded demurely.

"How did you ever get that effect?"

"An accident," Bessie responded and then told the story.

By the time dessert came, everyone at Claude's table knew why Harriet had chosen him. But it was Lyle who posed the question about why he'd chosen Harriet.

"We all love her," Lyle said. "And we all think she's a gem, but I was there when you met. You were so angry with Hubert because you thought he'd set you up, you were rude to Harriet. So what turned you around?"

"She did," Claude grinned. "And I can't for the life of me figure out how she did. I think I appreciated first her not getting in a huff over my ill-mannered treatment of her when we met. I relaxed when I realized Hubert had brought her along to teach him how to hunt. I thought this was ludicrous until we compared notes at the end of the first session.

After that, she kept surprising me. Her mind, her manner, her ideas, her attitude--there was nothing about her I didn't like."

"But those are the traits of a friend," Ed said perceptively.

"Well, that's the mystery, isn't it? My reason told me this would be a good person to have as a friend." He held up his ring finger. "We chose double bands. One band signifies friendship; the other, love. As for the latter, the heart choses and it doesn't consult the brain at all. I can't explain love, but I did recognize it when it hit me. I loved my late wife dearly, and until I met Harriet, I had no intention of marrying again."

"I understand," Ed said. "Beatrice had that effect on me too."

"Short honeymoon," Lyle commented.

"Oh, it's not over. Harriet says when it's over I have to get a job."

"I thought you just retired," Lyle said.

"I did. And I don't intend to depart from my retirement so quickly which is why as soon as this party is over Harriet and I are leaving to finish our honeymoon."

"Your home in Carbondale may not be safe," Lyle warned.

"I know."

"We don't know how these men are tracking everyone, but we suspect they're using computers," Lyle continued. "They had planted some pretty sophisticated tracking devices on the homeless men they targeted."

"I'll have Harriet leave everything she brought with her when she came to go hunting. We'll only take the new stuff she bought."

"What about her purse?" Ed said.

"She won't like leaving that," Claude said. "But she'll do it."

"I hate to be suspicious, but nobody has been guarding your plane," Lyle said.

"I'm buying a new one--one that I can fly without a copilot. Hubert knows someone selling one. The man will fly it up here this afternoon."

"Where will you be going on your honeymoon?" Lyle asked.

"I'm going to file three flight plans. Right now, I'm the only one who knows which I'll be using."

"Keep it that way," Lyle said. "With Harriet gone, we'll have a better chance of keeping Aleta and Martha safe. But you have to persuade your wife not to contact them. It could be dangerous not only for her, but for them."

"I'll take care of it," Claude promised, pleased to hear Harriet referred to as his wife.

As soon as people began to leave the tables, Claude took Harriet aside. "We need to talk."

She led him into the unfinished bedroom in the back. The only items in the room were boxes of books.

"Robert's law books," Harriet said. "I bet he's forgotten they're here."

"I've arranged to buy a smaller jet this afternoon," Claude said without preamble. "We leave right after the party. Chief West says if we do, that will help him safeguard Aleta and Martha."

"There is that," Harriet said. "Where are we going?"

"Trust me. You'll like our destination. I absolutely guarantee it."

"You know me that well?" she said wryly. "And if you're wrong?"

"I'll eat crow or anything else you decide," he grinned.

Suddenly, she put her arms around his neck and kissed him. "You are the world's most wonderful man!"

He embraced her and kissed her tenderly. "I do adore you."

Then he released her. "You need to strip."

She looked shocked.

"You're kidding!"

He laughed. "I am, but now that I have set the stage. You need to leave everything behind that isn't brand new."

"Not my underwear!"

"The Hepner brothers planted the bomb in your bedroom. Lyle is worried they may have made an intrusion into your bedroom earlier and planted a tracking device in some of your clothes. West believes that's how they knew you'd gone to Carbondale."

"You are serious," Harriet said. "You want me to strip."

"Only if you're wearing garments that aren't new."

"You know I am."

"I wasn't sure. But I had high hopes."

"I'm not going out there without any underwear on," Harriet announced. "In case you hadn't noticed this is a filmy dress."

"The slip is new. No one will know."

"Of course they'll know," Harriet insisted. "I'm wearing panty hose."

"I don't want to take any chances with your life," Claude pleaded.

Suddenly, Harriet began stripping. Claude was caught by surprise. She neatly laid her dress and slip on one box and then deposited her watch, her earrings, her necklace and her bra on another.

Claude came alive when she did that. Then she began to pull off her panty hose.

"I'm not taking a chance with your life, either," she said simply.

When she was done stripping, she turned to begin redressing. Behind her she heard a box moved along the floor toward the door. She was not surprised that as she bent over to pick up her slip to feel his hand on her waist. He turned her toward him and pulled her close.

When Harriet and Claude reentered the living room, Harriet noticed smirks on the faces of both Lyle and Hubert.

"We may be fast, but we aren't that fast!" she quipped. "Hubert, take Claude to see that plane while I buy some clothes."

Harriet handed Lyle her purse and asked if she could take some items in it with like her reading glasses, her cell phone and her credit cards. He said no to all of them and her money as well.

Hubert and Claude excused themselves and left.

When they were driving to the airport, Hubert told Claude about Aleta's wedding promise to Stanley and asked him if Harriet had made a similar promise."

"Not really," Claude said. "She never said obey. All she promised to do was honor me. Considering what just happened, I guess I got a promise."

"When Aleta doesn't want to do something and Stanley orders her to do it, she not only does it, she does it happily."

"Harriet said she would always receive any gift I offered. She considers my part of the sexual exchange a gift."

"She does put a unique spin on things," Hubert remarked, then switched over to discussing what he knew about the plane they were going to see.

Back at the house, Harriet sat down beside Aleta and told her what plans she had made and why.

"Grams, I hardly know him," Aleta said.

"Hubert's known him for years," Harriet said. "He and Lydia can answer more of your questions than I can. They think this is a good match."

"Where will you be? I hate not knowing you're alright."

"Lyle says if we communicate, it could be dangerous for both of us. You just have to believe this is God's plan for me. I do."

As she said the words, she knew they were true.

"Then go," Aleta declared. "Don't worry about Stoney or Keeper or Babe. We'll take good care of them. Of course,

Stanley may have a bit of adjusting to do, but he's getting used to his life being turned upside down."

Harriet turned to Martha. "I hate to be leaving you especially since they're going to put you back in the hospital."

"After what happened at your house, I want my house inspected thoroughly. I don't want to be blown up."

"But you'll be lonely."

Martha grinned. "Bernard says he'll visit me a lot."

"Bernard? You mean Dr. Chesney?"

"None other."

"You're not getting serious?"

"He misses his wife. He needs female company with no agenda. I'm it. Don't worry. My heart still belongs to another."

"Your speech is practically normal again," Harriet commented.

Harriet spotted Stanley and Robert in an earnest conversation with Chief West and decided to join them.

The men stopped arguing when she came near.

"Don't stop on my account," she said. "What's the argument about?"

"We aren't done researching case studies for our brief. We need to return to the office," Stanley said. "And Lyle says we can't."

"Why?"

"Because we've been here for this party and he can't spare the men to search the office and make sure no one's planted a bomb while we were gone."

"Work here," Harriet said. "And use Aleta."

"Grams," Stanley said slightly exasperated, "My law books are at the office."

"What's wrong with Robert's library? It's boxed in the back bedroom."

Stanley and Robert stared at each other.

"I forgot they were here," Robert said.

"And I can help Bertha with Aleta, and Robert can help Bertha with the dogs," Stanley mused aloud.

"Not you?" Harriet teased.

"There are five of them. Three are grown-up."

Harriet's smile broadened. "Dogs do that."

Stanley suddenly realized he was possibly complaining to the wrong person. "Don't worry. Aleta will see that I do things right when Robert goes home."

"Hey, I'm not going very far," Robert said. "You do remember that Jocelyn and I were living at my mother's too, don't you?"

Harriet looked at him questioningly.

"I'm staying in your RV. Jocelyn is staying with Bertha who'll take her to school in the morning. I'll pick her up after school and bring her here so she can ride her horse. When Bertha's done, I'll take them both to her house and, after supper, I'll supervise Jocelyn not doing her homework."

"You mean doing her homework," Harriet corrected.

"There's more 'not doing' than 'doing' with Jocelyn."

"I'm really sorry your things and hers got ruined," Harriet said.

"Jocelyn's ecstatic. She gets to buy a lot of new stuff."

There was a soft knock on the door. Harriet turned.

"Here's my clothier now."

"All he's got is a suitcase." Stanley observed.

"I told him what I wanted and asked him to pack the outfits in a suitcase for me," Harriet replied. "I told him about the fire."

"You aren't going to try them on?" Lyle asked.

"Mother doesn't shop," Robert said.

"Neither does Aleta," Stanley added.

"Shopping is a monumental waste of time," Harriet said. "On top of that there is no time to exchange anything. Besides he has impeccable taste when it comes to what would look good on me."

She left the group and went over to greet the clothier who told her he'd added several blouses he thought she'd look good in.

"I'm sure they will be perfect," Harriet said. "Thank you."

It wasn't until he left, she realized she hadn't asked for underwear.

Not long afterward, Harriet and Claude, under police escort, journeyed to their newly purchased plane.

"It's a honey!" Harriet exclaimed when she first saw it. Eagerly she mounted the stairs and went inside. Claude followed with the suitcases.

"You can go now," Claude told the officers as he was closing the door. "It'll be a while before we take off."

"Chief Milani said we weren't to leave until you were in the air. But take your time."

When the door closed, Harriet smiled at her new husband. "I gather we're going to christen her in our usual fashion."

"Are you in a receptive mood?"

"More than ever."

"You never cease to surprise me."

"Our matching sexual appetites is all part of God's plan for us. I'm not sure I could have been drawn away from Aleta by anything else."

"God's plan?"

"We need privacy. With my house gone, that was taken away, so here we are, leaving at a time of crisis. I think God is telling me it's time that I stepped down as leader and let the younger people try their wings."

"Well, I like this plan really well and if God increased our sex drive then I am truly grateful. Truly, truly grateful."

"Well, knowing you, you won't last until Denver unless we discharge same of that sexual energy now."

"How did you know we were going to Denver?"

"It's late in the day. It's getting dark in the east. Denver is the closest big city west of here that we can make before dark."

"I love a woman who reasons well."

"Then I guess you love me."

"You I love for other reasons."

"Show me."

And he did.

When they were in the air, Harriet asked, "How long are we going to be in Denver?"

"Overnight, only we can sleep in if you want."

"Then where?"

"Buchanan Field in Concord, California."

"I don't know anyone in Concord."

"But they have a huge Hilton there and we have a suite and I've invited Paul and his family to join us for dinner."

"My Paul?"

"I have a Dawn, a James and a William; but no Paul."

"You aren't going to have to eat crow or anything else you don't like after all."

"Don't speak too soon. We still have to see what Aleta's ultrasound shows."

"How often are you right?"

"I always guess a boy."

"Then you're wrong half the time."

"People love it when I'm wrong. They get a kick out of thinking what goop to feed me."

"Now you've surprised me."

"Paul was very nice on the phone. He was shocked, but he warmed up quickly when I told him I planned the visit as a surprise for you."

"He probably wondered why I never mentioned you."

"Not anymore. I told him we met Thursday and I was rude to you because I thought Hubert was setting me up, then on Friday we hunted together and I had to struggle to match your marksmanship so you'd agree to go hunting with me again on Saturday morning. We were married that afternoon and went to Las Vegas to make it legal that night."

"Was it really that quick?"

"I told Paul it was a long courtship and he just laughed," Claude said. "So I said you were a very decisive woman and he agreed."

"You're a decisive man, too."

"You can tell my kids that."

"When do we tell them?"

"When the time is right."

"Okay.

Later that night as they rested side by side in bed,

Harriet took Claude's hand and squeezed it gently. "I feel so safe here with you."

Claude rolled toward her, lifted her hand to his lips and kissed it. "We aren't safe yet. Your enemies are smart and mobile."

"But they have no idea where I am. There are no leaks this time."

"Now that we're safe and been put to pasture is God going to diminish our sexual appetite or my ability?"

Harriet laughed. "That's the strangest approach to lovemaking I do believe I will ever hear."

"You're wearing a nightgown," he commented.

"A satin one," she responded softly.

"Is that an invitation?" he asked, his hand following the curve of her waist.

"It is that, but only that," Harriet murmured softly. "God did not lessen my desire for you if that's what you're asking."

"I was," he whispered. "I know that nothing has changed for me. I feel the same as I did last night."

Harriet chuckled. "I'm glad you made the reservations with Paul for dinner. We're going to be getting a late start tomorrow."

"We have to vacate the room by eleven," Claude mentioned.

"There's always the plane," Harriet observed.

"Evidently God's going to let us enjoy His gift a while longer," Claude murmured.

He leaned over and kissed her tentatively.

Her response told him she was as ready as he was. His next kiss was just as tender but it carried the passion welling up inside of him.

She responded wordlessly, her rising passion matching his.

Their first coupling was a joyous reunion. Their second took place four hours later. Their third erased all worry in both their minds that God's gift was going to be withdrawn.

It wasn't going to happen.

And, Harriet thought, no one knows where we are. She slept soundly between sessions, waking refreshed and unworried each time he caressed her.

There was, however, one circumstance that no one foresaw. Aleta's younger sister Jocelyn and their first cousin, Lettie, were best friends and kept in constant touch via email. As a consequence, when Harriet's house burned down, Jocelyn had used her laptop which she carried with her as if it were a purse to tell Lettie all about it. And when Aleta's party got too dull, she holed up in the bedroom and emailed Lettie the news that they had a new grandfather, Claude Luther.

Lettie emailed that her dad just told her they were all going to meet him the next evening at the Hilton.

Jocelyn, not to be outdone, told her he'd bought a new plane so now he had two.

Lettie emailed that she'd asked her father why they had picked Concord as a meeting place. He'd told her that Grams and Claude were flying into Buchanan Field because the Hilton was nearby.

Jocelyn emailed that no one knew where they'd gone. Claude had kept his destination a big secret.

Lettie replied that her dad told her not to say anything to anyone, and asked Jocelyn just who did her dad think she was going to tell.

Fred Hepner laughed when he read that last exchange. He turned to Sam.

"Us. That's who."

"So what?" Sour Sam said. "They're meeting in California."

Toby turned to their younger brother.

"Fred, see if you can find out what room the newlyweds are staying in at that Hilton,"

"What are you thinking?" Sour Sam asked.

"One of us could fly out there," Toby suggested.

"And shoot her with our finger?" Sam scoffed.

"I can get the gun to California in a day," Toby lisped.

"So who's going?" Sam asked dourly. "I need Fred to keep track of the others."

"Well, you can't go, so I guess that means I'm going." Toby responded.

He turned to Fred. "Fred, bump someone off a flight to San Francisco and put me in his place. Have me pick up the ticket at the counter at the airport. And book me at the Hilton one floor below the Luthers."

"In a minute," Fred said. "The girls are still at it. It seems Martha Cook is going back to the hospital. Same room. Only she'll be alone."

"That means no one will expect a hit," Sam declared. "They all think Aleta Praetzel was our main target."

"We'll do her when I get back," Toby said.

Sam scowled. Toby was taking over the leadership again. He protested on that basis only. "No, we'll time it to coincide with your hit."

To his surprise, after a moment of thought, Toby agreed.

"Good idea!" Toby lisped. "They might beef up the patrols around old lady Cook after they hear about Harriet Locke going down."

Fred turned. "I get to shoot, right?"

Sam replied before Toby could, "I'll hold the elevator."

Toby nodded. "How can he miss from three feet?"

Chapter 21

Back in Arborville, the party long over, Stanley helped Aleta prepare for bed. The only use of her hands she was allowed was turning pages and eating. For everything else, she still needed help. There were movements her reinjured shoulders weren't ready to do.

Dr. Cook had reiterated this when he picked up his grandmother. Bertha hung on every word and he directed most of his words to her knowing she would see his orders were carried out despite protests from anyone, not that Stanley wouldn't comply, but Stanley was involved with the case and when Stanley was involved, he wasn't always as aware of his surroundings as he needed to be.

Aleta was an independent woman who was itching to break free of the restraints he was placing on her. There was just so long a person who was finally feeling close to well would believe such restraints were necessary. Although Aleta was still obeying his orders, in his estimation, she'd about reached the end of her willingness to comply.

When the last guest departed, while Bertha cleaned up, Robert, Stanley and Aleta got to work. The last hour before the end of the party Hubert and Lyle helped Robert and Stanley unpack the books. While doing so each brought up relative cases that came to mind. Lydia joined them and took notes. She added a few cases she thought of and when she mentioned them, the others generated even more references. The brainstorming session meant a long night of work for the three left to look up, study and extract relevant decisions and arguments. It had to be done that night.

It would take Stanley a full day to pull all the substantive background material into a cohesive logical argument. The brief would be long and detailed. In his conclusion, he would be expected to digest and simplify it.

And for Stanley, who had been immersed in child advocacy work since passing the bar, the preparation of a case in constitutional law meant digging deep into his memory banks for all he'd absorbed from his professors. He had no recent experience to draw upon.

To the family, he was the logical advocate, not because he was the most experienced, but because he had the drive and the deep belief in his clients' integrity that would spark his intellectual prowess into full flower.

In recognition of the heaviness of the task at hand, Aleta suppressed all her own desire for love and comfort and poured herself into aiding Stanley in his search through precedent after precedent. It wasn't just those that supported Stanley's position that needed to be explored, all opposing arguments needed to be examined and counter arguments prepared.

As midnight approached, Robert noticed that his daughter seemed to be weakening in her ability to function. He interrupted Stanley and told him to put her to bed.

Stanley woke up to his surroundings. The house was quiet. The dogs were all asleep. Bertha had long since made an extra pot of coffee and left, taking Jocelyn home with her. Stanley vaguely remembered saying goodbye and thanking her.

At least he hoped he'd thanked her. Aleta had proclaimed it was too early for her to retire so he'd promised he'd see she got to bed in an hour. He glanced at his watch. Surely, he hadn't made that promise five hours ago.

"Take your time," Robert said. "We both need a break." And having said that, he stretched out on the couch and closed his eyes.

Stanley had trouble leaving the task he was immersed in. His mind refused not to continue going over the arguments as he slowly helped Aleta change into the pajamas Bertha had laid out for her on the bed.

Both were conscious of the presence of the police contingent patrolling the grounds and knew Aleta needed to be clothed.

Realizing that Stanley hadn't rested at all in the last several days, Aleta decided that he should come to bed with her.

He demurred but she insisted that he take off his pants and lay under the covers beside her until she fell asleep. He decided he could manage that. She was exhausted. Sleep would come quickly. All thought of sexual activity had long since been sublimated to his single-minded focus on the case.

He lay down beside her and her hand come over and rested on his bare hip. He rolled toward her and kissed her tenderly. She was after all the reason he was working so hard. She was the center of his new universe. The lawsuit threatened to hurt her and he had garnered all his skill as litigator to protect that which was more precious to him than life itself.

"I'm glad you're home," he whispered.

As he had turned, her hand had brushed against his penis and her fingers encircled it loosely. When he tried to roll back, her grip tightened. It was as if she had hold of a handle. And in fact, she had. Instinctively, he knew he was being held captive.

He almost laughed aloud at the ludicrousness of the situation. The words 'she held me back' took on new meaning.

He decided to relax until sleep loosened her grip. He closed his eyes. He had to admit her touch was a pleasant one and it relaxed him completely. Later he would remember that as his last thought and have no recollection of falling into a deep sleep.

The opening of the back door and the subsequent yapping of the puppy in the family room woke him. He opened his eyes and saw that it was light outside. His wife's hand was in the same place it had been when he fell asleep.

You little minx, he thought as he lay trying to gather his thoughts.

He remembered Claude taking him aside and saying, almost in a whisper, "Your father told me that you believe that pregnancy has heightened Aleta's sexual desire, but take it from me, it's in the genes."

There hadn't been any time to explore that statement, but, upon reflection, Stanley found that it was complete. No wonder Claude had wanted to spirit Harriet away so quickly.

I could tell you, old man, he thought, there is no hope of taming these women or reining in the desire for them that they arouse. Just be grateful that they appear to have so narrow a focus. Aleta will never look elsewhere, he realized. She would find a new way to overpower him, just as she had last night.

He lay still facing her, afraid to roll over on his back for fear of pulling her shoulder. He leaned closer and kissed her.

She licked her hips but didn't open her eyes.

"Don't tease me," he scolded. "I need to get back to work. Bertha's here. I need to put my pants on."

She lay still. He sighed and kissed her again.

She still didn't move. Her hand stayed in place.

"When are you going to let me go?" he whispered, apprehensive that he would be heard by her father whom he feared was on the other side of the bedroom door.

"Never," she said, opening her eyes and smiling at him.

"Claude says your grandmother is just like you," he said impetuously.

She released him instantly. "Don't say that!"

"You don't want her to enjoy sex?"

"Not at her age."

"When exactly do you plan on giving up enjoying it?"

"Never."

"She has your mind set," he said rolling over before she took hold of him again. "And since I slept half the night, you need to loan me that quirky brain of yours this morning. And tonight I'm going to let Bertha put you to bed early."

"I'd work better with a bit of sex to start my day."

"Aleta!" he gasped. "Your father's in the next room."

"No, he's not."

She pointed out the window. Her father was walking toward the barn, the three Chessies and the pup romping in front of him. He was accompanied by one of Lyle's men.

"Well, Bertha's in the next room."

"No, she's not," Aleta said pointing at a half grown Lab emerging into view. "That's King. Bertha will be right behind."

"I'm half-dressed."

"Well, take off that dirty shirt," she ordered. "You never wear anything two days running. And since you have to take off my pajamas anyway, do that next."

"Then what?"

"We let nature take its course," Aleta grinned.

Stanley began to remove his shirt. There was no sense arguing with Aleta. The sleep had reenergized him. And he knew that once he'd removed Aleta's pajamas, all the desire he'd pushed down into additional energy to prepare the brief would overcome his reason and he'd want to take his wife completely.

He still had a choice, of course. He could turn his back on her, dress and send Bertha in to dress her; but that was a cruelty he wasn't willing to visit upon her.

He bent over and kissed her as he began to undress her. And, as she predicted, nature took over.

When they were done, Aleta told him to shower and dress and let Bertha help her with her bath. Stanley studied her face. She was setting him free without the guilt he would have dragged with him had he denied her.

"You are a most satisfactory husband," she said. "And I'm never letting you go."

He rose quickly and hurried into the bathroom. When he emerged he noticed her pajamas were on the floor.

"Do you want me to help you put your pajamas back on?"

"You mean so Bertha won't know we've had sex?"

"Well, yes."

"She would be disappointed if we didn't."

"What do you mean?"

"She always walks King before she comes."

"Why do you tell me these things?"

"To shake the cobwebs from your brain."

"I don't have any cobwebs."

"Sure you do. And this case needs a fresh approach, not some regurgitated rehash of other men's thinking."

"Is that what you think I do?"

"Not in your child advocacy cases, you don't. But here you're not on such solid ground. You don't trust yourself. You don't need to ingest anything more. Now you need to rethink this case."

Stanley went to the door and yelled, "Robert, are you in the house?"

Robert rushed from the family room.

"Your dad's here too," he called.

"Bring him in here," Stanley shouted.

"Stanley!" Aleta gasped. "I'm not…"

Stanley ran over and pulled up the sheet.

"What's wrong?" Robert asked bursting into the room.

Hubert rushed in on his heels.

"What do you need?" Hubert asked.

The two men saw Aleta in bed and immediately figured she was ill, especially as Stanley was tucking in his shirt as they entered.

"We can't waste time. I need her input and yours right now before her brain takes another holiday and wanders off onto other concerns."

"My brain doesn't wander," Aleta protested. "And I would think better dressed."

"No you don't!" Stanley declared. "You think better under stress than any woman I know."

"Really?" Aleta responded softly, obviously pleased.

"We could wait until she's dressed…," her father began.

"Sit!" Stanley ordered as he stuck another pillow behind Aleta's head allowing her to see those in the room. "Okay, Aleta, tell me again what I need to do."

"Stanley, we're in the bedroom and…"

"…and you're naked under that sheet which embarrasses you but it also frees your mind. You think more clearly in bed than anywhere else. And you are a notch above normal as it is. So let's get down to business. Why do I need to rethink the case?"

"For several reasons. First you need to establish that while we are not members of a recognized religious sect; we are nonetheless a sect, so defined by our ability to prophecy and to do so in tandem. We pray jointly for guidance and interpret it identically without collusion. The latter is important. We have no ulterior motive but are one in our desire to do God's will. We do not deny our prophecies. We do not hide them. We risk our lives to tell them. We expect no reward and in fact, as this lawsuit shows, subject ourselves to censure and ridicule."

She stopped and studied the stunned looks on the faces of the three learned men seated around her bed. Their eyes were fixed on her and their absolute silence told her that they had absorbed every word. Mouths that were open were suddenly closed and all three gulped simultaneously.

"Go on," Hubert said, his voice cracking slightly.

"Second, Jackman is suing the wrong entity. And I use that term exactly. He is filing suit demanding that we produce visions and share them. It is as if a person who has bought a pair of red shoes that she liked is told by the retail store that they no longer carry those shoes because the manufacturer is no longer making them. Jackman is like the man who is suing the retailer for not carrying shoes that the manufacturer is no longer making."

The three men spoke together and Aleta could tell their questions dealt with how we know that there isn't a pair of red shoes in the storeroom that the retailer is unwilling to sell.

"Third," Aleta went on, "there was our announcement that we would no longer prophesy. This is the reason for the suit. It does make it appear that we have a choice. And in truth we have. But only as to what to do when we receive a vision. We have no ability to generate one. And none of us knows when another receives a vision. So the two who did not receive the vision are to suffer just because they are in the class of prophets as defined by the suit. If this is the basis for the lawsuit, then we are being sued as a group and not as individuals. And yet the compensation is being levied against each of us individually. He can't have it both ways. If he is indeed suing us as a group, then my first claim--that we are a religious sect--is validated by his suit and we come under the protection of the first amendment."

"What about the argument that by not prophesying you are doing harm."

"It is our contention that his life and death are in God's hands. Our prophecies do not kill. They can prevent someone from dying if our warnings are heeded."

"Not good enough," Stanley insisted. "If you deny him warning…"

"If God tells us to do that, we do it. In the end it is not what is good or evil in the eyes of men, but what God wants. To obey God is the whole duty of man. That is our belief and under the Constitution we have the right to practice our religion without restriction."

"But if you receive a warning…," Hubert cut in.

That a prophet could refuse to share a warning was still a hurdle he felt Aleta had not satisfactorily addressed.

"There are three parts to this. First the court must declare that we always receive warnings about murders for there to be any proof that we denied to share one."

"They can't do that," Hubert said. "But Jackman might reasonably expect you to receive another warning about his."

"Only if there is a certainty that the Hepners' are going to try again."

"The fact is they did."

"And we didn't warn him," Aleta said. "That's because he didn't die. We don't prophesy near-misses."

"But it proves intent on the part of the brothers."

"But not that God sent a vision. And that's the other part. The court must declare we receive visions of near misses despite the fact that not one of us has ever prophesied about a near miss."

"It's obvious they can't do that either," Hubert admitted.

"That brings us to the third part which is based on three assumptions. The first one is that Mr. Jackman is going to be murdered. The second is that we are going to receive a vision foretelling his murder. The third is that we are going to refuse to warn him. Now just suppose he doesn't die. Are we liable for not envisioning a death that didn't happen? And just suppose none of us receives a vision. Are we liable for that which we did not receive? Finally, if one of us does, in fact, receive such a vision do we not have the right to follow the dictates of our God in that matter? God may, in fact, decide that we should warn Jackman. God may, in fact, tell us what He plans to do and not want us to reveal it. Our announcement was a warning to Mr. Jackman not to depend on our prophecies as a safeguard against death. He is now in the same boat as the rest of us. He doesn't know when or how he's going to die. He knows he has enemies out to kill him. We have those same enemies. None of us, even as prophets, can foresee our own demise. We must be vigilant. It seems to me that it is neither unfair nor unreasonable to tell Mr. Jackman that he too must practice diligence."

Aleta paused. "The basic premise here is that the right to decide cannot be restricted. We have that right. We cannot be punished in advance for something we might or might not do in the case of an event that might or might not happen. The court cannot dictate our decision in advance. It may only pass judgment after the fact."

Hubert stood up. "You did it, Aleta. I'm convinced."

Robert looked at Stanley. "Can we let Aleta get dressed now?"

Stanley rose. "I'll take care of her bath myself. You two know what case law I need. I'll be done in thirty minutes. Right now we will let Aleta's brain go fuzzy."

"My brain does not go fuzzy," Aleta declared.

The two fathers withdrew smiling. They shut the door. As they left, Stanley removed his shirt. He hated getting his clothes wet, so Aleta knew they'd soon both be completely naked. She wondered if thirty minutes would be enough time.

It wasn't.

When thirty minutes came and Stanley didn't appear, the two fathers looked at each other and smiled knowingly. Stanley was never late. But Aleta didn't care about his penchant for being on time. She weighed in all the factors and decided whether or not he needed to be on time.

"It's been a week," Hubert said. "If she's anything like her grandmother."

Robert raised an eyebrow and Hubert stumbled to apologize. "I didn't mean any disrespect. Claude says she's the most exciting woman he's ever met. When I asked him if she was demanding, he said no. He told me she aroused his passion."

"That I do believe Aleta would do just because she's Aleta," her father said. "Poor Stanley. He's in for a wild time of it."

"He loves that about her," Hubert said. "He's never been happier."

"She wasn't so alive with her last boyfriend. No passion at all. I was so glad when her grandmother spirited her away."

"Your wife didn't like Stanley much," Hubert commented.

"Not even after she found out he was rich. That surprised me. But then, she wasn't the wisest of women."

"And Bertha?"

Robert looked behind him. Then he heard her in the laundry room.

"She's a gem--my kind--sweet, pleasant, loving. She's what I need after years of deprivation."

"Does she excite you?"

"When she does, I busy myself with something. I have a long wait, you know."

"I know. I took a lot of cold showers when I was courting Lydia," Hubert confided. "Don't tell Stanley."

"I sometimes wonder how Aleta thinks she was conceived."

"They don't think about it," Robert finished as Bertha passed them. They looked at her and she assumed they wanted more coffee, so she brought it along with a plate of cinnamon buns.

"You read our minds," Robert said warmly.

"Aren't these the last of the batch?" Hubert inquired.

"I have another pan ready to go into the oven when…," Bertha hesitated, then finished. "I need to put them in the oven now. Mr. and Mrs. Praetzel will join you in twenty minutes."

"Thank you," Hubert said with a straight face.

"How do you know?" Robert asked.

"It takes Mr. Praetzel a while to bathe Mrs. Praetzel. He never rushes," Bertha replied then hurried into the kitchen.

"Everything about this argument looks good except the closing," Robert said.

"I think Stanley knows that," Hubert said. "But he has a great mind. And it'll find what he needs."

"He is brilliant," Robert said. "He's gotten me excited about the law again."

"So what area do you think you'll switch to?"

"If I were to apply for a job anywhere, I'd be pigeonholed into tax law. It's where my expertise lies. Stanley is letting me start over. It is such a gift your son has given me.

"Well, neither of you will be able to practice anything exclusively with Aleta in the mix," Hubert predicted.

Twenty minutes later, just as Bertha was pulling the rolls out of the oven, Stanley wheeled Aleta out of the bedroom. The Chessies, who'd been sleeping at the feet of the men seated at the table in the kitchen, rose to greet her.

Bertha looked up.

"Just in time," she remarked. "You two have noses as good as the dogs here."

Robert winked at Hubert.

Then he said, "We think we've pulled all the cases that support the first proposition that the three prophets are a religious group. We found the cases to support the proposition that non-traditional religions are protected to the same degree as traditional, organized religions: Lukumi Babalu Aze vs. City of Hialeah, Frazee vs. Illinois Dept. of Employment Security, and Callahan vs. Woods. Then in U.S. vs. Ballard, we have the decision that the courts will not judge the truth or falsity of any belief in doctrine."

Hubert picked up the cadence. "Supposedly free exercise of religion is protected by the First Amendment from intentional encroachment by the government under all circumstances.

"What about Employment Division vs. Smith?" Stanley asked. "The majority ruled that the free exercise of religion doesn't relieve an individual of the obligation to comply with a valid and neutral law of general applicability on the ground that the law proscribes conduct that his religion prescribes. I don't want to hang my case on the dissenting opinion that free exercise is an affirmative guarantee of the right to participate in religious practices and conduct without impermissible governmental interference even when such conduct conflicts with a neutral, generally applicable law.

"Stop right there!" Hubert said. "What law are our ladies violating?"

"Knowledge of a murder before the fact," Robert said.

"Are we saying all psychics must reveal their predictions or face criminal charges?" Hubert queried. "Because if we aren't, we can't hold these three to that standard. And so far, we haven't demanded that any psychic reveal his predictions or go to jail."

"It goes beyond that," Stanley said. "The government cannot force an individual to express himself contrary to his beliefs. These three women believe that obeying God is more important than life itself. It is not Jackman's belief. He believes his life should supersede their belief that obedience to God is the first order. It is a matter of one man trying to impose his belief on another. That gentlemen is what we argue."

The two men sat back and considered what he said.

"I think you have the telling argument," Hubert said.

"I agree," Robert said. "I think we are ready now to write the brief."

Aleta broke in. "You three can handle this. I need to talk with Martha and get her take on this."

"Tell Lyle," Stanley advised. "He'll see that you're properly escorted."

Dr. Chesney was with Martha when Aleta was wheeled into her hospital room.

"You're just the person Wayne and I need to talk to," Dr. Chesney said.

"Me?" Aleta questioned. "What did I do?"

"It's what we're going to ask you to do," Dr. Chesney said. "You wait here. I need help on this one."

Aleta smiled at Martha. "It must be something big. Any idea what?"

"None," Martha said.

"Before he comes back, I came to tell you that Stanley, with the help of my dad, his dad and me, has put together a great case."

"Now I know I'm in good hands."

"I came to go over a bit of it with you," Aleta said. "If either side loses, the other one will appeal."

"I trust you four."

"I still want you to know what I said that we three believe. They couldn't talk to us as a group, so I was the spokesperson."

"Aleta, don't worry. We all believe in obeying God. That's the whole of our case. I know that's what you said."

Aleta relaxed visibly.

"That's the crux of the case. We believe obeying God is the first order, the prime directive, the belief that supersedes life itself."

"If that's what you told them, then you echoed my thoughts exactly."

"They aren't going to deviate from that idea. Do you think Grams feels that way?"

"Remember when she let you, as she put it, enter the gates of hell because God told her to?"

"She even told me I had to."

"That should tell you where she stands. Obeying God is partly what took her away from your side yesterday. Of course, God sweetened the incentive in the form of a very attractive man, but mostly she went because she believed she was supposed to."

"Her house blew up," Aleta said. "She didn't want Claude hurt."

"All part of the mix. If they hadn't felt compelled to go to Las Vegas to get married, she'd be dead. She said she saw God's hand in all this."

"Did you know that Claude told Stanley's dad that she was compliant?" Aleta confided.

"That's not a term I'd ever have thought anyone would apply to her."

"Except that you and I know it applies to her when it comes to God."

"We're all of us like that. That's why our faith seems so odd to others."

"Do you think this court case…?" Aleta began.

"I don't try to understand God's purpose. But Aleta, whatever the two doctors are going to ask you to do, if God tells you to do it, no matter how hard it is, do it."

"What do you know?"

"Absolutely nothing."

"Where'd that advice come from?"

"It just popped out," Martha said, and then switched topics. "I enjoyed your party yesterday."

"So did I. Lauren really made it work. She has a real knack for that."

"I'll tell her you said that," Lyle said from the doorway.

"Don't you ever knock?" Aleta asked.

"Not when the door is open," he said jovially. "Glad to see you two made it through one more night. Ed is in Indianapolis and he's started his search."

"Where did he start? "

"The places that sell the kinds of rifles the brothers like to use. Remember we have two of their guns in our evidence room."

"We were expecting Dr. Cook and Dr. Chesney," Martha remarked.

"I know. They called me. I'm part of the package."

"What part?"

"The 'protect Aleta' part."

"So what kind of request are the doctors going to make?" Aleta asked.

"Oh, no you don't. It's their request, not mine."

"But you didn't veto it."

"I expect you'll do that and then I'll still be in good standing."

A few minutes later the two doctors arrived. They both pulled up chairs and sat down.

"We have a serious favor to ask you," Dr. Cook said.

Dr. Chesney interjected a correction. "He has a serious favor to ask you."

"Actually, it's not me either," Wayne Cook remarked. "I'm just a messenger. Dr. Taekman is calling in a favor. He'll send over a helicopter to transport you from here to Cook County Hospital at your convenience."

"He has a patient," Aleta guessed, "that can't speak. And he needs a translator."

"Wait," Wayne Cook said. "Don't answer until you hear all of it."

"What's wrong with the patient?" Aleta said.

"It's not what. It's who. The patient is Simon Jackman."

"The Simon Jackman that's suing me?"

"The same. But it's worse," Wayne added.

"How could it be worse?"

"He doesn't want to tell Jackman who he's bringing over."

"Then that's that."

"Not quite," Wayne continued. "It seems his lawyers need to discuss some matters with him and they aren't sure he understands their questions; so they want you to establish his cognitive abilities and they'll take it from there."

"Do the lawyers know I'm the translator?"

"Yes."

"And they see no problem with that?"

"No, because they only need to be sure Simon Jackman can make sound judgments."

"Give me one reason why I should help him?" Aleta challenged.

Lyle rose. "I told you she wouldn't."

"We had to ask," Wayne said.

"You do have a talent no one else has," Dr. Chesney said. "But you have the right to turn someone like this down."

"I know Dr. Taekman will understand. Jackman's your enemy," Cook added.

During the entire exchange, Aleta remained mute. Suddenly, she capitulated. "Tomorrow afternoon. I'll go over tomorrow afternoon. But I want Stanley with me. His lawyers have to get the continuance. Those are my terms."

"And I'm with her too," Lyle interjected firmly. "She comes with not only her lawyer but also her police bodyguard. And I don't stand in the hall. I'm in the room. Those are my terms.

"Wait here," Dr. Cook said. "I'll be right back."

"You're sure, Dear," Martha said after Wayne left. "It's not too late to change your mind."

"As we agreed earlier, obedience is our prime directive."

"Did you get a directive from God?" Dr. Chesney asked.

"Only the same ones we all have gotten. Love your enemies and do unto others. Nothing new. But He's pretty clear on it. If I would go to the side of a friend who needed my help, He expects me to go to the side of an enemy."

"I'm not sure Simon Jackman will be grateful," Dr. Chesney said.

"I'm absolutely sure he won't be," Aleta replied.

Chapter 22

Toby arrived in San Francisco mid-afternoon. Two hours later, he was settled in his room in Concord, one of the cities on the outermost fringe of the East Bay. Concord was fast developing into a city rivaling Berkeley and Oakland as a business hub, hence the relatively new Hilton near a small airport.

Toby was situated one floor below the newlyweds' suite. His packages were delivered to his room at five. He left at six to go to the dining room to eat.

He was sitting at the bar when Harriet and Claude walked in and were shown to a large table at the rear of the restaurant. He turned away as they passed him. He saw Harriet glance at the mirror above the bar and spot his freshly scarred face. He felt that the scar was enough of a disguise, so he hadn't attempted any other.

For some reason he sensed that while she hadn't actually recognized him, her eyes had hesitated briefly when they swept the faces reflected in the mirror above the bar. She might recall why he looked familiar in a moment, an hour, a day or never, but he decided not to give her a second look.

He left immediately, went to his room, ordered room service and began assembling one of the two guns he'd taken apart and shipped to himself in four small packages via an express package delivery service that guaranteed same day delivery.

Toby was ambidextrous and Sam told him he should have two guns just in case she had one.

"It's not Aleta," Toby had protested. "It's her grandmother."

"Well, maybe her new husband will have one," Sour Sam warned. "They're both hunters."

"This isn't a hunting party. They're on their honeymoon," Toby argued. "They're staying at the Hilton, for Pete's sake."

In the end, Toby agreed to pack two guns. One could misfire, he reasoned.

Now, as he was putting the guns together, he realized that he was glad he had two guns. There were two people. He might have to shoot both simultaneously

As they were about to sit down, Harriet asked Claude if he had his gun with him.

"It's in the plane," he said. "But how did you know?"

"When you come back tonight, bring it with you."

"What's wrong?" he asked.

Lyle West had told him not to brush off any hint of apprehension.

"These women have a finely honed sense of danger," Lyle had told Claude. "Stay alert and stay alive."

Harriet replied hesitantly to her husband's query.

"I'm not sure it's anything. I thought I saw someone familiar."

"You used to live in this area," Claude reminded her.

"He wasn't from here."

"How do you know?"

"Wrong clothes. Skin too pale."

"We are at the Hilton. It caters to travelers."

"It's probably nothing," Harriet repeated. "We'll ask Paul. If none of them has talked to anyone, it's probably my imagination."

"I can go get the gun now," Claude offered.

Harriet spotted her family coming into the restaurant.

"No, they're here. I think we're safe here."

As soon as her son and his family were seated, Harriet asked Paul if he had called anyone or told anyone that she and Claude were here. He said he hadn't even told his partners. Paul turned to Andrea.

"Did you call Jayline or anyone?"

She shook her head. "I only told the kids."

"Paul, what about you?" Paul asked his son.

"Mom said she'd kill me if I breathed a word."

"Lettie, did you make any calls?" Harriet asked.

Lettie shook her head.

"Tell any friends at school?"

Another head shake.

Harriet opened her menu, "I guess I'm worried for nothing. No one knows we're here but you four."

Lettie opened her menu and stared at it without seeing the print. Jocelyn knew. As she sat wondering whether to tell her grandmother that she'd told her cousin, she realized she'd be confessing to doing something which wasn't even bad. Jocelyn wouldn't hurt Grams. And she wouldn't tell anyone. They'd agreed. Grams wouldn't be worried about Jocelyn. That was one thing she knew.

"Your grandmother asked you what you want to order, Lettie," her father said.

Lettie tried to read the menu, but the words still didn't compute.

"I'll order last," she said, her eyes on the menu.

"You are last," her father said. "We're waiting for you."

"I can't decide," she said.

"How about spaghetti?" her father asked and Lettie nodded, eyes downcast, glad to no longer be the center of attention.

She looked up and found Claude staring at her. It was as if he could read her thoughts. She didn't like it.

Harriet barely touched on the bomb destroying her house and Lettie was disappointed. She wanted details of the carnage.

"You didn't even look?" the sixteen-year-old asked astounded.

Her tone was accusatory as if her grandmother had a duty to survey the scene.

"It would have been too sad," Harriet responded kindly. "So many things I brought with me from here were in that bedroom and living room. All my photos and books, my antique dresser and the rocking chair I used to sit in to rock Robert and Paul to sleep. The quilt my sister gave me. It had been mine as a child. My mother had stitched it together. It's bad enough I know they're gone. Seeing them charred and blackened or reduced to ashes would have dampened what for Claude and me is a glorious time in our lives."

"At least no one was hurt," Paul said. "Most of all you. The real treasures in our lives were untouched."

Unexpectedly, Harriet burst into tears. Claude put his arm around her. "It's been a difficult time for her, just trying to stay alive."

"What about that magic stuff you do?" Lettie asked.

Harriet dabbed her eyes and managed a smile at her youngest granddaughter. "I see you and Jocelyn still talk to each other."

Lettie nodded, thinking, I could tell her now that she and Jocelyn had discussed the visit, but she decided that what no one knew would be better for her.

Sometimes," she admitted. "But talking costs money so we only get to talk once a week."

She didn't mention the emailing. Her parents didn't know. The girls were afraid if they knew they'd cut off their phone calls. That neither set of parents guessed surprised them.

"They are so yesterday," they would remind each other.

"It's not magic," her grandmother went on. "Aleta and I are prophets."

"That's the word Jocelyn used," Lettie said. "What does it mean?"

"We can foretell certain future events."

"Like when people are going to kill you."

"Unfortunately, not those."

"Then what?"

"When someone is going to be murdered."

"Like you?"

"None of us can foresee our own death. If we're fortunate, we sense danger and can go on the alert. So far that's been enough. Of course, Aleta has been banged around pretty much in the process."

"How is she, by the way?" Paul asked. "We've heard so little from anyone out there lately."

"One reason is that our phones and computers have been tapped into. Nothing we communicate is private. That's why it was so important that none of you contact anyone. We're trying not to leave a trail. It's the only way we can stay safe until these men are caught."

Lettie paled when her grandmother mentioned that the men had invaded the computers.

They wouldn't have tapped into mine, Lettie reasoned. Grown-ups don't do that unless they're your parents. Otherwise they aren't interested in what you're interested in. And besides they don't think you know anything important anyway.

The salads and soup came and Lettie found herself with a salad she didn't want. She frowned at it partly because she didn't remember ordering it and only vaguely remembered her father saying she'd have the salad and milk. She didn't want milk either. She wanted iced tea. Milk was for babies.

The other reason for the frown was that it was possible that her email was being read by same stranger and she didn't like that. The stuff she wrote Jocelyn was private stuff--just between the two of them. She fretted inwardly that her space had been invaded.

Harriet saw the look of consternation on Lettie's face and suggested they might exchange plates if she wished she'd ordered soup. Lettie was too distraught to think about being polite. She just needed to change something. She handed her grandmother her salad and wound up staring into a bowl of clam chowder. It was her favorite.

"Thanks," she managed.

The talk became exciting after that. Harriet talked about Jocelyn and her horse and her buying Sterling for Stanley who couldn't be ridden and how she thought that made him a perfect horse and then Stanley took lessons so he could surprise Aleta at Christmas. She talked about Hubbs and Jezebel and Lettie wanted to go out and visit them all.

"After our honeymoon, when my house is rebuilt, Claude and I will fly out here again and take you and Junior back with us for a visit," Harriet promised.

"Don't you work?" Lettie asked Claude.

"Well, your grandmother says I have to go back to work when our honeymoon is over."

"What do you do?"

"I was a professor of economics."

"Sounds dull."

Claude laughed and Lettie began to like him.

"I agree," he said. "I thought maybe I'd find a new line of work. What would you suggest?"

"Airline pilot would be good. You already know how to fly."

"Any other ideas?"

"You could train dogs. Grams can teach you."

"Now that's a great idea!"

Lettie beamed.

Later, Claude took Paul Junior, Lettie and their mother for a ride in his new plane. Harriet and Paul sat in his car and talked. Harriet told him about everything that had happened. She ended with the wedding.

"I like him, Mom," Paul said. "And except for having these men after you, you seem happy."

"It's like starting life all over again. It's very exciting," Harriet said, then added, "you aren't going to ask me about whose money we bought the plane with, are you?"

"It doesn't matter. Your money is yours. By the way, I'm pleased you helped Robert. Don't think you have to even things out."

"Are you sure? I want to be fair."

"Being fair is unimportant to me. What's important is you helped Robert when he needed it. That's what's important."

Slightly embarrassed by her son's words, Harriet returned to the other monetary considerations. "We each signed a pre-nup. The plane is his. He bought it for us to honeymoon in. He owns a larger one already, but it takes two pilots."

Paul smiled. "And he didn't want to share you."

"That's it in a nutshell."

"I could tell he didn't want to leave you on the ground with me."

"But he did because he knew I wanted to have a good long talk with you. I hate that you're so far away."

"So do I, but you've made quite a life for yourself back there. I don't blame you for returning," Paul remarked, then added a question. "Not to be noisy, but if you're both rich and you trust each other, why the pre-nups?"

"He said his kids would be upset if there were none. He doesn't really want them to know how rich I am."

"They sound a bit greedy."

"I don't think all of them are. I think it's just one. As they're his children, we'll play it his way. Immediately after he signed the pre-nup, he signed a new will. I get half. I told him I didn't need his money and he said I could give it to anyone I chose, but I was his wife and that was the share his late wife said was right so that's what I get too.

"Why are you making him go back to work?"

"Because he needs to. He doesn't know it yet, but he needs some responsibility as balance in his life."

"So he can't just retire and live the good life?"

"He's doing that now. But it will wear thin if there's nothing else."

"Are you sure?"

"I'm always sure."

Paul leaned over and kissed her lightly on the cheek. "Yes, Mother, you are. You aren't always right, but you are always sure you are."

"Are you telling me I'm wrong?"

"I'm telling you to let Claude decide. He's been making a lot of good decisions lately. Don't throw a monkey wrench into the works."

"Is that what I'm doing?"

"He'll do it your way to please you," Paul said. "But wouldn't it be more exciting to let him find his own way?"

"I wanted to spare him any disappointment."

"He doesn't need you to mother him."

"I'm doing that?"

"It's habitual. You've been a mother longer than you were a wife. You need to learn the difference."

Harriet giggled. "And there is a difference."

"Mother!" Paul admonished. "Remember I'm your son. There are certain things I know that I don't need to know."

"Thanks Paul."

"You're welcome, Mother."

Later in the car, Andrea said, "Your mother was glowing."

Paul nodded. "We had a long talk and she was upbeat through all of it. Having Claude in her life has made a big difference."

"You hurried us off a bit soon I thought," Andrea ventured.

"They wanted to be alone," Paul answered.

"Nonsense," Andrea exclaimed. "They may be newlyweds, but they aren't spring chickens."

"You'd be surprised. You'd be really surprised at how often."

"You can't mean what I think you mean."

"Oh, but I do."

"She didn't tell you that!"

"Of course not; but I can read my mother. She said he was the most exciting man she'd ever met."

"He's not exciting," Andrea said. "He's pleasant and I like him, but he's just an ordinary man."

"My take exactly. And mother has met many men both at work and in the field hunting, and she's never said that about any of them."

Lettie leaned forward and burst out, "You mean they're having sex?"

"Lettie!" her mother gasped.

"Oh, Mom, grow up!"

"There are some things people don't talk about in mixed company."

"That's what you and Dad are doing. You're just using adult subterfuge-type lingo."

"They're on their honeymoon," her father said. "It's allowed after marriage."

"Is that why they got married so fast," Lettie probed. "He couldn't keep it in his pants?"

"That's enough!" both her parents yelled.

Lettie sat back. This was too juicy not to tell Jocelyn. Grams was having sex and lots of it. Wow! Talk about a scoop. Who would have thought it?

Back in Arborville, Aleta arrived home from her visit with Martha and found Stanley's secretary typing pages from handwritten sheets of yellow, lined legal paper while Robert and Hubert hung over her shoulder, scrutinizing every word. Stanley was busy writing.

Aleta couldn't bring herself to interrupt the process at so critical a stage. Arguments were like everything else. They could be lost if the mind was distracted by an equally compelling issue. And her visit with Jackman the next day was that kind of issue.

She busied herself petting her pup, a pleasure she'd been denied since he arrived. The pup seemed insatiable. Finally she sat on the couch and when he climbed up beside her, she let him stay and lay his head in her lap. He fell asleep there and Aleta stroked his head gently.

When he woke, she had Bertha accompany her to the barn so she could talk to Hubbs and visit with her horse. Both of the policemen at the door went with them as did all five dogs.

She saw Hubbs' quarters for the first time. Les Swekla had done a remarkable job. The room had the feel of the barn but it was warm and pleasant, the smell of hay was strong and fresh. She saw a bale of hay in one corner and Aleta guessed immediately it served as a chair.

Shadow neighed upon seeing her and she offered him a slice of apple. She then gave one to each of the other horses.

Hubbs was pleased to see her. She was obviously still not fully recovered.

She didn't talk much except to Shadow. Hubbs liked that. Animals needed to be conversed with.

She told Hubbs she'd forgotten to tell him he could ride Shadow if he thought it would help Shadow at all. He replied that he thought it might help now.

"It'd be the next step," he commented.

"And I can't do it yet," she told him. "Let's not wait. You do it."

"Yes, Ma'am," he said. "It'll only be around the barn a bit. Just to get him used to it again."

"He won't throw you?"

"He didn't throw you, now did he?"

"No, he just ran home."

"Well, then if I don't go far, he won't have far to run."

At that juncture, Bertha insisted that Aleta return to the house and rest. Aleta agreed that she was tired. She slept for hours. When she woke at midnight she discovered that the brief was almost finished.

A short time later as Stanley was helping her with her pajamas, she said slyly, "No sex tonight?"

"I'm exhausted."

"I never thought I'd hear you say that," Aleta said calmly. "I guess the honeymoon's over."

"Do you understand the word 'exhausted'?"

"Don't bother with the top then. Just drop your pants and climb in bed."

Stanley took off his trousers and carefully hung them up.

"Can't you just drop your clothes on the floor like normal men?"

"I am normal. I'm a normal man who's neat."

"You said you were exhausted."

"I am."

"You're incorrigible."

"In this area, I am," Stanley returned evenly. She was up to something, but he couldn't figure out what. It had to do with something she wanted him to do on the morrow. Yet, she knew he had a critical court appearance, on her behalf no less. Still, she was going to monkey with it somehow. That's why the blatant push for sex. He always agreed to anything she asked when they were making love. He couldn't understand where his rational mind went during that period, but he knew it went somewhere out of his reach.

He continued to methodically remove his clothes and fold them despite Aleta telling him he was the only man in the world that folded his laundry before it was to be washed.

He donned his pajamas and climbed next to Aleta in bed.

"Move closer," she said, "I want to hold your handle."

He knew exactly what she meant and he considered scooting away, but he didn't. Instead, he kissed her and asked softly, "Why?"

She grabbed hold of his 'handle' and held it tenderly but firmly.

"So you won't leave when I tell you what we're doing tomorrow," she explained.

"I know what I'm doing. I'm going to court and deliver the brief I've poured my soul into preparing. Then I'm going to argue the case."

"No, you're not," Aleta declared. "Jackman's lawyers are going to ask for a continuance."

Her hand kept him next to her. It wasn't really necessary. He wasn't even considering splitting.

"The judge won't grant it."

"Yes, she will. The circumstances are going to be such that she will."

He began to pull back. Her hand held him in place.

"And you know this how?" he asked, his suspicions taking form rapidly.

"Because tomorrow afternoon Jackman has an appointment with an interpreter."

"He can't speak, can he?"

"No."

He tried pulling away. She was ready for him. He gave in and settled back down, betrayed by his own love of that particular part not being injured and by his love for his wife. She could get away with this because she knew she could. He would never hurt her. And she knew he wasn't foolish enough to hurt himself.

"You can't go!" he protested predictably.

"Lyle's okayed it."

"He's not your husband," Stanley maintained.

"You're going with me."

"Are you crazy? Not only do I not want to help Jackman. This could jeopardize our whole case."

"There will be no discussion of the case."

"Why are you there then?"

"So his lawyers can determine whether he is competent to aid in the decisions that need to be made."

"Can't he nod or shake his head?"

"Yes. But they're confused. They want him to explain why he says no to things they know he wants."

"It's dicey, Aleta," Stanley proclaimed.

"That's why you're corning, so I can consult you."

"Why didn't you ask me?"

"Because God told me to go."

"How exactly did He do that?" Stanley challenged. "You can let go now. I'm past the stage where I'll storm out."

The hand stayed in place.

"It's stuck," she said lightly. "Just as surely as you're stuck with me."

"Okay. I'll stay put. Answer the first part of the question."

"The answer is in the conclusion of your brief."

"No, it's not."

"Our faith puts obedience to God above all else--even hatred of our enemies."

"So this is a love-your-enemy sort of thing."

"Well, I pretty much still hate him. It's pretty much a do-unto-others thing."

"You absolutely can't vent your anger tomorrow."

"Don't you wish I had a handle that you could hold onto to hold me in check?"

"Aleta, if our situation were reversed, I know exactly what you'd do to get me to release my hold," he said.

"But you don't."

He leaned over and whispered, "You are such a manipulator."

And then he kissed her. His hand went down and stroked hers and slowly her fingers released him. His exhaustion took a back seat as his passion grew.

What was it Claude said? "It's in the genes."

I'm a lucky man, he thought as he kissed Aleta again. She recognized the second kiss as the beginning and not the end of the most private part of this night.

It felt good to realize that despite the loss of hair, the multiple scars and the injuries that required special handling, he treated her as if she were the most beautiful woman in the world.

At that moment, on the fifth floor of the Concord Hilton, Harriet woke to find herself alone in bed. She listened for the sound of running water and when she didn't hear any, she rose and without putting on a robe walked into the second room of their suite.

There on the couch lay Claude trying to get comfortable.

"What's wrong?" she asked.

"I didn't mean to wake you." he said.

"You didn't. Your absence did."

"I could ask for… well… You're tired and I can't seem to get myself under control when I'm next to you."

She walked over and stood in front of him.

"And who asked you to do that?"

"I feel like such a kid."

"And so do I. Isn't it delicious?"

"Don't stand there like that," he said.

"Like what? I'm just standing."

"Shit!" he exclaimed.

She moved toward him.

"I've never made love on a couch before," she said softly.

"Come here, you! You are the most irresistible woman!"

"Talk about a turn on. Those are words a woman loves to hear.

"Let's try out this couch," Claude suggested. "If we like it we'll know exactly what kind to buy."

"You don't pick a couch for that!" she said as she settled in next to him.

"Poor Stanley," he murmured.

"How'd he get into this?"

"He has years of this ahead," he said putting his arms around her, drawing her closer.

"So, do you."

"At this rate I won't last until the end of the week."

"How much of a wager do you want to put on that?"

"No bet. If I win, I die and can't collect."

"But I might win."

"Then you and I will have had a glorious week," he said. "Scoot over."

"Ouch! What's my head hitting?"

"The gun."

"You put it under the couch cushion."

"I wanted it handy."

"To shoot who--me?"

"The safety's on"

"But it's loaded."

"Of course! What good is an unloaded gun?"

"Put it on the floor."

Claude reached in and extracted the handgun. He dropped it on the floor.

"Push it under."

He did so.

"Satisfied?" he quipped.

"Yes. Now come get your reward," she said softly.

Afterward they talked briefly about moving back to bed but after readjusting themselves slightly, they both fell sound asleep.

At four AM, the sudden onslaught of rain on the large picture window woke Claude. He found that Harriet had moved on top of him. He stroked her gently and she murmured something so softly he couldn't quite make it out.

"It's raining hard," he announced. "We won't be flying anywhere."

She wiggled a bit and then fell asleep again.

"So we can sleep in," he added as he closed his eyes.

Chapter 23

The storm which dropped a heavy load of rainfall on Northern California, Oregon and Washington was the second of two storms. The first had bypassed California and moved over the mountains dropping snow onto Montana and Idaho. It met another storm over the Midwestern states and pelted the Dakotas, Minnesota and Wisconsin with heavy snow, Iowa and Illinois and Indiana with sleet, hail and snow. The roads became frozen ponds. Power lines overcome by the weight of ice and the strong winds dropped to the ground in humble homage to the power of nature.

While Claude was sleeping on the couch, Harriet's weight kept his passion turned down to a slow simmer. He slept with pleasant dreams. When he woke those dreams were a reality. She was real. She was his. His contentment grew each time he woke.

He was sound asleep when a loud knock on the door of his suite, startled him awake and Harriet with him.

She tumbled off her husband onto the floor and lay there trying to think. She turned her head and spotted the gun under the couch. She pulled it out.

Claude meanwhile was pulling on his robe, shouting at the knocker to identify himself.

"Room service," came the call through the door.

"We didn't order room service," Claude shouted back.

"It be a gift," the voice called.

Harriet stood up and looked around. Through the door to the adjoining room she spotted her robe on the bed. Instinct told her not to go for it.

Claude looked through the peephole. He saw a young black man in the hotel uniform. Face and voice matched. Claude lost most of his apprehension.

"Read the card," he demanded nonetheless.

"It say 'Happy Wedding, Grams and Claude.' It be signed, 'Paul' "

Claude didn't know Harriet's sons never called her anything but 'Mother'. He'd heard the term 'Grams' often enough to believe it was the entire family's term for her. Thus, Claude without looking back opened the door. He then stepped back to let the young man roll in the cart. The steward pushed the cart through door, gave it a shove, then ducked sideways and took off down the hall.

Claude stared at the cart rolling into the room. He didn't notice that Harriet was standing beside the couch holding his gun. He did hear the click as Harriet released the safety. He started to turn toward her when a man rose from behind the cart, a gun in each hand.

Toby pointed one gun at Claude and as his eyes swept the room, he locked onto Harriet standing stark naked holding a gun.

"Holy shit!" Toby exclaimed. "Not again."

He then fired both guns.

Claude had begun his leap as the man's head was turning to find Harriet's whereabouts. He wasn't faster than the gun, but he was higher than Toby had calculated. The bullet brought him crashing down; however, when Toby caught Claude's movement out of the corner of his eye, he reacted. His hand swung minutely to the right as he squeezed the trigger. The bullet aimed at Harriet's head, grazed her scalp just above her left ear. Harriet's bullet, however, fired at exactly the same time, hit him in the middle of his forehead.

Toby went down soundlessly. Claude teetered for half a second, then fell on top of him.

Harriet, blood streaming from her head wound, ran to the two fallen men and bent over them as doors opened down the long hallway.

"Call the police," she yelled at the first person venturing into the hall. "Now."

Harriet felt the pulse in the neck of Toby Hepner as Claude rolled away, bleeding profusely.

"Is there a doctor anywhere?" Harriet cried. "Someone call an ambulance."

Quickly, she bent over her husband, untied his belt and yanked it through the loops. His robe fell open; but she ignored that as she tucked the belt around the top of his thigh.

"You're naked," he hissed.

"Don't worry about it," she said as she wrapped the belt around his upper leg and made a simple knot.

"Pull this end," she ordered.

He pulled and, as he did so, she yanked the other end. He let out a howl of pain.

"We stopped the bleeding," she said securing the knot.

"You didn't cut off the circulation to anything important did you?" he quipped.

"You're intact, you old reprobate, you!" she said. "How dare you leap unarmed at a man with a gun."

Harriet felt a robe being slipped over her shoulders.

She put her arms through the armholes and Claude smiled. He might be exposed; but finally, his wife wasn't.

Harriet borrowed a cell phone and punched in a well-remembered number.

"Paul," she started.

Claude put his hand on her arm.

"It's Lettie," he said. "She's emailing Jocelyn is my guess."

"Paul, it's your Mother," Harriet said. "Lettie is emailing Jocelyn and the emails are being monitored."

"Mother, I'm sure…" Paul began.

His mother interrupted him. "Don't let her do it anymore. Please!"

"Mother, are you sure?"

"Claude and I have been shot. We'll be taken to Mt. Diablo Hospital is my guess. It's closest. Can you come?"

"Yes, Mother!" Paul cried. "Yes, of course!"

"Take care of Lettie first."

"Yes. Oh, Mother, I'm so sorry."

"It's important she not tell Jocelyn what's happened. And please, don't contact anyone. Just come."

"Mother, don't worry. I understand--completely."

As he was speaking she heard him open Lettie's bedroom door and say sternly, "Lettie, if you push that send button, you won't ever get out of the shit you're in."

"Oh, Daddy, chill out. It's just Jocelyn," Harriet heard Lettie snap.

The next sound Harriet heard was a loud crash followed by screeching. She guessed that Lettie had just lost her computer. She closed the phone and returned it.

"You were right, Claude," she said. "Lettie may spend the rest of her days in the dog house."

"What'll Paul do?"

"Take away everything she is sure she can't do without--you know, computer, phone, television, music, radio, movies, shopping, snacks."

"All life's essentials, huh?" he quipped as the elevator doors opened and the paramedics rushed toward them.

Back in Illinois in the County Court House, the three hour time difference meant the court day had just begun.

After several minutes after nine, Stanley presented the judge with his brief. Jackman's lawyers asked for a continuance. As Aleta predicted, it was granted.

Concurrently, in Arborville, on the fourth floor of Tri City Hospital, Martha Cook was sitting in front of her hospital room window when a tech came in and told her they'd moved her therapy up an hour. The patient scheduled before her had called the hospital to report that he'd skidded off the road and had one wheel spinning in the ditch.

Martha rose from the chair only to find herself facing a wheelchair.

"I can walk, you know," she announced testily.

"Not yet you can't. A wheelchair is still ordered to take you to and from therapy."

"My grandson did this, I suppose," Martha sighed.

"Yes, Ma'am."

Martha sat in the chair. "He babies me."

"He babies all his patients. And they get well. He's one of our best doctors."

Martha smiled inwardly. She was so proud of Wayne.

As she left the room, both guards fell in step behind the tech.

"You don't need to come," she said. "Nothing's going to happen."

"We have our orders, Ma'am."

"Well, if you must, you must," she sighed again.

As she was ascending to the physical therapy level, in the basement, Sam and Fred Hepner, dressed in hospital garb, entered the service elevator.

"You're sure she's in her room now," Sour Sam asked.

"She has physical therapy at ten," Fred replied. "Where else would she be?"

"Visiting another room," Sam suggested without any conviction.

The elevator stopped and the doors opened. Fred stepped out and hurried to the room across the hall and slipped inside, his gun drawn. Sam held the elevator in place and waited.

Fred stared at the empty bed. She was gone. They'd made it this far on time despite the worsening road conditions and she wasn't in her bed waiting to be killed.

As he stood there undone by her absence, he remembered Sam's comment about her visiting another room. He rushed from the room and signaled to Sam that he was going to look in the next room.

He entered the room and stood stock still and stared with disbelief at the man in the bed. It was Foster Mize, their first target, the man whom he'd tagged as he wandered among the homeless, the man who had disappeared that night but hadn't been listed among the dead and hadn't shown up back at his house. They had read that he'd been hospitalized, but Sam had concluded that the story was a plant. And yet here he was.

Fred raised his gun. He wasn't Martha Cook, but he'd been on their list.

The man in the bed stared at the gun and tried to talk. His words came out a mumbled string of unintelligible words.

Fred listened for a moment, then he realized that maybe Mize knew where Martha was and so he asked him.

More garbled sounds came tumbling out.

"Slower," Fred ordered, "so I can understand you."

The mouth opened again. Suddenly, a small choking sound emerged. The eyes opened wide but no other sound emerged.

"Have it your way," Fred said.

He squeezed the trigger. From three feet away, he didn't miss.

He ran from the room and straight to the elevator as nurses and orderlies began running toward the sound of gunfire. Fred ducked inside the elevator just as the doors were closing. They jiggled open again. Sam hit the close button repeatedly. Within seconds, the elevator responded.

"So you got her," Sam said.

"Not her," Fred said breathing hard. "Foster Mize. In the next room."

"So that's where he's been hiding."

"He looked sick. Couldn't talk very much."

"Doesn't matter," Sam said jovially. "You got one of our targets. Good work, Fred."

As they left the building, Fred asked, "What about Martha Cook?"

When Sam didn't answer, Fred got worried.

"We could go back and check the physical therapy level. No one would expect us to return so fast. I'm game if you are."

"Do you know what just happened?"

"Yeah, I killed Foster Mize," Fred said, puzzled by the question.

"There were no police around at all." Sour Sam remarked.

"They were probably with Martha Cook," Fred explained.

"Mize was unguarded."

"So?"

"So, that means no vision by our ladies. We killed him and not one of the ladies prophesied that we would."

"Maybe they just didn't report it." Fred ventured.

"Which is even better."

"I get it. Either way we can act without interference."

"Now's the time to hit Jackman," Sour Sam proclaimed.

"We don't know our way around Cook County Hospital," Fred commented apprehensively.

"We'll go during visiting hours. Visitors are always getting lost."

Several of Milani's men picked up Stanley and Robert outside the courtroom and drove them back to Stanley's house.

"We aren't going to get to the office ever again, it seems," Stanley remarked.

"Well, at least I get to while away my time with Bertha," Robert said smiling. "It could be worse."

"Breakfast would be nice," Stanley agreed.

"I didn't think you were a breakfast man."

"I wasn't. Aleta has changed that and evidently my stomach likes her regime better than mine."

"Be sure you have lots of kids. Aleta would be too much mother for just one."

"I don't think I'm going to have much voice in the matter. Aleta will probably garner kids around her as she does everything else. We started with one dog and now we have five--granted four of them aren't ours, but that's how many we have. And I agreed to housing Jocelyn's horse and now I have five horses in my barn."

"It's not all Aleta's fault, you know."

"She's contagious. There should be vaccinations for whatever it is she does to people."

"You have a choice, you know," her father said.

"Just wait. She'll rope you into one of her cases as soon as you pass the bar."

"Glad to be part of the team," Robert said gratefully.

"You know if you want to join another firm, I'll give you a sterling recommendation," Stanley said.

"And miss all the fun."

"Isn't that Lyle West's car parked next to my house?"

"Maybe he's early."

"He's never early."

Chapter 24

"It's on all the news channels," Lyle said as soon as the front door opened. "I'm here to give you the real story."

"About what?" Stanley said moving into the house just far enough so Robert could squeeze in beside him.

"Harriet and Claude were in the hotel room early this morning. They opened the door for room service and Toby rushed in, a gun in each hand. He hesitated for a fraction of a second. Harriet did an 'Aleta' and his last words were 'not again'. That tiny hesitation allowed Claude to leap at him. Toby's bullet took him down mid-leap. Harriet says his other gun was aimed right at her head when it went off. She, however, didn't move. Her shot caught Toby right between the eyes. His shot grazed the side of her skull.

"Both are alive?" Robert asked.

"Harriet's wound is minor. It bled a lot so she looked bad. Someone got a video of her like that."

"And Claude?" Stanley asked.

"He's in surgery. The bullet nicked an artery. Harriet used the belt on his bathrobe to make a tourniquet." Lyle went on, "She probably saved his life."

"I sense there's something more," Stanley said.

"It seems Toby caught them before they got dressed."

"So what?" Robert said. "Lots of people wind up in pajamas escaping from burning buildings."

Stanley interjected a note, "When Toby Hepner said 'not again,' he was referring to Harriet pointing a gun at him while completely nude."

"My mother doesn't sleep nude," Robert insisted.

"You mother's on her honeymoon," Stanley put in.

"That part no one got on tape," Chief West said cautiously.

"Thank goodness!" Robert exclaimed.

"What part did they get on tape?" Stanley asked.

"She saw Claude bleeding heavily and immediately went to his aid--naked," Lyle reported.

"And someone filmed that?" Robert gasped in dismay.

"It's playing on all the news stations with the proper squares across well... You know."

"You said Claude had a robe on," Robert said. "Why didn't she...? Oh, hell. I don't even want to know."

"It's hard when it's your mother," Lyle said. "But she saved her husband's life. You've got to agree she came through in a crisis."

"Yeah, I know," Robert said soulfully. "Only why couldn't she have had on a nightgown. Mothers are supposed to wear clothes to bed."

"They're newlyweds," Lyle said.

"Don't remind me," Robert groaned. "I have trouble with that concept as it is."

"There's more," Lyle said.

"How could there be more?" Robert gasped. "You tell me my mother is appearing on all the major networks in her birthday suit. There is nothing more."

"The other two Hepner brothers shot Foster Mize this morning. We think they were after Martha and stumbled into his room and recognized him."

"Who's Foster Mize?" Robert asked.

"One of the first on their target list," Lyle said. "So that brings me to this afternoon's appointment with Simon Jackman. I think it's risky."

"Why are you telling us?" Stanley asked. "It's Aleta's deal."

"Well, I thought maybe you could…," Lyle began.

"Change her mind?" Stanley asked.

"You seem to be able to exert influence over her."

"Only when reason is involved," Stanley replied. "But this is not such a case."

"I don't understand."

"Aleta believes she received a directive from God," Stanley explained.

"Like a vision?"

"More like being reminded of several Biblical passages that provide guidance."

"Can't you re-guide her?"

"Not when she's interpreting the Bible in a reasonable fashion."

"She could get hurt."

"I know. But she doesn't care."

"We could get hurt."

"She cares about that. She won't let us die. That's all I know."

"Mr. Locke, can you persuade her?" Lyle pleaded. "You're her father."

"I haven't been able to change her mind about anything since she was two."

"I need to be re-deputized," Stanley announced.

"It's like baptism," Lyle smiled. "It doesn't wear off. Until I ask for the badge back, you're still sworn to uphold the law, protect and serve."

"I need a gun."

"You planning to shoot someone?"

"There are two of them. You and I are the best marksmen on the force."

"I'll have one for you before we leave."

On the West Coast, Claude had just been moved to his room when the phone rang. Harriet noted he was still a trifle groggy.

"I'll put it on the speaker. I imagine it's one of your children."

"How do they know?"

"We made network TV."

"Really?"

"The footage is of me putting the tourniquet on your leg. I can get the doctor to tell you I probably saved your life."

"I was there, remember?" Claude inserted.

"Vaguely."

Suddenly, Claude gasped.

"I was exposed."

Harriet grinned. "So, My Dear, was I."

"Where was the camera pointing?"

"Not down far enough to get a good view of you," Harriet responded tactfully. "They did, however, capture more of me than I would have liked."

"You...? But you were..."

"Exactly."

"And my kids saw that?"

"Shall we find out?"

Dumbfounded, Claude nodded weakly.

"Hello," Harriet said.

"Is this the bitch that conned my father into marrying him?"

"Well, you have two words wrong in that sentence," Harriet responded coolly.

"What are you an English teacher?" snapped the voice.

"Replace 'bitch' with 'lady' and 'conned' with... I don't know... Claude, what did I do?"

Claude shrugged.

"He's not sure either, but conned is the wrong word."

"We saw you on TV," the voice charged. "What lady would do that?"

"I guess one who was having marital sex with your father. It's difficult to do that fully dressed."

A twinkly laugh was heard. "Give it up, Will. How is Daddy?"

"Recovering nicely," Harriet said.

"Congratulations!" Dawn said. "I'm dying to meet you."

"So am I" came Will's harsh voice. "Although I have a really good idea what you look like."

"Will," Harriet said with a smirk, "they blocked out my best features."

Dawn giggled. "She's got you there, Will."

"Will," Claude said laughing, "give it up. She didn't marry me for my money."

His hint fell on deaf ears.

Will persisted, "Did she sign a pre-nup?"

"Alas, yes. She insisted."

"Good," Will gloated. "So at least she won't leave with all your money."

"If ever she leaves, Will, she'll take my heart, so don't wish for that."

A new masculine voice came on. "Sorry about Will, Dad. He doesn't speak for all of us. Congratulations! Did you really land the real Harriet Locke?"

"Harriet Luther now," came the response from Harriet.

"Dad has talked about you a lot over the years."

"James listens," Claude put in.

"Glad to meet you, James. We kept this a secret because I have enemies."

"Who?"

Claude spoke up. "Will, you have your computer at your elbow. Look up Cook Construction."

"Got it," Will said. "They just named a new CEO. I thought old lady Cook would never step down."

"Martha sent Harriet over to pick her successor and she fired one of the executive vice presidents and he tried to kill her. That's one enemy."

James broke in. "Evidently, she made a good choice. The stock was on a decline, but it taking off right now."

"Les is a good man," Harriet said. "He has integrity and real know-how."

"I thought Mike Carlson would be the new CEO," James said.

"You've done your homework. He was on Martha's short list, but he was arrogant and self-centered.

Claude butted in. "He didn't give Harriet any respect. This woman's got balls."

"Daddy!" Dawn objected. "Women don't have balls. I thought you knew that."

Will butted in, "Who's Harriet Locke?"

"He's a bit slow," Claude said aloud. "And he never listened when I talked economics. James hung on every word."

James answered, "Harriet Locke is one of the most successful investors of our time. She started with--what Harriet?--about twenty-two million--and catapulted that trust into a trust worth over a billion. I understand that even now, after everyone took out a huge hunk of money for non-profit enterprises that the Tontine is at the billion dollar level again."

"Why didn't you tell me this?" Will charged.

"I told you she wasn't after Dad's money."

"But you didn't fill in the details."

"You didn't ask."

"Did Dawn know?" Will charged.

"No. She just figured Dad wouldn't marry any woman who wasn't as great as Mom."

"He's right, Harriet," Dawn said. "I want Dad to be happy and I hear that in his voice. He was in mourning for so long."

"Not as long as I was, my dear," Harriet said.

"Why did you go west?" Will charged. "We're all in the east."

"My son Paul is an architect in San Francisco," Harriet started.

"My choice," Claude said. "I'm sorry you had to find out this way."

"How long have you two known each other?" Dawn asked.

"Forever," Claude replied.

Harriet laughed lightly. "Translated into real terms, about a week. Your father is a very decisive man."

"So is your new stepmother," Claude added. "We knew on the second day..."

Dawn burst in, "Not the first?"

"I was mad on the first day we met. I wouldn't even speak to her."

"Harriet, how did you get over that?" Dawn probed.

"I ignored his tantrum. He was worried I was another blind date. I didn't even know he was single. I went down with friends to hunt."

"You hunt?" Will jibed. "That'll be the day."

"She almost bagged the limit the first day," Claude inserted. "Hubert brought her along to teach him the finer points of duck hunting and he took her with him. Then Hubert's friend who didn't have much luck decided to go with her and her Chessie. It seems Lyle's Lab was giving him dirty looks every time he missed. And, to make a long story less long, I wanted to go out with her, so I offered Avery my guide. And so we had our first date."

"You gave up going out with a man with a trained dog?" Will sneered. His nasty attitude remained intact.

Harriet put her finger on Claude's lips and spoke firmly, "You know, Will, I have a granddaughter who has the same attitude you do. We're a stone's throw from where she lives, but I haven't called her. All my grandchildren have met Claude but her. He's too nice a person to be subjected to that kind of attitude. Be careful we don't decide not to visit you either. We are both of us too old to deal with any more shit. So until you can speak to us with some respect, don't speak to us at all. And, by the way, Stoney holds an AKC Master Hunter's title. He is better trained than any dog you've ever seen."

"Goodbye kids," Claude said. "Dawn, James, you'll see us as soon as I can fly again. These pain pills make it too dangerous for a while. Both of you are welcome to fly out here and spend time with us. We'll pay the fare. Love you. Love you too, Will, but we don't want to see you. Bye."

Harriet hung up the phone.

"That was pretty harsh," she said. "I thought my scolding was enough."

"He doesn't catch on quick. Typical salesman. He doesn't listen except to what will help him make his pitch. I wanted him to know that to offend you is to offend me."

"You are a love."

"What are we going to do now? No more honeymoon."

"I have no intention of having our honeymoon end until we say it's over."

She reached under the sheet and her hand found what she was looking for.

"What are you doing?"

"Just making sure it's still there."

"You could have asked me."

"You checked?"

"Of course, I checked."

"Okay.

"Your hand is still there."

"Just checking to see if it still works. And don't tell me you checked that out."

"We're in a hospital!"

"It still works."

"Now look at what you've done."

"Well, well. The pills didn't affect that any."

"Why did you do that?"

"To keep you from dwelling on Will's attitude and blaming yourself for the man he turned out to be."

"Well, make it go down before a nurse comes in."

"Me? It's attached to you."

"Then roll up the bed."

"Are you sure. It might make you dizzy."

"Just do it!"

Harriet pressed the remote that raised the head of the bed. "You know, I was thinking that maybe while you're lying here trying not to think about me, I'd sign up for flying lessons.

"Don't leave!"

She grinned. "Not today."

"I don't want you to go tomorrow or the next day or the next either."

"Okay, I guess we can watch the news then," Harriet said, picking up the television remote. "Maybe somewhere in the world something happened besides our shoot out."

She clicked on the television and saw herself bending over Claude.

"My God!" Claude gasped.

Harriet looked at him. "I told you…"

"You are a good looking woman!" he finished. "Wow!"

"Well, that's a positive response if ever I heard one," Harriet laughed. "We're never going to live this down, you know."

"Everyone at the university is going to see this," Claude moaned.

"All our grandchildren and their friends."

"Hubert and Lydia."

"We just won't go home," Harriet said.

"Yeah. We'll move to some tropical island that doesn't have cable," Claude decided.

"Okay. Meanwhile should I see if I can find us on another channel?"

"Yeah. Let's do that. We're still on our honeymoon, aren't we?"

"Why do you ask?"

"I don't feel up to looking for a job."

"I've been thinking about that," Harriet said seriously. "And I was wrong."

"Wrong about what?"

"I was wrong to make such a request."

"It was stronger than a request. More like an ultimatum."

"Well, I cancel it, whatever it was."

"What brought this about?"

"Someone asked me why I was deciding for you what would make you happy. And that's not something anyone can decide for someone else."

"So I don't have to get a job?"

"Not ever," Harriet said. "Not ever."

She leaned over and kissed him. "I love you. Just being with you makes me happy.

"You mean if I just lie around and vegetate, you'll be happy."

"You are and I am."

The phone rang. Harriet put it on speaker.

"Grams," Aleta said. "Lyle gave me your phone number after I told him I'd take your advice on a decision I've made."

"What kind of danger are you walking into? He must think it's grave to let you call me?"

"Ed's found the rabbit hole our three brothers have been holed up in. They aren't there right now, so they can't monitor this."

"At least you hope they can't."

"Grams, you've been on TV. Everyone in the whole world knows where you are."

"There is that."

"Around here they're saying you did 'an Aleta'," her granddaughter pushed on. "Evidently I've got a style. Tell me you didn't face him with only a gun in your hands."

"You want me to lie?"

"Claude got hold of a robe," Aleta pointed out.

"His was nearby. Besides I was getting the gun."

"Well, I am proud of you, but won't you please wear a nightgown to bed."

"You don't."

"That's my business!" Aleta huffed.

"Exactly," Harriet replied. "Now what is it you are about to do?"

"Visit Jackman. He can't speak."

"Wouldn't that compromise our case?"

"His lawyers only want to know what his head nods mean," Aleta explained. "Stanley will be there."

"So why's Lyle so worried?"

"The other two brothers tried to get Martha. They got Foster Mize instead."

"I didn't get any vision at all," Harriet said.

"Neither did Martha. Nor did I."

"Strange."

"Lyle's worried our prophetic powers are gone and he doesn't want to take any chances since two of the brothers are still at large."

"Can't the police guard you well enough?"

"It's the Chicago police. They said they'd allow only one man to accompany me. They don't believe there's any real danger. But Stanley will have a badge and a gun. He's still a deputy it seems. I asked for a gun, but Lyle wouldn't give me one."

"So Chief West thinks this is dangerous."

"I think he's right." Aleta went on. "But I think God wants me to go." "

Then go."

"Thanks, Grams," Aleta said. "Sorry about your honeymoon being ruined."

"It's not ruined."

"He's in a hospital bed."

"I can be just as creative as you."

"Grams! Behave yourself!"

"I am. Aren't I, Claude?"

"She's behaving perfectly," Claude said solemnly, then added after winking at his new wife, "sexy, provocative, willing, receptive, exciting and ultimately satisfying--oh, and she's absolutely gorgeous dressed and undressed."

"She has a mind too, you know," Aleta stammered, abashed.

"I've been too busy noticing the rest of her."

"Grams!" Aleta cried obviously distressed.

"Aleta, grow up. Passion isn't the bailiwick of the young."

"But you're a grandmother!"

"Exactly. And how do you think I got to be one."

"Immaculate conception is my theory," Aleta giggled. "I figure it's reserved for Mary and grandmothers."

"Seriously, Aleta. This venture will be dangerous. Please be careful," Harriet cautioned. "Call me when you get back home no matter how late."

Chapter 25

After leaving the Tri City Hospital in Arborville, the brothers traveled to the windy city. Sam insisted that he and Fred breakfast at a diner near Cook County Hospital.

Sam thought they should go in as hospital staff but when he noticed that everyone that came into the diner wore an identification badge, he worried about being stopped in the first twenty steps by some security guard or cop.

Fred worried with him.

"We could snatch a badge off a uniform in the locker room," Fred suggested, "but we need to get home to fix it to use."

"We could get lucky," Sam said.

"Yeah," Fred offered sarcastically. "Real lucky. It'd be just our luck to bump into a guard that knows the badge owner."

"You're right," Sam agreed.

They moved into another diner and ordered a second breakfast. The television news broadcast was on. Sam and Fred were sitting in a booth that had a full view of the screen. Fred almost jumped up when he saw the face of their dead brother flash on the screen. Sam, warned by the opening statement to which Fred had not listened, put his arm around his brother's shoulder and asked the waitress for more coffee.

"Calm down," he hissed. "We can cry later. Do it now and we'll be arrested."

"But it's Toby," he sobbed.

Sam squeezed his shoulder hard.

"Get hold of yourself."

The waitress poured the coffee and asked if she could help.

"It's our dad," Sam said. "He's in the hospital. He was operated on. It doesn't look good."

"Oh, I'm so sorry," the waitress said. "You just stay as long as you like."

"I loved him," Fred said, his voice breaking.

"Fred, don't mess up the story," Sam warned. "We have a job to do."

A young woman slipped into the booth beside them, "I hear you received some bad news about your father."

"That's true," Sam said. "Fred believed it, but I want to see his doctor first. Fred, what's the name of his doctor?"

Fred choked back his sobs and coughed out the name, "Taekman."

"Oh, I know him," the young nurse said. "He's one of the best neurosurgeons on the staff. Who is your father? Maybe I know him."

Before Fred could say something stupid, Sam answered, "Simon Jackman. He was shot in the head by same sons-of-bitches who think he owes them."

"Well, I don't know him personally, but I hear he's going to pull through."

Sam shook Fred. "Snap out of it. He's gonna make it."

Fred swallowed his grief and stared at the young nurse.

"Really?

"In fact, he's having a special visitor today. They're bringing her in by helicopter from Arborville. Some friend of Dr. Taekman's."

"Do you know who?" Sam asked. "We weren't told about it."

"I guess she's here to interpret his wishes to his lawyers.

"Oh, yes, the case," Sam said. "I was hoping it was another specialist."

"Well, she is sorta. I hear she can interpret the mumblings of stroke victims," the nurse said, chatting on since the two men appeared to be listening intently. "We aren't allowed to see her in action. Just security on the floor while she's here."

"When's she coming?"

"One o'clock."

"Just before visiting hours," Sam said. "I wish we could be there."

"Why don't you ask Dr. Taekman? I'm sure he'll let you come."

"Fred, let's go and see about that."

"Yeah, sure," Fred mumbled, getting up. He was having a hard time playing this game now that Toby was gone. It was fun with the three of them.

Once outside Sam began talking to him earnestly. "You've got to pull yourself together. I need you."

"Toby's dead," Fred said. "I'm not interested anymore. I just want to go home."

"You don't want to get back at the woman who killed him?"

"She's in California," he retorted.

"But her granddaughter's not," Sam said. "In fact, at one o'clock she's coming to us. All we have to do is be there."

"What the hell are you talking about?"

"The woman coming in by chopper. Who needs police guards right now? Right after we bumped off old man Mize and were a hair's breadth away from taking out Martha Cook? Who?"

Fred scowled angrily.

"I don't know and I don't care!"

"Aleta Praetzel!" Sam spit out triumphantly. "Maybe we can't kill her, but we can hurt her like she hurt us."

"She'll see us coming."

"You didn't listen to the commentators did you?"

"I didn't care what they said. They don't know the whole story."

"The reporter I listened to said he wondered if the ladies had lost their prophetic powers. They didn't prophesy about Foster Mize. They had the first time. Why not this time? That's the question he kept asking."

"Toby did hit her in the head," Fred said.

Sam couldn't follow his reasoning so he went on with his argument. "We gotta go ahead with the plan or Toby would've died for nothing.

"I get to do Aleta Praetzel," Fred determined.

"She's all yours. So is Jackman. You get to do it for Toby.

"Yeah," Fred said. "What's the plan?"

Back in Willow Glen, Stanley had just finished his late breakfast. Aleta called her meal lunch.

"Let me help you get dressed a bit early, Stanley suggested.

"You want to talk me out of going to see Jackman, don't you?"

"Yes, I do," Stanley said.

Robert pushed back his chair. "Bertha you want to walk the dogs with me?

"Yes, Sir," Bertha said politely; taking off her apron and reaching for her coat. "Now would be a good time."

Stanley and Aleta watched the pair through the large living room window. Robert's arm slowly encircled Bertha's waist and she leaned into him as they walked. Their steps got slower and slower until they stopped. A kiss followed.

"Don't they know we can see them?" Aleta said softly as Stanley's arm circled her waist.

"I think they think we're busy."

"Did you put a bug in my dad's ear?"

"No. He took advantage of the situation on his own."

"Are you planning to make love to me?"

"Would it help change your mind?"

"Probably not."

"Probably?" he queried. "I'll take probably as a chance."

"What would you have tried if I'd said definitely not?"

"We would have sat here and watched the snow fall."

"And what are we going to do?"

"Watch the snow fall, but from our bedroom."

"You probably aren't going to be successful."

"But I'm going to have fun trying."

"You love me even when I'm obstinate."

Stanley scooped her up and carried her to the bedroom. He laid her gently on the bed and closed the door.

Stanley knew she was going into a hostile environment. She needed to walk in confident in his love. Past experience had indicated that making love to her before a tough situation buoyed her up. He couldn't believe Jackman wasn't going to be nasty.

Aleta smiled timidly at him as he approached and he realized how much she needed to be loved right now. She was defying everyone to do what she felt was God's will.

And it well could be, he thought.

"Ladies choice," he said.

"What does that mean?"

"Anything you want," Stanley reiterated.

"Anything?" Aleta questioned.

"I want you to forget Jackman," Stanley said." I don't want you trying to quell your anger beforehand."

"But I could say things I shouldn't."

"First of all, Aleta, you're a lawyer. You don't need me except as someone to turn to when you're trying to think."

"I'm so angry right now."

"Well, I can't believe God isn't as well. He could have chosen a milder-mannered representative but He chose you."

"Why are we making love right now?"

"Because…"

"Don't take off your clothes."

"That's what you want?"

"Yes," Aleta said decisively.

"You've got it."

"They'll get rumpled," she reminded him.

"I'll change after."

"I'm not taking back my request just because you're willing you know."

"I know."

"How do you know?"

"Because this is a once in a lifetime offer and you won't let it pass by."

"How well you know me," she replied lightly. "My clothes, however, you can remove."

And he did.

Meanwhile in the Cook County Hospital parking garage, inside their van, Sam was checking out their new Tasers. "Advanced Taser M-18," he read, "utilizes compressed nitrogen to shoot two small probes up to 15 feet."

"Yeah," Fred said. "And it'll send the charge through two inches of clothes. Toby said these would do the job."

"How long will they be out?"

"Who cares?" Fred said. "When we shoot the guards, we're gonna tie them up anyway."

"I guess we can see how long it takes them to come to." "Just remember I'm as big as you," Fred said querulously. "I'm a size 42 too."

"Gotcha. Two 42's coming up."

Sam got out and put up the hood of the van and pretended to be checking under the hood for trouble. The first guard to emerge from the hospital passed right by with scarcely a glance. Sam shot him in the leg. He fell instantly.

Fred opened the side door and hauled the unconscious guard inside the van. He began stripping the clothes off him. When he'd finished removing all but his underwear, he taped the unconscious man's mouth shut, then his eyes. Finally, he secured his arms and legs.

He pushed him into the back corner of the van just as Sam opened the door and called for help. His shoulders wouldn't let him even move the guy who was lying on the ground near the van. Fred leaped out of the van to and dragged the comatose security guard into the van. This one was bigger than the last one and he struggled to get him through the door. Sam went back to the front of the van while Fred undressed the second man and bound him.

After both had changed, they checked the guards' guns.

"This one's dirty," Fred said. "It could misfire."

"Take yours," Sam said.

He looked back at the two men. Neither was moving.

"The Taser works," he announced. "Reload this one and check the other one."

"What do we do about these two?"

"Cover them with the tarp," Sam said.

"Suppose we want to get away fast?" Fred asked. "We can't take them with us."

"You got a better idea?"

"Yeah, we hide them now." Fred said. "And I know where."

"The chopper arrives at one." Sam warned.

"When do we go?"

"When the chopper approaches."

"Won't that be too late?"

"We can't afford to be early," Sam said.

"Then we got time," Fred told him. "Stop worrying."

The same words were being spoken in the front hall of the Praetzel house as Stanley fastened Aleta's cloak.

"Stop worrying," he said. "If he's too nasty, we will leave."

"Remember," Lyle said. "We both stay on the same side of the room."

"Why?" Aleta asked.

"Crossfire," Stanley replied calmly.

He folded the wheelchair and Aleta frowned in dismay.

"You're not taking that."

"You could get bumped," Stanley said. "And you can't afford another injury."

"My legs are fine," Aleta muttered. "I really don't need a wheelchair."

Stanley turned her toward him and kissed her lightly. "Aleta, you look like a person who needs a wheelchair, so it's not going to look odd."

"Are you going to order me to ride in it?"

"If that's what it takes," Stanley said firmly.

"That's what it's going to take."

"Then it's an order."

"So you're back to normal," Aleta commented.

Lyle looked at Stanley askance.

"Don't worry about it. I'm not going to explain."

"Are you up for this?" Lyle asked, worried.

"Don't worry, Lyle," Aleta responded gaily. "For an hour today Stanley let me hand out the orders. But that's over. I was just hoping I could push for one more thing."

"It's for your own protection," Lyle said.

"I know," Aleta said. "I'm ready, let's go."

The sound of the approaching helicopter brought both Hepner brothers out of the van. They passed through the security contingent easily after Sam announced that they were on extra duty on the fourth floor.

Sam headed for the stairs.

When they got to the fourth floor, Sam worried they might have beat the chopper group to the room and told Fred they would wait at the door for another five minutes before moving down the hall.

The Hepner brothers hadn't arrived early. Aleta had already been wheeled into the room.

Dr. Taekman left his patient's side and came over to greet her. His face showed his pleasure at seeing her.

"I see you're obeying orders," he said. "You're looking well."

"You did a good job," Aleta said, relaxing in his obvious delight that she came. "I owe you a lot more than this."

Lyle looked around. There were two guards posted out of sight at the door. As one entered the room, there was a short hallway that led past the bathroom. One had to turn the corner to see the bed and the man in it. Lyle made all three lawyers move to the far side in front of the window. He had Stanley wheel Aleta to Mr. Jackman's right. Stanley and he positioned themselves between her and the hall opening. Dr. Taekman stood in the corner next to both patients.

Simon Jackman watched the young woman being wheeled into his room. He stared at her bandaged head and saw that each arm was in a sling. Her obvious injuries didn't soften his attitude one whit.

This was his enemy and as soon as he had her attention, he was going to vent his wrath fully. He didn't really believe she would be able to understand him; but that didn't matter. The force of his fury would carry his message. When he was done, his silly lawyers would stop asking him if he wanted to settle. Settle? He wanted his day in court. He wanted to accuse her before the world. If she had told him he was going to be shot, he wouldn't have left the house and he wouldn't be lying paralyzed and unable to speak clearly.

She was going to answer for this. She let those bastards blackmail her into silence. She needed to pay for not doing her duty. Since when was a horse more valuable than a man? He had her by the balls and he knew it. If these stupid lawyers would just do their job, he'd have his revenge.

Dr. Taekman said this woman could understand people when no one else could. Well, he wasn't giving her the satisfaction. Even if she understood a word, he wasn't going to acknowledge it. His lawyers could figure it out themselves if they put their minds to it.

Aleta's voice was sharp and authoritative. She spoke before he'd gathered himself.

"You don't like me much," she said. "I believe you even hate me. You can nod so your lawyers know you can hear."

Without meaning to comply, he did so. Did the stupid lawyers think he was deaf? That would explain their shouting at him. Good God, what else did they think?

"They're still not sure you can hear, so let me try something you will shake no to. Do you want them to drop the case?"

His head shake was vigorous.

"Okay, so you can nod and shake your head and you can hear, so why are you confusing them?"

Aleta listened intently as a barrage of obviously emotional loaded mutterings poured out of Jackman's mouth.

Most of it sounded like gurgling to his lawyers. They shook their heads. They couldn't believe anyone could understand what he was saying.

Aleta listened intently and then turned to Dr. Taekman and said politely. "Please tell him to stop swearing. I won't repeat the swear words even though I can. And one term in particular he is not to use again."

A short outburst was followed by Aleta saying calmly, "That one!"

Dr. Taekman turned to Jackman. "You heard the lady. No swearing.

"Thank you, Dr. Taekman," Aleta said.

One of his lawyers popped up. "You're guessing."

"And you are who?" Aleta asked.

"Martin Zolinger," carne the reply.

"Ask a question you've gotten a confusing answer to."

Zolinger looked at the two senior men. They nodded. He cleared his throat and asked, "Mr. Jackman, why do you shake your head on questions we know you want to say yes to?"

Aleta spoke before Jackman started to speak. "I'm sure you don't want anyone to believe I can understand you and you're thinking about shaking your head when I repeat your words. If you call me a liar I'm out of here."

Jackman decided to give her an honest answer. There was no way she'd get it right and he'd shake his head and she'd be gone. Now that his stupid lawyers knew he could hear, he was sure they could communicate without her.

When he finished, Aleta commented. "I'm surprised they didn't figure that out on their own."

"What did he say?" Zolinger pressed. "We don't need your damn comments."

Aleta turned on him with fire in her eyes and steel in her voice. "Counselor, you will treat me with the respect I deserve. And ditch that arrogant air of yours. I gather you've been the main questioner."

"Please," Jules Barre, the gray-haired senior member said politely. "Tell us what Mr. Jackman said."

"He said you ask complex questions only part of which he can agree with. If you're confused, it's because you don't break them down into their simplest components; but instead asked the question with a new twist. You forget how limited his answers are."

Mr. Barre spoke directly to Mr. Jackman, "I apologize, Sir, for our obtuseness. It won't happen again."

Simon Jackman let out a barrage of words replete with anger that startled Aleta. She had expected a response to Mr. Barre. Instead she was castigated soundly for him being in such a state. How dare she come into his room and add insult to injury by ordering him and his lawyers around. She wasn't worthy to be a rug for him to wipe his feet an. He used the phrase to describe her that was foul to her ears, then laughed saying he could call her that because no one could understand him but her.

"You're so wrong," Aleta said, her anger rising to meet his. "God understands your words. Who do you think interprets them for me?"

"I don't believe in God," he retorted.

Aleta interpreted his words complete with the anger with which they were spoken and then let her own anger color her response, pausing so there was no question who's words were being spoken.

"I know," Aleta said. "Still He sent me."

"That's proselyting garbage."

"But I don't want you in heaven with me. I want you to rot in hell!"

The words were forcefully spoken and everyone's attention was riveted on the exchange. Thus Fred and Sam, having quietly dispatched the two guards at the door, entered the room unnoticed. Aleta, ruing her angry outburst, turned to ask Stanley to stop her before she said too much.

She spotted the two uniformed officers and would have granted them no more than a glance were it not that each one had a drawn gun in each hand. Her reason told her there was no danger inside the room. Her reason also told her there was no reason to fear a cop. But her instinct knew better.

Instinct drew her out of her wheelchair, her eyes staring as if at a television screen. Lyle and Stanley followed her gaze. When they spotted the two pseudo officers with their guns leveled at Jackman and the group to the left of the bed, both Lyle and Stanley fired.

Their guns fired only a fraction of a second after Fred's, but Aleta's arm was thrust out in front of Jackman a fraction of a second before the bullet that was aimed at Jackman's head was discharged from Fred's gun. It hit Aleta's arm instead.

She screamed when she was hit and fell across Jackman.

The shot from Fred's second gun was aimed at the group to his left. Sam had told him to fire low and his second shot hit Stanley in the thigh. It brought him down instantly.

Sam came in behind Fred and fired two Tasers at the lawyers on the other side of the bed. The youngest lawyer had seen the men coming through the short passageway from the outside door into the room with their guns drawn and was already dropping to the floor when the exchange of bullets took place. The Taser guns took out the two lawyers left standing.

Stanley's first shot had knocked one gun from Fred's hand; Lyle's first shot was to the shoulder nearest him and it pushed Fred backward into Sam. Fred steadied himself and leveled his second gun at Lyle. Stanley shot from the floor at the same minute Lyle shot from his position in front of the doctor.

Both bullets hit their target. Fred collapsed instantly. Sam's arms failed him when he tried to drag his brother from the room and he dropped him after a few feet.

Lyle started to follow when Aleta yelled, "No, Lyle. No!"

He stopped dead and stared at the woman lying on top of the patient on the bed. "Tell me you saw something."

Aleta nodded. "I did. He killed you and still got away."

Dr. Taekman moved forward and struggled to help Aleta off Jackman. She dared not use her injured shoulders to push herself up from the bed, so she couldn't help. Lyle, seeing this, carne back and added his strength to the process. He straddled Stanley lying in a heap on the floor groaning. When Lyle finished helping Aleta, he bent over coughing.

"Sorry," he apologized. "Dry throat."

When Aleta was settled in her wheelchair, Dr. Taekman bent over and examined Stanley.

Matt Zolinger pushed himself up and shouted at Lyle," Why didn't you go after him?"

"I was advised not to," Lyle responded calmly.

"By that nut!" Zolinger screamed.

"By the woman brave enough, sharp enough and fast enough to save your client's life. And probably yours as well."

"Mine?" Zolinger scoffed. "Don't give her credit where credit's not due. They were going to take us down with Tasers."

"Are you sure? They shot Stanley and Aleta."

"But not me," Zolinger said, a bit less certain. "They had no reason to shoot me."

"You're trying to get Aleta to predict their hits," Lyle reminded him with a cough.

The bluster faded completely. Zolinger looked at his comatose fellow lawyers. "You guys don't know how lucky you are."

"How is he?" Lyle asked Dr. Taekman who had turned from examining Stanley to looking at Aleta's wound.

"I think the bullet is pressing on a nerve. The sooner I operate on the leg, the less damage it will inflict."

"I want to take these two back to Tri City Hospital to recuperate. Is that possible?" Chief West asked.

"If you're willing to wait until I think they're stable enough to transport and Dr. Cook is there to meet them."

"I can have Dr. Cook here in thirty minutes," Lyle coughed.

"If he gets here in twenty, he can assist me with the leg."

Lyle spoke into his radio. "French, get Dr. Cook into a chopper and over to Cook County Hospital ASAP. Tell him he's going to assist Taekman in operating on Stanley Praetzel."

"Are you sending the chopper?"

"No time. Use the police chopper. And send me a couple men in full riot gear. Aleta was shot too."

"I'm on it."

"Arm them with Tasers," West said, coughing lightly.

"Yes Sir."

As French rushed downstairs to select the men, he realized he had only one experienced man at the station. He told dispatch to call someone at the hospital to get Dr. Cook ready to be transported to Cook County Hospital and to tell him both Praetzels had been shot.

Justin Conway jumped up. "Can I tag along?"

"No," French said. "Derrick, you're with me. Full riot gear and Tasers."

"I'll just go in the news chopper," Justin said. "But they'll insist on a cameraman coming with me."

"Sorry, I can't," French said.

"Check with Chief West. He owes me."

"If you're lying to me, you'll regret it."

Justin held up his hand. "I'm not. Honest."

"You wear a vest," French said.

Ten minutes later the chopper was in the air.

"Any idea why I'm being called in?" Dr. Cook asked. "I'm not a specialist."

"Don't know, Doc," Lieutenant French said, "but Chief West never does anything without a reason."

Dr. Cook looked at the tall black reporter. "Justin you look formidable. Have you joined the force?"

"No, Doc. Once in a while the police protect us reporters too."

"How'd you manage to hook a ride on this junket?"

"West owes me."

"He never owes anyone."

"He owes me," Justin stated with conviction. "They all do."

"You must've done them one hellava favor."

"I did."

"I sure like your articles," Cook commented. "You have a readable style."

Cook was escorted immediately to the scrub room. "Glad you made it, Wayne," Dr. Taekman said.

"Michael, why am I here? I'm no specialist."

"I thought you'd like a bit of drama in your life."

"I do," Wayne said, "but I want the Praetzels' to have the best."

"I am the best."

"I mean the best team."

"We are," Taekman said. "I wouldn't have called you otherwise. Stanley insisted on a spinal."

"Is he afraid you'll cut off his leg?"

"He says he needs to stay sharp. He's still planning on appearing in court tomorrow."

"You didn't tell him that wasn't going to happen?"

"That's the other reason you're here. I'm no match for him. I'm leaving his after care in your capable hands."

"Gee, thanks."

"Chief West insists they be taken back to Arborville tonight."

"What about Aleta?"

"Bullet in the arm. We do her next."

"She's waiting?"

"She insisted no one could touch her until Stanley was okay."

"And you let her boss you?"

"I want to do her. She's fun

Chief West scowled at Justin Conway who was quick to remind him that he owed him.

Then Justin added, "Aleta likes me. Let me get her side. She could use a friend in the press after this gets out."

Thus it was that Justin Conway wound up in pre-op talking to Aleta. The nurse frowned but as families were allowed and a police chief walked the black reporter in, no verbal protests were made.

After Aleta said it was okay, Lyle left the two. A spasm of coughing hit him as the door closed behind him and he wished he had a cough drop.

French was standing guard on the other side of the curtain in pre-op. He heard West coughing, but he didn't dare leave his post. The chief had been coughing a lot lately. He figured he'd say something when this was over.

Derrick was stationed outside the operating room. He took a bit of ribbing from the Chicago cop stationed with him, but he reminded him that two Chicago cops had been taken out by Tasers and it was the Arborville police who saved the intended victim. After that, the ribbing stopped and the cop wondered why, after a shooting, he wasn't in riot gear as well. His sergeant told him the perp was long gone and his duty was a formality.

Derrick, however, proud of his chief's actions, paid no heed to the alternative view. Men on his force had misjudged these particular brothers before and been embarrassed.

French had the same attitude. No one had seen the man leave. There were still two missing men whose uniforms wound up being worn by the attackers. There was a full scale search being conducted for the missing men inside the hospital.

Chief Lyle West ventured outside and looked around. He saw a variety of vehicles in the multi-level parking garage. He coughed as he went from vehicle to vehicle, glad he was where no one would be concerned about his continual hacking. The icy air burned his lungs.

He concentrated on vans. The Hepner brothers had traded their truck for a van. It was snowing again. That cut the sharp sting of the wind. He gave only a casual glance to any car with snow on the roof. It had just entered the garage.

Coughing, Lyle trekked up and down the rows looking inside van windows. His mind told him that the chances that the guards were in the van were slim, still he kept looking.

Sam was still suffering from having been shot in both shoulders. That's why Fred was doing the shooting. Sam couldn't even drag his brother out of the room, Lyle recalled. These brothers planned everything. They wouldn't want to take the security guards with him; but, suppose they had no choice. He kept looking. He came up empty.

Where would they dump them? He wondered. It had to be somewhere out of sight. His mind jumped back to the word dump as another spasm of coughing doubled him over.

I need to go back in and get some water, he thought. Just one more place. Despite the distance between the parking garage and the area where the dumpsters sat, he forced himself to walk over to the far end of the hospital complex.

That's where he found them, cold and stiff and unmoving. He thought they were dead, but when one of them groaned, he radioed for help.

"I guess he's gone," the hospital security captain commented as West was downing his third cup of coffee.

"Those three brothers were clever men," Chief West responded. "One's still around. I wouldn't relax just yet."

"I disagree. He's been made. He's on the run."

"Just to be safe, move Jackman to a different room," West suggested politely, stifling a cough, "and keep a guard on him."

"You've been a big help," the captain admitted, "but the danger's over. I'd appreciate it if you'd take your men out of here."

"They'll leave with the people they are guarding."

"Well, at least have them remove that riot gear. It's scaring people."

"I've already had one deputy shot. I'm not risking another one," West stated authoritatively. "The gear stays on."

"How soon will they be gone?"

"The doctors are operating on Stanley Praetzel now. His wife is waiting."

"Let's get a surgeon in there," the captain said.

"She won't allow it," Chief West said. "I wouldn't push it. She was, after all, injured in your hospital. And, she's a lawyer."

"Well, okay. I'll wait," the captain said reluctantly. "But that's as far as I go."

Meanwhile, downstairs in pre-op, Justin was ecstatically pulling all the details of the attack from Aleta when suddenly he stopped speaking.

Her face paled slightly and she appeared to be listening to a voice other than Justin's. The pause wasn't long; but she had stopped in mid-sentence. He had waited patiently believing she was simply hunting for a word or phrase.

When she looked at him after the pause, he could tell her mind was on something else. He saw her tense as she ordered him to fetch Lieutenant French.

He rose. "Do you want me to leave?"

"No, stay."

Justin poked his head around the curtain. "She wants to speak with you."

"I'm not supposed to leave my post," he said. "Can you tell me what this is about?"

"You better come," Justin said tersely. He sensed all was not right with Aleta.

French took a quick look around and told Justin to stand in the opening and tell him if anyone carne in through the doors thirty feet away. He went to the side of Aleta's bed.

He'd seen her before with her freshly shaved head showing several recent scars and a large bandage covering the newest one. But still he was startled. One arm lay strapped to a board while the slow drip from the IV kept her hydrated and added necessary electrolytes to a body about to undergo surgery. Some blood had seeped through the bandage on her upper arm. His sympathy was aroused instantly.

Her voice, however, was strong and commanding.

"Lieutenant French, I need you to help me save three lives."

Justin's attention to the door was instantly directed to Aleta's face. It was no longer pale and wan, but vibrant.

"Whose lives?" French asked.

"If you don't follow my directions exactly, Chief West will be the first to die."

"Let me call him!" French said.

West had said he was to be called if she had a vision or even if she sensed something.

"You will in a second," Aleta said. "But hear me out. He is heading toward Jackman's room. You must get Chief West to turn around this very minute and get down here as fast as he can. Do it now!"

French hesitated for a brief moment and then spoke into his radio. "Chief, Aleta says to come down here right now. Seconds count."

"What is it?" West asked.

"Are you turned around? Are you coming?"

"Yes, I'm coming, but how did you know I had to turn around?"

"Aleta told me."

"I'll be there ASAP," West coughed.

French looked at Aleta with a frown of consternation. Had he made a mistake?

"Now," she said, "you are to go to Jackman's room as fast as possible. As you are approaching you will see two guards on the floor. A third is about to enter the room. Stop him with your Taser. If he turns and runs toward the stairs, don't chase him. Someone will call 'Help.' Answer the call. If you do, you will save another life. Don't deviate from this plan."

"Gotcha!" French said rushing out.

"Justin, you stay put!" Aleta called to the reporter.

He hesitated. He wanted to follow French.

"Stop!" Aleta said sternly.

Her voice brooked no defiance. He couldn't afford to leave without at least telling her he had to.

He turned and Aleta spoke.

"You are to follow him--but not until I tell you."

Justin relaxed. She wasn't going to stop him. She was going to help him.

"After Lieutenant French shoots his Taser, he's going to be surprised because the guard doesn't fall. He doesn't know he has on a vest that's too thick for the Taser to penetrate effectively. The man will run toward the stairs. Lieutenant French will forget what I told him and start to pursue him. You will go into Jackman's room and find him on the floor and you will yell 'Help'. Peter will know what to do to revive Jackman."

"Now?" Justin said anxious to be off. He had to see if she knew what she was talking about. What an opportunity!

"Go!" she said. "Don't stop for any reason. Don't tell West. If he doesn't get here, I may die."

The last sentence almost stopped him; but this story was too priceless not to follow through on. Besides West was coming.

He ran through the door. He already knew where Jackman's room was. He was told it was off limits. And now she'd directed him to enter it. How lucky could a reporter get?

As he entered the stairwell, he met West.

"Where are you off to?" West asked.

Fearful that if he told him, West would forbid him to go, he blurted out, "Aleta says if you don't come, she'll die."

"And you left her?" West spat out angrily.

"Hurry!" was all Justin would say.

Nothing was going to keep him from this story. As he ran, he toyed with the idea of not yelling for help and see if French would wind up dead. It would make even a better story. He could see the headline: "Cop Ignores Warning: Dies".

It would sell a lot of papers. And French had been warned. It wouldn't be his fault if the prophecy carne true. She was very clear.

I won't yell help just because Jackman fell out of bed, he thought. I'll go to his aid and forget to yell "help". French is on its own.

Justin could see the sub-headline: reporter saves Jackman. He knew CPR. He could do it. He didn't need to yell for help. He'd seen a lot in his lifetime. He could handle this.

French would die in the line of duty. Or maybe he wouldn't die at all. He was warned after all. That might give him the edge he needed to survive. Not only survive, but capture the killer. What cop didn't want to be the one to capture a known felon that had eluded police in half a dozen cities? She was robbing him of his shot at glory. He would want to have that chance.

"Am I going to give it to him?" he questioned as he hurried up the remaining stairs. "French is an experienced cop. He can decide whether he wants to take the chance. I'm not going to stop him."

That decided, he burst through the door into the hallway leading to Jackman's room. As he ran down the corridor, Justin saw French fire his Taser and he saw the missiles hit.

Sam Hepner brushed them off his uniform, and then spotting Justin running toward him wearing a police vest, decided he was outnumbered. He turned and ran toward the stairwell at the other end of the corridor. French took off after him.

Justin, whose long legs had brought him within a stride of French, darted past the two fallen guards and into Jackman's room.

Sprawled on the floor, his mouth open, saliva mingled with blood drooling out of one side, laid the upper half of Jackman. His feet were still in bed. His neck was cocked at an odd angle.

Immediately, Justin was scared.

"Help!" he shouted.

It just burst out. It was real. It was loaded with the panic he felt. His panic forced another shout from his throat. It was louder, more desperate than the first.

Down in the basement, Aleta lay alone, waiting for Chief West. She didn't have long to wait. He rushed in breathless.

As he tried to catch his breath, Aleta said, "You're needed up in Jackman's room."

"That's where I was going," he puffed.

"I know," Aleta said. "But I needed you to give me your Taser or your gun."

"Are you in danger?"

"I don't know."

"I'll stay if you are."

"Jackman needs you. His neck's not broken. He wants you to take him to Arborville. That's what he's saying."

Lyle didn't move.

"I won't leave you if you're in danger," Lyle insisted.

"You've got to go. You've been told what he wants. You need to do it. As for me, I'm just nervous. I feel so helpless. Please let me have a weapon."

"Okay. Since it's you. You can have my Taser. Its range is twenty-one feet."

"How far is that?"

West paced it off.

"To here," he said, pulling over a chair.

"Now go! Run!"

"Geez," he muttered as he hurried away. "I was there and French was here. Why didn't she just tell me to stay there?"

Didn't she think I could be radioed? he wondered as he reached the stairway. He looked over and saw the elevator doors opening and he ran toward it.

He took a chance and it panned out. He caught his breath on the way up, but only after another spasm of coughing. He wondered what was wrong with him. He shouldn't be winded at all. He'd just traveled down the stairs, not up. And this cough was getting the better of him.

Later, he'd ask Dr. Cook to check him out.

When the elevator doors opened, he headed toward Jackman's room on the run. He forgot about his shortness of breath.

He passed the two guards lying on the floor.

Where were the nurses? he wondered.

He crept inside, gun drawn. Peter looked up. "You got here fast!"

"You didn't call," West said perturbed.

"I thought Justin and I could get him back in bed, but Justin won't touch him."

"His neck could be broken," Justin said.

"Did anyone call for a doctor or nurse?"

"I rang the buzzer over and over," Justin said. "Either it's broken or no one's around."

"Well, Aleta told me his neck's not broken," West said. "But just to be sure, let me ask Mr. Jackman a question."

"What good will that do?" Justin asked.

"It will tell me if Aleta's right about his neck," West said.

"If he moves, he could paralyze himself," Justin put in. "And he can't speak. I already tried talking to him."

"Mr. Jackman," West said, "Aleta tells me you want to be transferred to the Tri City Hospital in Arborville where you'll be under my protection. Is this true? I want you to…"

Before he could give him new instructions as to how to answer, Jackman began nodding his head vigorously.

French and West immediately lifted Jackman back into bed.

"Is anyone with Aleta?" French asked his chief as he watched Justin interviewing Jackman. Even though Simon Jackman's responses were limited, Justin, armed with the information Aleta had given him earlier, knew just what questions to ask.

"She has a weapon," West said. "I left my Taser with her."

"I shot the perp with mine and failed to stop him. He's wearing some thick armor under those clothes."

"Aleta said she was in no danger."

"I thought you said she couldn't foretell danger to herself."

"She senses it." Lyle explained.

"Did you offer to leave the Taser or did she ask for it?"

"French, take charge here!" West ordered.

Downstairs in pre-op, Aleta called the nurse to her bedside.

"Is there a closet nearby?" she asked.

The nurse frowned, puzzled. "Over there."

"Go get in it," Aleta said. "A man with a gun will enter in a few minutes. If he sees you, he will shoot you."

"I'll call the doctor," the nurse said.

The patient was exhibiting psychotic symptoms.

"What harm can indulging me for one minute do?" Aleta asked. "If he doesn't come, you can call a doctor."

The request was given in such a reasonable tone, that the nurse thought, I could do that.

Thirty seconds later, the outer door opened and Sam Hepner entered. While his appearance was changed because he was still in uniform, Aleta knew who it was instantly.

"I've been expecting you."

Sam quickly surveyed the room.

"The police are upstairs; the nurse is in the closet," Aleta said.

The closet door clicked shut.

"I'm here to kill you," he growled.

Aleta ignored the threat.

"I want to help you bury your brothers properly. You can't do it alone without getting caught, but I can."

"Bury my brothers?" Sam stammered.

"And you too if you insist on dying."

"Why should I believe you? You lied about not telling anyone about us coming after Jackman."

"I didn't tell anyone the first time. You ran into my police guard. They were there because Jackman's lawyers wanted answers and I was sent for. Bad timing on your part. However, I didn't know you were coming."

"Don't lie!"

"I'm not. I only foresee murder, not attempts."

"But the second time, just a few minutes ago," Sam snarled. "You stopped me."

"From killing my friend, Lyle. I will always protect him and his men. There is no threat strong enough to keep me from doing that!" Aleta said with such certainty that Sam believed her.

"Why didn't you guard yourself?"

"I chose to save others," Aleta said simply.

"People don't do that."

"Well, I do have a Taser, but I noticed that you stopped at the chair."

"I suspected you were armed."

"I could have asked for a gun, but I didn't want to kill you, only stop you."

"That's not going to happen," Sam decided.

"Put the burial details in the personal column. Address it to 'Taser' and I'll know it's for me."

"I want people at their funeral."

"I'll be at the graveside service. You can kill me then if you want to. I won't put anyone else at risk."

"I get what I want!" Sam shouted.

"Not with me you don't. God's orders supersede yours. He's giving you another chance. Take it. You've got the money. At least let me bury your brothers decently."

"Deal!" Sam said.

He holstered his gun and left quickly.

Within minutes, Chief West barreled through the door.

"Are you okay?"

"Nurse," Aleta called loudly, "You can come out now."

Lyle gasped.

"He was here?"

Aleta nodded.

"But you're alive."

"We made a deal."

"You don't deal. I know you," Lyle said.

"She told him she'd bury his brothers and he left," the nurse said.

"Why did you do that?"

"I wanted him to stop killing people. I wanted to give him time to think."

"You could have been killed!" Lyle charged angrily. "You had me running around like a puppy chasing a butterfly."

"Lives were saved," Aleta said without apology.

"Aleta, we need to catch this man!" Lyle rebuked her. "You set him free to kill others."

A spasm of coughing cut his scolding short.

"He won't kill again until after the funerals," Aleta said.

"How do you know?"

"I'm guessing he's going to want to see if I keep my word."

"You're playing with fire, Aleta. And I don't want you pushing me and my men around."

"Lyle, you're making a big mistake here."

"You shouldn't be messing around in police matters."

"I didn't," Aleta countered. "It was God's plan. That's why it was so complex."

"He's directing my police force now?" Lyle shot back.

"Not the whole force. Just you and French."

"I don't like it!"

"Hey, take it up with Him, not me," Aleta said. "I told Sam he can't stop me from interfering to save the lives of my friends, even at the cost of my own life. I think he believed me.

"Of course he believed you. You threw yourself in front of Jackman," Lyle said. "You have to stop doing that! And I know that was your idea not God's."

Aleta agreed a bit sheepishly that it was her idea.

"Suppose God wanted Jackman dead?" Lyle posed.

"Then He would be upset with me, except that He knew I'd do that. But, you're right. I'm pretty pleased with myself which I think He doesn't really like at all."

"Don't go twisting stuff around," Lyle said. "He liked what you did. You saved your enemy's life. By the way, have you decided to let them tape your eyes shut?"

"What brought that up?"

"Want me to arrange for headphones!"

"Don't do anything!" Aleta snapped. "Just let me be."

Lyle sat down beside her. "You're too brave for your own good, that's all. If you think being aware during your surgery will be difficult, let us provide aids that will help."

"Why are you suddenly being nice to me?"

"I just remembered what French said. You saved his life, didn't you?"

"His following the directions I gave him saved his life. And he did that because you told him to. You saved his life as much as me."

"I guess maybe you can push us around when necessary. Besides Lauren would kill me for being angry with you for keeping me safe. And don't worry. Ed is in Indianapolis waiting. It Sam Hepner shows up, Ed will call the police."

"He won't go home until after the funerals."

"A guess or a prophecy?"

"A reasonable guess. He let me live so I could make funeral arrangements."

"Who cares about how his brothers are buried?"

"Fortunately for me, he does."

"Are you going to do it?"

"I gave my word."

"But why?"

"I would do it for a friend. Why not an enemy?"

The reporter Justin Conway returned just as two orderlies were wheeling Aleta to the operating room. He stood in the empty pre-op area wondering where to go next when the nurse politely told him where the waiting room was.

"Pretty exciting upstairs," he commented for no particular reason.

"We had plenty down here as well."

"Oh?" Justin queried softly.

The nurse, desperate to talk about her experience, began her tale to this stranger who seemed so interested. When he opened his notebook and began jotting down her words, she remembered vaguely that he was a reporter, but she needed to tell someone, so she brushed that fact aside. She wasn't revealing any confidences. She was simply telling him what had happened.

He asked a few questions at the end, one of which was her name.

"Are you going to print this?"

"Probably. It's a pretty interesting story," Justin said. "And you told it well."

"Did I really?"

"I wouldn't change a word," he said and wondered briefly why he'd said that.

Chief West pulled Derrick Gardner from guarding the operating room and Peter French from guarding Aleta and posted them both outside Simon Jackman's room.

"Sam Hepner's still in the building," West proclaimed. "Jackman's not safe until he's in our hospital."

"But Chief," Garret asked, "isn't Aleta Praetzel still in danger?"

"Not today; however, Sam knows she's going to be operated on. He could use the opportunity to strike at Jackman again. I'm sure that despite him having struck twice, the captain of hospital security won't believe he'll do it again. But he's still here."

"He didn't just run?"

"He ran straight to Aleta," West said.

"And didn't kill her?"

"She bought herself a bit of time," he told his man, and so he wouldn't take him literally, added how.

"She's going to see that his brothers are buried properly."

"Smart lady," Garrett commented. "And he bought it?"

"That's because she keeps her word," West said.

Chief Lyle West entered the recovery room.

"What've you been up to while I've been away getting repaired?" Stanley asked.

"You don't want to know," Lyle said, knowing full well Stanley would pull out every detail.

He sat down beside his friend and asked jokingly, "They didn't cut off anything important, did they?"

He coughed twice.

"That doesn't sound good."

"Just a dry throat," Lyle said dismissing the cough. He coughed again and looked around. "My throat's dry. They have any water?"

"They love to put IV's in people here," Stanley joshed. "I'm sure I can get them to hook you up to one."

"You don't even have a glass on the stand next to your bed," Lyle complained.

"Why's your throat dry?" Stanley asked, ringing for the nurse who was only ten steps away.

"I've been yelling at your wife."

Stanley caught the nurse's eye as she approached.

"He needs water."

Lyle coughed again. "I don't know what's wrong with me."

He took the water and sipped it.

"Why?" Stanley asked. "What else do you have besides a cough?"

"Nothing, Doctor," Lyle quipped. "You want to talk about Aleta or discuss my dry throat?"

Stanley didn't reply. Instead he studied his friend's face. It was more than a cough. Lyle was sick.

Dr. Cook had told him Aleta's surgery would be quicker than his. Until the doctors were finished with Aleta, there was nothing he could do.

"Tell me what Aleta did," he decided.

"For the first hour, while I was outside looking for the missing guards, she talked to Justin Conway."

"Why were you outside?"

"I had a hunch. Everyone else was scouring the inside of the building; but if they were inside they were okay. But it's freezing outside."

"How long were you out there?"

"An hour I guess. I was chilled to the bone and I had a heavy coat on."

"Did the guards make it?"

"They're still working on them," Lyle said. A spasm of coughing stopped him again. He sipped some more water, and then began the story of Aleta's sending him running around the building receiving and sending messages.

"She has no appreciation for the communication devices we have, you know, cell phones, radios and the like."

"She had her reasons," Stanley put in. "That cough is sounding worse. Why don't you let me talk for a while?"

"About what?"

"My operation, of course. I was awake, you know."

"No way!"

But Stanley told him anyway.

Chapter 26

Several hours later when Stanley and Aleta were taken to Tri City Hospital by helicopter, they were the second ones to be transported in the police chopper. Simon Jackman preceded them along with Dr. Cook and Chief West.

When the helicopter carrying Stanley set down, Dr. Cook was there to meet it. Robert Locke was with him. There was a gurney for Stanley and a wheelchair for Aleta who was dressed to leave the hospital without ever laying in a bed.

As they entered the elevator, Dr. Cook told Stanley he was going to have a roommate.

"Lyle said he didn't have the manpower to cover the extra room," Dr. Cook explained.

"He's got it in for me," Stanley said sourly. "Just because I bored him with the details of my operation is no reason to stick me with Jackman. Can I forego police protection and get a private room."

"Your roommate asked the same thing," Dr. Cook responded. "You two recalcitrant patients deserve each other."

"I've been a model patient," Stanley protested.

"As long as Aleta was your roommate."

"So how long?"

"For you, probably five days. We need to keep that leg packed in ice for the next several days."

Stanley called back to Aleta, "We need a continuance for a week at least."

"Relax," Aleta responded. "I'll take care of it."

When Stanley was wheeled into the room, the curtain was drawn around the other bed. He was glad. He had no desire to even see Jackman. He shuddered at the thought of listening to the man's angry mumblings all day long.

It took a while to settle him in bed and rewrap his leg in ice. When the nurses were done, Stanley found he couldn't move at all. They raised his bed slightly and then, without even asking, pushed back the curtain.

Even though Stanley had heard coughing, he was surprised to see Lyle occupying the next bed.

"How?" he asked.

"Wayne threatened to call Lauren."

"So you're really sick?"

"Pneumonia," Lyle replied. "He says I won't rest at home."

"He's right," Stanley said. "And if my leg wasn't pinned by these packs, I'd be up and going home too."

Aleta was wheeled in.

"I called Lauren," she said. "I told her you were really sick and could die if you didn't stay put."

"Damn!" Lyle exploded.

Stanley grinned. "You were planning to persuade Lauren to spring you, weren't you?"

"Stop grinning!"

"Welcome to my world," Stanley said, still smiling. "Take it from me, it doesn't get easier."

"I've got to go, Aleta," her father said.

"I'll just wait here. He should be here any second."

"Have a good night, Guys," Robert said and then took off.

"Who's going to take care of you?" Stanley asked Aleta.

"Well, not my father!"

"Who then? Bertha?"

"She has Jocelyn to care for in the evenings," Aleta responded.

"You aren't taking care of yourself!" Stanley exclaimed.

"With my arm? Don't be silly," Aleta replied. "Your dad is picking me up. Your mom is going to help me get ready for bed. And Bertha will help me during the day."

"If Dad's coming here, I can ask him to get the continuance."

"I'll have him wheel me down to talk with Martha while you and he talk."

And that's what Stanley's father did.

When Hubert Praetzel came to pick up Aleta, Martha bade him sit down.

"There's been a change of plans," Martha said.

"You don't even know what the plan is," Hubert remarked.

"That's okay because it's been changed."

Hubert pulled up a chair. "Okay, Ladies, tell me what you cooked up while I was keeping Stanley occupied."

The next morning Hubert drove over to Aleta's house in his car. Robert had already loaded the wheelchair into the van. Aleta had on her cape and hood and was waiting.

"Did you clear your calendar?" Aleta asked.

"My partners understood. In fact, they're delighted our firm is taking part."

"What will I do if she doesn't let Dad help me?"

"Let me worry about that," Hubert said. "I prepared an argument to cover that contingency although I don't think I'll need it with Judge Cohen.

The courtroom was nearly empty when Aleta was wheeled in. Her father placed her behind the long table on the judge's right. At the other table sat Simon Jackman's three lawyers: Jules Barre, the gray-haired senior partner, Brad Scheff, a man in his late forties who was their top litigator and Martin Zolinger, the young agnostic whose zeal matched that of the three prophets.

All were surprised when Aleta was wheeled to the lawyer's table. They whispered among themselves and Aleta knew they were reminding one another that she hadn't passed the bar and therefore had no standing in this case.

When the judge came in, Robert helped Aleta to her feet. When everyone else seated themselves, Aleta was helped back into her wheelchair.

Judge Ellen Cohen banged her gavel and asked if the parties were ready to proceed.

Jules Barre stood and said in a clear deep baritone. "We are Your Honor."

Robert helped Aleta to her feet. "If it pleases the court, may I present my credentials and state that I am representing Harriet Locke and Aleta Praetzel in the matter before the court. As House Attorney for the Tontine Trust, I am empowered by the State of Illinois to represent any of its members in any legal action. Both Harriet Locke and Aleta Praetzel are members of the Trust. As Mr. Stanley Praetzel will not be available, due to an injury sustained yesterday, I respectfully request that I be allowed to continue in his stead."

Robert took the documents from the table and handed them to the clerk who handed them to the judge. She scanned them and asked the opposing lawyers if they had any objection. None was raised.

When Aleta asked for permission to have Robert Locke aid her physically and the judge granted the request, several onlookers hurriedly left the courtroom. The news spread rapidly that the case was going to be argued today and people began filing into the courtroom.

By the time Hubert Praetzel presented himself as the substitute council for Martha Cook, the courtroom was full and the bailiffs were denying admittance to more spectators.

Mr. Hubert Praetzel answered the judge's inquiry as to whether he was familiar with the case by telling the court he'd helped prepare the brief the judge had in hand and was prepared to proceed.

Judge Cohen ruled that the defense was going to be allowed to use a religious freedom defense.

Despite a feeling of elation, the lawyers at the defense table nodded politely at the ruling. They were only halfway home.

Jules Barre called a police officer as his first witness. Aleta Locke stood up. "The defense will stipulate that Mr. Simon Jackman was shot by one of the Hepner brothers and, as a result, suffered brain damage which caused loss of intelligible speech and left him with minimal use of his arms and legs."

Jules Barre then called Aleta Praetzel. Hubert had told her this would happen and suggested she allow it.

"Don't argue your case from the witness stand," Hubert advised. "Answer yes or no whenever possible. Let me object to the questions."

"You must promise me you will cross-examine me and ask the tough questions so that the truth can come out."

"Is there anything I need to know?"

"Just that Martha knows everything and said she concurs with every decision I made. You may be surprised, but you won't be embarrassed."

"There is something, isn't there?"

"Yes, and if we're lucky, they won't know about it."

"You don't intend to tell me?"

"I haven't even told Stanley," Aleta said.

That bothered Hubert even more; however, this woman would not have done anything illegal. He knew that. So she did something that might appear to be. As soon as that realization hit him, his worry became anticipation. She was counting on him to uncover the truth. And, for same reason, she believed that if he didn't know it, he'd do a better job.

He liked the freedom not knowing gave him. She was a sharp enough lawyer to have told him in advance if she'd done anything that would come back to bite them in the rear. This was something she wanted dug out in open court, not something she presented about herself.

Clever, he thought. She wasn't going to bring it up, but if they did, she had her defense ready.

She had said Martha knew about it, he remembered. She had said that to reassure him. Strangely, it did.

The lead attorney, Jules Barre, charged in immediately. "You say that Simon Jackman is interfering with your religious freedom, correct?"

"Yes," Aleta replied.

"And that you are not working in collusion with any one or all of the Hepner brothers?"

"Yes."

"Did you not meet with Sam Hepner secretly at the hospital?"

"That is two questions," Aleta said. "Simplify it."

"It is simple. Did you meet secretly with Sam Hepner yesterday?"

"Your client complained that you couldn't ask a question that could be answered yes or no. Evidently, you still haven't learned how."

"Object, Your Honor," Barre spat out.

"On what grounds?"

"Unresponsive."

"The response will be stricken. Answer the question."

"Yes, to the first part. No, to the second," Aleta replied.

"That is no answer," Barre argued. "Did you meet with Sam Hepner yesterday?"

"Yes."

"That's what I asked before," he protested.

"No, you didn't," Aleta said.

Brad Scheff whispered to Jules Barre and the elder man deferred to his younger partner.

"Was the meeting a secret?" Brad Scheff asked.

"No."

"The police weren't told about it."

"Correct.

"You kept it to yourself. I call that 'secret'. What would you call it?"

"I told someone which is why you know about it. I didn't tell her the meeting was a secret. Why don't you call your source and ask her?"

"Object, Your Honor. Unresponsive."

"Overruled. You asked her to explain."

"During this meeting, didn't you and Sam Hepner make a deal?"

"Yes."

"Did this deal include your not revealing any prophecies about Simon Jackman?"

"That deal was made before the meeting. It's a matter of public record."

"Did you not agree to arrange for the burial of his brothers? I believe the word you used was 'proper' burial."

"Yes."

"Who is paying for this?"

"I am."

"And did you not promise to attend the service?"

"Yes."

"Were these lies spoken to save your life?" Brad Scheff said. "Weren't you, in fact, in grave danger?"

"Your Honor, please ask counsel to ask his questions one at a time."

"Never mind. I'll rephrase," Scheff said. "Were these promises lies?"

"No."

"The man had a gun aimed at you from twenty feet away."

"Yes and no."

Unsettled, his rhythm being constantly interrupted, Scheff simplified his query. "He had a gun aimed at you, true?

"Yes."

"And he was twenty feet or less away from you. True?"

"No."

"How far was he?"

"Just over twenty-one feet."

"How do you know that?"

"Chief West measured it out for me and put a chair at twenty-one feet. That was the range of the Taser I was holding."

"Chief West gave you a Taser?" he asked before he realized he was departing from his agenda and moving over to hers.

"Yes."

Scheff felt forced to ask the next question. "Why did he give you a Taser?"

"I asked for it."

"And he gave you a weapon just because you asked for it?"

"Yes."

"But you didn't use it?"

"No."

"You never intended to use it, did you?"

"No."

Scheff concluded on that note.

Hubert wasn't sure what he was supposed to ask but he rose anyway. He decided to start with the witness.

"Where was the nurse during the meeting?" he asked.

"In the closet," Aleta replied.

"Why did she get into the closet?"

"I asked her to before Sam Hepner arrived. I told her he'd shoot her if he saw her."

"So she never saw the gun?" Hubert asked. Aleta had told him to ask the hard questions. This was one of those. If she didn't see the gun, no one did but the two principals.

"Correct," Aleta replied, seemingly undisturbed by this fact.

"Did he tell you the purpose of his visit?"

"Yes. He said he'd come to kill me."

"Why did he change his mind?"

"I told him I'd see to the burial of his brothers."

"And he believed you?" Hubert asked. It was the question on everyone's mind.

"I don't renege on my promises."

"But he was afraid you would. That's why you were a target. True?"

"Yes."

"How come he changed his mind?"

"He didn't. He just took a chance on me. He wanted his brothers buried properly."

"You knew he was corning?"

"Yes."

"Why didn't you tell Chief West?"

"I saw Chief West die and I assumed I would die too. If I was alone, only one of us would die."

"You lied to Chief West?"

"I told him I would be alright. And I was."

"Was the meeting planned?" Hubert asked, finally realizing where Aleta wanted him to go.

"No."

"But you knew about it?"

"I was able to see many future events that day. The meeting was one."

"Did you see the end?"

"All I foresaw was Chief West being shot to death. I have never been able to prophesy my own death."

"What about Mr. Jackman? Did you see his death?"

"No."

"But you sent help. Weren't you responding to a vision of him dying at Sam Hepner's hand?"

"No."

"What did you see?"

"First I saw Chief West get shot trying to save Jackman. I had Lieutenant French call him to my side. When I removed West from the danger, I sent Lieutenant French to Jackman's room. I did foresee him arriving on time to prevent Sam Hepner from entering Jackman's room but I also saw him shot and killed chasing Sam in the stairwell, so I warned him. Do you want me to go on?"

"Please do," Hubert said.

"I sent Justin Conway, who's a reporter, to remind French not to chase Sam Hepner down the stairs. I saw Jackman on the floor with his head twisted. I sent West back up to help with Jackman. You know why I did that?"

"You promised the Hepner brothers you wouldn't prophesy anymore."

"We promised not to reveal our visions. We cannot stop having them. They are not products of our minds. They are given."

"But you prevented Sam Hepner from killing Simon Jackman."

"I prevented Sam Hepner from killing my friends who were willing to die to save Simon Jackman. I told Sam Hepner he could never stop me from doing that."

"You were willing to die to save your friend, correct?"

"Yes."

"And when earlier, Fred Hepner shot at Simon Jackman; you jumped in front of him and took the bullet, correct?"

"Yes."

"Did you know that attack was going to happen?"

"No."

"Would you have told Simon Jackman if you did have such a vision?"

"No."

"Why not?"

"Because God told me not to."

"So you're leaving Simon Jackman to the mercy of Sam Hepner?"

"Our sole duty as men is to obey God."

"And do you have personal knowledge that Harriet Locke and Martha Cook hold this same view?"

"Yes."

"One final question," Hubert said. "On what basis did you decide to pay for the burial of your enemies?"

"It was God's idea."

Hubert asked for a recess and it was granted. The judge left the courtroom. Aleta was helped back into her chair and wheeled to her table. Her father held up a glass of water and she took several sips. Hubert leaned over and asked her if he'd failed to ask any question. She told him that this was a good note to end on.

"What about our opponents?" Hubert inquired.

"Zolinger will want a go at me, but Barre won't let him."

"Are we still putting him on the stand?" Hubert asked.

"Yes."

"Are you up to it?" Hubert said. She looked so fragile and beat up with the scars from several operations visible except for the most recent one still covered by a bandage. The slings were not for show, he knew. They supported badly injured shoulders. He knew she was in pain from the recent operation. She had refused painkillers and Robert told him she moaned half the night.

He knew the exhilaration of a courtroom battle. It would be easier to bear the pain if she was actively engaged than if she was forced to sit passively while he made arguments. This was her fight. She had the heart and brains for it. She was the best person to tackle Zolinger.

He had heard that the young lawyer, while zealous and prone to asking seemingly crude questions, was a savvy litigator.

Zolinger banked on being underestimated.

What he probably didn't know because no one had seen Aleta in action before was that she was not someone one could manipulate. That was the reason his son married her. She was his equal.

The opposition had gotten a taste of her mettle when they went after her on the witness stand. She came out ahead slightly if you considered their defense posture; however, her testimony proved their contention that she would not reveal a vision concerning Simon Jackman. They would not hammer away at the immorality of that decision, although they would allude to it often, thus keeping it unspoken but at the forefront of the judge's thinking, rather their focus would be on the illegality of her knowing that a man was in danger and her refusal to warn him. She was, therefore, aiding the man planning to murder someone.

She was walking a tight rope, Hubert thought, however, only she completely understood the nuances--she and his client, Martha Cook.

After the recess, both sides declared that they were finished questioning Aleta.

Zolinger was called to the stand. He was eager to get to speak. He'd show the others how to handle this woman.

"Mr. Zolinger," Aleta began. "Do you believe…"

"Objection!" Barre shouted. "Irrelevant."

"Let me rephrase, Your Honor," Aleta said quickly.

Zolinger smiled smugly. They had her.

Aleta, however, acted as if the objection was like an annoying fly one brushed away. She went on.

"There is an old adage 'Actions speak louder than words'. Do you think this is true, sometimes true, or never true?"

"Sometimes true."

"Spoken like a true lawyer," Aleta commented. "Now yesterday, Mr. Jackman was under attack twice. You were present during the first attack, correct?"

"Yes."

"Upon seeing the gunman, you dropped to the floor, correct?"

"Yes, but I knew there were…"

"Your Honor, instruct the witness to answer only the question I ask."

Hubert smiled. Point one for Aleta.

"You are so instructed," Judge Cohen said.

"You were aware that there were two armed men at the door and two armed men inside the door, correct?"

"Yes," Zolinger spat out. She was not going to get under his skin.

"So considering the fact that there were two armed men in the room when two men entered with guns drawn, a reasonable man, knowing that he wasn't the target, would hit the floor. Am I correct on all points?"

Zolinger could not find fault with a single word.

"Yes," he replied.

"If you had charged the men, it would have been reasonable to assume that you would have been shot, correct?"

"Yes."

"And, in fact, your two fellow lawyers, Mr. Barre and Mr. Scheff were shot, correct?"

"Yes, with a Taser."

"Answer only what I ask, please," Aleta chided him.

"When you saw the weapons in the hands of the two men, there were two kinds of guns, weren't there?"

"Yes."

"Did you know at the time that one man held two Tasers?"

"Yes, but the other…"

"Your Honor, please," Aleta pleaded.

"Mr. Zolinger. Answer only the question asked," Judge Cohen reiterated.

Barre scowled at his young associate. Stop defending yourself, the look said.

Aleta went on. Zolinger squirmed in his seat.

Hubert smiled at the interplay. She was getting under his skin. She was after something. He couldn't wait to discover what.

"The other man held two guns, the kind that kill people, correct?"

"Yes," he replied his resentment growing. He didn't like being led.

"So is it fair to assume you didn't know which guns might be used on you if you charged the men?"

"Yes," he said.

"Is it fair to assume that to throw yourself in the path of a bullet is an unreasonable act?"

"Yes."

"Do you consider my throwing myself between Mr. Jackman and the bullet an unreasonable act?"

Zolinger was stymied. He didn't want to go on record as stating that Aleta Praetzel acted unreasonably since that would shoot holes in their conspiracy theory. He was forced to spout out a resounding, "No!"

He fully expected Aleta would ask him to explain.

"Well, Sir," she said. "I agree. It was a reasonable act given my belief. Let's move on. Did Mr. Jackman ever tell you what religion he adhered to?"

"Your Honor," Zolinger began.

"Let me rephrase," Aleta said quickly. "Did Mr. Jackman, to your knowledge, ever accuse me of attempting to proselytize him, that is convert him to another religion?"

"I know what proselytize means," Zolinger snapped, annoyed at her patronizing attitude. "And the answer is yes, he did."

"Therefore, am I to assume that he does not adhere to my religious beliefs?"

Zolinger didn't like her being in control, but the fact was that Jackman didn't hold the same beliefs she did. He kept saying that it was all a farce, a fake belief. And he said so publicly. Zolinger knew that she would pull out articles quoting Jackman's views. He hated that he had no choice.

"Yes," he said reluctantly.

"Does it not follow then that if he does not hold my beliefs, he holds other beliefs?"

"He has no beliefs!" Zolinger spouted out.

"Everyone believes something," Aleta charged.

Zolinger snapped, "He doesn't and I don't. We don't believe God exists at all!"

"You are both atheists?" she asked calmly.

Zolinger wasn't happy being pigeonholed. And he could see from Barre's expression that he had stepped over the line. The only reason the man didn't object was because Aleta had asked a question and Zolinger could therefore adjust his statement.

"I am," Zolinger said. "Mr. Jackman is an agnostic. An agnostic is..."

Aleta interrupted him. "The court knows what the word agnostic means."

"I didn't think you did," Zolinger quipped.

"Object!" Hubert said. "Irrelevant and derogatory."

"Sustained. Mr. Zolinger's last remark will be stricken from the record."

Aleta turned to her father and asked for a drink. He poured a glass of water and held it for her. Until that moment Judge Cohen wasn't aware how helpless this young lawyer was. She had been very discreet.

"Mr. Zolinger," Aleta said, "is it true that while Mr. Jackman doesn't believe in God, he does believe in my prophetic power."

"That's too complex a question," Zolinger retorted smugly.

"I apologize," Aleta said. "Does Mr. Jackman believe I can predict his death?"

"That's why we're here," Zolinger quipped.

"You are wrong," Aleta said firmly. "Mr. Jackman doesn't believe I have any power at all otherwise he wouldn't have dared file this suit; however, being an agnostic, he's unsure and he's not willing to risk his life for what he truly believes. Is that a fair statement?"

"As I said before, I don't know what he believes."

"And you don't believe the lawsuit can be regarded as a declaration of his belief?"

"Objection, Your Honor," Barre said. "Asked and answered."

"Withdrawn, Your Honor," Aleta said. "I'm done with this witness. I defer to co-counsel."

Hubert rose slowly, took a sip of water and moved in front of his table.

"Mr. Zolinger, why was Aleta Praetzel involved in a conference between you and your client?"

"We couldn't understand him. Dr. Taekman recommended her as an interpreter."

"And was she able to interpret for him?"

"She seemed to."

"Is that a yes or a no?"

Zolinger glanced over at Barre who nodded his head. Hubert moved over so as to block Zolinger's view of the two men at the table. "I'm asking you these questions, Mr.

Zolinger, not Mr. Barre. So did she succeed in interpreting what he was saying? I can call Dr. Taekman or Chief Lyle West to reply if you can't remember»'

"Yes," he shot out. "Yes, she did."

"Did she at any time hear you discuss today's case?"

"No, we were careful."

"Did Mr. Jackman make any statement regarding her service as an interpreter?"

"I... um... That's confidential."

"The man couldn't speak, so how could what he said be confidential? She had to be there to interpret it."

"He called her some names and she wouldn't repeat them."

"But you know what he called her, don't you?"

"I have an idea considering how upset she was."

"What else did he say?" Hubert asked.

"That just because she came and helped him, she shouldn't think he was dropping the lawsuit because he wasn't."

"Are you telling me that while she wouldn't repeat his cuss words, she'd repeat his firm declaration for you to continue this suit?"

"She had no choice," Zolinger said.

"When exactly did she have no choice? She refused to repeat several terms hateful to her sensitive nature and still she told you to continue the suit. Why couldn't she have refused to pass along that piece of information?"

"She was there to help the man. She got angry with him, but only about his cussing her out."

"At any time did she attempt to solicit any consideration for her services?"

"Yes!" he stated firmly.

Hubert remembered Aleta's advice. Ask the tough question. So he did.

"What consideration?"

"She demanded he treat her with respect."

"She leaves the safety of her home to enter a dangerous situation to help her sworn enemy communicate with his lawyers so he can sue her and all she asks for in return is respect? No more question, Your Honor."

Judge Cohen glanced at her watch and called for a lunch break.

"Court will resume at one o'clock," she ordered. "Mrs. Praetzel, do not rise."

Aleta remained seated while everyone else rose and Judge Cohen left the courtroom.

The two Arborville police, who were waiting outside, made their way down the aisle and cleared the way for Aleta's wheelchair. Hubert led the way to his wife's courtroom. Hubert opened the door, went in and stood at the rear. Lydia called a ten minute recess and waved the group into her chambers. The police guard stayed at the door.

"How'd it go?" Lydia asked.

"Aleta and Hubert worked as if they'd been co-counsels for years," Robert reported enthusiastically. "The other team stumbled several times. I think they underestimated Aleta."

"I only have a few minutes," Lydia said. "Aleta use my couch and lie down. My cook prepared lunch. It's in my refrigerator and on the sideboard. Do eat a little, Aleta. I know you don't feel like it, but if you don't you'll feel weak mid-afternoon. Don't take my advice as a mother, but as a jurist."

"Thanks for letting us use your office," Aleta said as her father helped her lie down to rest while they set up the lunch.

Lydia left after a few minutes. Aleta asked Hubert who he thought would argue the case.

"Scheff," he replied. "He's their best litigator."

"Tell me about him."

"He likes to start by conceding all the paints you've obviously won. This rattles inexperienced lawyers. For the experienced, he dismisses same of their arguments in a cavalier style. This riles them so that sometimes they spend an inordinate amount of time in those areas, and overlook the fact that he is carefully building his case on his strongest point.

"What point will he chose?"

"That freedom of religion does not relieve a person from his or her obligation to comply with a valid law generally applied to all citizens."

"That's what I think too," Aleta said. "That's the argument I'd use."

"Let's eat," Hubert said. "Let your mind chew on the idea subconsciously."

"I hope there's milk. It settles my stomach," Aleta said.

"There is," Hubert announced. I think Lydia was more worried about nourishing the baby than settling your stomach."

"She's getting into this grandparent role, isn't she?"

"We all are," her father commented.

Chapter 27

Just before one o'clock, Hubert Praetzel gazed at Aleta lying on the couch. She looked pale and spent.

"I can argue this case, you know."

She gazed at the man so like the husband she loved, in both looks and manner. Stanley would have put it just that way. An offering. Not a suggestion that she couldn't. Not an admonition that she shouldn't try. Just as offering. No pressure. The choice was hers.

He could argue it as well, perhaps even better than she, but she wanted to do it.

He knows that, she thought. He wants to do it too.

"I know you can," she said. "If you don't think I can do it, tell me."

Hubert smiled. "There is no one who could do it better, not even Stanley."

In the courtroom, as Hubert predicted, Brad Scheff stood up to present their case. As Hubert had predicted, he conceded that the three women were a recognizable religious group, set apart from others by their prophetic powers. He agreed that Aleta had, indeed, performed a brave act by throwing herself between Simon Jackman and the bullet from Fred Hepner's gun.

He conceded that while there had been a meeting between Sam Hepner and Aleta Praetzel, apparently it was not planned and, while the deal Aleta Praetzel claimed to have made was an odd one, it did not in itself prove collusion. It did, however, bolster the theory that somehow they were working together. It was common knowledge that Martha Cook bitterly opposed Jackman's selection as CEO. The association between her and the Hepners could possibly be a loose one and, as such, difficult to uncover. It certainly would explain why the prophecies were so accurate. And as for the announcement about no longer prophesying, that might have been made necessary by a falling out between the two groups. With their information source cut off, the women backed off with their excuse that God wanted them to. Who could argue with such an excuse?

The gauntlet was thrown. Aleta looked at Hubert and nodded. She remembered his prediction. And Scheff had done excellent work. He'd riled her to the point where she wanted to deal only with that last issue—the attack on Martha's integrity.

Hubert had exchanged places with her father earlier and she wondered why. Now, when he offered her some water and leaned over and whispered in her ear, she knew.

"Don't fall in his trap," he warned. "If you do, we'll lose. Here comes his real argument."

Hubert sat back. His warning was well-timed. Aleta shook off her emotional desire to defend Martha Cook. She had been unprepared for an attack on anyone other than herself. While her grandmother and Martha Cook were named in the lawsuit with her, she was the most controversial of the three. She expected to be the focus of attention.

As Aleta listened to Scheff begin to cite cases with which she was familiar, her mind wandered back to Scheff's intimating that any of them had any ulterior motive in prophesying and whether it could be viewed as a form of revenge. Money was not an issue as the three of them were extremely wealthy. In fact, had they not been, no lawyer would have taken on so spurious a lawsuit. She was certain that the firm of Barre, Scheff and Cadean believed that the litigants would want to settle out of court. These were women who prized their reputation. A quick search into the background of each brought up a personal issue that two of them wouldn't want to come to light. That the women decided to fight them in court worried them until they discovered that the three had chosen a little known child advocate to represent them. His expertise in his chosen field would do him little good in this case.

Then he was injured and his ailing wife took over. Until they put her on the stand, they didn't realize she would be a formidable opponent. Who would have believed that a psychic would have a legal mind-set.

Scheff decided he had case law on his side. He started with the famous 1990 high court ruling in the case where the State of Oregon wanted to enforce its anti-drug laws against a Native American sect that used peyote as part of its religious ritual.

"In that case," Scheff said, "the justices wrote that the First Amendment's guarantee of religious freedom, and I quote, 'does not relieve an individual of the obligation to comply with a valid and neutral law of general applicability on the ground that the law proscribes conduct that his religion prescribes'."

He continued after a momentary pause. "Criminal law states that a person who has knowledge of a crime before its commission is an accessory before the fact.

"In response to that decision," Scheff went on, "Congress enacted the infamous Religious Freedom Restoration Act which the Supreme Court's decision in the case of Boerne versus Flores struck down the constitutionality of the controversial Religious Freedom

Restoration Act because it established one set of laws for private individuals and businesses and another set which was applied to churches and other religious groups on a selective, discriminatory basis.

"These three prophets," Scheff finished, "have declared that they will not reveal any visions pertaining to the death of my client. That their visions are accurate has been proven. The source is a matter of conjecture; however, that is of no moment. My client has the right to demand that they share all prophecies concerning any planned murder of him with him. Their withholding this information makes them culpable. The monetary award, while no compensation for his life, is just compensation for the emotional distress caused by their declaration that they have chosen this course to save the life of a horse. His value as a man has been estimated by them to be less than that of a horse."

Aleta had to admit the last was a clever note to end with. She had been wondering how they were going to justify the award they were demanding. And he tied it into the package neatly.

Robert rolled Aleta's chair out from behind the table. He patted her shoulder lightly as he left her.

The courtroom grew quiet in anticipation.

"Your Honor," she said. "It appears my worthy opponent has neatly narrowed the case to a single argument, providing, of course, I don't waste the court's time with the spurious red herring defaming the reputation of my two fellow prophets whose integrity has never before been questioned in a court of law without a smidgeon of factual evidence. That being said, let's move to the only valid point made by my esteemed opponent, that being that religious freedom is currently circumscribed by the needs of the government that wants all its citizens to obey all its laws. In other words, you can hold any religious belief you like as long as somewhere the government hasn't passed a law forbidding it.

"In detailing a history of religious liberty, Supreme Court Justice O'Connor said 'Our nation's founders conceived of a republic receptive to voluntary religious expression not of a secular society in which religious expression is tolerated only when it does not conflict with a generally applicable law."

"Add to that, please, the dissent in Employment Division versus Smith where freedom of religion--and I quote again here--'is best understood as an affirmative guarantee to the right to participate in religious practices and conduct without impermissible governmental interference, even when such conduct conflicts with a neutral, generally applicable law.'

"That, Your Honor, is our argument. We believe that our practices have done no harm to those outside our group and, in actual fact, have been responsible for saving a number of lives, including that of Mr. Simon Jackman twice.

"Mr. Jackman assumes that if we switch to his religion, we will bring our prophetic powers with us. He is mistaken. Our abilities are the result of our religious belief which dictates an obedience to God above all.

"All three of us received the same direction to save the horse. We didn't decide the horse was more valuable than Mr. Jackman. We foresaw it as the first in a series of threats escalating to the point where our children would be threatened. And yes, we all value our children more than Mr. Jackman. Personally, I like my horse a whole lot more than Mr. Jackman; however, twice I have laid down my life to save his. He cannot honestly say that I do not value him.

"It was God who directed us to acquiesce to the demands of the Hepner brothers and make the public statement we did. It was not a popular statement.

"Now if we are going to demand that we be held liable for Mr. Jackman's death we need to hold others to the same standard. For example, in Mr. Jackman's room yesterday, when the gunmen appeared in the short hall leading from the doorway to the room, only one person was able to see them approaching, Mr. Martin Zolinger. Mr. Zolinger knew that they were about to attack Mr. Jackman and perhaps others in the room including his associates. He did not cry out a warning. He simply fell to the ground. He had advanced knowledge of a criminal act and yet did nothing. He claims his was a reasonable act of self-preservation. Why isn't he culpable? If he had shouted, perhaps my husband wouldn't have been shot. And perhaps I wouldn't be sitting here with an arm that was ripped into by a bullet. If he had cried out, perhaps I could hold my own glass of water. Why isn't he culpable?

"The same law should be applied equally to the believer and non-believer, yet I am on trial and he isn't. Does the amount of forewarning matter? The law doesn't say. So who decides?"

Aleta paused and her father offered her a drink upon her signal.

"My esteemed opponents would have you make a decision on certain facts and disregard other equally compelling facts.

"Our visions have thus far been accurate. There is no guarantee they will continue however. Each is a surprise. We believe each is the last. We may never receive another relative to Mr. Jackman. Are we to be held liable for what we cannot produce? There are things out of the control of man. Prophecy is one of those things.

"Traditionally, God has given us visions with the implication we are to act upon them. Who is to say we will ever receive another?

"How can we be found guilty of breaking a law that we have not broken and may never break?

"Finally, I received no vision of Fred Hepner shooting Simon Jackman. Suppose I had followed the dictates of Simon Jackman's and Mister Zolinger's belief that self-preservation is the prime directive and not followed the dictates of my own religion? Had I done so, Simon Jackman would be dead. Isn't he fortunate my beliefs are different than his?

"And yet he would force his beliefs upon me."

Suddenly, Aleta was done. She couldn't remember if she'd made all her points or not, but her mind was a blank.

She bowed her head and Hubert moved forward and took hold of the wheelchair.

"Your Honor," he said politely, "Mrs. Praetzel has fainted. May I please remove her from the courtroom?"

"Court recessed for fifteen minutes. Bring her into my chambers. Bailiff, call the paramedics."

Hubert wheeled her into Judge Cohen's chambers. Robert trailed along behind the pair. With great care the two men lifted Aleta from her chair and laid her on the couch.

Hubert opened his cell and punched a single number. "Dr. Cook, Aleta collapsed in court. She'll be coming in by ambulance."

"Did she finish her presentation?" Judge Cohen asked.

"Most of it," Hubert said. "She wouldn't have ended on a personal note, however. I do believe I know where she was going."

"May we resume as soon as the paramedics come for Mrs. Praetzel?"

"Yes, Ellen, we may," Hubert said. "We used Lydia's office during the break. Aleta appeared wan then but I had no idea how close to collapse she was. I would have insisted an completing the case if I had."

"I think it's more than a faint," Robert worried aloud.

"Go with her to the hospital. I'll follow as soon as I'm done," Hubert said.

The attitude of the paramedics told Judge Cohen that Aleta was not putting on an act. Her concern for the young woman became genuine. The paramedics assured her Dr. Cook was one of the best.

After the paramedics left with Aleta, Hubert returned alone to the table. It felt so empty without Aleta. He moved over to her chair and perused her notes. Words and phrases. That's all. But from them he gathered how far she had gotten.

The judge entered and announced that Mrs. Aleta Praetzel had suddenly taken ill and her co-counsel Mr. Hubert Praetzel would continue the presentation.

"Your Honor," Hubert started, "we of the defense do apologize for upsetting these proceedings. There is just one more point I believe my colleague planned to make. It had to do with the fact that our founding fathers, per various state and colonial charters and the constitution, planned to permit religious exercise so long as it didn't violate general laws governing conduct.

"The key word here is conduct," Hubert said. "The First Amendment allows people to express themselves freely. It also tells the government it cannot force a person to express themselves in any manner, hold certain beliefs or belong to certain groups.

"Mr. Jackman is trying, via this lawsuit, to force his belief upon Mrs. Praetzel, Mrs. Locke and Mrs. Cook. He wants the court to force them to reverse what they declared publicly to be their religious belief.

"None of the prophets named in the petition before the court has conducted herself in violation of any law with regard to Mr. Jackman. It is our contention that illegal conduct must occur before any redress can be made."

Chapter 28

Hubert Praetzel called Robert Locke from the phone in his wife's chambers. He asked about Aleta and was told she was still comatose.

"Judge Cohen said she would have a decision shortly. I think she expects me to wait for it," Hubert said.

"There's nothing you can do here right now," Aleta's father told him. "I'm in the waiting room pacing. I haven't told Stanley. Dr. Cook called in a neurologist to help him read the CAT scan. He plans to tell Stanley as soon as he has some idea what's wrong."

"As soon as the judge renders her decision, we will come straight over. "Who's watching Jocelyn?"

"Bertha is. She and Jocelyn will stay at Stanley's place tonight and take care of the dogs and wait for news."

It was nearing the close of the court day when Hubert and Lydia Praetzel entered Judge Cohen's courtroom.

"The clerk said Judge Cohen was ready," Hubert said.

"It's been years since I've been in this position in a courtroom, waiting for a verdict, hoping for a win, scared of a loss," Lydia confided to her husband. "Aleta certainly has shaken up the calmness of our lives."

"Robert said Dr. Cook plans to tell Stanley now."

"Don't fret, Hubert. He's not alone. Not like before. He has friends now."

"We'll appeal," Hubert said. "We have a good case."

"Stop anticipating the verdict."

"Why is she taking so long?" Hubert fretted.

"Ellen knows this case will be appealed. She wants her decision upheld. She wants to word it just right."

"Aleta won't comply, you know," Hubert predicted.

"I know," Lydia sighed.

At that moment Dr. Cook walked into Stanley's hospital room. When Stanley saw Robert behind him, he immediately knew something was wrong with Aleta.

"Is she dead?" he asked.

Lyle looked startled. He had always been the first to hear such news. He didn't like being on the receiving end, but worse than that, he feared that his men had failed to protect Aleta.

"No," Dr. Cook replied.

"Shot?" Lyle asked.

His apprehension made him impatient. Cook could be so slow sometimes.

"No, she was in court and she collapsed," Dr. Cook said. "As yet we don't know why. She's in a coma."

"I must see her," Stanley said, throwing back his covers.

"You can't!" Dr. Cook said moving toward the bed.

"Try and stop me!" Stanley said moving one of the packs imprisoning his leg.

"Whoa, Stanley!" Lyle cried. "Use that brilliant brain of yours. Have them bring her here."

"This room's not big enough," Dr. Cook protested.

"Lyle will give up his bed," Stanley announced, putting the pack back in place.

Lyle's response was instantaneous. "No, Lyle won't. He's not spending one second with Jackman. Move Aleta next to Stanley or move her in the same bed he's in. I don't care which, but I stay here."

"I like the last one," Stanley said, sitting back.

"I'll have her bed moved next to yours," Dr. Cook decided. "It'll be tight; but maybe listening to you two spar is just what she needs."

He rushed out muttering.

"You two will be better than a porno film," Lyle quipped

"You watch those?" Stanley asked surprised.

"Never!" Lyle replied. "Lauren would kill me."

"Robert, what was happening when she collapsed?"

"She was toward the end of her summation," Robert said. "And suddenly she just stopped. It took us a few minutes-actually it took me a few minutes--your dad guessed right away she wasn't praying. He's not here because someone had to deliver her closing argument. She'd done so brilliant a job; we couldn't let it all be lost in a retrial."

"She argued the case?" Stanley gasped, stunned.

Lyle poked at him verbally. "Come on, Stanley. You can't tell me you didn't suspect."

"I knew she would want to; but she can't…"

"She only represented the Tontine personnel," Robert explained, "That is, herself and her grandmother. Hubert represented Martha Cook. Jackman's lawyers put her on the stand. Hubert cross-examined her. It was brilliant."

"Why did they do that?" Stanley asked, puzzled.

"Because she met with Sam Hepner."

"She did what?" Stanley's reaction spoke of his ignorance of that happening.

Lyle spoke up. "I meant to tell you someday. She sent me off to save Jackman. She knew Hepner was coming. I never would have left her if I'd known."

"That sounds like Aleta," Stanley said. "She must have thought you would be killed."

"That was her explanation," Lyle said. "Better one than two she said. I was furious with her."

"I know the feeling," Stanley said with equanimity. "How come she survived?"

Robert spoke up.

"That's why Barre put her on the stand. He wanted to prove collusion. He had a witness to the meeting. She made a deal."

"With what? She had no bargaining chip."

"She promised to bury Sam's two dead brothers properly," Robert revealed. It sounded a little like the kind of deal one would make with a friend."

"Which Sam Hepner is not!" Stanley declared.

"Which became so clear after Hubert did the cross that Scheff dropped the whole collusion idea in his closing," Robert explained. His tone changed suddenly and his speech waxed enthusiastic. "Stanley, she was brilliant in her summation. Reason and fire combined. It was so captivating that when she stopped Hubert wasn't prepared to finish. He said he would, but I know he was unsettled at the thought of doing so. Hers would be a hard act to follow. I don't envy him the position he was stuck in."

The noise in the hall told them the bed was corning.

Dr. Cook entered first. "This isn't standard procedure you know. I have to explain it to the Board."

"Blame me, Doc," Lyle said. "She's under police protection. So are the rest of us."

"I've got my grandmother alone in a room and Jackman alone in a room and I not only have three people in this room, but mixed sexes. Your police protection explanation won't cut it."

"Sure it will. I'm the police chief. I get to deploy my men. And I'm putting me in the room."

"Yeah, in a hospital gown," Dr. Cook quipped.

"I'm under cover," Lyle smirked.

"As soon as she wakes up, she goes back into the room with Martha," Dr. Cook declared before he began directing the orderlies where to place the bed.

Stanley turned his head as the bed carrying Aleta was positioned next to his. He studied her face for a long moment before the tears welled up, blurring his vision and running down his cheeks. He brushed them away and blinked repeatedly as if he could stop them if he just blinked enough. He took her hand in his.

Dr. Cook motioned to Robert to follow him and they left the room.

"Aleta," Stanley said softly, "you're with me and everything's okay. We both have some healing to do, but if you wake up we can talk while we're doing it."

"Doing it?" Lyle jibed. "What a promise!"

"For heaven's sake, Lyle!" Stanley said exasperated. "Get your mind out of the gutter. I mean while we're recuperating."

"If I were her, I'd like it better with the other meaning. If she's like her grandmother, that's what excites her."

"Lyle! You're talking about my wife!"

"Too bad you can't put your hand elsewhere," Lyle quipped. "That'd wake her up in a hurry!"

"Stanley, don't you dare!" Aleta declared.

"I told you talk about sex would do it." Lyle snorted, trying not to laugh.

"You're a rotten scoundrel!" Stanley declared.

"She woke up, didn't she?"

Aleta opened her eyes. "It is over? Did we lose? Did I mess up? Am I never going to be a lawyer? Are we going to be poor? Will you ever forgive me? I thought I could do it."

Before he could reply, his parents entered the room.

"I can't believe it!" Hubert exclaimed. "How did you ever pull this off?"

"They have a chaperone," Lyle said. "And, believe me, they need one. Stanley needs to keep that leg on ice."

"Did she postpone?" Aleta asked.

"She handed down her verdict," Hubert replied.

"I didn't finish."

"I closed."

"I'm sorry."

"You were a hard act to follow," Hubert said. "Oh, hell, why keep you in suspense. "You won!"

"I... We did?"

"Jackman may try to appeal, but his current firm won't handle it. Barre told me he doesn't think Jackman has a leg to stand on. Of course, that was off the record."

"We won... imagine that...," Aleta mused. "I can take the bar... I can practice law. .

"Is that what was worrying you the most?" Stanley asked.

"That and losing all your money."

"Stanley, don't tell me you haven't told her what you're worth?" Lyle asked.

"I know he's rich," Aleta shot back defensively. I don't need to know how rich."

"Evidently, you did need to know," Stanley said. "And since everyone here already knows, let me put it in reasonable terms. We are a bit richer than rich. The forty million on the line represents about eight percent of our total worth."

Aleta's brain sped through the calculation. "You're half a billionaire?"

"I never heard it put that way before."

"And you bought two rescue horses?"

"That's the first thing you think of?" Stanley asked, his mouth dropping open.

Lyle began to laugh. "Tell him why, Aleta."

"Because it means you haven't been spoiled by the money. You have great priorities. I love it!"

Stanley looked at Lyle askance. "How did you know?"

"I'm married to Lauren. That was her reaction only not about horses because we don't have any; but because we're living in an old house on an ordinary street in Arborville. It was her house and she loved it."

"I heard happy talking," Dr. Cook said coming into the room. "Tell me what the magic words were."

"Lyle, don't you dare!" Stanley growled.

"Sorry, Doc, It's a secret."

"Aleta just found out how rich she is," Hubert said.

"You mean she was worried about forty million?"

"That and not being able to be a lawyer," Stanley added.

"Well, Grams never told me how rich I was until I moved back here," Dr. Cook admitted. "I guess she thought it would spoil me. My advice to you two is not to tell your kids until they're your age. That means you have to live that long, you realize. No getting so hurt I can't fix you."

"Is that an order?" Aleta joked.

"Obviously you're well enough to move to a proper location," Dr. Cook observed wryly.

"Why not wheel Martha in here? Hubert was about to tell us Judge Cohen's decision," Aleta proposed, in an attempt to put off the move.

"We'll wait," Stanley said, squeezing Aleta's hand.

She tried to lean over to kiss him, but the IV held her in place.

"I'll get him to take it out as soon as he gets back," she promised.

"Don't," Stanley said. "Just having you here and awake is enough for me."

"I don't want to be moved."

"Hospitals have rules."

"But we're married," Aleta protested.

"Lyle won't move."

"Why not?"

"Because the only other male roommate under police protection is Jackman."

"Ugh!"

"Exactly," Lyle said.

"Well, we managed a week with Martha," Aleta reminded him.

"Yeah, an hour a day and we had to bribe her with headphones and TV," Stanley returned.

"Hush!" Aleta hissed. "Your folks are here."

"I thought you'd been pretty blatant," Stanley retorted.

"I had not!"

"Well, if they had any doubts what we were talking about, they don't now."

Lydia leaned over and whispered in Hubert's ear, "Maybe we should go."

Hubert shook his head. "And miss all the fireworks?"

"But that's not what happened!" Aleta protested.

"Well, Lyle is certain it is. He's seen your grandmother in action," Stanley remarked dryly.

"He has not!"

"How do you know?" Stanley challenged.

"Grams is discreet."

Lyle nodded. "Aleta's correct. And I'm sorry I made that inappropriate reference to your grandmother earlier. I thought it might make you angry enough to wake up and defend her."

"Thanks," Aleta said. "It did."

"Martha's here," Lydia announced.

"We won!" Aleta exclaimed as soon as Martha was in sight. "Hubert is going to tell us all how."

As soon as Martha was settled, Hubert began.

"We won on a point none of us thought to make," he said, "Although Aleta alluded to it constantly."

"Something so close I didn't see it?" Aleta queried. "Great lawyer I am.

"You were great, Aleta," Hubert responded with warmth. "You stuck to the truth and…"

"And it set us free," Martha added. "Well done, Aleta!"

"Give us the ruling," Aleta said. "Please."

"First, Judge Cohen castigated Simon Jackman and his lawyers for denigrating all that you did to save Simon Jackman's 'miserable'--her words--life. Not one ounce of gratitude from either the client or his lawyers despite repeated acts that went beyond normal kindness to the ultimate gift of self-sacrifice."

"Ellen appears cool on the bench, but she's a sensitive person," Lydia said.

"After that," Hubert went on, "she ruled. You can read the full text of the ruling in a couple of days, but basically her reasoning was that the prophetic power the three women possessed was not of their own making, a fact undisputed in this case. That they had no control over when they would receive the gift, according to Judge Cohen, was moot. The telling paint was that it was a gift. Not only a gift, a God-given gift. The government cannot demand that a person given such a gift share it. It is a religious experience which a person is free to express or withhold as his spirit dictates. There is no rule of law that demands a prophet make public his visions. There is no law that says that a group of prophets may not declare that henceforth they are not going to reveal their prophecies.

"As a matter of fact, she said, the only law that touches on the matter at all is the law of self-preservation. If the prophet's saw the threat to the horse as the beginning of a series of escalating threats to themselves, they had every right to protect themselves.

"The repeated attacks an all three prophets support their reasoning. There is no law that says that one man owes another his life. History is replete with examples of such willing sacrifice of one human for another. One was described in this trial. Such a heroic act should have been rewarded with gratitude not repaid with retribution.

"Then she ordered Jackman to pay all court costs," Hubert finished. "It was a glorious victory. I wish you had been there--all of you."

"Barre is ready to hire you," Lydia commented. "His is a prestigious firm. You really impressed him today. He said he'd go six figures."

"That's not a starting salary," Aleta commented.

"He knows you're past that," Lydia said. "Some important ground-breaking cases come through his office."

"Are you trying to sell me on him?" Aleta asked, surprised at the pitch.

"It could be a good career move. One walks through such doors when they're open," Lydia said. "You have options. Stanley won't give you any grief."

Aleta looked at her husband. "Do you want me to work for someone else?"

"That's not the twist I'd put on it, but Mother must have gotten a feel that Barre will give you a real foot up the ladder to a judgeship if that's what you want."

"A judgeship?" Aleta mused. "Really? A judgeship. I'd like that."

"You won't get it working for me," Stanley said matter-of-factly. "Mine is a small firm and I won't be unhappy if it stays that way. You are free to spin your career in any direction you choose."

"You have a real talent," her dad said. "I think you'd make a great judge."

"You need to get some tough cases under your belt. It won't happen if you're working for Stanley," Hubert said.

"Stanley doesn't need you to bring in business. He's got all he can handle," his mother said. "A few more cases like this one are all you need."

"I didn't do this alone," Aleta pointed out.

"You did do it," Stanley said. "You made the case. You have the mind to go as high as you want. I'll support you all the way."

"I collapsed at the end of the trial."

Dr. Cook spoke up. "You shouldn't even have been trying that case. I'm surprised you lasted as long as you did."

"Speaking of that," Aleta said, "can you take out the IV?

"Absolutely not!" Dr. Cook declared. "How did that come up?"

"You spoke," Aleta replied, "and I remembered what I wanted to ask you."

"I'm moving you tonight."

"Can't I stay? Stanley and I will be good."

"With you two in separate beds in separate rooms, I know you'll be good and I'll have a peaceful night. I deserve one."

"Why? You didn't cure me," Aleta retorted.

"Sure I did. I put you in here, didn't I?"

"Which was a good move, Aleta conceded, then added, "leaving me here is a better move."

"That isn't going to happen," Dr. Cook said. "Even if I could get you to promise to stay put, I have no such hold over Stanley. But with Grams as your roommate, he won't go travelling. His leg needs to stay packed and immobile until all possibility of tissue swelling is past. Tomorrow, after I've checked you out, you can spend the day with him if you like."

"Go on, Aleta," Stanley said. "Take the time to think about Barre's offer. We can talk tomorrow."

Later, after Aleta moved and Martha was back in her bed and the halls grew quiet as the nurses finished their final rounds, Aleta spoke to the ceiling because the nightstand interfered with her view of Martha.

"What do you think I should do?" Aleta asked.

"Look at your goals."

"Did you?"

"Not really. I always knew I wanted to make my husband happy. After he died, I kept doing that I thought he'd want. He had a vision. I made it mine."

"Stanley doesn't have a vision."

"Hasn't he?"

"I guess my idea of a vision is climbing to the top of the mountain."

"Isn't he already there?"

"He's an top of a small mound."

"It's growing under his feet."

"You mean because he hired me and Dad?" Aleta asked. "He's not building a firm. He's allowing each of us to practice whatever kind of law we want."

"Three individual practices under one umbrella. That's how corporations are structured."

"But it's not like that. We're each independent. We can choose to take any kind of case we choose."

"Do you like that?"

"It's wonderful."

"And if you go with Barre, Scheff and Cadean--what would it be like? Tell me."

"Well, the partners would decide what clients to accept. The case would have to be a moneymaker. But the cases would be big ones."

"And you'd be handling them?"

"Not for a while. I might sit in on a few but the partners would take the big ones."

"Suppose they took a case you didn't believe in?"

"A good lawyer must, of necessity, be able to argue both sides," Aleta explained.

"And if you were with Stanley?"

"I could turn down anyone I didn't want to represent," Aleta said. "And actually, considering how rich Stanley is, I wouldn't be pressured at all."

"So you could defend people hike Bessie Dobbins?"

"Yes, I could.'

"What about the Tontine Trust? Will Barre want you to bring that client with you?"

"I don't think... Do you think that's why...? He didn't want... But Harriet wouldn't take Stanley off..."

"I wouldn't worry about the Trust. Harriet is in charge, but if you're an associate of Barre, Scheff and Cadean, you can't have private clients."

"Dad could take over," Aleta figured. "I don't like corporate work and I've already approached him. He thinks he might like it."

"So then you're free to choose," Martha concluded.

"I would like to be a judge someday," Aleta said wistfully, "but I want other things too."

"Just because a door is open doesn't mean you must walk through it," Martha said. "Every choice you make influences subsequent choices."

"If I don't walk through this door, does that mean I'll never be a judge?"

"There is always more than one path to a destination," Martha replied. "Life is lived on the path chosen. For most of us the goal remains just that, but life is lived on the way."

"Life is lived on the way," Aleta mused. "You know I wasn't alive until I met Stanley."

"Love does that."

"I like being with him. I like what he does. I love bringing home a case and having him say, 'Aleta, I'm a child advocate. That's what I am. That's all I want to be.' He is so staunch in his attitude. I love to tease him with a case that gets him to spread his wings. I think he actually enjoys it although he won't admit it. But I don't want to change him. He is so good as a child advocate. He'd make a good judge. I wonder if he's ever thought of it."

"I doubt that that's his goal," Martha remarked. "He'd be more political if it were."

"I'd have to be political if I wanted to be a judge, wouldn't I?"

"I would think that's a part of it."

"Lydia is political, isn't she?"

"Yes."

"And Hubert goes along?"

"He has his own practice," Martha said matter-of-factly, "and his own good reputation."

"He was great today. He let me carry the ball even though he could have done it equally well, if not better. He helped me wholeheartedly."

"He loves you," Martha said simply. "He didn't want you to fail."

"Stanley has a nice family," Aleta said yawning. "Goodnight."

"Pleasant dreams, Aleta," Martha said.

Chapter 29

Sour Sam Hepner entered the basement of the hospital through the tunnel from the new wing. He headed straight toward the laundry room and picked up a neatly folded scrub suit, entered the locker room which was nearly empty as it was between shift changes, and changed clothes. He borrowed a pair of soft-soled shoes from an unlocked locker and entered the service elevator and punched the two. He left the elevator on the second floor, passed a number of rooms and took the corridor to the lab and control room beyond which was the huge MRI unit.

In his hand he carried a small satchel. He came prepared to complete his business.

"There were three people inside the room when he entered: two techs and an orderly. He brandished his gun and all three backed away.

He tossed a thick roll of wide adhesive tape at one tech and told him to tape up the female tech. He carefully explained to them that he didn't intend to harm anyone in that room.

He hesitated and then added, "But I won't hesitate to kill you if I think you've disobeyed at all."

The tech and the orderly, under Sam's direction, taped the hands, feet and mouth of the women. Joanna was stuffed inside a lower cabinet where she could scarcely move. She was warned to be quiet. Then the doors were shut.

Then Sam had the tech tape the hands, feet and mouth of the orderly. Sam opened his satchel and extracted a small silverish device which he fastened to the orderly's collar. He handed the tech another matching device and told him to fasten it to his collar explaining that these were sending devices. He would be listening to everything they said on their journey.

He told the tech to sit down and write an order for an MRI for Simon Jackman. The orderly stood bound in the center of the room.

"Who's the doctor who's the biggest prick in the hospital?" Sam asked.

"Dr. Trottner or Dunlap," the tech replied.

"They order a lot of MRI's?"

"Yeah, both do. They're neurologists."

"Have it be Dunlap who ordered this MRI," Sam said. "Don't hesitate. Tell him I had a gun on you."

As he spoke Sam took out a silencer and fastened it to his gun. "If I hear any strange noise, suspect that you are trying to signal anyone, the lady in the cabinet is gone and I'll be out of here before you get back. And I know where you each live. However, if you do what I ask, all three of you will live to report me, and no one will get killed. Do you understand?"

Both men nodded.

Sam gave out a few more directions and sent them on their way.

Meanwhile Aleta had been wheeled into Stanley's room. She insisted on the chair being set close enough so she could hold his hand. When the nurse left, he asked her if she'd made a decision.

"That's what I need to talk with you about," she said. "You know I love you with all my heart. If you ask me to stay, that'll be the end of it."

"Aleta, I want you free to follow your own dreams."

"I want to be a judge. I can't even explain why, but I do. I really didn't know how much I wanted it until your mother told me about Barre's offer. Until then I was focusing so hard on my immediate goal which is to pass the bar, I didn't give the future beyond February much thought, except for the baby, of course."

"I understand completely," Stanley said.

"It does mean we might have to be a bit more political than we have been."

"Whatever you want," Stanley said. "Mother would help you better there."

"Not a lot of events. Just a few. We'll both be busy lawyers and we'll have a baby to care for. I need to meet people."

"I'm behind you, Aleta," Stanley said.

"What kind of salary should I expect?"

"Mother said six figures."

"That'd mean working long hours."

"We'll manage."

"It means we'd have to squeeze in our love making whenever we had a minute, like now."

"Aleta, why are you switching hands?"

Lyle coughed. "You want me to get the nurse to draw the curtain?

"Just don't look," Aleta said.

"And don't even think what you're thinking because nothing's going to happen," Stanley quipped. "Tell him, Aleta."

"Nothing's going to happen," Aleta sighed. "Ah, well…"

"Why did you suddenly switch to silly from serious?"

"I was scaring myself with all the changes," Aleta said.

"You don't have to make them all today. You can work into them."

"Martha said there are many paths to a destination and I should choose mine carefully because I may spend my life on the path."

"Whatever you want, we'll make it work," Stanley said.

"You know what I want, Stanley?" Aleta asked. "I want you to know because it's important to me that you understand my decision. Ultimately, I want to be a judge, but I don't want to lose the chance to take any case I fancy, to be able to grab hold and see it through to the end, to turn away from any client I don't want to represent, to work in an office where I can take time off if my child needs me for any reason at all, to have partners that will work with me when I need help because they aren't in competition with me. That's what I want. I want to work with you in your office where I can bring my dogs and not make out a time sheet every day. I want to spread my wings in areas I don't even know about right now. I don't want a specialty just yet. All the things I want I will have working with you. I do, however, expect a raise in pay.

"You aren't generating any income," Stanley protested.

"And I may never generate any income, but I still want a good salary."

"On what basis?"

"Any basis you consider tenable."

"Me? You're going to ask me to decide why I'm giving you a raise?"

"That's what bosses do."

"Aleta, you're priceless!" Stanley exclaimed.

"I expect a really good raise on that note," she said pulling one hand out of Stanley's and laying her head on the bed.

"Aleta, are you alright?"

"Just terribly tired," she murmured.

She closed her eyes and Stanley suddenly felt her hand under the sheet.

"Shit!" he exclaimed.

"What's wrong?" Lyle said. "Should I ring far a nurse?"

"Don't. In fact, don't let a nurse come near me just yet."

"What's going on?"

"She's got hold of me," Stanley grunted.

"Persistent, isn't she?"

"This isn't sexual," Stanley insisted.

"That's a new one."

"That's what people will think, but it's not. She does this when she's upset or worried."

"You're her pacifier?" Lyle snickered.

"It's okay at home, but, Good Lord, we're in a hospital," Stanley cried softly.

"And you can't peel her off?" Lyle asked.

"Then she grips tighter."

"Can you wake her?"

"How? Our voices aren't doing it. If I shout the guard will come running in. All I can reach is her injured head and injured shoulder. I can't shake either one."

"So, you are in a pickle."

"Any ideas?"

"Maybe a doctor?"

"Wayne already knows more than I like, but see if you can get the guard to page him, only say it's for you."

"Sure, okay."

When Dr. Cook arrived, Lyle said, "Shut the door."

Dr. Cook waved away the nurse who'd followed him and shut the door.

"This better not be frivolous," he said.

"Stanley has a problem--an extremely delicate problem."

Cook moved over to the next bed and spotted Aleta. He went to her at once and set two fingers on the blood vessel in her neck.

"Pulse is strong," he said. "But she shouldn't be sleeping. I don't like it. I'm going to take her back to her room."

"You have to detach her first," Lyle said.

"Detach her?" Dr. Cook queried looking at her more closely.

"Stanley, what are you doing?" he scolded.

"Aleta did it," Lyle said grinning. "He's her pacifier when she's worried or upset."

"What's she got to be worried or upset about?"

Lyle grew sober. "Come to think of it, what indeed?"

Dr. Cook moved his hand along Aleta's arm and tried to pry her fingers open.

Lyle shouted for the guard. "Get French over here."

Stanley's cry of pain made the doctor stop.

"She doesn't let go, does she?" Dr. Cook noted.

"You can't force Aleta to do anything," Stanley told him. "This is embarrassing."

Dr. Cook went over and drew the curtain as Peter French came through the door.

"Something's wrong somewhere," Lyle said told his lieutenant.

"Where?"

"Aleta's not able to tell us. Check every room and everyone personally.

"Martha's up in therapy. Jackman's getting an MRI."

"Any of the people who came for them new?"

"No. Regular staff."

"Start with Martha."

"I'm putting a couple extra units on this floor," Peter said. "I'll set a second on Martha after I've checked things out. Same with Jackman. You rest, Chief. And don't worry."

Lieutenant French with two officers trailing him spotted the gurney entering the main elevator.

"Hold it!" French shouted.

"Can't!" one of the men said, punching the button that closed the doors just before French got there.

He was about to start swearing when the doors were reopened by the guard.

"No room," the tech said. "Can a couple of your guys take the stairs?"

French leaned over. "Is he okay?"

The angry mumbling told him Jackman was alive.

"He's pretty agitated, Sir," the tech said. "We need to get him in bed right away and call his doctor."

"Okay, you two take the stairs," French said as he stepped into the elevator.

He punched the button that closed the door and the elevator ascended. The two men accompanying the gurney rushed Jackman down the hall to his room.

"He's in his room," the tech said.

The orderly repeated the words.

"We're putting him in bed now."

French heard them as he entered the room. "What the hell's going on?"

"He's holding Joanna hostage down in MRI," the tech reported. "He's got us wired. He can hear everything we say."

"Who?"

"Someone who hates this guy really bad," the tech said, pulling back the sheet.

On top of the man's chest was a large brown envelope addressed to Aleta Praetzel. French took the envelope.

"He needs a doctor," the orderly said as he removed the folded sheet. The bottom was blood soaked.

French told the orderly to call Dr. Cook, and then he radioed his men telling them there was a hostage situation in the MRI room.

Dr. Cook answered his cell and rushed out.

"I'll be back," Cook told Stanley. "Just hang in there."

"Doggone it," Stanley muttered. "Aleta, you do get me into the weirdest predicaments."

He pulled the sheet over the problem just as French came around the curtain and handed Stanley the brown envelope. "This is for her. Cook said to give it to you."

"Shit!" Stanley exclaimed.

"French, open the curtain and close the door," Lyle ordered.

As French did what his chief ordered, he radioed his men not to move until he got there.

"Read the contents to her," Lyle said as soon as the door closed. "It's from Sam Hepner…"

"Damn!" Stanley exclaimed. "Don't say his name."

"Maybe what's inside will wake her up."

"There is no way this leaves this room," Stanley growled.

"I'm not laughing anymore," Lyle said. "This stays between the two of us. Go on. Read."

Stanley withdrew the sheaf of papers from the large brown envelope. He scanned the first sheet. "A power of attorney naming Aleta so she can claim Toby's body."

He turned to the second page. "And one for me so I can claim Fred's body here in Illinois. This Sam is no dummy."

"Ouch!" Stanley exclaimed.

"Keep going."

"There's a letter," Stanley said. "And a list of instructions."

"Instructions?"

"Mortuary, grave site, type of coffins, songs, type of service, flowers. He's thought this out," Stanley said. "And don't say his name. I have a vested interest in that part of me and, if she doesn't let go soon I'm going to have something else besides my leg that'll need ice packs."

"Read the letter."

"'Dear Aleta, you'll need these to carry out your promise. You said you'd be there. Please don't fail me.'" Stanley paused. "I'm not letting you go!"

"Is that all he said?"

"He signed his name," Stanley reported. "Oh, and there's a P.S. 'I've decided to do what you suggested.'"

"That's it?"

"What did she suggest?"

"How do I know?" Stanley quipped. "I'm her pacifier, not her confidant."

Suddenly, the hand loosened its grip.

"Aleta are you awake?" Stanley cried hopefully.

The head came up. "Did I doze?"

"Sam must be gone," Lyle concluded.

"Don't!" Stanley yelled.

Aleta pulled her hand out from under the covers. "Don't what? What's wrong?"

"Never mind," Stanley said. "We're going to have a long talk when we get home."

"I'm back," Dr. Cook said. "You're awake, Aleta. Good."

"What about Jackman?"

"One of my interns is stitching him up now. Someone carved a huge 'H' on his stomach. Not serious. But painful. He's very agitated. I need an interpreter."

Aleta paled visibly.

"What's wrong?" Dr. Cook asked.

"I just had the worst dream only I can't remember it. But I'm feeling shaky right now."

"Well, you just sit there while I check out your husband."

"Stanley? What for?" Aleta asked.

"She doesn't know?"

"We didn't tell her," Stanley said. "Can you do the exam privately?"

Dr. Cook moved Aleta back and drew the curtain around Stanley's bed.

Their voices were kept purposely low. Aleta had no idea what was being said. As the minutes passed her worry grew. The doctor left the room once and returned, but she was on the side of the room away from the door so she didn't see what he'd fetched. She sat silent, exasperated. She felt as if she was locked in a closet.

Finally, Dr. Cook said words she could understand. "This may be all you need, but you can ask for another if you need it or you can call for me."

"Someone tell me what's going on," Aleta demanded.

When Dr. Cook opened the curtain, Stanley said, "No one is going to tell you what's going on. If, however, you don't ask any questions, I will tell you when I get home and we are alone."

"But I want to know now!" Aleta insisted. "Is it serious, Dr. Cook?"

"Stanley, I'll be back to check on you this afternoon," Dr. Cook said and then left the room.

"You asked a question," Stanley said. "That'll cost you another day before you find out."

"But…," Aleta started.

"Are you going for a week?"

"I don't like secrets!" she exclaimed.

"How long it remains a secret depends upon you."

"What else is in the envelope?" Lyle asked.

"What envelope?" Aleta asked.

"Sam Hepner was here," Stanley said.

"Here?" Aleta burst out. "Did he hurt you?"

"That question makes it a week and a day," Stanley said.

"That's not fair!" Aleta protested.

"I'll take it back if you won't ask about my injury again."

Aleta didn't hesitate.

"Okay. I promise. Take back the week."

"The other contents?" Lyle pressed.

"There's an audio type," Stanley said. "I have no idea what's on it or if we should even listen."

"It's probably something he wants said at the funeral," Lyle suggested. "Everything in the envelope has to do with the funerals."

"Let's listen to a few words," Stanley said. "That'll give us an idea whether we want to listen to more."

"We need a tape player," Lyle said. "Tell Aleta about the other stuff while I send for one."

When the tape started, Aleta cried. "That's today's court session. He recorded me in court. Oh, Lord, he was there!"

Stanley took her hand. "Or he had someone record the session for him."

"Or he put a recorder under one of the seats," Lyle said.

"I'm not sure I want to hear this."

"I'll call the nurse to wheel you out," Stanley said. "Lyle and I want to hear this tape."

"No. No," Aleta protested. "I'll stay."

The three were an hour and a half into the tape when they heard the lunch carts in the hall. Stanley turned it off.

Lyle's first words both surprised and delighted Aleta. "Can I have a copy of her testimony? I want to use it as a training tape. Talk about effective witnessing!"

"I want to share this with Martha later," Aleta said. "I know she wishes she had been in court."

When the first tray was delivered, Stanley told Aleta he'd share his lunch with her, but it turned out that Dr. Cook had ordered a tray for her.

While the three were eating, in the next room Simon Jackman stared at his tray. He was too upset to eat. Why didn't they bring Aleta to him?"

Dr. Cook had said he'd ask and then never returned.

Everyone else just told him to calm down, that the danger was over. Little did they know. It wasn't over at all. It had just begun.

Sam Hepner had laughed when he told him his plans.

"Aleta won't ever agree to see you," he'd said. "You've treated her so badly. And no one else will understand a word you're saying."

He'd then taped the mouths, hands and feet of the men who rolled him into the MRI room and made them sit in the far corner. Jackman had expected to be killed, but Sam told him that he had to avoid that because Aleta would be able to foresee that.

He'd breathed a sigh of relief but his relief was short-lived. When Sam Hepner slapped tape across his mouth, he was suddenly afraid again.

Why tape the mouth of a man who couldn't speak? All he could do was scream.

And scream he did. Over and over. At every knife cut. Sam took his time. He chatted about stuff Jackman didn't want to hear. Sam's father had been a so-called good employee.

So had lots of others, Jackman thought. But he had to show a profit. Eliminating jobs was the quickest way to do it. He'd given every downsized employee a generous severance package. And yes, he did know that the pittance, as Sam called it, wasn't enough for a man with two sons in college, a man too old to start again.

Jackman would have shut his ears but he couldn't. The man wouldn't stop talking. And the cuts were burning like hell.

He let the words roll past his ears without assimilating any. The company's failure was old news. He'd moved on, much wealthier as a result of his three year stint as CEO.

Somebody would have taken the money. If not him, it would have been someone else. It was happening everywhere. Why shouldn't he profit from the inevitable downfall of a company? Maybe it could have been fixed, but it would have taken a great deal of work. He wasn't prepared to invest the time and energy it would take for a company with a 50-50 chance of survival. So he took the easy way out. Others were doing it. It was part of being a smart corporate exec--the leaving of a dying corporation with a big piece of the corporate pie.

This stupid Sam Hepner was only sour because he wasn't able to profit from the company's downfall personally.

Jackman decided that not a word he was saying was worth listening to. He focused on the retribution he was going to exact when this was over. This man was momentarily in power, but that was only temporary. He took note of every painful slice, counting them. He still screamed. That he couldn't help. He was not a stoic man. With each cut Jackman's resolve for revenge hardened.

He'd have the hide of the police chief that let this happen to him. He's take the hospital to the cleaners as well. He would be rich by the time he got through. He'd make sure everyone would suffer as he was doing now.

That thought brought a smirk under the tape that covered his mouth. When Sam Hepner looked at his face he didn't see the smirk. What he did see were eyes brimming with pure hatred.

And Sam sensed the hatred was overpowering Jackman's fear. It was then Sam had laughed and began to tell him of his plans, plans only he would know because no one but Aleta would understand what he was saying.

Jackman's mind absorbed the details. He would use these to force Aleta to be his voice. He couldn't believe his luck.

The man was done, Jackman figured. And he'd survived. Now it was his turn.

How Sam guessed what expression was under the mask Jackman couldn't fathom. But suddenly, he saw hate on Sam's face that matched his own.

"You're planning something!" Sam exclaimed. "And I don't like it. So I'm going to make one more point before I let you go. If you hurt Aleta in anyway, I will be back and this will seem like nothing!"

As he said that, Sam dragged the scalpel in deeper than before and carved another long line next to the first.

Jackman's scream penetrated the tape and sent chills down the spines of the two men on the floor. They began to sweat. They looked at each other, eyes wide with fear. There was a madman loose and they were at his mercy.

They'd heard the anger in their captor's voice and knew Jackman had incited him into a furious rage. Why couldn't the dumb, old man just take his licks?

"Do you understand me?" Sam yelled, slashing crossways with his blade.

Jackman's eyes registered his abject terror. "Oh, now I have your attention," Sam sneered. Jackman nodded vigorously.

"Do I have your promise?"

Jackman nodded again.

"Liar!" Sam said making one more long deep cut.

Jackman's screech filled the room. Both men sitting on the floor wet their pants. Joanna, stuffed inside the cabinet, fainted.

Tears flooded Jackman's eyes. His head nodded as if it was an a spring that was wound too tight.

"I think you're ready to go back now," Sam announced.

"Let's see. We need to hide all the blood until you're back in the room."

He undid the tech's hands as Jackman's body shook with sobs. "Untie your partner. You make sure that the guard doesn't see a speck of blood until you're back in the room."

"Yes Sir," the tech said. "We'll wrap him in sheets."

The orderly went to the cabinet and pulled out a stack. The two men wrapped Jackman, turning him over and over as if he was a store dummy, ignoring his cries which the tape was no longer muffling. Both were conscious of their stained pants but didn't dare say anything.

Just before they were about to leave, Sam noticed the stains.

"Any spare pants in here?" he asked.

Both men tore over to the cabinets. One pair was found. It was a small size. The tech held them up and then dropped his pants and briefs and pulled them on.

"Joanna has a pair on," the tech said. "Hers are bigger. They'd fit him."

"Get them!" Sam ordered.

As the orderly was changing, Sam went over the plan again.

"Get Jackman to his room and you're done. Stop for any reason and she's dead."

"Yes, Sir," the tech said as calmly as he could. "We'll do what you want."

As soon as the elevator doors had closed and Sam was certain the other officers were climbing the stairs to check on Martha Cook, he'd left the MRI room and headed for the locker room. He changed clothes, then strolled out of the locker room and watched the police surround the entrance to the MRI as he waited for the service elevator. No one stopped him.

That was hours ago. Simon Jackman had been stitched up by a pair of interns who had to put him in restraints because he was so agitated. He'd kept shouting obscenities and demanding they bring Aleta and saying he wanted her to see what her friend had done.

No one understood a word.

Dr. Cook had left shortly after examining him and calling his interns to take over. He'd said he had another patient he had to attend to.

The locals he was given had deadened the area, but nothing had deadened his wrath. He needed someone to understand him. He needed to yell at somebody.

Despite his protests, his stomach was neatly bandaged. He wanted to be able to lift his hospital gown and shock Aleta. He knew he couldn't pull off the bandage. He had barely any strength in his hands and arms to lift his spoon to his mouth.

His fine motor skills were gone He couldn't write even a simple sentence. The letters that formed words were lost partway between his brain and hand and the resulting scrawl resembled nothing. His hand went up when he wanted it to, but the fingers curled when he needed his hand to go down. The result wasn't even recognizable as handwriting. It was just a bunch of random jagged lines.

So, when he thought of writing a note, he knew the most he would be able to manage was a single letter. He wasn't sure he could do even that, but he decided to try.

He dipped his finger in his pudding and made a single line on the paper on his tray.

He looked at it. It was fairly straight and slightly angled. It was a start.

He shoved the dishes off the tray. Some of them wound up on his sheet, but he didn't care. He dipped his finger into the pudding again and tried to draw another line. It crossed the first and had a huge wave in it.

He was so upset he swept his arm across the table and swept the remaining dishes on the floor. His forefinger, pudding still clinging to it made a huge line across the paper.

He stared at it. He'd made an A!

He waved the paper in front of the nurse who rushed into the room. She ignored it, scolding him soundly for making such a mess. She called for housekeeping.

The cleaning lady tried to take the paper away, but he shook his head and held it to his chest. She let it go, but said nothing to anyone.

A nurse came in to check on him. He pointed to the figure on his paper, but she looked puzzled, shook her head and left.

Simon looked down at the paper. He mumbled angrily. It was upside down.

Mid-afternoon Dr. Cook returned to Stanley's room, drew the curtain around the bed and reexamined him.

Being shut out a second time annoyed Aleta. Whatever it was, Dr. Cook was taking it seriously.

The voices of the two men were unusually low. Her mind ran the gamut of possibilities. It couldn't light on any.

"That'll keep you until this evening. I'll stop back then," Dr. Cook said and then left.

He was back a few minutes later. He held up a rectangular piece of paper. Stanley turned off the tape. "What's that?"

"What does it look like?"

"Some kid trying to make an A," Stanley said.

"Or a man, unable to speak or write, trying to tell us he wants to see Aleta," Dr. Cook said.

"I won't let her go alone," Stanley said.

"If Wayne will let me use a wheelchair, I could go with her," Lyle offered.

"She needs someone to push her chair," Dr. Cook said. "Aleta, if you want to go now, I'll take you."

"Don't stop the tape. You can keep listening," Aleta told Stanley. "I was there."

"We'll wait," Stanley said. "We need a break."

Chapter 30

When they were in the hall, Aleta looked up into Wayne Cook's face and said, "I'm very uncomfortable about this."

"Aleta, I will pull you out the instant you tell me, no questions asked, okay?"

"Thanks," Aleta said.

Simon Jackman began talking as soon as Aleta was wheeled into the room.

"Look, I know you're mad at me because I sued you, but I didn't have a choice. But just hear me out. I've got a great proposition for you. I'm planning to sue the hell out of this hospital, that doctor standing behind you and the police chief of this hick town. I need you to tell my lawyers what happened to me. And in return, I will let you take your time paying me my forty million."

Aleta started. Didn't he know?

"Oh yeah, and furthermore, I will tell you where Sam Hepner planted all his bombs. He told me because he was sure you wouldn't ever come to see me, but he don't know you like I do. You can't help doing the right thing. I knew you'd come. And, much as you're gonna hate to help me, you'll do it because you like saving lives more than anything else."

He paused and Aleta turned to tell Wayne to take her out when she saw Barre outside the door in the hall.

"Excuse me, Mr. Jackman," she said coolly. "Your lawyers are here."

"Good!" Mr. Jackman said. "Don't want to hear them gloat. Face it, girl, you were outclassed."

"Let's go," Aleta said and Wayne spun her around and exited the room with surprising speed.

"Mrs. Praetzel," Jules Barre said extending his hand. He withdrew it quickly. "Sorry about that."

Aleta pointed toward Martha's room and Dr. Cook began to wheel her in that direction. Barre walked alongside her.

"Judge Davis told me that you were planning to offer me a position," Aleta remarked.

"I hope she put it in a good light."

"She made it tough for me to turn down your offer. Hubert and Stanley both urged me to take the position."

"And still you are going to turn me down."

"Not you personally, Mr. Barre. I have the highest regard for you. It would have been an honor to work with you and for you."

"They why?"

"I'm not ready for the structure of a corporate practice," Aleta said. "I've been there."

"Our offer would put you much farther up the ladder. It's a great opportunity."

"Of that I have no doubt. But I need more experience in trial work and I will get it where I am now. Besides my husband's office has fish. And the fish have names."

Barre grinned. "There's no competing with fish. But if you ever decide you want to swim at the deep end of the pool, give me a call."

"That, Mr. Barre, I will do," Aleta said. "And thanks to you I managed to wrangle a raise out of my husband as a result of your offer. Of course, he's still not sure he's going to give it to me, but I have great powers of persuasion."

"That you have, my dear," Barre returned. "See you in court."

Wayne turned the wheelchair into his grandmother's room. "I brought you a visitor."

"Wayne, is there any way I can use that other bed?" Aleta asked.

"You can even spend the night," Wayne said, helping her into the bed. "Later, I'll check on you and see how you're doing."

"He wore me out."

"Jackman?" Dr. Cook asked.

"Yes."

"Was he abusive?"

"I don't even think he knows he is, but that's not what's wrong. I need to have a talk with Martha."

"Okay, Grams, I'll see you later too," Dr. Cook said. He kissed his grandmother lightly on the forehead and left.

"Do you want to talk first or sleep first?" Martha questioned quietly.

"I'm tired because I'm weighed down with a huge problem," Aleta responded dispiritedly.

"I guess we pray first," Martha said.

"Oh, yes! Let's!" Aleta agreed enthusiastically.

Dr. Cook hurried down the hall. Barre ran into him in the hall. "Can Aleta come back and translate for us?"

"Sorry, she's had a relapse."

"She was fine a few minutes ago."

"Do you remember how quickly she collapsed in court?"

"Yes, but…"

"I released her too early last time. She wasn't ready to go back to work and take on a major trial. And a few minutes ago, whatever your Mr. Jackman said to her made her relapse again. I won't allow her in there again."

"He's not my client anymore," Barre said. "He's not taking that very well."

"He hasn't taken anything well all day," Dr. Cook remarked. "My advice is to say what you have to say and then leave."

He hurried on and entered Stanley's room. "I want both of you to stay put. If I have to put a guard in here to see that that happens, I will."

"You can't order my men around," Lyle said.

"Don't either of you tell me what I can or can't do or I'll put you both in restraints!"

"What's going on?" Lyle asked.

"Aleta's collapsed again," Dr. Cook replied. "She put herself back in bed. She doesn't know how close she is to a total collapse. Martha won't push her over the edge."

"I wouldn't do that!" Stanley retorted.

"She's worrying about you," Dr. Cook said. "That already burdens her."

"Then tell her."

Lyle butted in.

"Not now," Lyle said. "She's got too much an her plate right now."

"He's right," Dr. Cook agreed. "Remember, she sought out Martha. I will keep you posted, but the two of you stay right where you are. What I can't figure out is how Jackman could have caused such total devastation so fast. She was in there only a few moments."

Dr. Cook went to the door and spoke to the guard.

"If either of these two attempts to leave his bed, call me."

He ducked his head back inside. "I'm going to concentrate on Aleta, so if either of you moves, you'll be taking me away from her."

"We won't move!" Lyle said.

When Dr. Cook was gone, Stanley said, "I've never seen him so upset."

"Nor have I," Lyle agreed. "Do you suppose listening to the tape was a bad thing?"

"No, I think it was Jackman," Stanley said.

"What could he have said?" Lyle asked.

"We know Aleta about as well as anyone," Stanley said. "Why don't we see if we can figure it out?"

"It's gotta be something that affects someone she loves," Lyle said. "She's pregnant. She feels protective. And she didn't come back here. My guess is that it's one of us."

"Well, Jackman would sue at the drop of a hat," Stanley said. "He just lost a big one. I can't see him taking that calmly. But he wouldn't have a prayer of winning."

"So who else would he sue?" Lyle asked.

"After today? Just about everyone. The hospital, the Arborville Police, probably you, the techs in the MRI lab…"

"They were threatened," Lyle protested.

"He doesn't care. Maybe even Dr. Cook."

"What did he do?"

"Who knows?" Stanley replied. "Jackman will manufacture something. He knows who's got deep pockets. He'll settle out of court on that one."

"I thought your mother said Barre was letting him go."

"There are a lot of lawyers that won't mind representing any scumbag if there's enough money to be had."

"Aleta would just refuse to help him," Lyle said. "She knows she has that right."

"That's how I see it," Stanley said. "He's got something on her."

"Blackmail?"

"Maybe not that, but something. Only I can't think of anything that would make her agreeable to helping sue every friend she has here."

"It must be pretty powerful," Lyle said, "because she's all torn up inside."

"She always carries everything on her own shoulders."

"Let's listen to the tape. Maybe something will hit us." Stanley pressed the play button.

Aleta woke three hours later. Martha rang for the nurse and asked her to tell Dr. Cook his patient was awake. Her request was made so quietly that Aleta wasn't aware that it had been made.

"Feel better?" Martha asked.

"Did I sleep long?"

"A few hours," Martha replied honestly.

"I guess I was tired-er than I thought."

"Or your problem was too big to bear any longer."

Suddenly, Aleta remembered. "How did I forget?"

"It must be a pretty grave one for you to shove it that deep."

"Martha remind me what God wants."

Without asking why Martha began with loving and obeying.

"What if you're torn between two evils only one of which you can do anything about and doing the one will bring about the other?"

"What has God told you?"

"If He's speaking, I'm not listening."

"Why is that?"

"Because I know which way I want to go and I want it so badly, I can't think straight."

"Go with your heart. It's not evil."

"And if I'm wrong?"

"God will show you. Is either choice irreversible?"

"The one is. The other isn't."

"And which are you leaning toward?"

"Choosing to prevent the one that's not irreversible."

"Now that we've discussed generalities, why not tell me what your two choices are?" Martha suggested. "Not because I need to know, but because when you put them into words maybe your choice will become clearer."

Just then Dr. Cook appeared. "You're awake. Good. Your husband's medical condition is improving. You can stop worrying about that."

"But you aren't going to tell me what it is, are you?" Aleta returned. "Have you ever heard of such a thing, Martha?"

"It happens all the time," Martha replied sagely. "However, I'm a bit surprised that it's happening to you."

"He's going to tell her, Grams. He's even set the day," Dr. Cook interjected.

"Oh, then that's different," Martha commented. "He's not dying."

"Now, Aleta, let's concentrate on you," Dr. Cook said. "I'm not happy with these sudden sleepy spells."

"What spells? I was tired. That's all."

"You collapsed in court. You were in a comatose state for hours. Then this morning, you suddenly fell asleep while talking with Stanley, and then after talking with Jackman, you slept for three hours.

"I guess I'm just tired from the trial," Aleta explained.

"That's what I'm telling everyone else, but you aren't recovering from that experience normally. I need you to stay here a couple more days."

"In the hospital?" Aleta questioned. "Just because I'm upset?"

"Whatever is upsetting you, get rid of it. You aren't strong enough to deal with it."

"Take me to see Jackman. Let me talk to him. Then I'll stay the night."

"I don't want you in a coma," Dr. Cook said. "I'm afraid a confrontation is out."

"Do you know which choice you're going to make." Martha asked.

"Yes," Aleta said. "I know. And I'll tell you about it when I get back."

"Tell me now."

"I can't. Just like Stanley can't tell me, I can't tell you. There are reasons. I'll be able to explain later."

"Wayne, take her," Martha said. "God will give her the strength she needs."

"One last question," Aleta said. "Martha, have you gotten any visions today?"

"No. None for a week."

"Neither have I," Aleta said. "Thanks."

"Well, Wayne, what are you waiting for?" Martha scolded. "Go get the wheelchair!"

Dr. Cook walked out muttering, "I swear next holiday season, I'm taking my family to Cancun."

"He doesn't mean that," Martha said. "He likes challenges."

When Dr. Cook pushed Aleta into Simon Jackman's room, Jackman began babbling immediately. Dr. Cook moved around to the side of the chair to watch Aleta's face. She wasn't wincing although Dr. Cook was certain that Jackman was swearing at her.

Her face held a steely resolve--eyes hard, mouth grim, forehead clear of expression. He put his hand on her back but felt no trembling. There was a tautness. That was all.

When Jackman stopped for a breath, Aleta spoke. Her speech was without tremor or hesitation, her voice strong and steady.

"I do not appreciate being sworn at, Mr. Jackman. Perhaps your lawyers didn't make it clear enough, but prophecy is a gift. As such it is mine to dispense as I see fit."

Jackman babbled on. "That's irrelevant! That's past. So I lost. So the judge felt sorry for a banged up girl in a wheelchair. You don't think it was your brilliance that gave you the victory. Look at you. You're pathetic. I understand the judge was a woman. Women are softies."

"Mr. Jackman, your lawyer offered me a position with his firm. He didn't do that because I was brainless. And he certainly didn't do it because I was beautiful. As you said I look pathetic."

Dr. Cook was puzzled. She was repeating his insults.

She hadn't done that before. He wondered why she was doing it now."

"Barre is a jackass," Jackman went on. "He quit. But then you know that."

"I knew he was going to quit."

"You need to find me a new lawyer."

"I don't need to do anything for you."

"You need to tell that stupid doctor standing next to you that I want a new lawyer."

"He's really not stupid," Aleta replied. "In fact, Dr. Cook is brilliant."

"So he's your friend."

"Yes, Dr. Cook is my friend as well as my doctor. You have the best doctor in the hospital and you are too stupid to realize it. Do you want me to tell him you are discharging him?

Jackman stopped speaking and considered her suggestion. When he spoke it was to take her suggestion.

"I guess if I'm going to sue him, I should fire him first or else the lawyers will ask why I didn't fire him. You're right. Tell him he's fired. I want a new doctor. Who's the best neurologist in the hospital?"

"The chief of neurology is Dr. Lemmon, isn't he, Dr. Cook?" Aleta asked.

"Yes, he is."

"And Dr. Trottner is another highly regarded neurologist, isn't he?"

Wayne felt as if he was on the witness stand.

"Yes," he replied. Aleta smiled at him. She was up to something. The smile told him he was doing what she needed. Besides now was no time to discuss personalities.

"And Dr. Dunlap and Dr. Nokes are equally regarded," she asked.

"Yes" he said.

Aleta turned back to Jackman. "There! You have four possibilities. Do you want to discharge Dr. Cook? Nod if you do."

Jackman nodded vigorously.

"I guess you're fired Dr. Cook," she said. "Now Mr. Jackman, what order do you want him to call the neurologists?"

"Top guy to bottom guy," Jackman said.

"Lemmon, Trottner, Dunlap and Nokes. Is that the order?"

Jackman nodded.

"Next do you want to hire a private security guard, one that will learn your signals and do what you ask?"

Jackman nodded.

"Do you want to replace the Arborville police with your own security?"

Again Jackman nodded.

"Good thinking," he babbled. "This will bolster my case in court, won't it? I mean, the fact that the Arborville police failed so badly I was forced to hire my own security guards.

"You are correct." Aleta said simply.

"I should go all the way, shouldn't I and insist I be transferred out of here. I am going to sue the hospital too."

"Where would you like to go?" Aleta asked politely.

Jackman mumbled an unintelligible string of words. Dr. Cook couldn't understand a word. The only way he knew

Aleta understood what he was saying was because Jackman was responding to direct questions.

"Can't go back to Cook County Hospital, especially as I'm thinking I should sue them as well. So I guess I need a private hospital near here, one where those doctors have patients. Ask Dr. Cook which one they use."

Aleta turned to Dr. Cook, "Mr. Jackman wants to be transferred to a private hospital near here, one in which one or more of those neurologists I named have patients."

"Glendale Extended Care Hospital," Dr. Cook said. "But it's expensive."

"Screw the cost!" Jackman burst out.

"Did he say no?" Dr. Cook asked.

"No, he said 'screw the cost!'" Aleta replied. "What about his wounds?"

"Clean dressings every day is all that's required now. They'll do that. No problem."

"Just to be sure, Dr. Cook understands, you want to be transferred to Glendale Extended Care Hospital, correct?" Aleta asked.

Jackman nodded.

Aleta turned to Dr. Cook. "Will you take care of those matters for Mr. Jackman? I suggest you draw up the necessary paperwork for the transfer and have him sign it. He can make a scrawl and two witnesses can verify his signature."

"Paperwork?"

"Mr. Jackman, allow me to help Dr. Cook with this. We will be back shortly and we'll continue then," Aleta said. "Dr. Cook, let's go to administration."

When they got into the hall, Dr. Cook said, "Aleta what's going on?"

"Simon Jackman has an agenda. Is anything I'm suggesting detrimental to his care?"

"No, but…"

"Dr. Cook, you are a doctor. I am a lawyer. Let me protect you, and I promise I will stay in this hospital as long as you deem necessary without once questioning your decision. Do we have a deal?"

"So far you've done nothing I find any fault with. I don't understand Jackman's motives. They don't make sense."

"I can't explain them to you yet, but his decisions are not irrational ones, are they?"

"No, they aren't," Dr. Cook replied. "He was attacked. He wants to hire private security. He wants a specialist. That makes sense. He wants to leave here. That's his pattern. He left Cook County after he was attacked there. But what's all this paperwork garbage?"

"There were just two of us in the room when he made these requests. We need his desires in writing. This is vital. Please let me lead on this. Get me a typist and I'll draft simple letters of request for him to sign."

"Okay, Aleta. I'll send someone from administration to your room. I want you to rest."

"Whatever you say, Doc."

Dr. Cook smiled. "That's the attitude I want."

"You look relieved," Martha commented after Wayne settled Aleta in bed and left.

"So far I feel God is with me. I'm still walking a tight rope though."

"The decision hasn't been made?"

"I'm making little choices one at a time. I'm a bit surprised at them. So far they are good choices no matter what my final decision is."

A young woman entered the room. "You sent for someone to type some letters?" she asked Martha.

"Not me," Martha said. "Her. She's the one who can't use her hands."

The young woman's facial expression softened. "I can take dictation and type from my notes."

"Four letters," Aleta directed. "All dated. All addressed 'To Whom it May Concern.' All with the signature line at the bottom and the name Simon Jackman typed beneath the line. There needs to be signature lines to the side for two witnesses."

Aleta paused and waited for the woman to catch up. Then she started dictating the letters. One discharged Dr. Cook. Another authorized the hiring of a specialist. The third requested a transfer from Tri City Hospital to Glendale Extended Care Hospital and the fourth authorized the hiring of a private security firm.

"I need these as soon as possible," Aleta said.

"I'll have them back in forty minutes," the woman said.

"Thank you. That will be fine."

Martha admired the professionalism with which Aleta dispatched the business. She was startled that Wayne was fired in writing. She wondered how he would handle this.

She didn't have long to wait. He returned with the woman from administration.

"Let's go get me fired," he said jovially.

Martha suppressed her query. Obviously, he knew. And for some reason he was happy. That she couldn't fathom. But Aleta was in charge and was acting with authority which appeared to stem from a strength beyond her own.

Two nurses were called into Jackman's room to witness the signing of the letters of request. Each letter was read aloud and then Jackman made a mark. He tried to make a "J" but his hand wouldn't obey. All four scrawls were completely different; however, the nurses were told they were witnessing the fact that Mr. Jackman had made the mark.

Aleta had the nurse hand the letters to Dr. Cook. "Make two copies. The original goes to the interested party, one copy comes back here to Mr. Jackman and one copy is put in a folder for his new lawyers. Make the copies now and then come back to me."

"I'm sorry, Aleta. I'm not leaving you," Dr. Cook said.

He handed the nearest nurse the letters and repeated Aleta's instructions.

Jackman shouted at her. "I want him gone. Send him away so we can talk freely."

"I want a name. One name," Aleta said calmly.

Jackman smiled. "You'd like it to be Martha Cook, wouldn't you? She was at the top of his list. He said he hated her most of all. But I'm not giving you that one. In fact, I'm not giving you any. Not yet. Now send him away."

Aleta looked up at Dr. Cook and was about to ask him to keep what she said confidential and then decided he could be trusted. Still she spoke with great care.

"What you are asking me to do is evil. You worship one god. I worship another. I won't join you in the worship of your god."

"You're talking nonsense!" Jackman said. "You can't refuse."

"I can and I do refuse to translate anything further for you. All that you have asked thus far has harmed no one and been for your betterment. What you asked me to do when first we spoke was not something I can or will do."

"You refuse to find me a lawyer?"

"Yes."

"You refuse to tell anyone I want a lawyer?"

"Yes."

"You can't do that!" he shouted. Dr. Cook could tell he was becoming more agitated, but it didn't seem to result in Aleta appearing disturbed.

"People will die," he shouted. "You will be responsible for many deaths."

"No I won't be," Aleta said. "You will be."

"Martha Cook is one of them. You want her to die?"

"If it's her time, she's ready."

"You say you love her," he sneered. "I'm glad you're not my friend."

"So am I," Aleta shot back with a hint of ire. "You would let your friends die so you can get rich. Sam Hepner was right about you. Your self-centeredness is total."

Dr. Cook's slight movement caught Aleta's eye. She gazed up at him. He was beginning to understand. That wasn't part of her plan. Why had she let her temper come to the fore?

She took a deep breath and let Jackman roar on. His words were like the sound of a rushing river--unintelligible. She felt relief that she couldn't understand him. At first she thought she'd just blanked him out in her effort to control her emotions. When she finally calmed herself down, she stared at the man in the bed.

His face was contorted in rage and she could only guess that the words emerging were words she had once understood.

She turned to Dr. Cook. "Is this how he usually sounds?"

Startled, Wayne Cook sputtered, "Yes."

Aleta began to laugh and then cry. Dr. Cook turned her chair; but she shouted "No!"

She held up a hand, sling and all.

"Wait." she choked out.

He stopped.

Jackman babbled even faster. Angry expression after angry expression. His fury raged on and Aleta listened to it.

It's like a waterfall, she thought. Such an outpouring of hate. Thank you, God.

After several minutes she ordered Dr. Cook to turn her back around.

Simon Jackman stopped. His mumbling grew softer.

Aleta smiled at him. "Mr. Jackman, I can no longer understand a word you are saying. I have no reason to do as you ask now. God has removed my ability to understand you.

Jackman's face reflected his utter disbelief.

"I know you don't believe me." Aleta went on, "but He did it for me. It was the sign I asked for. You gave me a choice between two evils. He made the choice for me. He does not want me to use His gift to me to further your demonic desires. Mr. Jackman, I no longer understand a word you are saying. I am sorry for you."

She looked at Dr. Cook. "Take me to see Stanley. I want to tell him I'm going to be a patient for a while longer and he's not to worry. I want his leg one hundred percent so he'll be able to ride with me. You will see to it that he does everything he needs to, won't you?"

"I will if you order him to obey me."

"Me? Order him?"

"Why not? He loves you enough to obey."

"I'll ask him," Aleta said. "I only order when God tells me to."

"Are you ever going to explain what went on in there?"

"Maybe to Martha, but not to anyone else."

"Stanley and Lyle won't like that," he commented.

"They have their secret. I have mine," she retorted.

"The magnitude of yours precludes any comparison," Dr. Cook observed.

"I'll ask Martha," Aleta said. "But other than telling my secret, I will do whatever you ask."

"Exactly when did Stanley's command to obey me get lost and replaced by your promise?"

"It didn't, but my promise means I won't search for any loopholes. I'll obey just like a normal person."

"You wouldn't know how."

"Then I'll obey like a robot, without thinking."

"I'll take that."

A few minutes later, Aleta was wheeled into Stanley's room.

"It's over," Aleta told Stanley. "God took away my ability to understand Jackman. The man was so evil. By the way, I'm going to stay in the hospital. Dr. Cook wants me to and I said I'd do it. Don't worry. I don't think anything is wrong, but I know you and he would feel better if you were sure. Will you be okay?"

"Me?" Stanley chuckled. "I'm fine. Honest. I'm fine."

"So your power is gone?" Lyle asked.

"I don't know. It could be. It was always a gift, one I never counted on to last."

"So what was the problem?" Lyle asked.

"Dr. Cook will tell you," Aleta said looking at him.

"Now?"

"Sure. Why not now? You don't want me to tell them. They'd get angry with me and I don't know if I'm up to that."

"Men, I'll be back. Aleta is going to bed," Dr. Cook announced. Without another word he wheeled her out.

"Guess he doesn't like being manipulated either," Stanley said.

"He's one of us. He doesn't get trapped easily."

"Us and our redheaded wives. What were we thinking?" Stanley quipped.

"She wouldn't tell him, you know," Lyle said.

"I know. She told him she wasn't telling anyone," Stanley said. "It must have been a really rough decision. She's out of it, but she still thinks she did something wrong."

"Why do you say that?"

"Because I know her."

"You know, Wayne knows more than he thinks he knows." "And we're great interrogators," Stanley said.

"So let's."

"As soon as he gets back," Stanley planned aloud.

"Suppose he doesn't come back?"

"He has to. If not right away, later. To check on you know what."

"Remember he's one of us."
"Yeah, a husband with a pregnant redheaded wife."

Chapter 31

After Dr. Cook left, Martha asked Aleta what she'd said to annoy him.

"He's annoyed?" Aleta asked with feigned innocence.

"He took away our television privileges---mine as well as yours."

"He'll get over it, won't he?"

"It takes him a while sometimes," Martha commented. "We may be without TV the whole night."

"Did he leave the remote in the room?"

"He took it with him."

"Sorry about that."

Martha shrugged. "I'd rather have live company."

"Maybe after I tell you what I did you won't be."

"Well I know half of it," Martha said. "I heard you dictate the letters."

"The first suggestion I made resulted from something Jackman said and I had this urge to push it all the way."

"Wayne's firing."

"Jackman planned to sue him."

"Whatever for?"

"My guess is he was angry because Wayne had two interns sew him up."

"That's standard."

"Jackman expects more than standard," Aleta said. "And one thing led to another."

"He signed everything?"

"I gave him the name of the four neurologists that you and Dr. Chesney regard so highly."

"That was a neat touch," Martha chuckled. "Bernard will enjoy that one."

"Think they'll take him?"

"If Wayne puts the word rich anywhere near Jackman's name, they will," Martha confided. "You wanted him out of here, didn't you?"

"But without Wayne."

"I don't think he liked being fired."

"I gave him a bonus."

"What could you possibly offer him?"

"That I'd be a really good patient and not argue with him at all."

"No wonder you let them put you in a gown this time."

"He's worried about me. And I'm so tired; I'm ready for a couple days of rest."

"Battling evil can drain one of energy."

"Let me tell you my dilemma. When I first went to see Jackman he told me he was going to sue everyone and I was going to help him. He saw that I was reluctant so he told me Sam Hepner had told him his plans for a string of killings and had gloated because he said he wouldn't be able to tell anyone. Sam said I wouldn't help him anymore."

Aleta took a deep breath as if she had been running and then continued.

"I admit I was scared to go into his room. The atmosphere in there was heavy with hate. I could feel lt. And when he told me I was going to help him sue Wayne and the hospital and even Lyle and the Arborville police department who had guarded him so well and been willing to lay down their lives for him, it made me sick. He told me I was going to translate for him. In exchange he would tell me where the bombs were."

Martha listened without comment.

"When I went back, he thought I was helping him prepare his suit. I didn't say so. I answered his questions honestly. These were the steps a person would take before slapping a suit on anyone.

"I had made my decision, but I felt I should take care of these matters first, so I did."

"Jackman wanted each one?"

"I believe he did. He wanted everyone to know how angry he was."

"Then what happened?"

"Wayne insisted on staying with me. He couldn't understand a word Jackman was saying, but I knew that if he knew Jackman wanted a lawyer, he'd feel morally bound to provide one, so I had to be careful. That's why I can't tell him or anyone. I can tell you because I trust you to honor God's will in this."

"Go on. I will honor your decision in this," Martha said.

"I told him I would not take part in his scheme that I considered it evil. I told him we each served a different god and I wasn't going to be forced to use my God's gift to serve his master." Aleta paused and smiled a bit sheepishly. "I sound so noble. The truth is I'm not. I fell back on religion because my own reasons seemed so much weaker."

"I gather he brought up the people whose lives were in your hands."

"I told him they were in his hands, not mine," Aleta went on. "I don't remember much until he mentioned your name. He said you were at the top of Sam Hepner's list. I still said I wouldn't help and he asked if I was willing to see you dead."

At this juncture, Aleta began to cry, "Forgive me, Martha."

"I forgive you, child," Martha said kindly. "Go on."

Aleta swallowed back the sobs welling up and finished her tale. "I said you were ready to die."

"That's true, Aleta, I am ready."

"And then he said he was glad he wasn't my friend. And he hit a nerve and I spat back something about him being willing to let friends die so he could get rich and that's when the river came in."

"The river?"

"The sound of it. I shut out his babbling and let his words rush by me. I concentrated so hard on getting back my composure that I only heard the sound with no meaning attached. My brain told me it was a river."

Again she paused to take a breath.

"And when I was able to listen again, all I heard was unintelligible babble. I listened for a long time. Then I knew I could no longer understand him," Aleta finished. "I told him God had taken back His gift. Jackman didn't believe me. I said I was sorry but I couldn't help him any longer."

"And now you're worried about me, huh?" Martha queried quietly. "A bomb, huh? Do you believe that?"

"I don't know why Sam would tell him that. Sam's a shooter. Besides he wrote me a note and sent it back with Jackman. He said he was going to take my advice."

"Which was?"

"To quit killing. Take the money and leave."

"Well, he didn't do it," Martha said.

"He didn't kill him," Aleta countered, "but I think his rage demanded he do something."

"Jackman hired security people," Martha said. "He must be afraid Sam Hepner is coming back."

"You know," Aleta said thoughtfully, "he said Sam hated you most of all, but Sam didn't. I know he didn't. And

Sam knew I knew he didn't. Sam was sending me a message."

"What message?"

"There aren't any bombs."

"You mean I don't have to worry."

"Ask Lyle to check your house and car again anyway," Aleta suggested. "Sam Hepner was here after all. So he's in the area. Your house has been empty all this time."

"What about the others?"

"The incident will make the papers," Aleta said. "That'll be warning enough."

"Some lawyer will smell lawsuit," Martha predicted.

Aleta laid back and closed her eyes. "I can't fix everything."

"It's about time you realized that," Martha said. "So you're going to stay in private practice."

"How did you know?"

"I'm a good guesser."

"I love working with Stanley. I'd like to be a judge someday, but I need lots of experience before that can happen. Let's hope a few choice cases come my way."

"There are people with serious grievances that can't afford a good lawyer. Sam Hepner's father was one," Martha said. "There are good cases out there. If you want, I can send you some."

"Would you?"

"Sure, I would. Remember, though, what I may think is a good case may be a trivial matter."

"I need to pass the bar before I can even advise anyone," Aleta cautioned.

"Well, since you're going to throw a party when that happens, I won't send anyone until the day after the party."

"That would be good," Aleta said yawning. "Why am I tired again?"

"Again?"

"Tell Wayne to bring you the court session. Sam Hepner gave me a tape. I don't need to hear... it... with..."

Martha rang for the nurse. "Get Dr. Cook at once."

"What's wrong?"

"At once!" Martha said sternly.

Two rooms down, Dr. Cook had just finished listening to Stanley and Lyle expound their theories as to what had been bothering Aleta and he'd said that Aleta had been extremely vague except for the last sentence she spoke to Jackman before she lost her ability to understand him.

Dr. Cook's cell vibrated. He pulled it from his pocket and opened it. "Dr. Cook, fourth floor emergency."

Then he sprang up and rushed out of the room saying for the thousandth time. "Stay put!"

"Should we?" Stanley said.

"Do you want to spend the night in restraints?"

"He wouldn't!"

"He just tamed Aleta. He's drunk with power," Lyle commented.

"Who do you suppose it is--Aleta or Martha?" Stanley asked, not wanting it to be either.

"It's who you think it is," Lyle replied. "He won't let us in there. Better we wait here."

"I need to pace."

"I wouldn't try that right now. Tear out your hair or bite your nails or crack your knuckles."

"My knuckles don't like being cracked, my nails are already short enough and, in case you hadn't noticed, my hair is too short to grab," Stanley snapped back.

"Then yell at me," Lyle suggested.

"Why should I do that?" Stanley barked.

"It'll pass the time and relieve some of that tension."

"I don't yell at people for no reason."

"You're doing it now," Lyle said calmly.

Stanley stopped short. "I am, aren't I?"

"Yep."

"Well, I'm all out of stuff to be mad about."

"Good. Let's look at the bright side."

"What bright side?"

"We're already at the hospital and her doctor was thirty seconds away."

The two heard scurrying in the hall and the wheels of a gurney rolling by. Dr. Cook poked his head into the room.

"I need you to sign a consent form for surgery if it's indicated," he said to Stanley. "The nurse will bring one by."

"She signed one a week ago."

"But she was discharged. We have to start over. She may not need it, but let's have it in place."

"What's happening now?"

"I've ordered an MRI and put Dr. Taekman on alert."

"Again?"

"When she fell on Jackman, how much of a jolt did she sustain? Taekman says he thinks that may have caused the vessel to break open again."

"Do they do that?"

"People don't usually engage in such violent activity less than ten days after brain surgery," Dr. Cook said. "I'll have an answer for you after I see the MRI."

"I gather she's unconscious," Stanley said.

"She is."

"I'll sign. Just save her. This time I'll make sure she stays in bed forever and a day."

"Celibate?"

"Anything."

"That'll be the day."

"You'd be surprised what I can do."

Dr. Cook looked at the distraught man in the bed and he remembered that Stanley had a power over Aleta no one else did except maybe God Himself.

"Let's hope God doesn't send her on another mission," the doctor said before he left.

"Didn't she have an MRI when she was brought here from the courthouse?" Lyle asked.

"A CAT scan. It was faster."

"So here we are again," Lyle said. "I think I'm going to get a new friend, one whose wife doesn't need so many brain surgeries."

"Come on, Lyle. Last time you were on duty. You had to sit somewhere. And I listened to your whole life story."

"Just the Lauren part," Lyle shot back. "I must admit that this is good planning on your part. I don't have anywhere to go tonight either."

"So we can lie here and worry together."

"I do the lie here part, but you get to do all the worrying."

"Why me? She's your friend too."

"Wayne said she mentioned Hepner being right. And she accused him of sacrificing his friends for money. She was talking about the present."

"We already suspect he was going to sue us all and she wouldn't want to do that," Stanley responded.

"What's the only reason she'd agree?"

"If someone's life was in danger," Stanley answered. "Especially if it was someone close to her. That would make the decision practically impossible."

"She could explain it if she was saving the life of someone close to us," Lyle said. "So it must have been the lives of people she didn't know. That would be harder."

"Wayne said she was cool up to the last minute."

"What did Jackman say to rattle her?" Lyle pondered.

"She's not easily rattled. He must have hit a nerve."

"She had two choices," Stanley said. "Wayne said she refused to help him. So then what would Jackman do?"

"Tell her that one of the victims is someone she cares about," Lyle said. "And Dr. Cook was standing right there."

"Martha?" Stanley ventured.

A nurse walked into the room.

"Any word?" Stanley asked. "About my wife?"

"The doctor will tell you as soon as he knows anything," the nurse replied. She handed Stanley a clipboard. "I have a permission form for you to sign."

Stanley signed the form and handed it back.

"Mrs. Cook has two requests," the nurse said. "She would like to hear the tape if you're finished with it."

Stanley picked up the tape player and rewound the tape. "Tell her we can finish later."

"And Mr. Chief," the nurse said, "she told me to tell you she'd like you to check her house again."

Lyle smiled. "We guessed right. Tell Mrs. Cook I will have my men take care of it."

The nurse rushed away.

"We have another worry," Stanley said. "Aleta promised Sam Hepner she'd take care of the funerals for his brothers."

"We have Sam's written instructions."

"How are we going to get Toby's body back from California? Aleta's not here to authorize a transfer."

"Wasn't she named after her grandmother?" Lyle remarked, "and didn't he use her full name Harriet Aleta Locke Praetzel?"

"The Praetzel will be a hard one to get past."

"Not for a person with a brand new marriage license. Harriet can claim Sam Hepner didn't know her new name. It was a simple mistake."

"She won't lie," Stanley declared. "Think of something else."

"Guard," Lyle called.

"You don't know his name?" Stanley accused.

"There was a shift change."

Derrick Gardner poked his head into the room. "Yes, Chief.

"Tell French I want to see him."

"Can I help you, Chief?"

"If you leave your post, I'll fire you."

"Yes, Sir," Derrick said. "But Sir, the lieutenant told us not to disturb him while he eats dinner."

"Tell him I said a chief is available twenty-four seven and an acting chief is twice as available."

"Yes, Sir."

French arrived so quickly after being called; Lyle greeted him with, "Did you use the siren?"

"Derrick sounded close to panic," Peter said.

"He was caught between my orders and yours."

"It was my mistake," Peter said contritely. "I won't make it again."

"If it's any consolation, I told my men that same thing early on and one day I wasn't called," Lyle commented. "You should probably have a second in command."

"I do, Sir. Derrick is that."

"He's standing guard."

"At your door, Sir."

"Martha wants…"

"She called," French said. "I've already scheduled a crew to go over the house tomorrow."

"We should maybe contact the other board members."

"Already done, Sir. Also, the police chiefs in their districts. Chief Milani and Chief Peets helped me, Sir."

"Aleta was given funeral instructions and…"

"I've already alerted the mortuary and they will handle retrieving Toby Hepner's body from the California authorities and get the graves prepared and the notices in the papers. I will bring them the specifics tomorrow."

"Where'd you get the information for the notices?"

"I asked Ed Ornstein for it. He came up with a couple of nice bios."

Stanley held out the brown envelope. "The paperwork's in here. Aleta will want to add same touches of her own."

"Will she be attending the service?"

"That's a chopper landing," Stanley said. "I guess Aleta's going to have another brain surgery after all."

"What about Mr. Jackman?" Lyle asked.

His new security guard service took over an hour ago. Jackman will be transferred by ambulance tomorrow."

"You seem to know everything," Lyle said. "Who's his new doctor?"

"Dr. Lemmon," French said. "Derrick is kept fully informed, by the way."

"You mean he could have answered most of my questions?"

"Yes, but the paperwork for the funeral is something that only I should handle."

"You're even a diplomat," Lyle commented. "I'm already obsolete."

"Not true, Sir. Everyone is working hard so you'll not worry and get the rest you need."

"Is Cook going to come back and tell us what's going on?" Stanley worried.

"Do you want me to fetch him?" French asked.

The offer gave Stanley pause.

"No, just go tell him we heard the chopper," he said. "He can operate first, then talk to us."

"So now we lie here and worry," Lyle said.

"Now we lie here and worry," Stanley responded.

Chapter 32

Hours later Aleta opened her eyes and saw Dr. Cook and Dr. Taekman smiling at her.

"Dr. Taekman, are you married?"

Startled, he blurted out, "No, I'm a widower."

"How long ago did you lose your wife?"

"Eight years."

"Ever think of remarrying?"

"I asked someone six years ago. She turned me down," Dr. Taekman said. "Why this interest in my marital status?"

"Because if you were married, you'd have better things to do than fly over here and open up my skull."

"I don't mind."

"I do. I want you happily married," Aleta retorted. "Now we have a pair of great matchmakers in this town. And I'm going to have a welcome home party in what, Dr. Cook, a week?"

"Ten days to two weeks."

"Why so long?"

"You run into things when you're on your own."

"Well, okay. I did promise not to give you any grief this time around, only I didn't expect you to chop open my skull the minute I fell asleep. So, Dr. Taekman, can you come to my party? There will be three single ladies there; two spinsters and one widow."

"Is the widow available?"

"She's pretty tied up right now helping Dr. Chesney get over the death of his wife."

"Chesney?" Taekman said looking at Cook who was smiling broadly at the exchange. "He's too young for her."

"How do you know who I'm talking about?"

"Wayne is grinning," Taekman said. "You are talking about his grandmother, aren't you?"

"Well, she's retired now and so she's got time to concentrate on finding you a good mate. Why did that woman turn you down? You're intelligent, compassionate, handsome, pleasantly tubby and wealthy. You're a dream catch. What was the woman like?"

"Intelligent, compassionate, attractive, slightly older and very busy with work. She said she had no time to be a wife."

"That was it?" Aleta gasped. "And you let her go?"

"She stopped taking my calls and, well, she had made up her mind I should be free to find a woman with more time."

"So she's stubborn. Well, there are other women. Martha will find you a good one."

Taekman turned to his fellow doctor. "She just plows right in, doesn't she?"

"Obviously, we didn't affect her mental abilities."

"I should hope not," Aleta quipped. "If you had, I'd fire the both of you."

"Aleta, there's something you should know," Dr. Cook began.

Aleta, still looking at Dr. Taekman, said, "So you'll come to my party and meet Martha and my grandmother who should be back from her honeymoon by then?"

"I'd be delighted."

"Grams is Aleta's roommate," Wayne Cook revealed.

"She might not want me to see her now."

Aleta mulled over that sentence and suddenly said. "You asked Martha Cook to marry you?"

"Boy, she is quick. I see why she won that court case."

"And she turned you down?" Aleta queried.

"Can I still come to your party?" Dr. Taekman asked.

Aleta didn't answer. Her mind was busy with another train of thought.

"She must have been in her mid-eighties. You're more than slightly younger."

"I'm older than I was."

"She's ninety!"

"She's going to live another twenty years," Taekman smiled. "Why not with me?"

"She won't leave Arborville."

"She still in that beautiful, old house her husband built?"

"Still there," Wayne said. "You know, she could use a visitor now. Someone besides her four doctors."

"Dr. Chesney is one of them," Aleta clarified.

"Four?"

"She had a stroke," Dr. Cook explained. "Dr. Chesney was in house delivering a baby. I needed another doctor and Chesney called the whole list before he got to Kurland who not only rushed right over but brought his partner. He was dying to take on a woman who had her first stroke at age ninety."

"I'm surprised they all didn't come running."

"Chesney said the woman was a special patient of mine."

"They assumed it was a clinic patient?" Dr. Taekman observed.

"Well, it was Christmas Eve."

"And when they found out who it was?"

"Chesney and Grams had fun with that." Dr. Cook relayed.

"Kurland is a good man. So's Hughes."

Aleta spoke up.

"Yes, you can come visit Martha and me. Bring chocolates. We like chocolates."

Wayne grinned. "Dr. Chesney keeps them supplied. If you interrupt their supply of chocolate, you'll be off to a bad start."

"Anything else?"

"You do know she's five years older than she was."

"So am I," Taekman returned. "I'll remember the chocolates."

"Maybe we should go tell Stanley he's got his wife back good as new," Dr. Cook suggested.

"He doesn't know?" Aleta asked.

"We came here first."

"What about Stanley's medical condition? Who's taking care of that?"

"I'm sure he's fine," Dr. Cook said.

"What medical condition?" Taekman asked. "Did anything happen to the leg?"

"The leg is coming along nicely. He developed another problem, a minor one."

"I'd like to check the leg."

"Of course. You'll never guess what happened to him while he was lying in bed."

They were out of earshot before Dr. Cook began the explanation. Aleta heard Dr. Taekman hoot as the elevator doors closed.

Chapter 33

Aleta came home in the late morning, two weeks after her latest operation. Her welcome home party was scheduled for that evening. Her father helped her out of the car. Stanley was still on crutches. He followed the two in.

"You only have one arm in a sling," Bertha noted. "Do you still need the same kind of assistance as before?"

"I need help dressing, changing and bathing still," Aleta said. Spotting the wheelchair, Aleta added, "And I'm confined to that thing longer than I think is necessary."

"How long is that, Ma'am?" Bertha asked rolling it closer.

"Four weeks," Aleta replied as Bertha helped her to sit down. "And I'm not to push it myself."

"That will be difficult for you, Ma'am."

"It will, but Dr. Cook doesn't want a repeat."

"Remember I'm available for your needs first. Don't hesitate to tell me whenever you need anything."

The puppy jumped in Aleta's lap. "Thank goodness I can pet my little chocolate fella. Huh, guy? Miss me?"

Scooby licked her face.

"I guess you did," Aleta said. "Unless you greet everyone this way."

"No, he doesn't," came the familiar rough voice of her grandmother. She walked over and gave Aleta a light kiss.

"Claude and I are staying in your new guest room."

"I have a guest room?"

"We have a guest room," Stanley corrected. "Two, in fact."

"But your study?"

"Intact."

"The baby's room?"

"Will be added this spring," Stanley said. "We have guests now."

"Are the rooms finished, paint and all?" Aleta queried.

"Yep, paint and all."

"What color?"

"Lauren picked sage green for one, pale blue for the other."

"Claude and I are in the green room," Harriet put in. "It's quite lovely."

"Where is Claude?" Aleta asked.

"Out walking the big dogs. I didn't want them to knock you over. Besides I wanted to talk to you about something."

"I'm pretty available," Aleta chuckled.

"I'm adding Robert as a Tontine lawyer."

"What a great idea!"

"He said you were wasted with office work. He said you're a born trial lawyer. I had already decided to move more work to him to free you up."

"I'm not sure I'll get to do much trial work," Aleta said. "I'm pretty unknown."

"All the Tontine trial work will be shunted your way. And Martha is lining up clients as we speak."

"Suppose I don't pass the bar?"

A gale of laughter greeted that query.

"You don't think the trial board knows about your brilliant work with the case of the three prophets. It made the papers big time," Harriet said.

Stanley explained Aleta's surprise at the bit of news.

"Dr. Cook kept her in a cocoon-like existence. He was so afraid she'd stress out over one thing or another."

"He even limited my visitors," Aleta added. "Thank goodness Martha stayed until Stanley was mobile."

"I hear she had a reason for hanging around."

Aleta smiled. "He visited us every day. And he brought great chocolates. And flowers. He came in on a chopper. If Martha heard it, she cut her therapy short and rushed back to the room. He told her he could live here and commute by chopper. It got serious fast."

That evening as Chief Alan Peets helped his pregnant wife from the car, he asked, "Now there isn't anything you haven't gotten around to telling me, is there?"

"No, why?"

"Every one of Aleta's parties somehow manages to have a surprise built in," Peets said. "I just don't want it to be me again."

"Well, they know about the baby. What else is there?"

"We're not moving, or having twins, or anything?"

"Stop worrying. This group is all out of surprises."

"Don't count on it."

Dinner went as usual with Lauren's place cards dividing the couples and mixing the men and women.

Dr. Taekman found this unsettling until he found himself seated beside Harriet's new husband Claude who confessed that the first time he didn't want to be separated from Harriet but that it had worked out well.

Michael Taekman found it fascinating to be seated with Chief Peets and Judge Davis and the artist Bessie Dobbins and Lauren West. He enjoyed talking to Bessie about the restoration of her home after the fire and Lauren about the genetics involved in the arrival of a chocolate pup from two black parents and Alan about his children's first ride on a horse. Claude and he shared the same interest in the others at their table and both brought out the captivating side of Lydia Davis, who at their polite urging, shared a few of the highlights of her career on the bench.

After desert was served, the wine glasses were refilled. Harriet rose.

"Someone has a surprise announcement to make."

Peets sought out his wife's eyes and nodded an I-told-you-so.

Harriet noticed Peets' nod and responded. "I see Alan Peets knows. Leave it to a police chief to ferret out a secret."

His wife laughed aloud. "He hasn't a clue!"

"I asked you before we came in if you had anything to tell me and you said no," Peets accused.

"And I didn't and I don't. I just know that you haven't a clue or you wouldn't have interrogated me so thoroughly."

"It was just a couple of questions!" he protested.

The whole group laughed.

It was Aleta who spoke out first, "Alan, don't be upset. I'm practically the hostess and I have no idea what my grandmother is talking about. Anyone else in the same boat, raise your hand."

Most of the hands in the room went up.

"See, everyone is in the same boat. Now, Alan, tell us what you deduced."

"Four people besides Harriet know the surprise."

"How many of you deduced that? Raise your hands. Every lawyer's hand went up as well as those of the two other police chiefs.

"Okay, Harriet, that's as far as I can go. What is it you and Martha and Evelyn know that I don't?"

"Why did you leave out the men?" Harriet asked.

"Because they're both doctors. Doctors never tell you anything, do they Dr. Cook.? They just open up your skull and fiddle around and hope they remembered to put back all the parts."

"I told you we should have left a sponge in there, Michael. Something to absorb this wit."

"Doctors are nice," Evelyn said aloud. "One just asked me to marry him and I accepted."

Alan Peets noticed the surprised look on Harriet's face, the smile on Bernard Chesney's, the frown on Michael Taekman, together with the freshly filled wine glasses and his mind put the pieces together.

He sprang to his feet, raised his wine glass and said loudly, "A toast. To Dr. Bernard Chesney and to Dr. Michael Taekman and to their prospective brides Evelyn Barnes and Martha Cook, respectively."

He glanced at Michael's face and knew immediately he was correct. The knot in his stomach loosened instantly and he smiled as he finished his toast. "May both couples enjoy all the delights marriage has to offer."

Glasses clinked and the toast drunk.

"What delights are those, Alan?" Lyle West asked.

"If you don't know, who am I to enlighten you?" Alan jibed.

"Oh, he knows!" Lauren quipped. "I'm living proof!"

This time the laughter was directed at Lyle. Alan relaxed even more.

Claude leaned over. "Nice recovery, Alan. I mean the toast. And I might suggest you never signal your wife across the room again. These Locke woman are uncanny at catching such."

"So I'm learning," Alan murmured ruefully.

"So, Michael," Lydia asked, "how long do you plan to be engaged?"

"Not long."

"Martha won't want a big wedding, but we all want to be there." Judge Davis said

"I thought we might do it like Harriet and Claude here--fast and simple."

"Ours was out of necessity," Claude said.

"She was pregnant?" Lydia asked with a wry smile.

Claude reddened. "I usually don't put my foot in my mouth like that."

"It seems this is the table with foot in the mouth disease," Alan commented.

"Oh, I don't know," Lauren said. "I'm guessing there are several wives here who'd kick their other halves under the table if they heard what they were saying."

"Well, at least Harriet didn't hear me," Claude said.

"If she had, she'd have laughed and said, 'That's right!'" Lydia pointed out. "We were with you two, remember?"

"I don't understand," Michael said.

Lydia looked at him askance.

"You aren't that old." Claude jumped in. "You said you wanted a short engagement."

"Well, that's because I don't want to give her a chance to change her mind."

"No other reason?" Claude said.

"Well, yes there are other reasons," Michael said. "I love her. I want to be with her day and night. I want to go to bed with her as my wife."

"That's how I feel about Lyle," Lauren said quietly.

Late that night when Stanley was helping Aleta undress, he listened quietly to her talking gaily about the party. Stanley, standing on one leg, gently removed her sling. The arm was still tender where the bullet had been removed. The shoulder was trying again to recuperate from the injury sustained when it was thrown violently in front of Jackman's head.

Stanley knew the sling would be kept in place longer than necessary to dissuade Aleta from taking charge of her wheelchair. He didn't object to the restriction. It would keep her quieter than if she had full use of both arms. To him keeping Aleta restricted was almost a mandate.

He didn't understand her complete compliance. It was as if she'd added a new directive to the one he'd given which he knew was still in place. Even Bertha had mentioned the difference.

"It's not that her spirits been broken," Bertha had confided. "It's more like she's keeping a pledge."

"I'm really feeling good," she told Stanley. "I'm worried about your leg. Should you be waiting on me at all? And do I need to wait another day?"

"Another day for what?"

"Never mind, I'll wait," Aleta said as he helped her lay back on the bed. "Did you know that when Fred shot Foster Mize he was already dead? The autopsy confirmed he'd died only minutes before he was shot. That's why we didn't get any prophetic warning. He died of natural causes."

"I knew," Stanley said, sitting to undress himself.

"I didn't," Aleta said. "I thought our prophetic powers were gone."

"Is that why you were so troubled about Jackman's threat?" Stanley asked as he folded his shirt neatly. She smiled at watching him engaging in his habit of folding clothes destined for the laundry.

"Yes. I didn't think there was any way to save those people except by cooperating."

"Yet, you chose not to."

"It was so hard when he mentioned Martha."

"I know."

"How?"

"Lyle and I figured it all out."

"No wonder neither of you ever questioned me."

"Neither call would have generated censure from us. Either call would have been justifiable."

His last item of clothing neatly folded, he began to dress tor bed.

"Now, looking back, only one was right," Aleta said.

"When Jackman taunted me about not caring about Martha I got angry. That's when I lost the ability to understand him. I know God was angry with me and so He took it away."

"You felt He was guiding you up to that moment?"

"Yes, I did."

"So why not afterward?"

"I got angry."

"So did Jesus. He upset the tables of the moneychangers. He caused a fig tree to shrivel up and die. Anger is a normal human emotion. It's allowed. Maybe God even wanted to let Jackman know how displeased He was with him."

"I hadn't thought of that."

Stanley climbed into bed and lay down beside his wife. His voice carried assurance. "It's wasn't a punishment. It was an aid. When you lost the ability to understand Jackman, his list became worthless. You were free to do as you wanted."

"So it's possible we three still have the ability to prophesy."

"It's possible," he said, leaning over and kissing her lightly.

"That's it?"

"I made a promise to Dr. Cook."

"What kind of promise."

"Celibacy."

"Does he know you promised this?"

"Yes."

"How long?"

"Until you're well."

"That's forever!" she exclaimed. "Well, I didn't promise."

"I promised for both of us," Stanley said firmly.

"Then that's that."

Slowly the tears began to flow. In the dark Stanley didn't see them. Even though she was silent, he sensed her misery. He rolled over and touched her cheek.

"I'll tell you the secret a day early," he said. "It will make you laugh."

Her curiosity rose to the surface. Her tears ceased. In hushed tones Stanley told her what had happened when she was dreaming.

"And Dr. Cook tried too?" she gasped.

"You were very determined," Stanley said. "He didn't believe me until he tried."

"How long were you sore?"

"Several days."

"No wonder you don't want to touch me."

"Aleta, I want to touch you. You are more desirable than ever. I'm not sure I can keep my word, especially since you insist on sleeping in the nude.

"Now you have a choice," Aleta said. "Your promise versus my need to feel loved."

Stanley took her hand and placed it gently on his most vulnerable part. "You may use it anyway you want."

"Stanley, you are the King Solomon of this generation," she said. "When we are both well, we will have a second honeymoon. Now fetch me my nightgown."

Once settled back in bed, Aleta took hold of Stanley's hand with the comment that, if she squeezed too hard, he could squeeze back.

"I won't do that."

"Why not?"

"You only tighten your grip when you're frightened. I won't add to your fear."

"I hear women in labor squeeze, pretty hard."

"And for good reason. The pressure you'll exert won't be even close to what you're experiencing."

"I'm sorry I didn't wait until you were free, but the doctor was there, the machine was close by and I was already in hospital garb."

"And your curiosity couldn't wait."

"He'll do another anytime you want."

"Are you okay with having a boy?"

"He'd just better look like you. I deserve to get some of what I want. Has your father decided on a name yet?"

"He's still vacillating. Right now it's between Gerard, Andrew and August."

"I like them all. I think Gerard is especially nice," Aleta said.

"He won't settle on one until the baby's born."

"It'll be Gerard."

"How do you know?"

"I'm psychic."

"You thought it was going to be a girl."

"Are you going to hold that over my head for the rest of my life?"

"Of course."

"How many weeks of celibacy do we have?"

"Four weeks less one day," Stanley responded.

"You're counting?"

"Aren't you?"

"Yes."

The Prophet Series

* to be released